E.G. FOLEY

THE GRYPHON CHRONICLES, BOOK FOUR:

RISE OF ALLIES

Books by E.G. Foley

The Complete Gryphon Chronicles Series:
The Lost Heir (The Gryphon Chronicles, Book One)
Jake & The Giant (The Gryphon Chronicles, Book Two)
The Dark Portal (The Gryphon Chronicles, Book Three)
Jake & The Gingerbread Wars (A Gryphon Chronicles Christmas)
Rise of Allies (The Gryphon Chronicles, Book Four)
Secrets of the Deep (The Gryphon Chronicles, Book Five)
The Black Fortress (The Gryphon Chronicles, Book Six)

50 States of Fear Series:
The Haunted Plantation (50 States of Fear: Alabama)
Bringing Home Bigfoot (50 States of Fear: Arkansas)
Leader of the Pack (50 States of Fear: Colorado)
The Dork and the Deathray (50 States of Fear: Alaska)

Credits & Copyright

Iron sharpens iron.

~Proverbs 27:17

TABLE OF CONTENTS

PART I

Prologue: The Black Crystal.. 1

Chapter 1. The Long Man.. 3

Chapter 2. Merlin Hall.. 12

Chapter 3. The Proving Ground 22

Chapter 4. The Rival & the Prodigy 35

Chapter 5. Lightrider Material? 44

Chapter 6. My Own Private Stonehenge 58

Chapter 7. Sweet Dreams & Nightmares 67

Chapter 8. Strange Creatures 74

Chapter 9. Spy Hunting 88

Chapter 10. Headless & Boneless 100

PART II

Chapter 11. Born on Beltane... 113

Chapter 12. Sorted... 118

Chapter 13. Lightriding 101 132

Chapter 14. The Trouble with Trolls 140

Chapter 15. There Be Dragons 150

Chapter 16. The Tower... 161

Chapter 17. Great Minds Think Alike 170

Chapter 18. *Dracosaurus Silvanus*.. 176

Chapter 19. Jealousy 187

Chapter 20. Smoke on the Wind... 196

PART III

Chapter 21. A Shocking Accusation 211

Chapter 22. The Enchanted Gallery 227

Chapter 23. The Queen's Flag 240

Chapter 24. Art Appreciation 254

Chapter 25. Explosions 274

Chapter 26. Landscape with Monsters 290

PART IV

Chapter 27. The Secret War Council 310

Chapter 28. And So It Begins 321

Chapter 29. Calm before the Storm 338

Chapter 30. The Battle of the Bugganes 347

Chapter 31. Nixie's Nightmare 362

Chapter 32. Bagpipes at Dawn 367

Chapter 33. The Crystal Ball 378

Epilogue: The Captive 392

Next Up!

About the Authors

PART I

PROLOGUE

The Black Crystal

Samhain. The great feast of the dead and the dying of the old pagan year. From time immemorial, it had fallen on October thirty-first, and was known to mortal peasantry as Hallowe'en, but few of those fools grasped the depths of its power.

On this night, as on all sacred quarter-days, the veil between the Realms grew thin. The stars stood in alignment in the sign of Scorpio, ruled by Mars, god of war.

And as war was their hunger on this darkest of nights, the thirteen warlocks of the Council took advantage of the veil's thinning to seek guidance on their plans from the terrible powers and principalities on the other side.

Those beings, their immortal allies, had always been willing to help them—for a price. A true sorcerer never shrank from paying it. What use was a soul, anyway?

The subterranean chamber reverberated with the chants rising from the ring of tall figures in long, black, hooded robes. Their cruel, haughty faces cloaked in shadow, they concentrated all their powers on the perfect, round ball of obsidian in the center of their circle, and willed their guest to come.

All had been prepared for his arrival.

The scrolls lay open. The blood offering had been made. The ancient words churned the air, and the torchlight writhed, throwing monstrous shadows of the men all across the stone walls.

They were eager for his counsel. Their combined power was vast, to be sure, especially since they had recently acquired the oldest of the scrolls, with secrets unseen since the days of the pharaohs. But even they were nothing compared to the creature they summoned through the dark crystal ball.

Blacker than a dragon's heart, it collected their obscene supplications, until at last, their prayers were answered from Below.

The first sign of a response was a vein of flame-colored orange cracking through the solid obsidian. The cracks splintered and grew.

Shining, red-hot slivers of a fiery glare pierced the darkness. Then the smell of sulfur filled the room.

The leader of the Dark Druids raised his voice above the deep, rhythmic chanting of the others. "We call to thee, O Shemrazul, servant of the horned king! Join us from your stronghold in the deep. Once again, we seek your guidance!"

A bestial roar came from the cracks in the obsidian ball. Smoke poured out, rising straight up and making even the druids' soulless eyes sting. Amid the smoke, the demon came, his claws outstretched, his baleful eyes full of wrath, his face grotesque. His garbled voice was almost more than mortals could bear to hear, and live.

"Greetings, my lords. I, Shemrazul of the Ninth Pit, bring you tidings from Below. And oh, yes. I have news for you, indeed..." Mocking laughter escaped his fanged mouth. "But you aren't going to like it!"

"Speak, O spirit!" the leader implored.

"As you wish," he said with a sneer of a smile and a hiss. And then, floating in his column of foul smoke, Shemrazul proceeded to explain to the overlords of the Dark Druid Council how they had recently been bested.

By a twelve-year-old boy.

CHAPTER ONE

The Long Man

Six Months Later, Beltane Eve

Springtime blossomed in England like a shy young girl who had only just realized she was beautiful. Orchards donned crowns of pink and white flowers. In the patchwork fields, lambs skipped and grazed. Timid hares ventured out to nibble the shoots of clover. The cuckoo sang atop the meadow grass, and honeybees zoomed about, glutting themselves on their annual feast of flowers.

Winding all the while through the dreamy Sussex countryside, the road the travelers' carriage took was muddy and long, but every puddle reflected the opalescent sky.

Jake Everton, however, the boy Earl of Griffon, could not be bothered with pretty scenery (nor with pretty girls, for that matter) when the whole weight and consequence of his future was at stake.

He stared intensely at his tutor, Mr. Henry DuVal, who sat across from him in the family's crowded traveling chariot.

"So, if I fail the test," Jake said slowly, every muscle taut, "that means they'll never choose me to become a Lightrider?"

"Jake, it isn't a test, as I've told you," Henry answered in a mild tone. "'Tis only an Assessment."

"What's the difference?" he nearly shouted.

"The difference *is*," Great-Great Aunt Ramona said, arching an elegant silver brow at his cheeky tone, "there is no right or wrong in this for you to pass or fail. Becalm yourself, Jacob! The Assessment merely serves to show the Elders of the Order who you are, what you can do. That way, your education henceforth can be set on the proper track."

"Her Ladyship is quite right," Henry said with a nod at the Dowager Baroness Bradford. "The Old Yew simply wants to see what abilities the new crop of magical children have been born with. It's really just a formality."

Jake shook his head, still in doubt. "I can't believe my fate rests on convincing a *tree* I'm worthy," he muttered.

"The Old Yew is no ordinary tree," Aunt Ramona chided. "And for that matter, he's not the only one who'll be watching your demonstration."

"What? You mean I'm going to have an audience?"

"It is the custom that anyone in attendance at the Gathering is welcome to watch the Assessments. The Elders want to see how our young people will hold up under pressure. You are the future of the Order, after all."

"Blimey." Jake did not scare easily, but he was not used to putting on a show before a crowd. In fact, that was his idea of torture. "Right. So if I don't impress them today, I'll be doomed to mediocrity forever."

Her Ladyship let out a fond chuckle. "Oh, my dear lad, I assure you, mediocrity is not *quite* the word that comes to mind when one thinks of you." The teasing note in her voice hinted this was not necessarily a compliment.

He snorted.

Thankfully, his very patient cousin, Isabelle, seated across from him, sent him a sympathetic smile. "Don't be nervous, coz. You'll do fine."

"My sister's right." Archie nudged Jake with his elbow as the carriage bumped along. "Izzy got through her Assessment two years ago with flying colors. If she can do it, shy as she is, so can you."

"Aye, stop being such a bloomin' Nervous Nellie," Dani O'Dell muttered. "It doesn't suit ye."

The little Irish redhead's brusque tone startled a wry smile out of Jake in spite of himself.

The others chuckled at her observation, too, for they all knew the carrot-head was right. It was completely bizarre for Jake, of all people, to be acting so unsure of himself when he was usually so confident.

Maybe a little *too* confident at times.

But didn't they understand? He had one, single, driving dream in life—to become a Lightrider for the Order of the Yew Tree, like his parents had been.

If he messed up his Assessment, he might as well throw himself off the Tower Bridge. Of course, with his luck, the blasted Thames water nymphs would probably save him and toss him back up onto the land like a tuna.

"How long before we get there, Lady Bradford?" Dani asked Aunt Ramona. "Is it very much farther?"

"No, my dear. We're almost there." The Elder witch glanced out the carriage window, then pointed. "Merlin Hall lies just beyond that hill."

"Really?" Dani searched the horizon for the medieval spires of the Order's ancient headquarters, as Archie and Isabelle had described them earlier. The two aristocratic Bradford children had attended many Gatherings before, but for Jake and Dani, this would be the first.

It was terribly exciting.

The venerable Order of the Yew Tree had been created a way-long-time-ago, in the tumultuous days of the Renaissance era. It had been founded by Good Queen Bess herself, establishing an alliance between mankind and magical folk of goodwill.

The Order had a simple purpose—simple, but not easy: to protect the fragile balance between the world of humans and Magic-kind, so that neither side should harm or exploit the other. Lightriders were the Order's elite agents who carried out this mission all over the world.

As for the Gathering, it had been taking place at Merlin Hall on Beltane for an age. Indeed, it was one of the great events on every magical family's social calendar.

There were festivities and games, contests and entertainments, feasts and fireworks, parties, teas, and soirees for the adults, culminating in the annual Crystal Ball, to be held in the great, gilded ballroom.

All of this jollification helped to strengthen the magical folk and humans' bonds of friendship, both personally and politically—which was why Queen Victoria herself would be in attendance.

The sovereign was always the nominal head of the Order of the Yew Tree. Besides, Her Majesty was also (at least on paper) the godmother of all magical children born within the borders of her Realm.

This arrangement allowed the powers-that-be to keep an eye on them.

Jake had had the honor of meeting Queen Victoria privately once, when his relatives had first found him. The stern little queen *was* admittedly intimidating, but nonetheless, he admired Her Majesty and was very proud to know her.

In any case, the Gathering was not all fun and games. Between festivities, the grownups held a great parliament, where representatives from all the major groups of magic-kind and their human counterparts met to discuss matters of importance.

And for the kids who had come of age enough to shed the Kinderveil since the last Gathering, there were the dreaded Assessments.

Nobody could tell what magical powers might be lying dormant in a child born into a magical family. Their abilities would only emerge once the Kinderveil wore off, usually around the age of twelve. The Kinderveil was the rarest kind of magic: a naturally occurring spell that protected all magical children from those who would harm them. It masked babies born with magical powers from the scrying stones and seeing bowls and other magical devices of the Dark Druids.

Who liked to kidnap them.

The Dark Druids, of course, were those unpleasant folk who had refused to join the alliance long ago. Not everybody wished to keep the balance between worlds, after all. The original Dark Druids had been thirteen warlocks, sorcerers, and alchemists who had, in their arrogance, rejected the offer of peace from ordinary humanity.

They and their modern descendants saw no reason why they should not use their powers to dominate and rule everybody else. Again and again over the centuries, the Lightriders (and their trusty warrior friends known as Guardians) had thwarted the Dark Druids' wicked schemes.

That was why being a Lightrider was, in Jake's view, the best, most exciting, most adventurous life in the world, and he was determined it should be his life, too. Gazing out the carriage window, daydreaming as he often did about what it would be like to finally serve as a real Lightrider—going on secret missions, trouncing evil foes and whatnot—he was suddenly taken aback by a dark thought that occurred to him.

He turned to Aunt Ramona. "Do the Dark Druids ever try to wreck the Gatherings, ma'am? Or even attack...?"

"Oh, gracious, no! With the whole Order there? They'd be mad to try it. We outnumber them greatly, Jacob. Never you mind about that. Of course," she added with a wry look, "they may send a spy or two to try to find out what the Order is up to these days."

Jake's eyebrows shot up. "Spies?"

"Indeed. We always have to be on the lookout for the evil ones' spies. They sent a bear shapeshifter last year, but we caught him in short order and tossed him in the same dungeon where we locked up your Uncle Waldrick. No, no worries, children. You'll be quite safe."

Who cares about safe? The others looked a bit scared despite her reassurance, but Jake thrilled to the prospect of doing a little spy-hunting on this journey. After all, he had not been on an adventure since Christmas, and besides, the thought of hunting spies at least gave him something else to occupy his mind other than his horrible, looming test.

Aunt Ramona noticed the concerned looks on the others' faces. "Now, don't worry your heads about it. Merlin Hall is *extremely* well protected by many layers of enchantment. I'd venture to say it's one of the safest places on the earth."

"If we ever get there," Dani muttered.

"What do you mean? We're almost there," Henry said with a casual nod toward the window—and a twinkle in his wolf-gray eyes. "Can you not see it yet? It's just beyond that rise."

Dani looked out again, then scrunched up her freckled nose. "No."

"Neither can I," Jake said, mystified.

"Look closer," the tutor suggested. "Hmm, maybe you two need to get your eyes checked."

"You're funning with us, Henry!" Dani leaned to stare out the carriage window once more, squinting into the distance. "I don't see anything! Well, except that giant drawing of the Long Man on the chalk hill."

"Hang me!" Jake said when he turned curiously and looked out the other window in the direction Dani was pointing. "Would you look at that!"

The huge chalk figure would have been hard to miss, considering its bright white outline stretched all the way up the green hillside.

While Jake and Dani marveled at it, having never seen one of England's famous, ancient, hill drawings before, Aunt Ramona smiled at the Long Man like an old friend.

As the carriage rolled on, Archie, with his scientific bent of mind, proceeded to explain how the ground in these parts contained the same, pearl-white rock layer as the famous White Cliffs of Dover farther up the coast.

To create the bright white outline of the Long Man brandishing his pair of tall spears, the green turf and layers of brown dirt had been ripped up to expose the white stone underneath.

Several such chalk-hill drawings dotted the south of England, the oldest and most famous being the White Horse of Uffington, which was thought to be as much as two or three thousand years old.

Nobody really knew what the hill figures meant.

Like the stone circles and burial mounds across the British Isles, the giant chalk-hill drawings had been a mysterious feature of the landscape, even before the Romans had invaded and established their outpost at old Londinium.

"It was probably the Celts who made them in the Neolithic age, possibly with later contributions from the Anglo-Saxons," Archie said. "We know they were here before the Romans came, for they mentioned these drawings in their writings. I imagine those centurions were as puzzled by them as we are today."

Dani shook her head in amazement as she stared out the window at the Long Man. "How could Stone Age barbarians figure out how to draw something so big while standing right beside it? I mean, he's as tall as Big Ben! How could they see what they were doing?"

"How, indeed?" Aunt Ramona's mouth twitched with amusement. "Hmmm, 'tis a mystery."

The redhead turned hopefully to her. "Could we perhaps stop for a moment, Your Ladyship, and have a closer look before we pass?"

"I want to stop, too!" Jake seconded her.

"If you wish," Aunt Ramona said. She leaned her head out the window and ordered her driver to take them closer.

As the coachman headed straight for the feet of the giant chalk figure, Jake noticed the mirthful glances that passed between his aunt and cousins and Henry.

He eyed them in suspicion. "What?" he prompted.

But even if they had told him, he would not have believed what happened next if he had not seen it with his own two eyes.

As they approached, a ponderous creaking sound filled the air like the groaning of a huge, old ship in a storm crossed with the scraping of fingernails on a chalkboard.

"What was that?" Jake started, but then his jaw dropped as the Long Man sat up slowly from the hillside, and rose stiffly to his feet, chunks of turf and dirt and chalk dust raining from his towering, lanky body.

"Who goes there?" he boomed down at them.

Jake and Dani shrieked.

The others burst out laughing.

Archie nudged him merrily in the ribs. "We got you!"

"Good morning, Aelfric," Aunt Ramona called politely through the window.

"Ah, Your Ladyship, good morrow!" said the giant, see-through, chalk-outlined man, leaning on his spear.

"Good to see you, old friend. Would you be so kind as to let us pass? We're in a bit of a hurry this year, you see. My great-great nephew here is keen to get on with his Assessment."

Aelfric let out a deep rumble of a laugh. "Oho, have we another brave stripling for the test, eh?"

I knew it was a test! Jake thought, despite his heart-pounding shock at such a sight.

"He is to make a demonstration of his telekinesis *and* his mediumship," Aunt Ramona said with considerable pride.

"Verily! A doubler, is he, now?"

"Yes, he inherited both his parents' powers. We're very proud. Jacob, don't forget your manners," his aunt said firmly. "Give a greeting to the Watcher on the Hill."

Jolted out of his astonishment by her command, Jake craned his neck to peer out the window. "Er, good morning, sir."

"Good morrow, young master. Fare ye well," the Long Man said with a slight bow. "Maidens, masters," he added, nodding to the others. Then he took a slight step back. "Go ye and make merry at the Gathering, and a blessed Beltane to ye."

"Thank you, Aelfric," Aunt Ramona replied.

And with that, the Long Man lifted the spear in his right hand upward, just high enough to reveal the opening of a carriage-sized tunnel hidden behind the chalk spear's base.

"Drive on!" Aunt Ramona called to her coachman, who seemed quite familiar with this bizarre procedure.

The driver clapped the reins over the horses' backs, and the carriage rolled on, toward the waiting hole in the hillside.

Archie and Isabelle waved cheerfully to Aelfric as they passed by his massive feet, but Jake and Dani could only stare up at the towering figure in open-mouthed shock.

"What a pleasant fellow," Aunt Ramona said, leaning back in her seat. "He's really very kind."

"He's, he's, he's—" Dani attempted. But no words followed.

Aunt Ramona smiled. "I told you Merlin Hall was well protected."

"I should think so, with *him* on sentry-duty!" Jake burst out.

"And he really doesn't like the Dark Druids," Henry added with a wink.

"W-what about the White Horse of Uffington, then?" Dani stammered, finally finding her voice as they neared the dark tunnel. "Does it come alive, too?"

"Why, yes, dear. That's been Aelfric's horse for millennia. Stormwind is his name, and a trusty steed he is."

They stared, agog, as the Long Man—obliging fellow—stepped back into his usual position after they had passed. When he lowered his spear, the tunnel closed behind them.

Underneath the hillside, things suddenly turned pitch dark. Jake was still in shock. He shook his head to clear it. "That's...impossible."

Aunt Ramona chuckled. "You're going to see a great many impossible things over the next few days, my dears. Best prepare yourselves." She murmured a magical command to the quartz crystal that hung from her necklace.

It began to glow with a soft, bluish light, enough to illuminate the tunnel, and the first thing Jake saw was Archie's grin. "Ha, ha! We fooled you two! You should've seen your faces!"

"I can't believe this one actually kept his mouth shut," Henry said, nodding at the boy genius in amusement.

Everybody knew that Archie couldn't tell a lie to save his life. "I can keep a secret when it's all in fun," he insisted. Then he turned back to Jake and Dani, obviously relishing the prank they had pulled on them.

Not that Dani and he would have believed their companions if they had admitted in advance that the Long Man was actually a living *person.*

But then, why should they be surprised, Jake thought wryly, considering he was about to be interviewed at his Assessment by an ancient talking yew tree.

Archie beamed in the half-light from Aunt Ramona's crystal. "Everybody thinks the Long Man's holding up two spears, but he's not, exactly. He's standing in the outline of a doorway."

"A doorway between worlds," Aunt Ramona specified. "The veil is thinner on the quarter-days. With Beltane tomorrow, it's easier for those without magical abilities to get through so they can join us."

Up on the driver's seat, the coachman urged the horses on through the darkness of the cold, clammy passage underneath the hill. Delicate sunshine beckoned to them from the end of the tunnel, the sprawling woods and ancient spires of Merlin Hall slowly rising into view.

Jake sat forward, his heart beating faster with excitement as the carriage moved quicker. The horses galloped through the darkness toward the opposite end.

All of a sudden, the tunnel spit them out on the other side, over the threshold between worlds...

Into the realm of the Fey.

CHAPTER TWO
Merlin Hall

Brilliant sunshine blinded them as they burst out of the tunnel. The spring day was just as beautiful here as it had been on the other side of the hill, but Jake could instantly feel the tingle of magic in the air.

The horses also reacted to the sudden shift in the atmosphere as they moved onto supernatural ground. It made them buck and balk and whinny, spooked, but the driver soothed them with a cluck of his tongue. A moment later, the glossy team of bays settled down and trotted on, following the winding gravel road into the vast, green acreage surrounding Merlin Hall.

There were woods and fields, meadows and marshes, sparkling ponds and quaint stone caretaker cottages with thatched roofs dotting the grounds here and there.

Merlin Hall, the great palace itself, stood proudly in the distance with the Queen's flag flying over the roof, a signal that the sovereign was in residence; Queen Victoria and her entourage had already arrived.

As they rode on, Aunt Ramona explained that the sprawling medieval palace had hundreds of rooms to accommodate all the dignitaries, guests, and VIP's arriving for the Gathering—at least those who preferred to sleep inside. Not everybody did, like the pod of water nymphs they saw frolicking in the deep brook as the carriage clattered over an old, arching bridge.

The naiads—freshwater mermaids—were congregating around a half-submerged stone gazebo built for them in the middle of the small river, velvet moss creeping up its sides.

As they passed, Jake and his friends couldn't help staring at the beautiful guardians of all the lakes and ponds and inland waterways.

Watching them in wonder, Jake was aware that long ago, a group of them had saved his life, though he could not remember it. He had been just a baby at the time.

They drove on, and Archie pointed out the stables and the menagerie of magical animals as they passed. Next, Jake pointed at the cluster of small, colorful tents, gypsy wagons, and wheeled market stalls gathered in the middle of a misty field. "What's that?"

Her Ladyship eyed the camp in distrust. "That, my children, is the traveling fairy market, and I strongly advise you to stay away from it. Not all fairies are as beneficent as our dear Gladwin, nor as civilized as the royal garden fairies you're used to."

"Fairy market?" Dani stared at it in wonder. "What's that mean— that you can buy magical stuff there?"

"Precisely," said the baroness. "But afterward, the cost usually proves higher than one ever wished to pay."

They weighed her warning with care.

The coach rolled on toward the wide, graveled courtyard outside the magnificent entrance of Merlin Hall, with its carved stone curlicues and soaring arches. As they approached, however, the carriage slowed. Jake saw they'd have to wait in line behind many other arriving guests. In the meantime, he craned his neck this way and that, for there was still a lot to see.

On the sunny, green lawn beside the palace, some servants were putting up a maypole. May Day was tomorrow. Its old name was Beltane, the great celebration of spring and all the new life it unleashed.

It also happened to be Jake's thirteenth birthday.

He couldn't believe it had been almost a full year since his relatives had found him. He had just turned twelve when his magical abilities had started coming out, much to his bewilderment. How his life had changed since then!

Dani suddenly poked him in the arm and beckoned to him to look out the window on her side. He leaned closer, staring at the massive garden maze she was pointing to.

Its thick green walls towered over twenty feet high. Newly arrived guests were streaming into the opening of the maze. Jake turned to Aunt Ramona in amazement. "Is that the entrance to the Yew Court?"

She nodded. "The Old Yew lives in the center of the maze. He's well protected there. That's also where the Assessments take place—on the Field of Challenge."

"So that's why everybody's going in there," Dani remarked, watching the parade of guests heading into the maze.

That's a lot of people. Jake gulped at the crowd, the Assessment never straying far from his mind. "Do I have time to visit Red before I have to do this?"

Being with his Gryphon always helped to calm him down.

The baroness shook her head. "Afraid not. You'll only have time to change into the Assessment uniform and freshen up before we must appear."

"Poor Red," Isabelle remarked. "I wonder how he's feeling."

"Not happy, I should think," Jake replied.

The Gryphon had departed from their company a week ago to take shelter at Merlin Hall once he had realized that he had started molting.

Poor thing. It was very embarrassing for such a noble beast, but it was merely a consequence of his being half-eagle. Aunt Ramona had explained that though gryphons could be deadly when angry, they were at their most vulnerable when they were going through that miserable process—couldn't fly, couldn't really fight, and certainly couldn't heal anyone with their magical feathers, once they all started falling out.

When Red had realized it was time for him to go through this again, he had flown off at once to Merlin Hall to wait out the uncomfortable process in a safe place. The last Jake had heard, all Red wanted was to be left alone until his unpleasant ordeal was over.

Jake wondered *where* exactly his poor, balding Gryphon had chosen to take shelter here. *Perhaps some high, rocky section of the magical zoo,* he mused, anxious to check up on him.

Then, at last, the coach ahead of them pulled away, and it was their turn to get out. Eager to be freed from the cramped confines of the vehicle, Jake and Archie jumped out first. Henry stepped down after them and turned to assist the ladies.

Aunt Ramona emerged grandly, looking every bit as regal as her old friend, Queen Victoria. Isabelle and Dani followed, while the coachman took their baggage down from the roof and handed them to the rugged gnome servants of Merlin Hall, each clad in little red hats and blue coats.

Scores of the sturdy little fellows scurried about at knee-level, attending the throng of arriving guests. Jake and his friends followed

Aunt Ramona, who walked ahead proudly, her chin held high.

Tall and silver-haired, the Elder witch did not look a day over seventy, though rumor had it she was about three-hundred years old. Of course, a lady never told her age, so no one knew for sure.

Hurrying on through the massive front doors, Jake found the crowded, soaring entrance hall abuzz with activity. Excitement hummed in the air. The din of countless voices all talking at once echoed under the high, painted ceiling.

Knowing his Assessment was closer by the minute, he could barely focus amid the noisy hustle-and-bustle all around him. His pulse felt fluttery. His mouth was dry. His palms sweated; he wiped them on his trousers in case Aunt Ramona introduced him to some important person and he had to shake hands.

To be sure, there were all sorts of strange folk in the busy crowd around them. Robed wizards greeted tall, mysterious wood elves with long, sleek, shining hair.

Half a dozen dwarves in kilts recounted some recent, merry adventure to a friend they apparently hadn't seen in a while—a Green Man with a leafy beard and bark-like skin.

A few ghosts glided over the heads of the people streaming into the next room, some sort of fine art gallery. Jake wondered if the paintings in that collection were magical, as well. Maybe they moved, like the portrait of Queen Elizabeth back at Beacon House, the Order's base in London.

Then he forgot all about the paintings when he saw a pair of well-dressed centaurs clip-clopping down the grand, curved staircase. Centaurs, of all things! He stared. Then, *whoosh!* A djinni went sweeping by on a flying carpet in a great hurry. Jake turned to his friends in astonishment and saw Dani staring at the crowd with her mouth hanging open.

A giant passed, bending low to fit under the ceiling. Pixies scampered up the bannister of the grand staircase, and an angel leaned casually against the wall some twelve feet off the ground, arms folded, watching over everyone with a slightly bored smile. There were Magic-folk that Jake couldn't even identify.

And of course, all races of men visiting from every corner of the earth—even those few parts that did not belong to the British Empire. Jake marveled at them, studying all the strange varieties of foreign dress.

Archie and his sister knew all sorts of people, human and otherwise, and greeted them politely. They seemed unfazed by all the strangeness—though Isabelle was looking a little overwhelmed.

The highly sensitive empath avoided crowds whenever she could, but of course, this wasn't always possible. Fortunately, even as Jake watched her, she seemed to steady herself, shaking off the onslaught, refusing to absorb other people's emotions.

He smiled, proud of her.

Having just turned fifteen, the Keeper of the Unicorns was much stronger now than she used to be. He liked to think he had been a good influence, helping to toughen up the sheltered aristocratic girl; but a lot of the credit had to go to Dani, who was always looking after her.

Dani O'Dell had no magical powers to speak of, but was blessed with superb common sense, not to mention the most unshakable loyalty. She had been Jake's friend through thick and thin when he had needed one most—during his years as a penniless orphan in London.

Once his rich, highborn relatives had found him, Dani had been hired on to serve as a lady's companion to Isabelle.

Her rookery toughness balanced out the older girl's gentle ways. Though the little Irish redhead was even shorter than Archie, she wasn't afraid of much. Back in the rookery—a place where Archie's colleague, Mr. Darwin, could have well studied his notions about survival of the fittest—Dani's wild tribe of brawling elder brothers had taught the wee lass how to defend herself.

In any case, she was even more protective of the tenderhearted Isabelle than she was of Jake.

As for Archie, though he shared the same magical bloodlines as his sister, his brilliant scientific mind was all-natural.

Of course, Archimedes James Bradford had only just turned twelve himself, so it was possible that the Kinderveil might still be on him, masking some dormant magical ability yet to emerge in the boy genius.

Jake thought that might be pretty funny, especially since Archie wanted no part of magic for himself. He was a *scientist*. Instead of spells, Archie loved his gadgets, and if he could not find a tool he needed to build some new invention, then he invented the tool, too.

Just then, a familiar face appeared, albeit a very small one. Everyone exclaimed with delight, greeting Gladwin Lightwing as she came zooming over to them. The little fairy's sparkle-trail was particularly bright that day, betraying her excitement over the Gathering.

"Oh, my friends are here!" she said in her tinkling voice. She hovered before them, her iridescent wings beating too fast for the human eye to see. "Have you been assigned your rooms yet?"

"No," they said.

"Henry, you have to go over to the butler's table set up over there to get your room keys," she informed him.

"Oh, very good. Thank you, Gladwin. I'll go, my lady," he said to Aunt Ramona before turning to the children. "Don't you lot go wandering off. I don't want anyone getting lost." The tutor then left them, squeezing through the crowd to join the queue of guests waiting for their room assignments.

Gladwin beamed at them. "I'm so happy you all are here at last. We're going to have such fun! Jake, are you nervous about your Assessment?"

"No! Well—yes. A little," he admitted. Frankly, he didn't even want to think about the ordeal ahead.

He brushed the reminder of it aside, longing for the stoic, patient presence and steadying words of his rugged mentor, Guardian Derek Stone, who had been helping him get ready for the test for some time. "Gladwin, have you seen Derek?"

"Hmm. No." The royal garden fairy fluttered up a little higher and glanced around at the crowd. "Actually, I haven't. I'm not sure if he's here yet."

"He is coming, though, right?"

"Of course he's coming! Jake, Guardian Stone would never miss your Assessment. He was your father's best friend! He'll be here for you. Never fear. A Guardian always arrives just when he's needed, as *you* know all too well."

"I suppose," Jake moped.

"Oh, come!" The fairy flew closer and gave him a familiar, teasing tug on his blond forelock. "Stop looking so nervous! I'm sure Derek's around here somewhere."

"He's probably off flirting with Miss Helena," Dani said with a grin.

Aunt Ramona pursed her lips and pretended not to hear that. Miss Helena DuVal was Henry's twin sister, and the girls' governess. A governess was not supposed to have a beau. It wasn't strictly proper.

But then, a Guardian was not supposed to have a sweetheart,

either. It was thought that such romantic attachments would only distract the Order's warriors from their missions. It was not quite forbidden, but definitely frowned upon.

In any case, the carriage could only hold six people, so Miss Helena had come down ahead of them the day before, bringing a large trunk of fancy gowns with her, not just for Isabelle to wear throughout the Gathering, but also a few specific, long, dinner gowns that Izzy's mother, Lady Bradford, couldn't fit into her baggage.

No doubt the governess had not minded her task of delivering the dresses, since it would likely give her some time to be alone with her not-boyfriend, Derek.

"Oh, there are your parents!" Gladwin said brightly, pointing toward the art gallery.

"Mother! Father!"

Instantly, Isabelle and Archie went rushing off to see the terribly glamorous Uncle Richard and Aunt Claire, Lord and Lady Bradford. They did not get to see their parents very much, since they were often traveling as diplomats for the Order.

Jake and Dani hung back, remaining with Aunt Ramona and still waiting for Henry to return with their room keys.

As Archie and Isabelle ran to hug their parents, Jake could not deny feeling a twinge of—well, not exactly jealousy. Insecurity, perhaps. It was a pointed reminder that he had no mother and father to cheer him on in his Assessment.

No sign of Derek. No time to go and see Red beforehand...

He didn't realize he was scowling about it until Dani elbowed him. "Would you stop looking like you're chewin' on a toothache? You'll be fine."

"Easy for you to say! You don't have to do this."

"Oh, thanks for that reminder that I'm just a plain, boring, ordinary person."

"You know that's not what I meant," he said at once.

She humphed. "Calm down already. You've got nothing to worry about, Jake. I mean, c'mon! This silly test is *nothing* compared to some of the stuff you've already done. You bested Loki, for goodness sake, a Norse god!"

"Thor bested him. I just stood there trying not to get killed," he said morosely.

"What about our visit to Wales, then? You blew up Garnock the

Sorcerer! The very founder of the Dark Druids!"

"Shhh!" Jake shushed her with a glare.

Thankfully, Aunt Ramona was greeting a friend and had not heard her say it.

He leaned toward her, lowering his voice. "We're not supposed to mention that, remember? Mind your tongue, carrot!"

"Sorry! If I was you, I'd be braggin' about it to the whole bloomin' world."

"Yes, but that would get me killed." Jake usually relished bragging, but in this case, he saw how it could be *unhealthy.* "Aunt Ramona doesn't want the Dark Druids tracing that bit o' business back to me."

Dani sighed. "Don't worry, I'm not goin' to tell anyone. I'm just sayin'. If you can get through *that,* your Assessment's easy-breezy."

"We'll see." Jake hoped she was right. Even if she wasn't, her words made him feel a bit better.

Then Henry beckoned to them, their room keys dangling from his hand.

"Here we are, children," Aunt Ramona said, spotting the tutor. "This way."

Jake followed at once, desperate for a quiet moment of solitude in his room to prepare himself for the test ahead.

* * *

Following him, Dani paused, still glancing around in wonder at all the varieties of Magic-folk, when she suddenly noticed a peculiar-looking girl about her own age who had just arrived.

With pale white skin and jet-black hair, the girl was dressed all in black, from the spiky bow in her raven hair, to her knee-length taffeta dress, to her black wool stockings and lace-up boots. She had arrived alone, no parents, no servants, no friends with her.

Clutching the black satchel on her shoulder rather like Archie's ever-present tool-bag, the girl glanced behind her with an uneasy air, dark circles under her eyes. Suddenly, she jumped as though startled, and warded off one of the little gnomes who offered to carry her bag for her.

Dani watched as she refused the help, shaking her head with a none-too-friendly glare at the waist-high gnome.

After her brief pause in the doorway, the girl headed for the butler's table—presumably to collect her room key.

"'Oy, carrot!" Jake called. "Hurry up! We're leaving!"

Dani shook off her distraction, glared at him for calling her that in public, then hurried after the blockhead and his aunt.

* * *

Nixie Valentine was utterly exhausted. She could not believe she had to have her Assessment in such a frazzled, sleep-deprived state.

Finally reaching the front of the line, she accepted her room key from the butler. She headed on her way, glad to leave the entrance hall. The crowd was getting on her nerves. She dragged herself up the grand staircase and followed the stupid printed map until she finally found her room down some distant hallway on the fourth floor of the east wing. Unlocking the door, she leaned over the threshold for a wary look around before she stepped inside.

With only one foot in the doorway, she nearly moaned aloud at the sight of the big, beautiful, fluffy canopy bed waiting for her.

Sleep!

"Hullo, gorgeous," she mumbled to it. Then, satisfied there were no traps laid for her, she walked in, dropped her bag, and just stared at the waiting bed.

Of course she didn't dare lie down yet. If she did, she would probably sleep through the whole Gathering and miss her Assessment. She shook her head firmly. *Later.*

A glorious long nap would be her reward once she had got through her Assessment.

Already Nixie felt lighter, now that she had reached Merlin Hall, with all the powerful spells protecting its borders.

The Bugganes would not find her here.

True, those little meddling gnomes gave her the creeps. But at last, she might actually be safe. The things that hunted her surely could not sneak past the Long Man...

Could they?

With a hard swallow, Nixie cast a nervous glance around the perimeter of the pretty bedchamber she had been assigned. Should she bother putting salt across the doorway and the windowsills? she wondered.

Not that it ever really helped.

No, she decided. Her little witch-in-training spells were nothing compared to the old, old magic that enveloped Merlin Hall. She told herself to relax. At least to try.

She was safe here, surely. Besides, the pretty chamber she had been assigned was loads nicer than the musty corner of the gypsy wagon where she usually slept.

Merlin Hall would protect her.

Maybe she might even make a friend.

Well, probably not, she amended. She didn't dare, actually. She could not tell anyone her secrets. The curse the hag had put on her was real. She had learned that the hard way.

Anybody who tried to make friends with her was only courting doom.

At least now, here at Merlin Hall, she could get knowledge that might help her solve her problem. Learn new spells. Find some way she hadn't tried before to escape the torment that had become her life.

Feeling a glimmer of hope for the first time in months, Nixie took a deep breath, then took out the uniform and changed into it, grimacing at having to wear white. But once she was dressed in the required garb for her test, she got her best wand out of her black bag.

Gripping it like a weapon, she headed for the door.

With one last, longing glance over her shoulder at the lovely bed with its sweet promise of sleep, she steeled herself and stepped out, heading for the maze.

It was time to go and dazzle the Elders—because, actually, she was pretty good at magic.

Maybe a little *too* good.

Much to her regret.

CHAPTER THREE
The Proving Ground

"This way, children!" A short while later, Aunt Ramona beckoned them on. The opening of the giant maze yawned before them. As Her Ladyship marched ahead, they had no choice but to follow.

Jake managed to keep his jittery nerves under control as they joined the crowd of guests streaming into the great, green labyrinth.

The adults wore finery fit for a Sunday afternoon picnic in the park or a bit of seaside frivolity, the gents in patterned promenade suits and jaunty straw boater hats, the ladies sporting an astonishing collection of wide-brimmed, complicated bonnets.

With the festival atmosphere enlivening the sunny afternoon, an observer might have thought the well-dressed spectators were hurrying on to watch a polo match or some long-awaited game of cricket.

A few of the kids, however, including Jake, wore the athletic garb required for the Assessment: a simple uniform of tan boots, loose-fitting ivory trousers (or skirts for the girls) to allow ease of movement, a white shirt, and a brightly colored sash tied around the waist to signify the category of supernatural talents the candidate possessed.

Several people, seeing his clothes, smiled and wished him luck as they progressed through the labyrinth. Some raised an eyebrow to note the *two* colored sashes tied around his waist: blue for his gifts as a medium, red for his telekinesis.

On Henry's advice, he had twisted them together like a rope before knotting them at his hip. The loose ends fluttered in the breeze like battle pennants as he walked.

In any case, Jake tried not to feel too irked at all the fun everyone else seemed to be having when, for him and the other candidates, this was all but life or death. Tension was giving him a headache, so he was grateful for the shade the towering shrubbery walls cast as they followed the flow of the crowd.

The grassy aisles inside the maze were so broad that there was room for eight or ten people walking abreast. Of course, this depended on what sort of people.

Dani discreetly held her nose when they found themselves downwind of the horsetail end of a few centaurs. Archie elbowed her and gave the carrot-head a scolding look.

"What?" Dani retorted while Isabelle fought a giggle and hid her face behind the striped pink parasol she was using to protect her milky complexion from the sun.

"Behave," Henry warned from behind them. He was bringing up the rear to make sure they did not lose anybody along the way.

Jake was grateful for that. It would have been very easy to get lost in the maze if one wandered off; his nervousness had quickly left him disoriented as the paths twisted this way and that.

Fortunately, Aunt Ramona knew the way well. Of course, if they had got separated from her, the small, wizened gnomes posted at the intersections were helping to guide people, blocking them from going the wrong way.

As their group turned a corner into another aisle that looked exactly like the last one, Aunt Ramona explained how the maze had helped to keep the Old Yew safe for many years. Even if someone with ill intents managed to penetrate the labyrinth, the intruder was not likely to get out alive.

While she went on describing the various magical and mechanical devices designed to protect the old father tree and his eldest tree children who lived in the center, it dawned on Jake that she never talked this much—and when he heard a thunderous cheer erupt from somewhere beyond the green walls ahead, he realized, aghast, that she was merely trying to distract him.

The noise got louder with every step. Jake's stomach promptly clenched with dread. Obviously, the audience today was larger than he had anticipated, judging by the roar of the crowd.

A cold sweat broke out across his forehead. For a second, he felt like a gladiator waiting to be sent up into the Coliseum to fight a wild boar. Blimey, it sounded like a small stadium full of spectators in there.

And, in fact, it was.

Sure enough, to Jake's surprise (or perhaps, horror), the next turn revealed a huge, grassy lawn in the center of the maze, its borders clearly marked with thick chalk lines. Inside the Field of Challenge, an elaborate magical obstacle course had been set up.

This took him greatly by surprise and brought a fresh surge of anxiety, but he let his gaze travel on. Bleachers lined the long ends of the field. The seats were packed with cheering people—parents, family, friends of the poor souls facing their Assessments.

The side of the field nearest the entrance—where Jake and his companions currently stood—was left clear of seating, so that spectators could have some room to mill about, and more easily come and go.

But on the far end, the Elders in their long, ceremonial robes were seated with the VIPs in the shade on both sides of the towering Old Yew.

Jake realized they had built the Field of Challenge around the "Father Tree" so he could watch all the goings-on. When Jake spotted Queen Victoria and her entourage arrayed in a place of particular honor right next to the Old Yew, he felt the blood drain from his face.

Great. The Queen herself, along with her court followers, would be watching his every move. He slowly scanned the sea of faces.

He was not a shy lad, per se, nor did he lack confidence on the whole. But by Jove's elbow, he had not expected an audience anywhere near this large, and no one had said anything to him about this insane obstacle course.

It took everything in him not to turn around and flee.

Of course, he'd probably end up getting lost in the maze, with his luck, he thought, his pulse pounding. Well, he refused to disgrace his parents' memory with a show of cowardice.

Oh, yes, he was well aware that everyone was curious about him because of the strange circumstances of his life, how he had gone missing as a baby after his parents' murders and how he had finally been found again. No doubt all the world wanted to get a look at him, which made him feel doubly pressured to impress them all.

With a slight gulp, Jake prayed the earth would open up and swallow him.

It refused. All he could do was remind himself that he *had* to go through this if he wanted to become a Lightrider someday. Indeed, there might be a few Lightriders watching in the stands even now.

Another reason to conduct himself to the best of his ability, Jake thought. He had never met a real, live Lightrider before, but Aunt Ramona said he might be introduced to one or two at some point during the Gathering. Shoring up his courage, Jake thrust self-doubt out of his mind as best he could and followed his kin.

With Aunt Ramona leading the way and Henry in the back, they headed for the bleachers.

"Your Ladyship, they have a chair for you over there with the other Elders," the tutor called, pointing.

"Thank you, Henry, but I wish to stay with my nephew for now. I shall join my colleagues later."

Jake sent the old woman a grateful smile.

She put a reassuring hand on his shoulder. "Up there. Where the gnome's waving to us, see?"

More gnomes posted around the bleachers were serving as ushers, though they were barely tall enough to manage the steps. One was beckoning them to an empty bench a few levels up. Aunt Ramona lifted the hem of her long, ruffled skirts and proceeded up the steps, leading the way to the seats the gnome had found for them.

Jake let the girls go ahead of him, finally learning to have some manners. Archie's influence, no doubt.

Walking up the bleacher stairs, Jake warily eyed the long rows of fashionable humans and magic-folk that he passed. The crowd seemed reasonably friendly and supportive, clapping for the unfortunate lad who was currently enduring his Assessment on the Field of Challenge.

Jake paid him little mind as they reached their seats. The gnome had directed them to a spot near a family of shapeshifters. Although they looked like ordinary people at first glance, the truth soon became obvious, thanks to the antics of their horrid children: triplets—two boys, one girl—about ten years old.

The young shapeshifters had no interest whatsoever in the Assessment in progress. Instead, they kept turning themselves into half-human half-skunks and torturing everyone around them with their wild laughter and squabbling.

Unfortunately for Dani, she was sitting closest to them, and it wasn't long before the pests took an interest in the redhead.

She didn't even notice at first, but eventually she sensed them: three beady pairs of eyes looking curiously at her, studying her in devilish speculation.

Sizing her up.

She tried very hard to ignore them. She was good at ignoring people when she tried. Jake knew that firsthand.

Several minutes later, she let out a startled yelp.

Jake looked over, wondering what they had done to her. Apparently somebody had pulled her hair. When she turned around and glared at them, the shorter boy stuck his tongue out at her. Then, laughing, they all three turned themselves into full-fledged skunks and ducked out of sight, snickering at their own antics.

"Try that again!" she warned them, holding up a fist.

Jake rolled his eyes and shook his head. He didn't have time to worry about that. Dani could take care of herself. Still, it was too bad the skunkies' parents were oblivious, eagerly absorbed in the Assessment.

Jake put the troublemakers out of his mind and focused on getting the lay of the land. *Right,* he told himself after a minute or so. *This ain't so bad. If that mumper out there can do it, so can I.*

"Egads!" Archie lifted his telescope to his eye. He never went on an adventure without it. The king of gadgets always took his whole trusty tool-bag with him, just in case.

Before Jake could ask what Archie was egads-ing about, Isabelle snatched the telescope out of her brother's hand, to everyone's surprise. "Let me see that!"

Sitting up primly with the parasol in one hand, she lifted the telescope to her eye and stared intensely at the tall, black-haired boy on the Field of Challenge.

Jake and Archie exchanged a blank look.

Such unladylike behavior was most un-Isabelle.

"I say," she whispered rather breathlessly after a moment, the telescope glued to her face.

Jake arched a brow, but when he took the trouble to focus on the young man's progress for himself, he saw why everyone was cheering.

Blimey. Is that the level of skill I'm up against? A sense of dread slowly overtook him as he watched the lad negotiate an airy wall of magic floating rings.

The sturdy hoops drifted up and down gently and waved a bit from side to side, which made jumping onto the next one ever more treacherous as the boy climbed higher.

Jake's heart began to sink. His first thought was, *Oh, please, don't make me go after him.* Whoever he was, that lad would be one hard act to follow. He wore a brown sash, but Jake wasn't sure which talent that meant.

"Nobody said anything about an obstacle course," he muttered. "Somebody could've warned me!"

"Oh, don't worry, coz, that's not for you," Archie said cheerfully. "They'll change the field when it's your turn. Guardians always get the obstacle course."

"Guardian? Oh, is that what he is?" Jake asked in surprise.

Archie nodded. "Brown sash—signifies strong as oak."

"Ah." Relief flooded through Jake upon hearing that he would not have to risk his neck climbing up that bit of treachery.

As he watched, the boy reached the top row of the wall of floating rings and vaulted up onto the small levitating platform above it.

The crowd drew an audible intake of breath as the lad steadied his balance on the precarious perch many yards above the turf. He had no sooner picked up the bat waiting for him on the platform when a barrage of clay balls started swooping at him.

The missiles flew at his head and body from all directions, trying to knock him off his precarious perch. He ducked and kicked a few away, but mostly used the bat to pulverize them with a look of great intensity. He seemed to relish the satisfying smash as he shattered each target.

Well, Guardians *were* the warriors of the Order, Jake mused. He was not easily impressed, but even he could admit that this kid probably could've held his own against all five of Dani's elder brothers at once.

Even without the brown sash, it probably should have been obvious that the lad was a Guardian-in-training. Though only a lad, he already had the tall, muscular build for the role. But then, his height and filled-out breadth might have been due to his age. He looked a few years older than Jake—closer to Isabelle's age—sixteen or seventeen.

Hmm. Jake wondered why the boy was only having his Assessment now. Maybe it had taken a couple of extra years for his Kinderveil to wear off.

Then he shrugged the question off, still too nervous about his own ordeal to give the other contenders much thought.

"May I *please* have my telescope back?" Archie demanded of his sister, just as Dani let out another yelp.

"Ow!" She whipped around again as the skunkies retreated and pretended to be engrossed in the Assessment, even though they were clearly fighting laughter.

Now Dani was incensed. "Henry!"

Sitting on the far end of their row, Henry leaned back, saw her point to his fellow shapeshifters acting badly, and called sternly to them, "Excuse me, children!"

When they looked over, Henry gave a rough shrug and jerked his neck, promptly turning his own head into that of his wolf form.

He growled at them in warning with a show of fangs.

The skunkies shrieked and ran away.

Henry shook himself again and returned to his usual self in a heartbeat, the mild-mannered tutor in a bowtie. "That should do it."

Dani beamed at him. "Thank you, Henry!"

"Any time, Miss O'Dell."

Jake always found it a bit strange to think of Henry, of all people, turning into a wolf, since in his human form, the bespectacled tutor was the most civilized chap anyone could want to meet.

One might have expected a wolf side from someone like Guardian Derek Stone, wherever he was. But Derek was just Derek.

Aye, heart of oak, Jake mused. It fit. The phrase had always been the highest of compliments in England, signifying strong, steady courage, and indeed, the color brown was well chosen for the Guardians.

Simple, honest, unyielding men. *Were there female Guardians, come to think of it?* Jake wondered. He didn't know. But to be compared to any sort of tree was praise indeed when the whole magical world of the Order centered around the ancient Yew Tree.

Where is Derek, anyway? Jake scanned the crowd in frustration. Honestly, he was a bit annoyed that the hero he idolized had not even bothered showing up to wish him luck. He'd been hoping for a little encouragement, maybe a few last-minute words of advice. But maybe some important mission had come along...

"C'mon, Izzy! Give me my telescope back!" Archie demanded. "I don't want to miss the next part!"

"In a moment!" She followed the black-haired boy's every move through the lens.

"Why? What's the next part?" Jake asked just as the clay balls ceased their attack and gave the lad a brief chance to catch his breath.

"They'll want to test his Guardian instincts," Archie said eagerly.

"Y'know, sensing when his assigned charge is in danger. This chap's really good. I wonder who he is."

"So do I," Isabelle murmured with unabashed interest.

Jake frowned toward the field, feeling increasingly intimidated. Then a thought struck him. "Say, Isabelle, I know you're busy ogling him, but do me a favor and read his emotions for a second. Was that kid scared about his Assessment, too?"

Please tell me I'm not the only quake-buttocks coward sitting here today.

Izzy tried, then shook her head. "Sorry, can't read him. Must be too far away, or there are too many other people here, too many emotions getting all mixed up together."

"Well, you'd better stop gawking at him before Aunt Ramona sees you. Her Ladyship will not approve," Archie warned his sister.

Isabelle handed him back his telescope. "Fair enough. But please note I'm not the only one," she said wryly. "If you haven't noticed, every girl here is staring at him. He's gorgeous."

"No, they're not," Jake said indignantly, for he was the one who usually got all the girls' attention. He pretended to hate it, of course, but...

"Give me that, I want to see him." Now it was Dani's turn to snatch the telescope out of Archie's hands. "I'll tell you if he's good enough for you, Izzy." After a moment, she said, "Hmm..."

Jake huffed. "Et tu, carrot?"

Dani handed Archie back his telescope and flashed Isabelle a grin. "Well, he's not ugly. But whether he's worthy of our Isabelle, it's too soon to say," she reported. "We'll have to figure out some way for you to meet him!"

Isabelle turned beet-red. "I couldn't possibly!"

"But we have to," the younger girl said reasonably. "You can't like him until we find out if he's boring or an idiot or rude like most boys. Ahem." Dani sent Jake a look.

He smirked at her.

Isabelle shuddered. "No, Dani. That's not how it works for a young lady of my station. I mean, I can look...but my parents will introduce me to any boys that I'm allowed to talk to."

"Or none, according to Father," Archie remarked.

"Father's only joking when he says that, I'm sure!" Isabelle retorted, her cheeks still as pink as her parasol.

"Huh. Well, I'm sure he and Mother have already composed a long list of requirements for any future suitor who, for some strange reason, would want to court my sister," Archie muttered.

"She's not old enough yet!" Jake reminded them, protective of his delicate empath cousin. "She's only fifteen. Miss Helena says she's got another year yet before her debutante ball."

"Excuse me, I'm sitting right here. Must you rudesbys discuss me as if I were not present?"

"Isabelle's in *loooove!*" Archie announced in a singsong.

Jake guffawed and then joined in, and both boys enjoyed teasing her for a while.

"Ohh, look at the handsome Guardian!" they mimicked.

"I am going to throw the two of you off these bleachers," the aristocratic miss said politely through gritted teeth.

They laughed harder when she turned and glared at them from underneath her parasol.

"Hey, Arch, she's turning redder than my Gryphon. If this continues, think her head might explode?"

"Maybe! Izzy, if your head explodes, can I dissect your brain? Please? For science, sis. It would only be for science. I don't believe a thorough dissection of an empath's brain has ever been conducted."

"Leave her alone, you pair o' heathens!" Dani warned while Isabelle hid from all the world behind her parasol.

"Aw, don't worry, Iz," Jake relented with a grin. "I'm sure the glorious Guardian kid doesn't want to meet you, anyway. You know their kind, all business. Your undying love would go unrequited, and then you'd catch consumption and waste away like a tragic heroine in a penny dreadful."

"I am going to strangle you." Isabelle peeked out from behind her parasol with a scowl. "At least I'm not jealous of him!" she shot back.

"What?" Jake retorted.

"You're jealous of how talented he is!"

"Don't be daft, I'm not a Guardian!" he said, though now, it was *his* turn to turn a bit red.

There was no fooling an empath when it came to whatever one was feeling. Of course, that did not stop Jake from scoffing in denial. It was really no fun having his insecurities called out in front of the others.

"I'm not in competition with that mumper," he grumbled, no longer laughing. "I'm going to become a Lightrider, remember? Lightriders outrank Guardians, anyway. Whoever he is, he's good at what he does. For that, I give him credit. Beyond that, I couldn't care less."

"Maybe you should care, actually," Archie remarked in a thoughtful tone, waiting to watch the final challenge in the boy's Assessment. "After all, if you become a Lightrider and he becomes a Guardian, he might save your life someday."

"Fat chance o' that!" He scowled at the boy genius. "You're supposed to be on my side, Arch, and what do I need him for, anyway? I'm the one who killed Garnock the Sorcerer, remember?"

"Shhh!" Dani scolded.

"Just sayin'. I don't need some idiot Guardian kid watching over me. I've got Red and you lot, and besides, I can bloody well take care o' myself."

"Sorry!" Archie exclaimed. "Cheese it, Jake, don't be so touchy. No offense intended."

Dani had turned to the lady sitting on the other side of her. "Excuse me, do you know that boy's name?"

The woman consulted the program and gave her an answer, though the applause was too loud for Jake to hear what she had said.

"Ah, thank you. Maddox St. Trinian," Dani echoed, turning back to them. "A good name for an Order knight." She gave Isabelle a big, unsubtle wink, and once again, the older girl's face turned strawberry-red.

Jake snorted. Girls really were the silliest creatures. Determined to ignore his dread over whether he would be called next, he folded his arms across his chest and stoically waited to see the final bit of torture that the Elders had planned for Maddox St. Trinian.

Better him than me.

Still standing on the levitating platform high above the ground, Maddox waited while one of the Elders waved a wand, raising four columns in the distant corners of the field. The stone pillars surged up out of the turf like weird, fast-growing trees, and Jake was startled to spy a gnome standing on top of each one.

The columns stopped growing when they reached half the height of the platform on which the aspiring Guardian stood; he was in the middle, well above them.

The Elder walked out to the center of the field and spoke a quick spell to the ground right beneath his feet.

"That's Sir Peter Quince," Archie told Jake and Dani. "He's a frequent master of ceremonies for the Assessments."

Sir Peter was an ordinary-looking, middle-aged man, a bit doughy, with short-cropped hair, tortoiseshell-rimmed spectacles, and an orange bowtie to match the orange trim on his long black scholar's robe, signifying his status as a wizard.

With another wave of his wand, Sir Peter caused a fifth pillar to rise, fatter than the rest, in the very center of the Field of Challenge. He stepped onto it and let the growing column carry him straight up until it came alongside the floating platform where Maddox St. Trinian waited. With a broad smile, Sir Peter beckoned to the Guardian-in-training to join him. Maddox did so, stepping off the platform with an air of total self-assurance.

"How are you feeling so far, Mr. St. Trinian?" Sir Peter asked in a rather smarmy tone through a metal speaking trumpet.

He held it up to the boy's mouth next so the crowd could hear his terse answer: "Good, sir."

"Typical Guardian, man of few words," Archie remarked while everyone applauded to encourage the lad through his final test.

Sir Peter smiled. "I think the crowd likes you."

"I don't," Jake opined in a mild tone.

But at least he could see why they chose Sir Peter to serve as master of ceremonies. His amiable manner no doubt helped to put the candidates at ease.

"So, let me explain the final step in your Assessment, Maddox," he said. "In this challenge, we will test your most vital Guardian instinct: the ability to sense when your charge is in imminent danger."

Sir Peter gestured around at the nervous-looking gnomes perched atop the four columns. "Do you feel you've been able to establish the necessary bond with the temporary charges we've assigned to you?"

Maddox leaned toward the speaking trumpet. "Yes, sir. They've been following me around for the past two days like baby ducks."

The crowd chuckled at the serious boy's humble tone. The girls giggled, charmed.

Jake rolled his eyes.

"Good," said the Elder. "Well, what we're going to do is release four identical battering rams at the same time, Maddox, one aimed at each column."

"Battering rams, sir?" Maddox echoed in surprise.

"Not castle-storming size, only about yay long." Sir Peter held up his hands about four feet apart. "Just big enough to destroy the columns the gnomes are standing on. The trick, however, is that only one of these battering rams is real. The others are a harmless illusion. It's up to you to determine which one is real, and which of your 'baby ducks' is in true need of rescue.

"As you can see, the columns are too high and the gnomes are too small to get down by themselves. So, choose well, young Guardian, for you'll have only a few seconds to decide which of your charges is in actual danger."

"Yes, sir."

"You'll swing to the gnome's rescue using the ropes provided—oh, and avoid getting hit by the battering ram yourself along the way. Your goal is to rescue your gnome before his column is destroyed and he, er, falls to his death."

A worried murmur ran through the stands.

"Don't be alarmed, ladies and gentleman," Sir Peter assured everybody. "We have a full medical team on hand in case of any...unfortunate accidents. The danger has to be real to activate the Guardian instinct. Let's have a round of applause for our brave volunteers. Ladies and gentlemen, the gnomes of Merlin Hall!"

Everyone clapped for the suicidal gnomes who had agreed to go along with this. Jake somehow doubted they had been given much choice, no matter what Sir Peter said.

"All right, then, if everybody's ready—stand back, please, audience. Any onlookers will please clear the edges of the Field of Challenge! Yes, very good, thank you very much. Safety first. We don't want anyone losing fingers or toes or hoofs or wings or tentacles or what-have-you."

The few stray spectators who had been standing around the edges for a better view took a big step backwards.

Sir Peter nodded. "Excellent. Now then."

With a shouted spell and a big wave of his wand, he caused a sturdy metal framework slightly like a cage to rise out of the ground around the borders of the field, surrounding the four columns. In a wave of sparkling magic, the steel posts sprouted higher and the horizontal beams stretched until the sturdy metal framework grew together over the middle of the field.

With the top part firmly locked into place, there was a second's pause, and then various long, thick ropes descended, dangling here and there, each one tied around the crisscrossed beams.

No one line was long enough to reach the columns, which meant Maddox would need to swing from rope to rope to rescue the endangered gnome.

Then the Elder worked a final spell, and four menacing battering rams materialized out of thin air, resting up into the metal framework, waiting to be released.

"Good luck to Maddox St. Trinian!" Sir Peter said through the megaphone. Then he jumped off the towering center pillar and, robes flapping in the breeze, floated down gently to the ground. He strode off the field, returning to his seat by the Old Yew.

Up there on the middle column, Maddox closed his eyes and lowered his head, looking inward, no doubt, to find whatever his Guardian instinct was telling him. Jake had seen that look of quiet concentration on Derek's face many times.

All four gnomes appeared extremely nervous. They probably hadn't been told, either, which of them would be in mortal danger so that none of them would accidentally give it away.

The whole crowd held its breath as a great, ominous rumbling sound came from the metal framework overhead.

Maddox's eyes flicked open with blazing intensity. He leaped off the platform, caught hold of a rope dangling to his left, and swung with all his might toward the north column, even as the four identical battering rams were released.

CHAPTER FOUR
The Rival & the Prodigy

The gnomes screamed.

It was impossible to tell which battering ram was real as their long chains uncoiled with an ugly, clanking hiss overhead. Simultaneously, they plunged out of their moorings.

All eyes were on Maddox as he flew through the air with the battering ram chasing right behind him. He had made his choice and there wasn't any chance of turning back or changing his mind. It was all or nothing. Even Jake held his breath as the aspiring Guardian turned his hips and kicked his legs sideways to swerve toward his destination.

He landed on the column just long enough to grab the terrified gnome and lift the little fellow up onto his back. At once, it reached its arms around the lad's neck and braced its feet in the back of his brown sash, freeing Maddox's hands for their immediate escape.

The battering ram barreled straight at them.

Maddox dove off the column and caught himself on a rope hanging nearby. Just as he went arcing away, the battering ram smashed into the column and turned it to rubble.

Everybody gasped. The three fake ones burst into colorful explosions of feathers like confetti.

But it wasn't over yet. Maddox still had one final challenge: a long, hair-raising jump from rope to rope with the gnome on his back. A Guardian, after all, must always transport his charge to safety in an attack situation, as Jake knew from Derek saving his neck in the past.

He didn't let himself blink as he watched Maddox make the gravity-defying spring between ropes without dropping the frightened gnome.

He did it!

Isabelle and Archie and even Dani cheered. Thunderous applause erupted as Maddox grabbed hold and clung to the last rope in relief, steadying the gnome and then letting it climb up to sit on his shoulder.

As Maddox stepped down onto solid ground, Jake applauded like a good sport along with everybody else. The kid deserved it, he admitted in begrudging admiration.

"Oh, good show! Well done!" Archie cheered, clapping madly. "Well, sis, I approve."

Isabelle was staring raptly at Maddox St. Trinian through the telescope again while Dani grinned like the cat who had eaten *two* canaries.

On the field, Maddox put the gnome down, shook its hand, then bowed to the Old Yew and marched off the field. Panting and sweaty, he picked up a waiting canteen and swigged some water.

At least he had the decency to look a little shaken up after what could have easily been the wrong choice and a total disaster.

Jake started to make a wisecrack. "Don't faint, Izzy. No one brought the smelling salts..." But the rest of the words died on his tongue as he saw what happened next.

Maddox St. Trinian was shaking hands with Derek Stone.

Down there on the edge of the field, Derek was beaming at him, clapping the boy warmly on the shoulder like they were old pals. He was obviously congratulating the younger Guardian on a job well done, and Jake realized at that moment that Derek had been sitting in the front row all along, watching Maddox carry out his Assessment.

Jake was utterly taken aback. He let out a great, indignant huff. *Well, that's a fine how-do-ye-do! Derek's supposed to be* my *mentor!* If he wasn't jealous of Maddox St. Trinian before, he certainly was now. *I think I hate that kid.*

"Uh, I guess Derek knows him," Archie said as tactfully as possible, for it was not difficult for the others to guess Jake's reaction when they, too, saw Derek making a great, proud fuss over the lad.

"He must be training him," Dani offered.

Jake couldn't hold back. "You'd think he would've said something about it—warned me!"

"Steady on, coz," Archie advised. "You need to keep a clear head in case they call you next."

Jake suppressed a growl.

Archie was right, and they both knew it. Within moments, the next victim would be called down.

Even now, Sir Peter waved his wand at the obstacle course and made it disappear, clearing the Field of Challenge for the next Assessment.

The metal framework, the columns—even the rubble from the one that had been smashed—dissolved and vanished as if they'd been no more solid than a morning mist.

Weird, Jake thought. Then he did his best to follow his cousin's sensible advice and ignore the fact that he was totally intimidated by this tough older boy with such outstanding skills. A boy that his own hero, Derek Stone, had obviously been more concerned about than *him.*

Jake felt small and unimportant, forgotten. Abandoned. He had come to know that feeling well growing up in the orphanage, but it had been a while since it had plagued him.

Leaning forward on the uncomfortable bench, he rested his elbows on his knees and clasped his fingers loosely, refusing to look at Derek or his great Guardian protégé anymore. It was too vexing. Like Archie said, he had to stay calm. Out there in that field, it was going to be him against whatever obstacles the Elders deemed appropriate for a boy who could see ghosts and move things with his mind.

What stupid talents his own gifts seemed to him at the moment. He would have much rather have been a dashing warrior like Maddox. Now *that* was what a real hero was supposed to be like, rescuing others, not lounging around chatting with ghosts and other invisible friends—

"Stop it, Jake," Isabelle said with a knowing sigh.

"*You* stop it!" he snapped. "Quit reading my mind. Empaths!" he huffed.

"She doesn't read minds, she reads emotions, unless you're a dog," Dani pointed out, for Isabelle only had true telepathy with animals.

"I wish I was! Then I wouldn't have to go through this torture!" he burst out.

"Excuse me, I turn into a wolf now and then, and I had to go through it, too," said Henry, glancing over at his outburst.

"Oh, everybody leave me alone," Jake muttered.

"We're on your side, coz," Archie told him earnestly.

"Just—nobody talk to me until this is over, all right?"

"Gladly," Dani said under her breath.

The others leaned away from him while Jake stared broodingly at the Field of Challenge, waiting to find out who would go next.

"I've never seen him like this before," he could hear them murmuring to each other. "He's a wreck."

"He'll be fine," Dani assured his cousins. "He just really wants to dazzle everybody. You know, so they'll pick him for a Lightrider someday."

Hands sweating, Jake laced his fingers together. *Please don't pick me next. Please don't pick me next,* he repeated over and over in his mind. *I don't want to go after Maddox St. Trinian.*

Down by the Old Yew, Sir Peter now held an envelope in his hand. He opened it, read the note inside, then lifted his speaking trumpet to his lips. "Our next demonstration will be from..."

Jake squeezed his eyes shut and grimaced, braced to hear his fate.

"Nixella Marie Valentine: witch!" Sir Peter boomed through his speaking trumpet.

Jake nearly collapsed at this temporary reprieve. *Oh, thank you, thank you.* Spared again.

"Where is Miss Valentine?" Sir Peter visored his eyes with his hand and scanned the field and bleachers with a pleasant air. "The next candidate will enter the Field of Challenge, please. Ah, there you are! Right up here, my dear, if you please."

A murmur of anticipation ran through the bleachers. The audience looked around to find the next contestant, a grim-faced girl marching out onto the field.

"Hey, it's the gloomy girl I saw before!" Dani said.

"What sort of name is Nixella?" Archie murmured.

Dani nodded. "Even *sounds* like a witch. Hmm, she doesn't look quite so pale now that she's not wearing all black."

"All black? Like Queen Victoria?" Jake asked. "Maybe she's in mourning."

With the orange sash of the witches and wizards tied around her waist, the girl walked out onto the field as warily as a stray cat.

Jake's heart pounded with relief for himself—mixed with sympathy for the girl.

When she arrived before the seating area for all the VIPs, she made a deep, formal curtsy to Queen Victoria, the Elders, and the Old Yew. The skinny, raven-haired girl looked tiny in front of the massive trunk of the several-thousand-year-old tree.

The Old Yew asked her a few questions privately before Sir Peter once more took matters in hand.

"Welcome, Miss Valentine." With a broad smile and firm grip on her shoulder, he forced her to turn around beside him and face the crowd, his speaking trumpet at the ready.

She blanched as she looked out over the audience.

"So! Are you ready for the day's challenge, my dear?" he asked, pleasant as ever.

She quickly lowered her head and nodded, as though she could not bear to look out upon the endless sea of faces.

Jake felt for her.

"Great! And do you enjoy being a witch?"

"Very much, sir," she said into the speaking trumpet. Then she lowered her head again, toying nervously with her long, cream-colored skirts. She fingered the wand tucked into her sash as if it were a good luck charm.

Sir Peter chuckled. "I believe Miss Valentine would like to get this over with, ladies and gentlemen."

She gave a more vigorous nod. "Oh, yes, if you please, sir."

"Very well. Let's get you all set up, then." He gestured to a pair of gnomes nearby.

Jake believed these were different ones than the last Assessment, but it was hard to be certain. They all looked alike.

Between them, the two gnomes carried out a tall metal brazier onto the field. It had a flat stand as its base; a single pole about five feet tall; and a wide, shallow basin on the top, mounded with unlit coals.

While the gnomes carried the brazier out to the middle of the Field of Challenge, Sir Peter surveyed the audience with his speaking trumpet to his lips.

"Ladies and gentlemen, as some of you know and others will remember from firsthand experience, as I do, the Assessment for the magic-working group requires young witches and wizards to demonstrate their progress in mastering the four elements." He counted them off on his fingers: "Fire. Water. Earth. And air."

"Aunt Ramona, did you have to do that for your Assessment when you were a girl?" Isabelle asked.

The Elder witch laughed. "Oh, child, they hadn't even started doing Assessments yet when I was her age."

Jake supposed that was a very long time ago, indeed.

"I've watched more of these things than I can remember," the Elder witch added. "Even served on the panel of judges dozens of times, doling out scores for our young hopefuls."

"Since this is a very challenging Assessment," Sir Peter continued through his trumpet, "the one aspect we really hope to see is that the coals in the brazier be lit by any magical means the candidate wishes to employ."

As the gnomes hurried off the field, Sir Peter glanced down fondly at the wide-eyed witch. "We're ready if you are, Miss Valentine."

The scared girl nodded and marched out onto the field alone, clutching her wand tightly in her hand.

Sir Peter returned to his place and fluffed his ceremonial robes out of the way as he sat down again.

Nixella took a moment to concentrate, and a hush fell over the watching crowd. Then she lifted her hands to the sky and began murmuring a spell under her breath.

For several seconds, nothing happened.

Jake and the others were already starting to cringe for her, but then, dark clouds began forming over her head.

"Well, that's appropriate," mumbled Dani. "Since dark clouds seem to follow her."

The thunderclouds gathered and grew over the center of the field where Nixella stood; they started swirling, slowly at first, but spreading and thickening as they churned faster and faster.

Jake was suddenly rather uneasy. This was serious power to find in the hands of a kid, and Miss Valentine was only getting started. Demonstrations like this certainly showed why the Order kept as close an eye as possible on all magical children. Especially when it came to witches and wizards.

Just as the oak-sure Guardians were always the reliable ones, the Order's stalwart loyalists, witches and warlocks were the type most likely to go astray.

At least, that was what Jake had heard. Too often, rumor had it, their power seemed to go to their heads.

Jake hoped Miss Valentine was a good person because even he could see that her abilities were formidable, though she only looked about Dani's age.

Lifting her wand in a straight line above her head, Nixella made the clouds she had formed obey her, ordering them into a small, intense, whirlwind.

The crowd oohed and aahed and applauded in amazement as the outer bands of wind from her magic-born tornado messed up everybody's hair.

"I guess that counts as air," Dani said loudly over the gale, her red hair flying in her face.

"It's a wonder she doesn't blow away!" Archie cried, just before somebody's lost program whipped flat against his face. He peeled the wind-tossed paper off him with a splutter.

"Oh!" Isabelle cried as her pink parasol suddenly flipped inside-out in the stiff breeze.

Nixella Valentine flicked her wand at the sky with a throwing motion and shouted, *"Incendia!"*

A huge lightning bolt streaked across the afternoon sky, as if Zeus himself had thrown it down to let her borrow it.

Crackling in shades of blinding gold and jagged silver, it pierced the thunderheads, rocketed down through the center of the funnel cloud, and struck the metal brazier.

Instantly, the coals burst into flames.

The applause was immediate, accompanied by astonished cheering as the lightning disappeared and the fire atop the brazier blazed.

"I bet she practiced this a lot," Archie said admiringly.

Even Aunt Ramona had sat up and taken notice, despite all the innumerable Assessments she had watched over the centuries. "*That* is a very talented girl."

Jake agreed. Thankfully, their talents were different enough that he didn't feel as threatened by the little witch as he had by the daring warrior-kid, Maddox St. Trinian.

Aunt Ramona was applauding and shaking her head in surprise. "This is extremely advanced work for one so young."

"Do you think she ever smiles?" Archie asked.

"I doubt it," Dani said. "She looks like she hates the world."

Having proved her thorough study of the element of air and succeeded at the main task of lighting the brazier by magical means—which obviously counted as fire—Miss Valentine now turned her attention to the element of water.

The lightning had receded to its invisible dwelling place in the sky.

She calmed the winds, dispersing her tornado before it blew out the brazier flames. All that was left now were the dark clouds she had started with.

Jake watched in fascination as she took her wand and tapped her left hand with it, then did the same thing to her right. This interesting bit of magic apparently allowed her to dispense with her wand and use her hands instead. She tucked the wand into her orange sash and then lifted her hands toward the thunderclouds above her.

Like a sculptor working a hunk of clay—smoothing, rounding, shaping it—she compacted the clouds down into a tight, shimmering ball of water.

It hovered about six feet off the ground. She took care to step back out of the way and then, with artful flicks of her fingers, she began making drips of rain leak off the watery sphere here and there.

Drip, drip, drip.

They fell faster and faster, until she clapped her hands together loudly. The water gushed out in a torrential downpour that soaked the circle of grass below it and turned it into mud.

The people applauded her flamboyant show madly, but Nixella was in her own world. Obviously, the girl loved her craft. The final element left now was earth. She seemed to brace herself as she took out her wand again, like she was worried about this one.

Too low to hear, she spoke an incantation of some sort over the mud puddle, then whisked the air above it with her wand. Again, she took a tentative step back, as if she were not quite sure herself what might happen next.

Something began stirring in the mud puddle.

Archie laughed aloud as a brown, misshapen, mud creature rose up out of the puddle. It stood taller than the girl, with big thumping legs, little stunted arms, and wonky long ears.

"What is it?" Dani cried.

"A rabbit!" Isabelle exclaimed as the giant mud-hare twitched its whiskered nose and hopped three times across the grass, before collapsing back into a large squishy puddle again.

"Brilliant," Jake breathed.

"Oh, bravo!" Archie applauded with unabashed admiration. "Isn't that what they call a golem, Aunt Ramona?"

"Correct," she said in distraction. She looked almost alarmed at the child's display of magic.

Nixella Valentine gave the Old Yew a quick curtsy before hurrying shyly off the field.

Archie started to make a comment about the girl, but before he could speak—and *quite* before Jake was ready to hear it—Sir Peter Quince raised his speaking trumpet and boomed out the words that he had been dreading.

"Jacob Xavier Montague Charles Everton, the seventh Earl of Griffon! Will you please come forward?"

CHAPTER FIVE
Lightrider Material?

J ake froze.

"You're up, man, go, go!" Archie urged, clapping him on the shoulder.

His friends and even Henry began applauding wildly, cheering, as Jake stood up, dizzy, from his seat. He felt as though his knees were made of jelly.

From the edge of the field below, Derek turned and pointed at him in greeting, as if to say, *There you are!* Beside him, Maddox St. Trinian studied Jake with a long, intent stare—until he noticed Isabelle. Then he looked at nothing else.

But Derek waved and started clapping heartily. "Hear, hear for Lord Griffon!"

Jake practically scowled at his mentor. It was a little late for Derek to be giving him the encouragement he had so desperately needed before. Ah, well. Now he would find out if he could indeed get through this on his own.

No parents. No Derek, no Red. No Henry and Helena to watch his back. No Aunt Ramona, no Gladwin. No Archie or Izzy or Dani helping him out in their own particular ways.

This time, it was just him and the moment of truth, with the whole world looking on. But he supposed that was the point of all this, anyway. He was growing up, and it was time to find out what he was really made of.

His limbs felt wobbly as he squeezed across the aisle in front of the others, reached the steps, and then walked down the aisle to the field.

"Good luck, Jake!" Dani called.

"Be calm, stay centered," Aunt Ramona had advised him earlier.

Easier said than done.

Isabelle waved her handkerchief in a ladylike show of support, but Jake still felt like he wanted to puke.

Down the bleacher stairs he went in a daze, across the gravel surrounding the Field of Challenge. Then he took his first momentous step over the thick chalk line.

And tripped a bit, of course.

Nervousness made him clumsy as he stepped onto the field. *Humiliating! Can't you even walk right?* He paused, remembered to breathe, his heart thumping like the mummers' drums of May Day. Then he squared his shoulders, steadied himself, and marched on, beginning to feel more normal.

Until he got close enough to the Old Yew to make out, for the first time, the gnarled old-man face in the ancient tree trunk. *Good Lord.* Jake took one look at it and stopped in his tracks.

He had known the Old Yew was a person, but for some reason, he had not thought about a face. That was how it was with trees, though. Sometimes you could see the faces in them, other times not.

It was most disconcerting, in any case. Especially since the Old Yew was staring right at him, matter-of-factly.

Somehow Jake collected his wits again and pressed on until he reached the spot where he bowed to all the powers-that-be.

Meanwhile, Sir Peter was clearing the Field of Challenge once more with another wave of his wand. Nixella Valentine's ruined mud-rabbit and the puddle that had spawned it both evaporated.

"Ah, there you are," Sir Peter greeted him brightly after completing his spell. He laid hold of Jake's shoulder and spun him about none-too-gently.

Jake gulped as he beheld the sprawling sea of spectators. There must have been a thousand people watching.

"Not yet, Sir Peter, we should like to speak to the boy for a moment," a deep, scratchy voice said behind him.

"Why, of course, Your Serene Leafiness." His captor whirled Jake around again.

The row of Elders in their elevated chairs were inspecting him with curiosity, and Sir Peter gave him a slight shove toward the Old Yew.

"Go and pay your respects, boy," he ordered under his breath.

"Y-yes, sir."

The towering tree in the center of the Elders' seats studied Jake with an unblinking stare.

As he moved forward, he kept a respectful distance, mindful not to step on the Old Yew's toes, as it were; its gnarled roots spread out for some yards around the massive trunk.

"So...Jacob Everton, the Lost Heir of Griffon," the ancient tree greeted him in a deep, raspy old-man voice, with slightly mulchy breath, while the spring breeze stirred in its branches, from which birds came and went as they pleased.

Jake blinked.

"And now he has been found," the tree said in a reflective tone. "I hear it is your birthday tomorrow, lad. Born on Beltane, yes? That is a very good omen, you know. 'Tis said a Beltane babe is born lucky. Happy birthday to you, boy."

Humph, I don't know about that, Jake thought, but he answered with respect. "Thank you, Your Serene Leafiness. And, er, if you don't mind," he added gingerly, "may I pass along a greeting to you from your Norse cousin, Yggdrasil, the Tree of the Universe."

The Old Yew's mossy eyebrows shot up. "You met Yggdrasil?"

Jake nodded, rather pleased with himself. He hoped the showoff Maddox was using his extra-powerful Guardian senses to hear this part. He felt rather important.

"We had to help a giant find his way back to Jugenheim a few months ago. Up Yggdrasil was the only way to get there."

"Indeed," the Old Yew marveled. "And how is the old Viking oak these days, eh?"

"Happy to say he is thriving, sir, according to the three witches who water him. They, too, send their best."

"By my buds and branches! You met the three ferocious Norns and lived to tell of it?"

"Why, yes, sir. They served us tea, actually."

"I say." Now it was the tree's turn to look entirely astonished at *him.*

"Begging your pardon, Your Leafiness," a furry-faced Elder with whiskers and small, pointy ears spoke up. "We really should try to keep to the schedule. The Griffon heir is not the only candidate today." He cast Jake a sour look. "And while we're all *very* impressed to hear these tales of his exploits—uncorroborated tales, I would remind my colleagues—perhaps the lad believes that chatting up His Leafiness will make the panel show a certain favoritism. Hmm?"

"No, sir!" Jake exclaimed in offended surprise, turning to him. *What is that fellow, anyway? Part rodent?*

The Elder in question studied Jake through beady eyes, his little pink nose twitching ever so slightly. The Old Yew looked askance at the furry Elder. (Of course, the tree could not turn his head very much to look at people beside him; all he could do was peer at them out of the corners of his eyes.)

"If you have questions for the boy, then by all means, ask them, Lord Badgerton."

"Very well," Lord Badgerton said crisply. "We hear that before you were found, you spent a few years as a pickpocket in London, Lord Griffon. Is that correct?"

Jake winced to hear the embarrassing secret of his thieving past announced to the entire magical community. Though his cheeks turned red, he stood stiffly, his chin high. "Yes, sir," he admitted.

He could hear the murmurs that ran through the audience and the row of Elders.

The Old Yew's woody face rearranged itself into a frown. "I trust your trainers will make sure to rid you of any worrisome old habits, Jacob. See that they do."

"Yes, sir." Everything in him longed to say something in his own defense, but somehow Jake knew it would only come out sounding like an excuse. So he kept his mouth shut and merely nodded.

Sir Peter Quince returned to his side. "Now then, Jacob. Are you ready to begin?"

Jake nodded, though it was really more a command than a question.

The smiling fellow whipped him around roughly once more to face the crowd and then proceeded to conduct a smarmy public interview of him. "Well, well, dear lad. Sounds like you have some big shoes to fill. Two talents!" He pointed at the red and blue sashes entwined around Jake's waist. "I hear you have inherited both your parents' abilities. Is this true?"

"Yes, sir. My mother could see ghosts, and my father had telekinesis."

"And they both were Lightriders," Sir Peter confided to the crowd through his speaking trumpet. "I am told you have high hopes of following in their footsteps someday?"

Jake blushed. "If I am found worthy, sir."

"Well, you're going to need quite a few more birthdays before you'll be ready for that, I warrant, but I'm sure the panel will keep you in mind," he said in amusement, and many in the audience chuckled at a mere boy's dreams of becoming a great hero.

"To be sure," Sir Peter continued, "two gifts must keep you very busy. When did your powers first begin to show? Do tell. Everyone's very curious about you, Jake."

"They are?"

"Charming." Sir Peter chuckled, and the crowd followed suit, which Jake found a trifle bewildering.

"Well, um, the Kinderveil wore off about a year ago, a few weeks before my twelfth birthday."

"Did both your gifts emerge at the same time?"

"Yes, sir. I didn't know what to make of it. I was on my own at the time. Thought I was going mad."

"No doubt. Then Guardian Stone found you, didn't he?" he narrated for the benefit of the audience, many of whom were craning their necks to gawk at Jake or watching him through field glasses. "Rescued you, I believe, when your Uncle Waldrick tried to kill you in his wicked conspiracy with that odious sea-witch, Fionnula Coralbroom."

The mere mention of that name brought a visceral reaction from many of the Elders. It was clear she was still very much hated and feared.

Jake nodded.

"You are lucky to be alive with enemies like that, young man. Fortunately, ladies and gentlemen, Fionnula Coralbroom is well contained in her cell at the bottom of the North Atlantic. Ah, what's the matter?" the Elder asked Jake, looking askance at him with a smile. "Does she still make you nervous? She would me."

"No, sir. I just didn't...realize the world knew about all that."

"Are you jesting?" he exclaimed. "Your story was front page news in the *Clairvoyant* for weeks last summer. Oh, yes, my lad, we read all about you. And now, finally, here you are among us, in the flesh. On that note, perhaps we should get started with the ghosts now. What say you?"

He nodded resolutely. "I'm ready."

"That's the spirit! Ha—spirit, ghosts, get it?"

The whole crowd groaned at Sir Peter's bad pun. He sent around a scowl of mock indignation at the bleachers, then beckoned to one of his colleagues before turning back to Jake. "I now leave you in the capable hands of Dame Oriel, one of our top mediums, who will conduct this portion of your Assessment. I cannot do it myself, for alas, I do not share that gift. Best of luck to you, young man."

"Thank you, sir," Jake answered in a tight voice.

Dry-mouthed with knowing his Assessment was about to begin, Jake noticed several ghosts materializing here and there on the Field of Challenge.

Sir Peter handed off his speaking trumpet to Dame Oriel as he returned to his chair. She was a trim, older woman with a serious demeanor, her elegant figure draped in the satin teal robe of an Elder psychic. She had piercing gray eyes and short, silvery-pink hair.

Jake promptly learned that Dame Oriel was all business, with none of Sir Peter's chitchat.

"How do you do, Jacob. I am Lady Oriel," she said. "Let us begin."

"Yes, ma'am."

She lifted the speaking trumpet to her lips and explained: "We enlist Merlin Hall's resident ghosts to assist in our young mediums' Assessments. This helps us gauge how clearly the candidates are able to see and hear those on the other side of the Veil." She addressed her next words toward the field. "Any spirits present are now asked to proceed as we previously discussed."

The crowd looked on, intrigued.

Lady Oriel turned back to Jake. "Your goal is to learn each ghost's name. In addition, several of them will give you either a message to convey or some small task to carry out. If you repeat the correct words and perform the correct actions, then we'll know beyond all doubt that your powers are authentic."

Jake nodded. It sounded simple enough.

"Any questions?"

"No, ma'am."

"Good luck, then. They're all yours." Lady Oriel handed him the speaking trumpet and marched back to her seat.

Heart pounding, Jake turned to face the Field of Challenge. This didn't seem too difficult. At least dealing with ghosts did not drain him, like using his telekinesis did.

Clutching the speaking trumpet, he walked across the sunny green toward the nearest ghost of the five he saw arrayed around the field.

She was a rather familiar sort of ghost—a Gray Lady in medieval garb, as could often be found haunting old castles.

Like all the waiting ghosts, she had generated her own little setting out of the ectoplasm mists that spirits could manipulate, acting out a scene. In her case, she had created a spiral staircase inside a castle tower. Several feet off the ground, she kept gliding up and down the tower stairs.

She stopped and stared at Jake as he warily approached. "Pardon, ma'am. Might I ask your name?"

She gave him a dirty look then ignored him and kept going up and down her misty stairs.

"Please? It's rather important."

"Why do you want to know?" she countered.

Confused, Jake turned toward Dame Oriel. "I thought these ghosts were supposed to cooperate."

"What ghosts?" Dame Oriel answered with a pointed smile.

Jake nodded with understanding, then cast the Gray Lady an imploring look. "Help me out here, please? I'm under enough pressure already."

"Fine," the ghost huffed. "What do you want?"

"I need to know your name."

"I am the Lady Rachel, who was called fair," she whispered, her spectral voice sounding hoarse with tears.

Staring at her, Jake realized why she had been rude. The Gray Lady seemed distraught. "Um, are you all right?" he ventured.

"Of course I'm not all right. I'm dead, you fool!" she snapped. "Snuffed out before my time, at the height of my beauty—or haven't you noticed I'm a ghost?"

"Sorry, I didn't mean to offend—"

"Do you really think I'd bother haunting anything if I were sitting on a cloud playing a harp somewhere? Instead, I'm stuck here, going up and down these steps all day long. Am I all right, he asks. What a stupid question. But what else should I expect from a male?"

"I beg your pardon," Jake uttered, taken aback. He glanced uncertainly at Dame Oriel, but her face gave nothing away, offered no clues about how to proceed.

He looked at the Gray Lady again, recalling Oriel's instructions about how he was to inquire if the ghosts had a message or a simple task he was to perform, so he could prove he was not just talking to thin air.

Lady Rachel had turned her back on him and was gliding slowly back up her tower stairs once more.

"Um, my lady, do you have any message for me?"

"Only one." She glanced bitterly over her shoulder. "All men are faithless swine. Chivalry is *deeeeaaaaad!*" she shouted, leaping out the tower window at the top of the steps.

She disappeared, and her ectoplasm with her.

Jake blinked. "Well, then."

Turning toward the Elders, he lifted the speaking trumpet to his lips. "Ah, that was Lady Rachel the Fair. Kind of a shrew. I think she had a falling-out with a knight or something."

"Why do you say that? Did she have a message?" Dame Oriel called.

"Yes, ma'am. She said all men are faithless swine, and chivalry's dead."

Dame Oriel nodded at her colleagues, confirming his accuracy. "The boy is correct."

"Bravo!" Sir Peter started clapping for him in approval, and the crowd followed suit.

Jake headed for the second ghost, surrounded by its cloud of spectral mist, and mused that this all must have looked very strange to the audience.

Some of them were surely psychics and mediums like him, but for most, it must have looked like he was standing in the middle of a field talking to himself, like an escapee from the lunatic asylum—or like Archie muddling his way through an especially hard equation.

Ah, well. His Assessment was too important to bother much about his dignity. Nevertheless, the next ghost rather startled him when he spotted it hopping about in the cloudy scene it had created.

Jake peered into the ectoplasm, searching the wispy ship's deck for any *other* figure he was supposed to talk to, but no.

There was only the one.

"Something wrong, Jake?" Sir Peter called amiably from his chair.

Hesitating, Jake lifted the speaking trumpet to his lips. "No, sir, it's just... Well, um, it's...a parrot."

The audience laughed, and Jake jumped as the large, showy, but quite dead bird let out a shrill squawk.

"*Je m'apelle Pierre!*" It swooped straight at his head.

He ducked instinctively, though he knew a ghost-parrot could hardly peck him. He glanced again at the Elders. "It speaks French. Problem is, I don't. But I think it might have just told me that its name is Pierre. Maybe it belonged to a French pirate or something?"

"Just report on whatever you hear it saying, Jacob," Dame Oriel instructed from her seat in the shade.

He nodded and turned to the ghost bird again.

It cocked its head and looked at him from its perch on the ship's ectoplasm rails.

"Come on, say something," Jake muttered. "I haven't got all day."

The parrot spoke, and when Jake repeated the "message" aloud in French as best he could, he realized it was a foreign swear word by the audience's mixed gasps and laughter.

"Sorry about that," he added through the speaking trumpet as his cheeks turned red.

The rascally ghost parrot flapped away and dissolved, along with the deck of its old pirate ship.

Well, that's that.

Jake took a deep breath and headed for the third ghost near the middle of the field. As he approached, he could already hear the music coming from the ornate theater stage the spirit had created. No orchestra was visible, but the tune seemed familiar—although once again, Jake did not understand the words. This time, they were in Italian.

An opera.

A dark-haired, bearded ghost of rounded proportions was walking about on the stage, rehearsing a song, as he must have so often done in life.

"La dona e mobile,
Qual piuma al vento,
Muta d'accento—e di pensiero..."

As Jake approached, he could see the man's smile and his dark, expressive eyebrows working up and down as he practiced the playful tune.

"Pardon, sir!" he called. "Sorry to interrupt, but I'm in the middle of my Assessment, so might I ask your name?"

The opera man glanced at him in surprise, then sang his response: *"I am Constanzio, the King of the Tenors!"*

"Oh, thanks," Jake started to say, but the King of the Tenors was not done.

"*CONNNNNN-stanzio! Zio, zio, zio, zi-OOOOOO! Constanzio eees my naaaaaame!*" he finished with a grand Italian flourish.

Jake waited.

Constanzio bowed.

Right. Jake turned to the Elders. "His name is Constanzio," Jake reported through the speaking trumpet.

"The King of—" the opera star insisted.

"King of the tenors," Jake dutifully added.

"Ahem!" Constanzio coughed. "Boy, bring me my wine. I must wet these golden pipes."

The large man gestured impatiently to the small ectoplasm table at the edge of the stage. It held a misty platter laden with grapes, cheese, bread, and cold cuts of meat. Beside it sat a bottle of ghost wine with half a goblet poured. Jake went over to the table and "picked up" the wispy ghost-goblet as best he could and carefully brought it over to Constanzio.

To the audience, it must have looked like he was just pretending.

"Grazie!" The ghost swigged with gusto.

"Er, Mr. Constanzio, is there any message you have for the living today?"

He swallowed the rest of the wine with a thoughtful gulp, then nodded vigorously. He had a deep, resonant speaking voice and an infectious laugh. "You tell that rogue, Sir Peter, that he still owes me twenty guineas over the wager we made shortly before my death."

"What sort of wager, sir?"

"Ha! That skinny fellow bet me that I could not eat a whole double-chocolate almond cake by myself, and I did! Though, in hindsight, maybe I really shouldn't have. Go on now, take yourself out of here, *ragazzo*. As you can see, Constanzio must practice his art. I have a huge concert in the Afterworld tonight. Greatness doesn't grow on trees, you know."

"Break a leg, sir," Jake said, and as Constanzio disappeared, he passed along the message to Sir Peter, who had apparently been great friends with the opera star before his demise.

The wizard Elder laughed aloud to hear his old chum was alive and well, in a fashion, on the other side of the Veil. The crowd clapped uncertainly, realizing by Sir Peter's reaction that Jake had been successful once again.

Glancing around the field, he saw there were two more ghosts to contend with—or was it three?

Jake wasn't sure what to make of the shapeless blob hovering in the shadows under one of the bleachers. He narrowed his eyes and studied it briefly, puzzled.

The being appeared to be made of a denser sort of ectoplasm, so it must have been a spirit of some kind. He did not doubt that the Elders would happily throw in some sort of a trick to challenge him. But given that the creature was lurking under the seats rather than joining the other ghosts on the field, he wasn't sure if it had anything to do with his Assessment, after all, whatever it was.

It had no face and did not act like any ghost he had seen before, showing no signs of turning itself into an orb or one of those little spiral shapes that spirits sometimes took to conserve their strength. (It took a huge amount of energy for a ghost to manifest itself as a full-bodied apparition, Jake had learned.) But not this one.

If anything, the mysterious blob reminded him of those tiny amoeba creatures that Archie had showed him under his microscope once, only it was about three feet tall and floating in midair.

Weird. Well, this is Merlin Hall, he thought with a shrug. *Anything might happen.*

Putting the blob creature out of his mind for now, he moved on with his Assessment.

The next ghost tried to terrify him by transforming into ghoulish shapes when he asked its name: a ragged skeleton with flesh still hanging off the bones here and there; a huge, growling black dog; a cloaked grim reaper that swung its scythe at him.

"Look, I'm only trying to find out your name!" he insisted, taking a backward step for caution's sake, though he wasn't really scared at all.

It was only a test.

Finally, the ghost gave up the game and materialized in the form of a simple farmer. "Did I scare you?" he asked hopefully.

"Not really. Sorry. Please, I need to learn your name for my Assessment."

The ghost sighed. "Very well. They call me the Cantankerous Caretaker. I worked here at Merlin Hall on the grounds for many years. Lived in a nice cottage and minded the acres assigned to me. Kept the woods nice and tidy for the unicorns. Dredged the brook every spring for the water nymphs. Ah," he sighed, "it was a very good life."

"Then why were you so cantankerous?" Jake inquired.

"Bad feet," he said. "No arches. Bunions, too."

"Ahhh," Jake said. "But you still haven't told me your actual name."

The old, rugged farmer-ghost chewed a length of hay. "Aye, I'll tell ye. But first I've been instructed to make you carry out an action so the Elders know your talents are real."

"Very well. What would you have me do?"

The Cantankerous Caretaker told him.

"Really?" Jake protested. "You're going to make me humiliate myself in front of all these people?"

The old ghost cackled. He really was a grouch. "Can't have you gettin' too full of yourself, now, can we, Milord-Two-Talents-Who-Inherited-a-Goldmine?"

"Fine." Jake heaved a longsuffering sigh. Honestly, some people treated him worse now that he was an earl than when he had been a homeless thief. What else could he do?

Dutifully, Jake followed the Cantankerous Caretaker's instructions, turning three clumsy cartwheels, followed by three somersaults.

Humiliating.

Maddox St. Trinian would have never stood for this.

When he rose to his feet again, Jake's cheeks were scarlet with embarrassment. The whole audience was laughing at him, but Dame Oriel nodded in approval to confirm he had successfully carried out the silly instructions that she and the Cantankerous Caretaker had agreed upon earlier.

"Real name's Garvey," the old ghost conceded, vanishing as Jake dutifully reported the ghost's name through the speaking trumpet.

"Well done, Jake!" Sir Peter called.

"Hold on, I've got one more ghost here." He marched toward the last ghost on the field, a hunched old crone stirring a cauldron.

There were different kinds of witches, but she was clearly one of the nasty sort. She looked very much like a wicked witch from a fairytale. But she couldn't be truly evil, Jake realized, or they wouldn't have allowed her to stay at Merlin Hall.

When he joined her, she barely acknowledged him, absorbed in her cooking, mumbling to herself all the while. He eventually figured out that her "message" consisted of the names of all the strange ingredients she was adding to her potion or stew or whatever it was bubbling in her cauldron. Jake quickly started calling out the names of the items as he heard them.

"Er, toadstool...bat's claw...goat's tongue," he echoed with a wince, though the old witch mostly ignored him. "Frogs' feet. Powdered pixie. Wait—powdered pixie? Blimey!"

He had met a tribe of pixies in Wales. He'd had no idea the tiny folk might be caught and turned into a powder.

She looked up and cackled at his reaction. "Baby's tears," the witch continued in a raspy voice. "Dead man's toenails."

Jake repeated these, too, disgusted. Then she spit into the cauldron, and he reported that, too.

"What is that you're making, ma'am?" he ventured.

"Why? Would you like to try it, dearie?" She offered him a spoonful.

Jake stepped back, shaking his head. "No! No, thank you, ma'am. But I would know your name, if you please."

"Oh, come, try my little potion, and I'll tell you," she wheedled him.

He glanced at the pot boiling away, but grimaced. "Sorry, I don't think I had better. I don't trust you."

She laughed. "Then you are wise for I am Mother Mehitabel! Beware the Boneless, young Jacob," she added, then disappeared in a puff of smoke.

Huh?

Beware the Boneless?

Oh, wait...

Maybe her mysterious warning concerned the shapeless blob apparition he had seen lurking underneath the bleachers. *So that thing is part of my Assessment, then!*

But why would the old crone see fit to warn him about it? On second thought, he *had* noticed that each of the ghosts seemed more challenging than the last. Maybe the Boneless would prove to be the trickiest one yet. Well, he wasn't scared. Not anymore. He felt like he was on a roll now.

When he reported the old hag's name through the speaking trumpet, Dame Oriel rose from her chair with a smile and walked toward him. Sir Peter followed her, ready to resume his duties.

"Very well done, Lord Griffon," Dame Oriel congratulated him, offering a handshake. "You got all five, a perfect score!"

"Ah, but what about number six?" he countered, not about to fall for the Elders' trickery.

"Six? No, there were only five," Dame Oriel said, tilting her head curiously.

"No, the blob thing. I still need to talk to him, don't I?"

She shook her head. "No, that's all the ghosts we have for you today."

Jake suspected they were putting him to the test. "But it's right over..." He started to point toward the bleachers, but the Boneless had vanished.

Dame Oriel chuckled. "Shake my hand, Jake, there's a good lad. You passed part one of your Assessment with flying colors. Now, I shall hand you over to Sir Peter once again to complete the telekinesis portion of your testing. Well done. Goodbye."

"Goodbye, ma'am, thank you," he mumbled, a bit puzzled, but he supposed he must have been mistaken about the strange creature.

Still, if it wasn't anything to worry about, he wondered why Mother Mehitabel would have warned him to beware.

CHAPTER SIX
My Own Private Stonehenge

"**N**ow, Jake," Sir Peter said to him and the crowd, "I've heard the longer one uses his telekinetic powers, the greater the strain becomes. So, since it is our purpose to put all our candidates under the most intense stress of their young lives, we are going to test you first for precision and then for strength. How does that sound?" Not waiting for an answer, Sir Peter beckoned to the edge of the field. "Gnomes, your assistance, please."

Jake waited nervously and watched along with everyone else as a row of four gnomes trudged out, two carrying a quiver of arrows between them, the other two hefting a round target painted with the usual array of colored circles.

"We're going to have you demonstrate your skill at archery, Jake—with one small twist. Instead of using a bow, you will fire these arrows using only your mind."

The crowd reacted to this interesting challenge with oohs and aahs. Jake nodded, grateful for the chance to make up for the silliness of his earlier cartwheels and somersaults with a more manly display.

"Farther, go, go!" Sir Peter waved the gnomes carrying the target halfway down the field. "Stop! There."

It was now very far away, but Jake wasn't worried in the least. He already knew that he could do this.

He practiced this sort of thing back home at Griffon Castle all the time, at Derek's suggestion.

"Excellent!" said Sir Peter. "Now, then. Your first task, Jake, is to fire ten arrows into the target in rapid succession. We want to see both speed and accuracy, so we'll be timing you. *And* you are not to step across this chalk line. See?" Sir Peter pointed at the line by Jake's feet.

The first two gnomes set the quiver of arrows down nearby. Things got a tiny bit more complicated when Sir Peter told the gnomes on the far end of the field to hold the target higher.

One climbed up onto the other's shoulders and lifted the target up over his head. The wee fellow barely cleared the tip of his pointy red hat. The target wobbled as the gnomes struggled for balance.

Jake looked at Sir Peter in alarm. "Are they going to stay there, in the line of fire?"

"Well, that target isn't going to hold itself up now, is it?" he asked lightly.

"Yes, but...doesn't that seem dangerous?"

"Then you'd better watch your aim, I daresay," Sir Peter answered with a wink. "Don't worry. Gnomes are very hardy. And if you kill these two, we've got plenty more. Good luck, Jake."

As Sir Peter walked away, Jake took a deep breath and focused all his concentration on the arrows by his feet. He had learned by trial and error that a clear mind was everything in getting objects to move without touching them.

Bringing up his hands, he made the first arrow slip out of the quiver and rise up off the grass; it hovered in midair, awaiting his command. *Please don't skewer those poor gnomes.*

Jake knew that nervousness usually made him put too much force into his telekinesis—which, in turn, threw off his aim. So he pulled back on the intensity as he sent the first arrow on its way with a cautious flick of his hand.

The arrow gathered speed as it traveled down the field. With nine more to go, he decided to take them in threes. This was as much as he could manipulate at one time.

His attention was already split between the first arrow nearing the target and the next three rising off the grass like angry hornets, lined up and hovering in midair.

Turning forward, Jake homed in on guiding the first arrow toward the bull's-eye. It did not help that the gnomes could barely hold the target steady. With one sitting astride the other's shoulders, they wove to and fro and tilted back and forth.

Jake scowled and concentrated harder as the arrow gathered velocity. *Better aim high.* Maddox St. Trinian hadn't killed any of *his* gnomes, and Jake did not intend to be the first.

Thunk!

The arrow struck the target nowhere near the bull's-eye. The crowd clapped for him anyway, but Jake was irked to have only hit the upper arc of an outer ring.

He wasted no time, but sent the next three arrows whizzing down the field all at the same time.

Starting to get a better feel for what he was doing, he stared at the target until he picked up the rhythm of how the gnomes were tilting back and forth under the strain of their heavy burden.

Thwack, thwack, thwack!

His next arrows slammed into the target in quick succession. He'd managed to get them inside the red and blue rings, but still, none of them had hit the yellow bull's-eye.

"Come on," he said under his breath and hurried onto the next three, since he was being timed.

The secondhand was ticking.

Whoosh! The next trio of arrows shot forward, faster as they flew toward the target. All three hit at once, and now Jake's temples were beginning to throb with the effort of using his gift in such a concentrated way. Again, no blasted bull's-eyes, but the middle one was pretty close—and the gnomes were still alive.

Three more arrows remained. This time, Jake took them one by one in quick succession instead of launching them all together. They flew toward the target, nose-to-tail, but he gasped as the lower gnome stumbled and started to drop the fellow on his shoulders. The whole target started falling down.

Blast it, this was his last chance to impress the Elders!

Eyes blazing, Jake did not take his gaze off the bull's-eye, but pointed his finger, directing the arrows as the target fell toward the grass.

The eighth hit the blue ring. The ninth hit the red. But the tenth arrow bit deep into the yellow bull's-eye as the gnomes toppled onto the grass.

Yes!

Jake visored his eyes with his hand to make sure neither of his little assistants had any holes in them. One had lost his hat, but picked it up and put it on again.

Whew. The gnomes climbed to their feet, unscathed.

Jake finally noticed that the whole audience was clapping for him, including some of the Elders. To his surprise, even the Old Yew waved his branches in approval.

A smile spread across his face.

Sir Peter returned to the field, his robes flowing with each stride. Since the smarmy master of ceremonies had not yet reached him, Jake had a brief moment to sweep a searching glance across the bleachers. *There they are.*

He saw Aunt Ramona beaming with pride, Henry clapping with a grin, and his cousins and the carrot-head cheering wildly for him. His biggest fans. The sight of them renewed his strength. If only Red could be here, too.

At least Derek was watching, applauding, and whistling loudly in approval from where he stood at the edge of the field. Even Maddox St. Trinian, who was sitting idly in the front row, looked somewhat impressed.

Ha, thought Jake. Then he turned to Sir Peter as the wizard rejoined him.

"Well, well, that was extraordinary, Jake."

"Ah, it was nothing, sir," he said into the offered speaking trumpet with a grin.

The crowd laughed.

"Any sense of the wobblies yet?" Sir Peter inquired in amusement.

"Not really," he answered, though he was not being entirely honest. In truth, he could feel the headache starting to pound in his temples from the exertion. And it seemed like the sun was in his eyes when it hadn't been before. The glare hurt, but he could ignore it for now. His Assessment was too important to let pain bother him.

"Hmm, we'll have to try harder," said Sir Peter. "Maybe the next task will get you good and green around the gills."

Jake chuckled and waited to hear what they wanted him to do next. After his success with the ghosts and getting at least one bull's-eye, he was feeling much better about all this, especially since he could feel the crowd's support. The people seemed to like him, and that made it almost kind of fun. It wasn't really as bad as he had thought, being the center of attention.

A lad could get used to this, actually.

"I'm ready, sir," he told him with a nod.

"Good. Up to this point, we've looked at the speed and precision with which you can manipulate objects. But now comes the hard part. For your last task of the day, we're going to test your strength. Tell me, what is the heaviest object you have ever lifted using only your mind?"

The question took him off-guard. "Um, I once got stuck in a mausoleum behind a sealed granite door. I had to blast the door off to get out of there. I really wanted out," he added.

"A mausoleum? With dead bodies? Egads, I can imagine you did!" Sir Peter feigned a shudder for the amusement of the audience. "In that case, I think you're going to enjoy your final task today—if it's not too painful." With that, he stepped back, lifted his wand, and conjured a new feature on the field.

Jake's heart pounded as he waited to see what might materialize from the wizard's incantation. But when a pile of huge boulders took form, the color drained out of his face. He stared in shock at the haphazard rubble of massive rocks.

Sir Peter turned pleasantly and said, "Build me a Stonehenge."

"Pardon?"

Sir Peter cast the crowd a crafty smile. "Geoffrey of Monmouth once claimed the real Stonehenge was made by our great forebear, Merlin, who transported the stones magically all the way from Wales. Do you know who Geoffrey of Monmouth was, Jake?"

He shook his head, blank with terror at this impossible assignment. "No, sir."

The Elder chuckled. "Neither do I, really, but whoever he was, he was right. So show us how Merlin did it. In miniature, of course. The real Stonehenge has many more stones than we're using here and bigger ones, of course. Did you know the heaviest one is judged to be about thirty tons! Can you imagine?"

Jake paled.

"Don't worry. We wouldn't ask a mere boy to move a thirty-ton stone. The largest one we've given you today is only a tenth of that."

Jake looked at him, appalled. *You want me to lift a three-ton rock in one go? I can't possibly do that. I'm going to fail,* he thought, horrified by the sudden prospect of public humiliation.

"Good luck, Jake." Sir Peter gave him what Jake saw as a sinister wink, then walked back jauntily to his seat.

Jake turned and stared up at the pile of boulders in a sickening daze. *Where on earth do I begin?* He had never been to the real Stonehenge, but at least he had seen pictures.

He walked around the pile of stones to count them and try to see how he might arrange them. There were twelve large, gray, flattish boulders and eight short, lumpy ones with blunt points on top, like crude teeth.

He knew from pictures that Stonehenge had a ring of massive doorway-looking things. Each of those would take three of the big stones: two for the uprights and the third for the lintel resting across the top. He didn't even want to think about how hard it was going to be to heave the lintel stones up into position using only his mind.

Counting twelve big stones told him the Elders wanted four such doorways in his finished product. Merlin probably would have lined them up with the four cardinal directions. Wizards liked that sort of thing.

Rubbing his mouth in thought, he walked around the pile again and finally started seeing how to start. He nodded. *Very well.* He did not yet have any idea what to do with the smaller stones, but he glanced at the sun and did his best to judge which way was east, then west, north, and south. He'd have to get all the uprights in place first, he decided. There was no time to lose, so he got right to work, knowing full well it would be horrible.

And it was.

One by one, inch by painstaking inch, he raised the massive boulders off the pile like they weighed no more than a feather. With a wave of his hand and intense concentration, he adjusted them so that they stood vertically in midair, rather than horizontally. He moved them into position—north, south, east, and west, each with its partner a few feet away from it; and then—*slam!*—dropped them into place.

It was exhausting. Soon, sweat stood out on his forehead. His chest heaved; his temples ached. The earth shook each time one of the great standing stones dropped out of the air into position, but thankfully, none of them toppled over, which would have forced him to redo it.

Twenty minutes later, his kid-sized Stonehenge was coming along all right. But for his part, he was feeling very poorly.

There is no way Merlin could have done the real Stonehenge in one day, he thought, his breath ragged.

Sweat now covered most of his body, and all his limbs felt shaky. His head throbbed like a star being born inside his skull. He felt queasy and dizzy, unsteady on his feet. But though his brain screamed for him to stop, he refused.

He'd either become a Lightrider one day or die trying.

It took a long time, but he had put the standing stones of all four doorways into place.

The audience was silent. He had forgotten about them. All that mattered was proving to the Old Yew that he was worthy to follow in his parents' footsteps.

Why, maybe his father had even had to perform this same feat at *his* Assessment. Jake did not know, but the possibility gave him fresh strength.

Then it was time to wrangle the lintels. There were four of them— about as welcome as the four horsemen of the apocalypse.

Lifting the first one with his mind drove Jake to his knees with a low cry of pain. It still wasn't high enough. He held his head with both hands, squeezing his eyes shut—the brief respite of darkness helped to soothe his raging migraine—but he had to open his eyes again to aim the thing and guide it into place.

Feeling physically ill, he lifted his hand weakly until the boulder rose high enough to top the standing stones. He managed to lower it onto the east doorway, then fell onto all fours in the cool grass for a moment.

He hung his head, heaving for breath. His skull felt like it might explode. No position he tilted it in was comfortable. His eyes felt dried out, burning, and glassy; with all the world watching, drool ran out of his mouth as he panted, head down. He wiped it away with his sleeve, beyond embarrassment.

He couldn't *believe* he still had three more to go. *No.* It wasn't worth this much pain. What cruel-hearted madman had planned this assignment for him, anyway? He was going to fail, and he wasn't sure he even cared anymore. Why had he ever wanted this so badly in the first place?

Logic then posed a simple question: If he was going to fail, then why keep trying? *Please just let it be over.*

And right when he had all but decided to quit, a high-pitched voice with the hint of an Irish brogue suddenly yelled out across the silent field: "Keep going, Jakey! You can do it!"

He groaned, recognizing Dani's voice. *Leave me alone!* he thought in irritation. Then he heard Isabelle and Archie join in, urging him on, and Derek shouting encouragement while Henry let out an insistent wolf-howl.

An angry sound tore from Jake as he realized he couldn't

disappoint them.

He couldn't let his parents down, either, if somewhere, somehow, they were watching, too.

Failure was one thing, but quitting was another matter entirely. A Lightrider could never quit. *Argh!* He shook his head violently, trying to cast away the pain.

The whole crowd cheered when he climbed to his feet again and focused his bleary gaze on the second lintel stone.

The slight break had helped give him back a little more strength. Sixty seconds later, he had the west-facing lintel in place. Now for the north.

He took a deep breath and whipped his hands out in front of him, pushing the air forward and underneath the boulder. It rocked but did not rise. He shut his eyes and concentrated harder, his heart pounding.

Move!

It just sat there in all its rugged bulk, huge, obstinate, and silent.

"I said, you *move*," he whispered to the stone.

Refusing to be stopped now after having come so far, Jake decided to just drag the ponderous brute across the grass with his telekinesis, only heaving it up off the ground once he had got it close to its standing stones.

It worked well enough, though it was slow going. By the time he crashed it into place, he was having tunnel vision, the blackness closing in.

The crowd was silent, holding its breath. Jake knew that, somewhere out there, Dani had her fingers crossed for him. *One more to go...*

The last stone waited, surly in its immobility.

He had already given up on doing anything with the smaller stones. A boy had his limits. But by Red's last feather, he'd get that final lintel up onto the south gate if it killed him. He merely took a moment to catch his breath.

The end was in sight.

Then he focused all of his remaining strength on the last big rock. His hands were shaking as he held them out, commanding the stone to rise.

It floated up off the ground at once, to his surprise.

The hope that this would soon be over must have given him one last kick of power. It wasn't much, but it might just be enough...

Then, as he made the lintel stone climb through the air to surmount the last towering pair of standing stones, he felt a sudden blinding stab in his skull.

A cry wrenched from his lips, and he almost dropped the stone completely. Somehow he held it aloft until the moment's agony had passed. Dry-mouthed, his stomach heaving with nausea, he had to fix the position of the lintel as it hovered over the uprights, manipulating it in midair with his hands.

Engrossed in his task, he did not notice the crowd already on its feet, cheering him on to victory. Indeed, he was so bent on finishing this and not passing out that he did not even notice the trickle of blood coming out of his nose or another from his ear.

The moment the lintel stone crashed into place, its unfathomable weight released from his control, Jake staggered backward and started to turn unsteadily toward the Elders to confirm that it was done. Black dots veered across his vision, and then he felt something hot dripping out of his nose.

He wiped it away and saw his hand coated in crimson.

Why am I bleeding? he thought in alarm, finally noticing it.

The crowd had gone silent, staring at him in dismay; some of the Elders had risen to their feet.

But the sight of them faded into darkness as another wave of pain hit him. Jake doubled over with a cry, clutching his head, and the crowd gasped in horror as he collapsed, unconscious, on the field.

CHAPTER SEVEN
Sweet Dreams & Nightmares

Nixie thought her Assessment had gone pretty well, except for the stupid mud rabbit, which had flopped into a ruin much too soon. She was too tired to fret about it, though, and had shuffled straight back to her assigned bedchamber to claim the reward she had promised herself, at last.

Luxurious sleep!

Maybe in a few hours' time she would get up and go down to supper in the dining hall. Or maybe she would just sleep on till morning like a hibernating bear.

She was snoring the minute her head hit the pillow and would have happily remained so till dawn—except that it wasn't long before she learned her enemies had found her, after all.

Boneless glided out of the wall and flew right through her, cold and wet and faintly slimy, waking her like a tendril of spiteful fog.

Past the point of horror at their unrelenting haunting of her, Nixie could almost feel her heart breaking to think they had found her even here. Still, she refused to believe it, refused to open her eyes.

She told herself it was just a draft. She tugged the covers up higher against her cheek and buried her face further into the pillow.

But when she heard the slow, ominous footfalls of the Headless Highlander walking across her room, she started shaking and pulled the covers all the way over her head.

Just a bad dream. They can't come here. They can't get into Merlin Hall. Too many protective spells...

But apparently no one had told that to Nuckalavee. *Oh, please no,* Nixie whispered in her mind, wincing in revulsion as she heard the gory creature's horrible whinny.

That Nuckalavee should have left his refuge in the water told Nixie just how angry the Bugganes were at her attempt to escape them.

Just a dream, just a dream, she kept telling herself with a small whimper under the covers.

But the Bugganes did not intend to let her ignore them. Not after they had tracked her all this way.

Squeezing her eyes shut, Nixie braced herself, hearing Nuckalavee's horrible, wet, squishing hoofbeats gallop across her room as the skinless bogey-beast charged her beautiful canopy bed.

In the next moment, her attempt to pretend they didn't exist was shattered. She screamed as the monster rammed the corner of her bed and made it spin.

"Stop, please!" she cried, coming out from the covers to grab onto the headboard to keep from flying off the whirling bed and splatting into the wall.

A witchy cackle filled the room as the leader of the Bugganes, Jenny Greenteeth, stepped out of the mirror, already mocking her. "Oh, please!" the hideous hag mimicked her cry. "Thought you could give us the slip, eh?" she taunted, then she made the spinning bed levitate off the floor.

"You can't do this to me here!" Nixie wailed as the torment went on.

But it seemed they could.

Just another day.

* * *

Dani never knew how to feel each time Jake nearly died.

She wanted to punch him and hug him at the same time, neither of which he would've welcomed, so she did neither.

Instead, she went quiet, still clutching her rosary in her pocket, even hours after it seemed fairly clear that the blockhead, as usual, would live.

Why, oh, why could he never be careful?

His brushes with death had always happened with distressing frequency, even during his pickpocket days, but now they were all the more common. He never seemed to mind. She could've sworn the glock-wit practically enjoyed it.

He was just *like* that, she thought in frustration, always taking risks, charging headlong into danger. But to think that this time, he had done it to himself—all for his stupid Assessment! It made her want to strangle him.

She kept her mouth shut, however, only relaxing a tiny bit when he regained consciousness long enough to sip some water. Then she and Archie and Isabelle were herded off to wait in the next room while the physicians treated him with medicine, both human and magical.

Alas, not even Red could help him this time, for word came that the molting Gryphon had no magical scarlet feathers left to give at the moment.

Jake's cousins and she looked at each other in alarm when they overheard Her Ladyship shouting at Sir Peter and Lord Badgerton for giving a mere boy such an assignment.

Even the Elder witch was scared that her great-great nephew might not make it, and that had frankly terrified the three of them.

But of course he survived. That was Jake. Nearly indestructible, Dani thought in shaky relief. At least *he* seemed to think so.

She wasn't quite sure.

Eventually the doctors came out and told them the bleeding had stopped and he was resting comfortably. They still weren't allowed to see him, though.

He slept for the rest of the day. Then Her Ladyship went in to check on him around half past four in the afternoon and found him doing much better.

Relief washed through their whole party when they heard that Jake had sat up in bed and announced that he was hungry.

That was always the sign that he was back to his usual self. The boy was a bottomless pit. Now that he could have food any time he wanted, he had grown half a foot taller in the past six months.

In any case, the three of them waited anxiously in the next room while Jake got dressed to go down to supper.

At last, he stepped out of his room, still looking pale and moving slowly, and Dani and his cousins encircled him in one huge hug. He insisted he was fine, but the color only began returning to his cheeks after he had finished the meal that they all ate together in the busy dining hall.

Throughout supper, Dani was annoyed at all the strangers who congratulated him as they passed their table. She scowled at them all. *Don't encourage him.*

Jake, of course, loved getting the hero treatment.

At length, he proposed going out for a walk. Spending most of the day in bed was not the young adventurer's custom, to be sure, especially not while they were in such an interesting place. He said he wanted to stretch his legs and get some air, and more importantly, now that he was well enough, he wanted to visit Red.

Dani knew that being near the Gryphon always made Jake (and all of them) feel better. His large, wise pet was probably the only one who loved the blockhead even more than she did.

But sometimes, oh, Lord, she wanted to kick him.

Red was so lucky he hadn't been there to witness the awful sight of Jake lying motionless on that field.

Lord and Lady Bradford refused to let them leave the table until Jake promised to take it easy. Archie assured his parents he'd look after him, and Isabelle explained their intent to see how the Gryphon was faring. Her mother told her not to wander off too far, since Isabelle was to attend her first real, grownup ball tonight in the company of her parents.

The Floralia was the annual, flower-themed gala, a Beltane celebration that officially kicked off the Gathering each year, according to Miss Helena. Dani was depressed she couldn't go, even though she was only eleven. Sometimes she hated being the youngest of the group. Always the baby!

It was just something else to be annoyed about. She wished Teddy were here to console her, but Merlin Hall was the one place Lady Bradford said she couldn't bring her dog. She'd had to leave the little brown Norwich terrier in the care of servants back at Bradford Park. She knew they'd take good care of him, but she missed him anyway.

Ah, well. With so many strange folk about, it was probably safer for him there. It would not have surprised her if some breed of these creatures ate lapdogs as a delicacy.

At last, the four kids gained their freedom. It was now about six-thirty in the evening. The western sky glowed gold, and the sun cast long shadows across the emerald grass.

"Whew, I am *so* glad that whole ordeal is over," Jake was saying as they walked toward the arched entrance of the magical zoo.

His cousins flanked him on both sides, while Dani followed a few steps behind, still in a bit of a mood.

"Now I can just relax and enjoy the Gathering," he added.

"And your birthday tomorrow," Archie reminded him.

"Honestly, how do you think I did on my test?"

"Coz, you were amazing!" the boy genius exclaimed.

"But was I good *enough*? I didn't put those smaller stones in place. Do you think I did enough of what they wanted to be considered for the Lightrider training someday?"

"I'm sure of it," Isabelle said in a comforting tone. "Of course, you'll find out for certain tomorrow, depending on what group they put you in."

Oh, the groups, Dani thought with another scowl.

Tomorrow morning, all the magical children were to be broken up into groups, each headed by an adult expert in their respective magical domains.

Henry and Helena, for example, would be lecturing the shapeshifter children; Derek would be talking to the young Guardians.

"I hope they don't put me with the psychics," Jake was musing aloud. "It's not that I don't want to meet them. It's just that I've pretty much got the whole ghost business in hand, you know?"

"Well, *I* hope they don't put you with the telekinetics after what just happened," Archie countered.

"Poor things, they're all probably terrified after seeing what happened to you," Isabelle agreed, "wondering if the same could happen to them if they ever overuse their gifts." She shuddered at the memory.

"Which group do you go with, Izzy?" Jake asked, glancing at her. "Empaths or those who can communicate with animals?"

"Oh, they've always put us empaths into a catch-all group of the general healing arts," she said with a shrug.

"I see," Jake said, but when Dani let out a morose sigh, he turned around and smiled at her. "What's the matter, carrot?"

She threw away the blade of grass she had been tying around her finger like a green ring. "Nothing."

"Oh, come on, out with it," Jake teased.

"Well—it's just that I'm going to have nothing to do tomorrow while you're all off with your groups! I'm going to be all alone again."

"You can come with me!" Archie offered brightly. "I don't have a group, either." He tapped a finger to his temple. "These brains are all-natural, remember? We no-talent types have to stick together!"

She offered him a rueful smile, but a boy his age who already held two doctorates from Oxford could hardly be called talentless. "Thanks,

Arch. Maybe I'll take you up on that. What did ye have in mind?"

"I'm going to the library!" he said eagerly.

She rolled her eyes and let out a groan.

Isabelle chuckled fondly then put an arm around Dani's shoulders. "Ah, don't fret, dearest. You love books, and the library of Merlin Hall is actually rather fascinating."

"That's not the point," she muttered. *Why do I always have to be the odd one out?*

Jake simply didn't get it. "Don't worry, carrot, we'll be done with our groups by noon and then we'll make sure and do something fun all together. It is my birthday tomorrow, after all."

"We know!" they said in unison.

He ignored their retort and forged on, more concerned with his own affairs than Dani's shaken-up feelings. "So, if the Elders liked my performance today, maybe they'll put me with the future Lightriders! I mean, it's possible, isn't it? What will the Lightrider group talk about, I wonder? What it's really like traveling through the Grid, saving the world every day?"

"Ugh!" Dani burst out at last, stopping in her tracks just inside the entrance of the zoo. "If I have to hear you say that word one more time, I am going to *scream!*"

"Huh?" Jake gave her a startled look. "What word? You mean Light—"

"Jake," Isabelle chided.

Dani glared. "Yes. *That* word."

The blockhead frowned, looking utterly confounded. "What? Why?"

"Stop me, Isabelle," Dani said through gritted teeth. "I'm gonna give him another nosebleed."

Jake snorted at her. "What's wrong with you?"

Fuming, Dani stared at him.

"She was really worried about you, Jake," Isabelle said with her usual tact.

"Aw, c'mon, carrot." The rascal grinned in his annoying way and took a step toward her. "I'm all right! See?" He held his arms out at his sides.

"Jake, you had *blood* dripping out of your ears and nose, like you got caught standing too close to an explosion! It's only the first day of the Gathering, and already you could have died. As if you don't already have enough enemies out there, this time you did it to *yourself!* Why didn't you just *stop*?"

"You're the one who told me to keep going!" he exclaimed. "I nearly did quit, but then I heard you cheering for me. So I kept on."

Dani pursed her lips. Maybe that was why she was so angry at him. Angry at herself was more like it. He could have died, and it would have been at least a little bit her fault.

He gazed at her, no longer looking quite so cocky. "You know how much this means to me."

"Aye, that's why I told you to keep on," she admitted begrudgingly. "But, still. Is it really worth your life?"

"I pushed myself too hard. I realize that now," he cajoled her. "Believe me, I have no desire to do that to myself ever again. But these were special circumstances. I had to impress the Elders."

"Hang the Elders!"

"Ah, come on, don't be such an old mother hen!"

"Mother hen? Ugh! Boys are so *stupid*!"

"Hey! I'm not," Archie protested innocently as Dani shoved past him in frustration.

Marching ahead of her companions into the zoo, she passed under the arched entrance.

She had taken only a few, angry strides up the wide center path when she stopped short, turned, and stared into the first cage. She blinked rapidly, then shook her head to clear it. She looked a second time, certain her eyes were playing tricks on her. But, no.

The impossible sight remained.

Slowly lifting her hand, she pointed and asked: "What the deuce is *that*?"

CHAPTER EIGHT
Strange Creatures

J ake and his cousins ran to catch up to her. He was keen to see what had her looking so befuddled. It was better than stewing over her yelling at him again—as usual.

What a nag! But he brushed off her scolding with only a slight twinge of guilt. He did not need Dani O'Dell's permission for whatever he wanted to do in life.

Still, he hadn't meant to scare everybody like that. He was well aware that Dani thought she couldn't live without him, but he had no intention of dying anytime soon.

Then he put her typical-girl's oversensitive reaction out of his mind and raced into the magical menagerie with his cousins.

A placard on a wooden post near the entrance was painted as a map, showing how the green, quiet refuge of the garden-like zoo was divided up into habitat areas suitable for the animals inside. The first enclosure on the right, Jake discovered, was made into a swamp.

This was what had got Dani's attention.

Mysterious dead trees without branches stuck up from the murky water here and there, and when Jake looked at them, he had the same reaction she did.

He blinked, shook his head, then wondered if there had been something stronger in that headache powder than ordinary medicine.

"That...can't...be," he said slowly, staring at the slimy brown fish climbing up the dead trees, inch by slow, wriggling inch.

Archie and Isabelle, who had been to the magical zoo before, exchanged a knowing glance and started laughing.

"But they're fish! How can they..." Jake started. "Fish can't climb trees! Shouldn't they be swimming?"

"How can they even breathe?" Dani asked wonderingly.

"Their gills have adapted! Come, there's loads more to see!" Archie beckoned them on, his dark eyes twinkling behind his spectacles.

"But, Archie...there are *fish* in the *trees*," Dani said.

"I know. Isn't it marvelous? Hurry up, before it gets dark. They'll be closing soon."

They ran after him. The next habitat was a dusty corral that held five huge tortoises, each one big enough to ride on. Unfortunately, none of them were moving, asleep inside their shells.

"Is that all they do?" Jake asked, unimpressed.

"What, do you want them to dance?" Archie countered.

"Hey, wake up, turtle! We want to see you!" Dani picked up a tiny piece of gravel and tossed it at the nearest one. The pebble plunked off its armored shell.

"Don't do that," Archie chided.

"What?" she retorted with a shrug.

"Hey," said Jake, frowning at the placard posted by the big, boring turtles' pen. "Whoever made this sign is an even worse speller than I am. That's not how you spell tortoise, is it?"

"It's spelled correctly," Archie said, smiling. "They're not tortoises. They're Tritoises."

"What?" Then Jake let out a yelp. The creature Dani had thrown the pebble at woke up, but when it peered out from under its shell, not one but *three* leathery turtle heads emerged at once.

"Tritoise—a three-headed tortoise!" Archie said triumphantly while Dani nearly screamed, jumping back from the fence. She clung to Isabelle, giggling wildly in shock, but Jake just stared in disbelief.

Archie and Isabelle greatly enjoyed their reaction. It took a while for them to get over the three-headed tortoises, but eventually, they moved on to the next cage—and this one was very much a cage. It was as big as a large room, but had very strong metal bars.

"The Common Yeti," Jake read aloud from the sign, then he glanced again at the ape-like creature sitting silently, sullenly in the corner, picking insects out of its light-brown fur. "That's odd. The yetis we saw at the North Pole last Christmas were white."

"That must be his summer coat," Dani remarked. "Maybe they only turn white in the snow."

Jake looked askance at her. "What, like rabbits?"

Archie grinned and pulled them on to see the next amazing

creature. They exclaimed in surprise at the sight of the High-Grazing Heifers stretching their long necks up to eat the leaves off the trees like giraffes—only, they were cows.

The six-legged Oliphants with their long ivory tusks were a wonder to behold in the next, well-fortified pen. The kids watched them shoveling hay into their mouths with their trunks while their gray ears flapped slowly to ward off the evening's mosquitoes.

The only beast that really scared them was the horrible Venomous Tython, whose cage came next. The front half was a tiger: furry feline head, tufted ears, great fangs, and front paws with scythe-like claws. But the back half of the Tython was that of a giant serpent, though its tiger stripes continued down the scaly, snake half of its body. Thankfully, the sign said the creatures only existed in the deepest reaches of the Asian jungles.

It hissed at them from behind the bars, a forked tongue darting out of its tiger mouth as it dragged itself closer.

They all stepped back.

"The Tython's bite is poisonous," Archie explained. "Like a serpent, it dispenses venom through its fangs. There's no known antidote."

"Ew," said Dani.

"I hope that's a very strong cage," said Jake.

Almost as horrid was the nearby Fairy Stinger, a scorpion as big as a beagle, with long, green mossy-looking hair to camouflage it perfectly in the sorts of forests where fairies loved to dwell. An odd, glowing lure dangled off the end of its deadly tail, and as it huddled against the big rock in its cage, they could hear a weird, purring sort of hum coming from the creature.

"Am I insane, or is that thing singing?" Jake asked.

Archie nodded. "That's how it lures fairies in. They hear the song and are drawn by the light on its tail, and as soon as they fly close enough—*wham!*" He lunged at Dani, pretending to catch her in big scorpion claws.

She screamed, and the Fairy Stinger fled behind its rock and went quiet.

Archie laughed heartily. "Got you."

Dani smacked him, but couldn't help laughing, too.

"What is that thing thinking about, Isabelle? Just wondering," Jake said.

She shook her head. "I can't read insects."

"Arthropods. Honestly," Archie said in a longsuffering tone. "Don't you people know anything?"

"It's scary, whatever it is," Dani said.

They moved on, but halted when they came to the wide, open pasture where the Dreaming Sheep were bouncing around, guarded by a winged sheepdog.

"Crikey, those things can jump." Jake tilted his head back to follow the long, arcing trajectory of one of the woolly, cloud-white sheep floating far above. Most of the flock were only jumping about six to ten feet off the ground.

"They only have one-eighth of our normal gravity," Archie said.

The shaggy, winged dog barked at the floating sheep to come back down, and when it didn't listen, he flew up after it and herded it back to the others.

"They're only getting started for the night. They're mainly nocturnal, obviously. By midnight," Archie added, "they'll be leaping up over the towers of Merlin Hall."

"Well, they'd better not accidentally land in that thing's cage." Dani pointed back at the terrifying Tython.

"The angel dog won't let them," Isabelle said.

"Hey, there's the zookeeper or veterinarian or whatever he is!" Jake said suddenly, pointing. "Maybe he can tell us where to find Red before they close. C'mon!"

They hurried toward the tall fellow in a white lab coat, who had just thrown some food into another lightly guarded habitat with a tranquil pond.

Archie was the first to call to him. "Excuse me, sir, would you be able to help us?"

"Oh, hullo. What can I do for you children?" When the zookeeper turned to them, Jake and Dani stifled gasps.

He was a Green Man, about seven feet tall with a mossy beard, barky brown skin, and twigs and branches coming out of his head like wild hair. Vines twined here and there around his body. Jake tried not to stare, recalling what Archie had told them about these folk in the carriage on the way here.

Green Men had existed in Europe for centuries, he had said. In pagan times, they had been treated as demigods. You could tell the females by the flowers that sprouted from their heads.

The Green Folk had often been mistaken for airy nature spirits, but Archie had explained that was a misconception. They were as solid as any flesh-and-blood being, but could *seem* to disappear because they could conceal themselves as trees and, by holding perfectly still, could go unnoticed by any passersby.

Very gentle souls, they helped things grow, obviously possessing a green thumb to match their green bodies. They could coax the earth to produce bumper crops, but they also were good with animals.

In the carriage, Archie had also told Jake and Dani a bit about the Green Folk's ancient ways: They slept standing up and barefooted, letting the vines and shoots that twined about their legs root down into the ground each night as they rested. They'd sip water, but were never seen eating food, for they fed on sunlight through the green leaves they had for hair.

Lastly, they were terrified of fire.

A sudden, discreet jab from Isabelle's elbow reminded Jake to quit staring.

"We're closing for the night soon," the Green Man said.

"Yes, we know," Archie started to say when Dani interrupted with a gasp.

"Ho! Wasn't there a lizard on that branch a moment ago?" She scanned the pen. "Where'd he go?"

The Green Man glanced into the cage, then smiled at her. "Oh, he's still there. He's just being shy." He tapped the placard on the cage: *Invisimeleon.*

"We don't mean to interrupt your work, sir, but we're looking for the Gryphon that arrived a few days ago for his molting. This is his owner." Archie nodded at Jake.

"More like he owns me," Jake said wryly as he finally recovered from the shock of meeting a Green Man up close.

"You're Lord Griffon?" The Green Man stared at Jake as if *he* were the oddment. "How do you do? I hear you had quite a time of it with your Assessment today."

Blimey, did the whole world know he had fainted today like a little girl? His smile was half a wince. "I'm just glad it's over. I was hoping to check on Red—?"

"Certainly, I'd be glad to show you to him. I'm Dr. Reginald Plantagenet, by the way. I'm the keeper and all-round veterinarian here."

"So, you are the right person to ask about how Red's been doing?"

Jake asked.

Dr. Plantagenet nodded and beckoned for them to follow him onto the path that wound uphill to the right. "The molting process is always difficult, especially for a gryphon. You know how proud they are. In his current state, he's probably only going to want to see his master. I think he's really embarrassed."

Dani stifled a giggle. "Is he bald?"

"As a plucked chicken, my dear."

"Oh, my goodness, the poor thing!" Isabelle exclaimed.

"We don't wish to cause the poor beast any extra anxiety," Archie said. "Why don't the rest of us wait here and let Jake go up to see him alone?"

The girls agreed to this, but Dr. Plantagenet warned them not to leave the path. "The animals start getting restless as the sun goes down," he said rather ominously.

They nodded, wide-eyed.

Then Dr. Plantagenet escorted Jake alone the rest of the way up the hill. "He made a nest up here among the boulders as soon as he arrived," the Green Man remarked, pointing as they climbed the slope.

"Is he eating all right?"

"His appetite seems a little less than normal for a gryphon of his size. He's finished off half a salmon daily."

"Not bad. Thanks for taking care of him, Doctor."

"That's what I'm here for." When the walkway ended, a small trail led deeper into the woods. "Up that way about twenty yards. Best not to stay too long. We don't want to strain him. He's got to conserve his energy for growing his new plumage."

Jake nodded, then continued up the trail alone.

Through the trees, he soon found that the small woodland path ended at the foot of a rock formation. It seemed he had some climbing to do, not that he was surprised. Gryphons, being half-eagle, preferred to build their aeries in high, rocky places like this, secluded from the world. Back home, Red's nest was tucked away among the stone towers of Griffon Castle's rooftop.

As Jake approached the rock climb before him, he tilted his head back and called toward the topmost boulders: "Red? Anybody home? It's me! I've come to see you!"

He started picking his way carefully up the pile, but found himself tiring quickly after his earlier ordeal. As he found another handhold between the folds of rock and pulled himself up, he reflected on the day's events.

Dani being cross at him was a clue to how bad it must have looked from the outside. Maybe he had come closer to death than Aunt Ramona or the physicians had cared to tell him. All the more reason to spend some time with Red.

A chunk of rock rolled away under his foot as he stepped up onto the next outcropping, but he caught his balance and moved on.

Thankfully, he could barely remember the moment when he had noticed the blood trickling out of his nose. Honestly, it had been pretty horrifying. He had thought he was going to die there and then.

Everything was foggy after that, but at least he had shown his mettle. Besides, what had happened wasn't his fault. He had only been doing what the Elders told him.

Aye, they jolly well *ought* to put him in the Lightrider group tomorrow to make up for nearly killing him like that, he thought. Especially since tomorrow was his birthday.

At last, he reached the top, where he immediately spotted the Gryphon's nest wedged between two boulders. Built of mud and straw, the nest was waist high, with about a five-foot circumference. Red didn't even bother getting out of it when Jake joined him.

The poor beast—usually his mighty defender—merely peeked over the edge of his sickbed as Jake approached, dusting off his hands after that climb. "Hey, big fella. I came to see you. How are you feeling?"

"Becaw," Crafanc-y-Gwrool answered with a plaintive note, his golden eyes soulful with misery. Today, the usually magnificent creature wasn't at all living up to his royal Welsh name, which meant Claw the Courageous.

Indeed, Jake's eyes widened as he realized there wasn't a feather left on the Gryphon's head. Dr. Plantagenet hadn't been jesting.

But for a few scraggly patches of sorry-looking feathers and baby-chick fuzz, the mighty Gryphon's eagle parts were as naked as the Christmas goose. Even his lion body looked mangy.

Jake couldn't help staring.

"Caw!" Red protested, using his beak to pull his blanket up to hide himself.

"Aw, I'm sorry, boy. No offense intended. It's all right. You don't have to be shy with me. I'm your master, and I'm here to make sure they're taking good care of you." Jake climbed up onto the edge of the nest and sat there to be close to him. "Is that blanket warm enough for you?"

"Becaw," Red said, resting his beak on the edge of his nest with a gaze full of woe.

"Try not to worry," Jake encouraged him. "This will pass before you know it. Besides, it's not like you've got some disease. This is *supposed* to happen to you every now and then, right? Just think how magnificent you're going to look when your new feathers grow in. You're going to be handsomer than ever. Don't worry," he added, "I won't leave Merlin Hall until you've got through this."

Jake patted the Gryphon's chicken-skin head, wondering if it unnerved Red not to be able to fly for the time being. His pet seemed comforted by his presence.

Jake proceeded to tell Red about his Assessment to distract him from his condition. He played down the bad part, of course, not wanting his currently helpless protector to worry about not having been there.

"So now I get to see which group they'll put me with tomorrow," he rambled on. "You know my preference, I'm sure. I'd love to hear the lecture from whatever mentor they've got lined up for the Lightrider group. I wonder if they'll talk about what it's like to fight the Dark Druids, or how it feels traveling through the Grid..."

He shrugged after pondering it for a minute longer. "Ah, well. I'll just have to wait and see."

Jake stayed with Red until he heard Dr. Plantagenet calling him from the bottom of the rocks. "I'm going to have to ask you to come back down now, Lord Griffon! We're closing up for the night."

"Be right there!" he yelled back. Then he turned ruefully to Red. "Looks like I've got to go. But I'll be back tomorrow evening to see you, promise. They're going to be keeping us busy all day."

"Becaw!" Red said. It was always difficult to know exactly what he was trying to say without Isabelle there to translate telepathically, but Jake was fairly sure his loyal pet wanted to be the first to wish him an early happy birthday. Red nuzzled Jake's hand with his large, golden beak.

"Aw, thanks, boy. Get a good night's rest. This whole molting business will be over before you know it. Bye for now." Then he climbed back down the boulders, retraced his steps along the wooded trail, then rejoined the others out on the main path.

They wanted to know at once how Red was doing. Jake reported to them on his pet's condition while Dr. Plantagenet escorted them back toward the entrance of the menagerie.

Along the way, they passed an intersection with another path and heard a banging sound coming from one of the pens. When they looked over, they saw a huge, human-like creature on the loose.

Dani gasped and pointed. "Dr. Plantagenet! That one got out of its cage!"

"Oh, er, that's not one of the animals, strictly speaking," he answered. "That's Og."

"Og?" Jake echoed.

"Ogden Trumbull. He's building a new fence around one of the pens for me. He helps out around here."

They looked at the Green Man in surprise, then stared at the towering figure, who was pounding thick wooden posts into the ground using his fist for a hammer.

Wearing nothing but tattered brown trousers that were much too short for him, Og had leathery, grayish skin the hue of stone. His thighs were like tree trunks and his massive arms seemed too long for his body; he did not have proper human hands, but only three thick, crude fingers.

He was bald-headed, with a broad, dull-witted face, a low brow, and no discernible neck, just massive sloping shoulders. His large, slightly pointy ears flopped outward at the tops.

"He's so big," Dani murmured in trepidation. "What *is* he, Doctor?"

"Well, er, he's half-troll," Dr. Plantagenet admitted in a delicate tone.

"Half troll?" Archie cried.

"Shh! You don't want him to hear you! No need to hurt his feelings," the veterinarian chided.

"I don't understand." Archie turned to him with that familiar fascinated scientist glow coming into his eyes.

"Og lives out here at the edge of the zoo. I wouldn't dream of caging him, of course. He's half-human, after all, and thus has human rights, and so far, has done nothing to earn a prison. Still," the Green Man explained softly, "although Og is *reasonably* civilized, he's not fit for...shall we say, an indoor life. Out here, he can have at least some supervision and a purpose for his existence. He's quite good with some of the larger animals."

"You're attempting to civilize a troll?" Archie asked in dubious amazement.

"Half-troll," Dr. Plantagenet corrected.

"How'd that happen?" Jake drawled.

The Green Man sighed. "Og is the result of an unfortunate experiment by one of our more misguided wizard-scientists."

"You mean somebody made him?" Dani asked in surprise.

"In a laboratory, yes, I'm afraid." The twigs on Dr. Plantagenet's crown waved as he shook his head in regret. "He's a little bitter about it, truth be told. But honestly, wouldn't you be? Poor, young Og will never have a normal life, being neither fully troll nor fully human."

"That must be very lonely for him," Isabelle remarked.

The Green Man nodded. "The animals here are his friends. As am I. If I could just get him to quit trying to ride the Oliphants," he added wryly. "Like many youngsters his age, he's quite obsessed with horseback riding, but of course, there's not a horse alive strong enough to carry him, poor lad."

"Well, I'm not sure I want him going anywhere near my Gryphon," Jake said with a worried frown.

"No, I've told him to leave the Gryphon alone until he's done molting. Og understands that."

"Good."

"But I still don't understand," Archie persisted. "Why would anyone want to tinker with breeding a better troll?"

"I don't know, but it cost the wizard his powers. The Elders sentenced him to have his magic removed by the Extraction Spell as his punishment for crimes against Mother Nature. I suppose the wizard's intentions were good, at least in his own warped mind. You know how they tend to go astray."

The kids nodded.

"Apparently, he was trying to create a super-strong hybrid servant. To elevate the rock troll into a useful species. They're not very nice, in general."

"I'll say! Trolls are known for their tempers. And occasional bouts of cannibalism," Archie said.

Jake and Dani looked at him, aghast.

"Don't worry, Og's not going to hurt anyone," Dr. Plantagenet assured them. "I work with him every day to teach him how to behave. He's *reasonably* civilized. Besides, he's barely your age—just a boy, himself."

"A troll boy," Dani echoed dubiously.

"Half-troll." Jake quirked a brow at her. "Who's seven feet tall, several hundred pounds of muscle, and could rip your arms off if you look at him wrong."

"Right," said Archie. "Think we'll keep our distance."

The Green Man winced. "That is probably for the best."

They had reached the arched entrance of the menagerie by now and started to say goodbye to Dr. Plantagenet, when suddenly, Jake witnessed the strangest phenomenon in the distance.

Out on the wide, green lawn that stretched between the palace and the zoo, a large, upright circle of bluish light appeared in a sudden, brilliant flash.

"What's that?" he cried, pointing to it as it glowed, pulsating with energy.

"Oh, you've never seen that before?" the Green Man countered. "That's a portal opening up—a gateway to the Grid. One of the Lightriders must be coming in."

Jake drew in his breath. "Lightrider?"

In the next heartbeat, he was running as fast as his legs would carry him to see this marvel up close.

"Jake, wait up!" his friends called, but there was no chance of slowing him down.

He had to see this, and he wanted a front-row seat to whatever was going to happen. As he neared the portal on the lawn, he could see it better. Pliant and plasmatic, the portal swelled and shrank slightly, like a living thing breathing. A strange sound came out of it as it throbbed, a deep, vibratory hum.

Skidding to a halt a few feet away, Jake confirmed that it was, indeed, a flat circle, maybe eight feet in diameter, like a giant round mirror.

The golden-white light coming from the portal was shot through with moving swirls of pink and blue, like the colors on the fragile membrane of a soap bubble. Beyond its glowing surface, he caught a tantalizing glimpse of a tunnel.

Meanwhile, Jake wasn't the only one who came running to see the Lightrider about to make his entrance. Other guests crowded around to view this rare and fascinating spectacle.

Sir Peter Quince happened to be passing by and rushed over to take control of the crowd. "Stand back, ladies and gentlemen! I implore you, give him room! It isn't safe!" he yelled at the spectators, flapping his arms in his long black robes to shoo them off. "For your own safety, move away!"

Jake resented being pushed back. "Why?" he called. "What will happen?"

Sir Peter turned to him in surprise. "If you get too close, you could be sucked into the portal, and without the proper authorization, you will be instantly vaporized! Care to try it?"

"Ah, no." Jake backed up a few feet, as did everyone else. But Sir Peter failed to give the Lightrider coming in off the Grid quite enough room, himself.

They heard the incoming agent before they saw him. A strange word echoed to them through the pulsating tunnel of light.

"Yeeeeeee-haaaaw!"

A second later, a tall, lanky man in a cowboy hat and a long leather coat burst out of the portal with a loud whoop and barreled straight into Sir Peter, knocking him flat.

As the cowboy fell forward on top of the sputtering wizard, Jake gasped to see several arrows sticking out of his back, another bristling from his thigh.

A tumbleweed rolled out of the glowing circle after him.

He looked up slowly, tipped his hat to the people, and said, "Howdy, y'all."

"Get off me, Josephus!" Sir Peter spluttered, still struggling at the bottom of the heap.

"Hold on, Pete," he answered, "afore my guests come a-callin'." Not even bothering to climb off Sir Peter, the new arrival calmly pulled up his left sleeve, exposing a tattoo like a complicated star on the inside of his forearm.

It was inlaid with tiny chips of light that glowed around the points; he started punching these like buttons with his fingertip in a seemingly random pattern as he spoke. "Folks, y'all better step back in case them Apaches on my tail take a mind to send a few more arrows my way. They didn't ken to my strayin' on their territory..."

From somewhere beyond the pulsating portal of light, the Apaches' whooping war cries were growing louder. Jake could hear a thundering of hooves.

"Hurry, Agent Munroe, they're coming! Close the portal!" an

anxious centaur lady cried, poised to gallop off to safety.

"Hold yer horses, gal, I'm a-tryin'."

Wide-eyed, Jake leaned forward, trying to see through the portal into the wild, dusty land where the Lightrider had come from, but he ducked back with a startled gasp when a real-life Indian arrow whizzed right past his nose.

To his own surprise, Jake reacted automatically with his telekinesis, knocking the arrow upward so nobody was hit.

As it rocketed off over the people's heads, the cowboy looked over at him, sizing him up in a glance.

"Nice move, kid," he drawled.

As soon as he stopped pressing the glowing buttons in his arm, the portal disappeared. "Whew. Ma'am," he added, tipping his dusty hat to Miss Helena, who had just come hurrying out to fetch Isabelle to start getting ready for the Floralia.

Then the pincushion cowboy promptly passed out from blood loss. Sir Peter struggled out from under him, moving gingerly, given the Lightrider's wounds.

"What *is* he?" Dani asked in wonder as she and his cousins arrived.

"A Lightrider!" Jake said in awe.

"That's not what I meant."

"I think he's...an American," Isabelle whispered tentatively.

Dani and Jake looked at each other in astonishment.

An American? This was one type of creature none of them had ever encountered before.

"Worse!" the centaur lady whispered, sounding slightly scandalized. "That one's a *Texan.* By my troth, they're the worst kind!"

"Well." Archie grinned and put his hands in his pockets. "Enter: the cowboy."

Then they all gazed down at the unconscious, long-haired gunslinger, from his ten-gallon hat to his alligator boots.

Sir Peter deposited the wounded cowboy on the ground and quickly beckoned to some gnomes. "Get him inside at once. Take him straight to the healers!"

In moments, a dozen little gnomes had lifted the unconscious Yank up onto their shoulders and sped him off to Merlin Hall to have the arrows pulled out of his back.

"Too bad Red's all out of healing feathers, 'cause that's gonna hurt," Jake said.

Dani turned to him, visibly distraught again after seeing the agent at Death's door. "Still want to be a Lightrider now?" she demanded.

Jake just looked at her. He pressed his lips together, but said nothing.

He didn't think she'd like his answer.

CHAPTER NINE
Spy Hunting

That night, Isabelle stepped into view at the top of the gilded stairs wearing a celestial-blue silk ball gown with a garland of pink rosettes adorning the skirts at knee-level. With a matching rosette tucked into her blond hair, the almost-debutante looked picture-perfect.

Dani jumped to her feet when she saw her, clapping her hands eagerly. "Oh, Isabelle, you're so *beautiful!*"

Even Jake and Archie nodded in approval.

"Not bad, sis."

"Thanks, if only I could breathe! Mother laced me up so tight." She smoothed her corseted waist with a giggle, her face shining with excitement at the prospect of attending her first ball—the famous Floralia, no less.

The flower-themed gala had been celebrated since pagan times to welcome the dawning of Beltane. According to tradition, the adults would be staying up all night at their party to watch the first rays of Beltane illuminate the great St. Michael and St. George Ley Lines that ran right through the center of England.

Isabelle didn't plan on doing that, since she would be going out with the other young ladies at sunrise to share in another ancient tradition: gathering the Beltane dew. This was supposedly a powerful ingredient in beauty potions.

The ballroom on the first floor continued filling up as magical folk of all kinds streamed in, bedecked with flowers, corsages, boutonnieres, gowns in flowered prints, or flowered hats, and glittering with flower-shaped jewels.

Jake and Archie were relieved at being spared this event, but Dani was a little disappointed.

The three of them had been loitering in the sprawling foyer of Merlin Hall to watch all the people going into the ball. They stood out of the way, admiring the smartly dressed adults of their party who now caught up to Isabelle.

Her tuxedoed father, Lord Bradford, took one of Izzy's gloved hands and tucked it into the crook of his elbow. "There you are, my dear." He beamed with his lovely daughter on one side of him and his glamorous wife on the other.

Jake smiled at his uncle, younger brother to the mother he had never known.

Next came Henry, escorting Great-Great Aunt Ramona. The Elder witch looked magnificent in a dark green gown with a flowered shawl and pearls around her neck. A flower-shaped jewel of some sort glowed brightly in her upswept silver hair.

Black-haired Miss Helena trailed behind them, wearing a gown that shimmered like a field of dark purple wildflowers.

"How smart we're all looking, eh?" Derek Stone greeted them with a grin, sauntering across the entrance hall in a tuxedo, his dark mane of longish hair tied back in a small queue.

Jake was startled to see the muscle-bound Guardian looking so debonair in his formal attire. "Evening, everybody. Ah, Jake, glad to see you're on your feet again. Say, before we go in, there's someone I'd like you all to meet."

Jake glanced sourly at Maddox St. Trinian, who had followed Derek over. He was *not* dressed for the ball, but wore ordinary street clothes with a short black jacket.

"This very promising young Guardian is Mr. Maddox St. Trinian. I believe you witnessed his Assessment earlier today," Derek said.

"Indeed, most impressive," Aunt Ramona told the lad.

Then Derek went around the circle, telling Maddox each of their names.

"Great work saving that gnome!" Archie congratulated him. But when Derek introduced his protégé to Dani, the redhead merely sent Isabelle a sly smile.

Jake looked over with a scowl and realized Maddox hadn't heard anybody's name except for Isabelle's. She, in turn, was standing stock-still, staring back at him, her blue eyes round as Wedgwood saucers, her cheeks the scarlet hue of Red's now-shed feathers.

"And this is Jake," Derek finished, gesturing to him.

"Hullo?" Jake said in a loud, purposely rather rude tone, stepping in front of the boy to make him stop ogling his pretty cousin. "Nice to meet you!" he said in his face.

His pointed greeting jarred Maddox from his daze. "Er, likewise," he growled, but the irked stare he gave Jake made it clear that their instant hostility was mutual.

Determined to enjoy the evening's festivities, Derek opted to ignore the tension between his two aspiring heroes-in-training and smiled fondly at Miss Helena. He offered her his arm. "Stunning as ever, mademoiselle."

"*Merci.* You, too." She gave him a kiss on the cheek.

"Aren't you going to the ball, Maddox?" Dani simpered with a glimmer of matchmaking mischief in her eyes.

"I don't dance," he said flatly.

Isabelle's face fell.

He glanced at her one last time, then withdrew with a slight bow to the family, and walked away.

"Well, then. Shall we?" Lord Bradford proposed, and with that, their party proceeded toward the ballroom.

Before they could go in, however, they had to wait in the line of guests arriving. That way, they could be formally announced by the butler as they entered the ballroom. While the adults in line stood chatting, Isabelle beckoned the three of them over.

"What is it?" Archie asked.

Dani bounced on her toes, already knowing somehow exactly what Isabelle wanted. "He saw you! He's so *cute.*"

"I can't believe he's not going to the ball!" Izzy whispered.

Jake rolled his eyes. "Try not to be too disappointed, Izzy. Maybe you could dance with the Troll Boy, instead."

"I'm not allowed to dance with anybody yet, you dolt," she shot back in a hushed tone. "I haven't officially made my debut yet, remember? This is just a *practice* ball for me. Mother just wants to present me to some of her lady friends. Supposedly, they'll help me when I make my debut in London next year."

"And I thought Assessments were bad," Jake muttered.

"Listen, I want you to do me a favor." Blushing again, Isabelle lowered her voice to a whisper to avoid her father's overhearing. "Find out if Maddox already has a sweetheart."

"Uh, why?" Jake drawled, but Dani bounced again and clapped her hands.

"We will! We will!"

"Well, we've got nothing else to do tonight, I suppose," Archie said, nodding decisively. "Very well, sis. I shall see it done. But you'll owe me one."

"Thanks," she whispered to her brother.

"First of all, who cares, and second, I can tell you right now that kid doesn't have a sweetheart," Jake said flatly. "I mean, look at him. He's weird."

"Jake!" Izzy scolded.

"For all we know, he could be the Dark Druids' spy! Remember, Aunt Ramona said they might try to send one?"

Dani turned to him in exasperation. "Honestly."

"What?" Jake said.

Then Lady Bradford gave Isabelle a nudge. It was their turn to step into the ballroom. "Come along, darling."

None of the younger kids were allowed beyond that point. Izzy waved them off and mouthed the word, *"Go!"*

Archie, Jake, and Dani withdrew into the entrance hall again and looked at each other.

"Well," Archie said, "it seems we have our mission for the night."

"I like him," Dani said. "He seems nice."

"How could you possibly tell? All he did was stare at Izzy! Pretty rude if you ask me," Jake huffed, folding his arms across his chest.

"We didn't," Dani said. "Are you coming with us or not?"

Jake frowned. Of course, he had no desire to wander around by himself all night. He was no troll.

"Tell you what," he countered. "You two can find out if Mr. Vainglorious has a girlfriend. I'm going to investigate whether he's our spy."

Archie looked at Dani. "Maybe my cousin's still a bit out of his head after the day's ordeal."

She nodded. "Probably right. C'mon, Jake, we'll look after you, my little demented friend. Let's go *spy* hunting," Dani said indulgently.

"Hey, I'm serious! What if he is?"

She grabbed hold of his jacket and pulled him along after them. "Quit dawdling. We've got to find him before he disappears."

"If only," Jake muttered.

A moment later, they burst through the main doors of Merlin Hall, out into the cool, black night—the last night of April. Reveling in their glorious freedom from parents and chaperones, they savored the night's adventure—especially since it wasn't a serious one and none of their lives were at stake.

They paused in the courtyard and glanced around, searching for their quarry. They could see the Beltane fires burning here and there around the dark landscape, the maypoles waiting for the morrow's festivities.

Dani looked around. "Which way did he go? I saw him come outside."

"There!" Archie pointed. "Hurry, we've got to catch up."

"I wonder why Maddox doesn't want to go to the ball," Dani mused aloud as they crossed the courtyard some twenty yards behind the Guardian kid. "He's old enough."

"Isn't it obvious?" Jake answered. "It's the perfect time to break into people's rooms so he can collect, you know, secret spy information."

Dani rolled her eyes at him. "You *have* noticed that we're outside? He didn't go up to the floors of the palace where the bedchambers are."

"He might still! He could be going *around* to the back of the building or something. Don't look at me like that! You saw him today! Well, you have to admit he has the sort of skills that would make a good spy."

"Jake, Isabelle can sense people's feelings," Dani said in an oh-so-reasonable tone. "Do you think she'd like him if he were some slimy liar of a spy? And what about Derek's Guardian instincts? Don't you think he could tell if Maddox was a fraud?"

Jake frowned. "I guess you have a point," he grumbled after a moment.

"You don't *want* to like him, that's all," Archie said. "Walk faster, he's getting away." He drew a breath to call out to Maddox, but Jake stopped him.

"Shh! No, don't! Let's just follow him for a bit first and see what he's really up to."

"Why?" Dani asked.

"Because I said so! And it's my birthday tomorrow—"

"We know!" they said.

"Well, that means you have to do what I say! So, come on, then!"

Archie and Dani looked at each other and shrugged, deciding without words to humor him.

It was more fun sneaking, anyway.

The process of stalking Maddox St. Trinian actually proved pretty amusing. Deep down, Jake supposed he knew quite well that no protégé of Derek's could ever be a Dark Druid spy, but Archie was right. He didn't *want* to like him. Just looking at the older, stronger, faster boy made him feel abysmally inadequate.

He wasn't used to feeling so insecure and didn't like it one bit. It was much easier making fun of his newfound rival from a distance.

Archie and Dani could not resist the sense of mischievous fun as Jake, barely suppressing his own laughter, led them dodging from shrub to shrub, and tree to tree amid the shadows, following the Guardian kid.

What little sense of mock-danger they could muster in their stealthy pursuit was nearly lost altogether when they heard a dog barking from straight above them.

They looked up and saw the winged sheepdog chasing one of the Dreaming Sheep across the starry sky. They broke down in laughter at this unlikely sight. A few fairies flying by on their way to the ball looked askance at them. Dani waved, still laughing. "Say hello to Gladwin for us!"

Jake clapped a hand over her lips and yanked her back behind the tree with his cousin. "Shush, bigmouth! He's gonna hear you!"

"Where's he going now?" Archie whispered. "If only I had brought my telescope."

"There! He's going over the bridge!"

"Ooh, look at the pretty water nymphs! They're having their own party, too! Why aren't we ever invited to anything?" Dani heaved a sigh.

"Because we're *children.* Just as good as lepers," Archie answered dryly.

"Shh!" Jake ordered. "C'mon."

They hurried after him.

As they sneaked over the bridge, Jake happened to glimpse a strange sight a fair distance downstream from the naiads' revelries. He paused and squinted in the darkness. *What the—?*

He could have sworn for a moment that he saw a strange creature lolling in the water, its rounded back and long body glistening wetly in the moonlight. Red eyes glowed among the pussy willows by the river's edge. He could just make out a pair of pointed ears like a horse's or a mule's. He hung back, peering over the bridge to try to get a better look.

"Jake, hurry up! Target's on the move!"

"We're going to lose him!" his companions prompted.

He jolted back into motion, chasing them. "Archie? Do naiads have horses?"

"Hmm, I don't think so. The ocean mermaids have seahorses, naturally, but not the freshwater nymphs. Why do you ask?"

"No reason." Jake glanced over his shoulder at the river, but the hulking form hiding in the reeds wasn't there anymore—if it ever had been.

Perhaps it was no more than a trick of the moonlight.

"Get out of sight!" Dani warned. "He's going into that building!" She pushed the boys behind another large tree.

From there, they spied: three heads in a vertical row.

She was right.

Their mysterious quarry had stepped into some kind of a shed with three walls and a chimney with a great, roaring fire.

"That's a blacksmith's forge!" Archie whispered.

"What the deuce does he want in there?" Jake murmured.

Maddox St. Trinian shook hands with the large, leather-aproned blacksmith, who ushered him in with a welcoming gesture. The older boy took off his black jacket; put on a leather apron, a pair of goggles, and big fireproof gloves; and then picked up a long pair of blacksmith's tongs.

The three spies watched in bemusement as he used the tongs to stick a small chunk of metal into the fire.

"Wot's 'e doing?" Dani whispered.

"Making something," Archie said with a shrug.

Jake shook his head. "I told you he was weird. C'mon. I think we can get closer."

Creeping ahead with the utmost stealth, they took up a position behind a pile of split logs meant to feed the fires of the forge. Peeking over the top, they watched intently as Maddox pulled the glowing metal out and placed it on an anvil. He picked up a large hammer and proceeded to pound the piece of metal thin.

Sparks flew at every bang. At length, he tossed the hammer aside and examined his handiwork by the firelight of the forge.

The night got very quiet when Maddox quit banging. But they should have realized they were dealing with someone who possessed a Guardian's supernatural senses.

Tipping the goggles up over his forehead, Maddox sauntered to the edge of the shed, drawing off his oversized gloves. They could see him clearly in the moonlight.

"Hey, idiots, you can come out now," he said, sounding dully amused.

Jake whispered "Blast!" and winced in chagrin. Archie and Dani glared at him in reproach.

"I know you're spying on me," Maddox called. "Just a bit curious as to why."

"We just *had* to listen to you," Dani muttered to Jake.

"How embarrassing." Archie was the first to stand up from behind the woodpile. He cleared his throat, smoothed his vest, and started forward. "I say! Good evening there, ol' man."

Maddox arched a brow at the gentlemanly greeting.

Dani stood up next with nearly equal dignity, brushing her hair behind her ear. "We were, um, just out for a stroll."

"Of course you were," Maddox said obligingly.

"We were!" she lied.

"Ahem, what's all this, then?" Archie inquired, awkwardly changing the subject with a nod at Maddox's work.

"Made myself a dagger," the Guardian kid said. "Want to see?"

"Really?" Archie ran to look, suddenly talking a mile a minute. "Oh, this is brilliant! Where'd you learn to do this? You know, I'm always keen to find people who can actually help me build the inventions I design..."

Dani hurried after him to the edge of the blacksmith's shed, no doubt determined to carry out her mission for Isabelle. But only after Maddox had turned away and headed back into the forge did Jake swallow his pride enough to come out of hiding, too.

Trying his best to look casual, he strolled up to the edge of the blacksmith's three-sided shop, hands in pockets.

Maddox was holding up the knife he had fashioned. "It needs a lot more work, of course. Smoothing and polishing. But a Guardian's got to learn how to make his own weapons."

"That sounds hard," Dani said.

Maddox shrugged. "I always found working in the forge kind of relaxing, actually."

"Well, you must have needed it after your Assessment today," she answered, obviously trying hard to draw him out.

Which was pointless, Jake predicted. Guardians preferred to be the strong, silent types.

"Were you nervous out there?"

Maddox shrugged. "A little."

"You really were one of the best of the day!" Archie enthused. He started praising him again for his Assessment, much to Jake's annoyance. "How did you know which gnome was going to be the one that was truly in danger?"

"No idea *how* I knew. I just did. Instinct."

"Right," Archie murmured, head bobbing.

Maddox eyed him more closely as he turned to reach for another odd tool. "So. You're Miss Bradford's brother."

"Yes, he is, and I'm her lady's companion!" Dani said proudly.

"And I'm her cousin," Jake interjected with a warning stare. Maddox glanced at him with a flicker of mild curiosity, but Dani ignored him altogether.

"Actually, Maddox, Isabelle was *very* impressed with your Assessment, too," she informed him like a little busybody.

"Really?" The serious lad almost smiled. "She saw me?"

"Mm-hmm!" Dani said, nodding. Jake could tell the carrot-head was loving her assignment.

Girls were so daft.

"And guess what?" Dani charged on. "Isabelle's an empath!"

Maddox drew back in alarm. "She can read people's minds?"

"No, only their emotions. Well, except for animals. They're all heart, anyway, so she can communicate telepathically with animals of all kinds. But not insects and I don't think fish."

"Well, they probably don't have much to say, anyway," he murmured with a half-smile.

Dani laughed like Maddox's low-toned quip was the funniest thing she had ever heard in her life. "You want to know something else about Isabelle? She's a Keeper of the Unicorns! Isn't that amazing? You have to be a really special girl to get that post, extra-nice and extra-good, 'cause unicorns won't accept just anybody."

"I suppose not." Maddox pondered this while Jake considered giving Dani a discreet kick before she blabbed everybody's whole life story to this stranger.

"So, Maddox," Dani wheedled, "do you mind if I ask you a question? Do you have a special sweetheart here at the Gathering? Or maybe back home?"

He frowned at her. "Sweetheart? Of course not." His cheeks colored at the question. Then he ducked his head and returned his attention to the knife he had made. "Guardians don't have time for that sort of nonsense."

Finally, a sensible answer, thought Jake.

"But you're not a real Guardian yet," Dani pointed out in her oh-so-helpful way.

Maddox looked a little irked at the reminder. "No," he repeated, "no sweetheart. Nor do I want one." He shook his head. "I don't have time for girls."

Good! Jake thought. *Then stay away from Isabelle.*

Dani's mouth tilted sideways at this unfortunate news. She was obviously not looking forward to passing this along to the older girl.

"Well! Let's not interrupt the man's work. A Guardian has his duties," Jake said in a brisk tone.

"Lord Griffon," Maddox said as Jake turned away, prepared to drag the two younger ones out by force if need be.

He glanced back warily.

"Your Assessment today. Building the Stonehenge. Most people would've let the pain stop them. You kept going. 'Twas well done."

Jake was startled by the compliment, and then quite pleased. It was one thing to have loads of random strangers congratulating him at dinner earlier, but this unexpected praise from a lad who possessed such excellent skills himself carried a greater significance.

He gave Maddox a stilted nod of thanks, but all he could think of to say was: "Derek Stone doesn't train quitters."

"True," Maddox agreed.

Still, hesitating, Jake could not bring himself to tell Maddox that he had done an outstanding job today, too.

Instead, they took leave of him.

"Isabelle's going to be *so* disappointed," Dani said as they headed back to Merlin Hall. She looked askance at Jake. "I told you he was nice."

"I guess he's not *that* bad," he admitted. "Especially since he's got no designs on Izzy, after all."

"And especially since he's not a spy for the Dark Druids, hmm?" Archie taunted, elbowing him.

Even Jake laughed at his earlier suspicion. It *did* sound a bit silly, now that they had had a conversation with the Guardian kid.

Of course, Jake still did not particularly want Maddox St. Trinian for a friend, any more than he wanted him for an enemy. He just wanted the interloper to keep his distance and not try to push his way into their close-knit group. Because if he did that, Maddox might make him look bad.

In truth, being around the older boy made him feel like a bit of an idiot, hiding behind woodpiles. Maddox seemed so mature and superior by comparison. It irked him.

Putting the whole matter out of his mind, Jake accompanied his companions back across the bridge and made sure to look again for the strange creature he had seen in the brook, but it was gone.

They paused on the bridge to listen raptly to the gathered naiads singing before they continued on their way. In the ordinary world, a mortal might be dragged underwater and drowned for daring to listen to the water nymphs' songs, but at Merlin Hall, such hostile traditions were suspended.

"Maybe we should go have a peek at the fairy market," Dani suggested at length, gazing at it across the fields.

Colorful lanterns winked and beckoned. Accordion music invited them to dance. Bursts of laughter echoed from the carnival games on offer amid the vendor stalls. But the veiling fog that twisted around the camp gave its allure a tricksy air of danger.

Archie shook his head. "Aunt Ramona told us not to."

"I know, but aren't you the least bit curious what might be for sale over there?" Dani asked.

"Only things that would get you into trouble," Archie said.

"Come on," Jake urged his companions before Dani took it into her head to insist. "Let's go."

Heading back toward Merlin Hall, they chatted idly about what they might like to do next, but Jake paused when he heard eerie music coming from the woods. "Wait—do you hear that?"

"Hear what?" Dani asked.

"Somebody playing a bagpipe. You don't hear that?"

Archie squinted at him. "I don't hear anything, either. Maybe you're still not right in the head, coz—"

"I'm fine," he retorted, all the more intrigued.

Logically, if only he could hear it, it would seem to mean the piper was a ghost...

Curiosity got the better of him. He headed for the woods. "Wait here, I'll be right back," he said.

Famous last words.

CHAPTER TEN
Headless & Boneless

Leaving his friends behind, Jake strode to the woods on the far end of the moonlit meadow.

He spied a path among the trees and ventured down it, until, amid the doleful wailing of the bagpipes, he heard slow, heavy footfalls marching ominously ahead. Back and forth they trod, in time with the dark song.

He moved closer. "Who's there?"

In the forest shadows, he could just make out the spectral form of a tall, brawny figure in a kilt. The piper turned, and Jake's eyes widened as he realized the ghostly Scotsman didn't have a head!

Though the bellows of the bagpipe was tucked under his arm, the long, flute-like reed was merely propped against the top of the ghost's neck, just above his neck-cloth. Considering that the headless Scot could somehow play the bagpipe without a mouth, perhaps Jake should not have been surprised to discover that the ghost could also sense him there somehow, even though he had neither eyes nor ears.

Indeed, if the headless ghost had possessed a face, Jake might have been able to read the angry expression there and realize the spirit did not wish to be disturbed. But as it was, he got no prior warning that this ghost was a murderously angry chap. Not until the bagpipe in the Highlander's hands turned into a great, sharp claymore.

Without warning, his giant long-sword in hand, the mighty Scot came charging at him like he was in the midst of fighting the bloody Battle of Culloden.

It was one of those rare occasions where Jake was so taken off guard that he responded in a most un-Lightriderly fashion: He screamed and ran away.

"What's wrong?" Archie yelled as Jake came barreling out of the woods and raced breathlessly across the meadow.

"Run!"

Dani screamed, too (just because), and both of them immediately did as he commanded.

To his relief, however, strangely, the Scot stopped chasing as soon as Jake rejoined his friends. When he looked back, the Headless Highlander twirled his broadsword impressively and slung it on its strap across his back.

He produced his ectoplasm bagpipe once more out of thin air and resumed playing, marching slowly back into the woods.

"Sweet peat moss!" Jake panted, bending forward to prop his hands on his thighs as he strove to catch his breath. Then he started laughing in belated humor and relief.

"What did you see?" Dani cried.

He told them, concluding with this advice: "Probably best to stay off that particular path." He pointed at it. "The ghost seems to think that's his territory."

"Somebody ought to put up a sign to warn people off!" Archie said indignantly.

Jake agreed with a rueful nod. "At least I can see why Lady Oriel didn't use that ghost in my Assessment. He's mean."

With that, he suddenly remembered to tell his friends about Constanzio, King of the Tenors, who had been his favorite ghost of the day by far. Jake's loud, off-key attempt to imitate the opera ghost's singing soon had all three of them laughing again after that brush with danger.

Nevertheless, Jake wondered privately if a ghost with a sword could really hurt anyone or just scare the blazes out of them. *That* much the Headless Highlander had certainly accomplished.

At last, the three of them stepped back into Merlin Hall, where the chandeliers blazed with light, chasing off the darkness outside.

The orchestra's music boomed through the closed doors of the ballroom. Only a few servants and bored kids stood around here and there in the grand foyer, excluded from the adults' festivities.

"Well?" Archie turned to Jake and Dani. "What now? I don't want to go to bed yet."

"Me neither. It's too early."

Dani pointed at the art gallery off the entrance hall. "Let's go see the paintings."

The boys followed as she led the way, her patent-leather shoes clicking over the marble floors, the busy rhythm of her footfalls echoing under the high ceilings.

Soon they were admiring the great classical paintings hung upon the red walls in ornate, gilded frames. Every palace this size had an art collection, Jake supposed, but he wasn't sure why these particular paintings should be hung at Merlin Hall. They did not look magical to him.

He was soon rather bored, especially when Archie started explaining the various paintings to him and Dani. Jake only half-listened.

First was a fairly typical foxhunting scene of some aristocrat jumping his horse over a hedgerow while a pack of sleek hounds flowed around him, chasing after some unfortunate fox.

Next came a Turner painting of a beautiful old sailing ship sinking in a storm; then an unsmiling portrait of a Dutch merchant sitting in his kitchen, looking overly intense beside a bowl of potatoes and a dead rabbit meant to be for dinner.

Fourth was a frothy French rococo fantasy, with giddy shepherds and ladies in huge fluffy skirts chasing each other around some garden, while a cupid hovered in the clouds shooting arrows at them. Jake rolled his eyes at that one, then followed as Archie moved on.

The next scene was more his style, full of action, danger, and adventure: Mount Vesuvius erupting. As the volcano spewed fire and brimstone all over the Italian islands, tiny people were fleeing into their boats to try to escape their ancient doomsday.

"Wouldn't want to be them," Jake remarked.

The sixth painting could only be described as disturbing in the extreme. Jake and Dani looked at each other and blanched.

It was by some demented medieval chap whose name Archie gave as Hieronymus Bosch. Monsters, devils, and grotesque creatures worse than the Venemous Tython were depicted gleefully torturing wicked souls in the afterlife.

"Ew," said Dani, moving past it with a shudder.

In sharp contrast to the hellish scene by Bosch, the last painting on the narrow end of the long gallery showed an idyllic farm landscape on a lazy summer's afternoon, with a field of sunflowers in the foreground, and a grove of trees in the distance, a soft blue sky overhead.

The peaceful country scene made you want to lie down in the tall grass and snooze in the sunshine.

They stood around staring at it for a long moment.

"It looks so real," Dani remarked, tilting her head.

Archie gave a slight yawn. "This one makes me sleepy." He checked his fob watch. "Well, it's ten o'clock now. Getting late."

"Maybe we could send down to the kitchens for a snack before we head off to bed," Jake suggested.

"Do you think the kitchen gnomes are still working?" Dani asked hopefully.

He shrugged. "Worth a shot," he answered.

The others agreed to this, but when they all turned around to leave the gallery, they promptly learned that the adventures of the night weren't over yet. For, at that moment, the formless, shapeless blob that Jake had seen earlier today on the Field of Challenge floated right out of the gallery wall and hovered in midair in front of them, blocking their way in a menacing fashion.

"What the dash is that?" Archie shouted, pointing as he skidded to a halt between Jake and Dani.

"You can see it?" Jake exclaimed.

Even Dani nodded. "Aye, but what the devil is it?"

"Not a ghost, apparently," Jake mumbled in confusion. "It showed up earlier at my Assessment. I thought it was some sort of spirit, but if you two can see it, too, it must have some sort of substance..."

"I say!" Archie marveled, studying it. He took a step toward the creature. "Hullo, what are you, then? Hold still, let me have a look at you..."

Whatever it was, it didn't like the young scientist trying to come closer.

"Archie, be careful!" Dani cried, but her warning came too late.

As Archie reached out to try to touch the thing, the boneless blob attacked, engulfing the boy genius in the mass of its thick gray fog.

An angry, non-human, yet oddly comical face formed on the surface, glaring at Archie.

"Get off o' him!" Jake and Dani both reacted at once, trying to pull the creature away, but their hands went right through its cold, clammy cloud of a body.

Inside, Archie waved his arms wildly like someone trying to escape a swarm of mosquitoes.

The blob retreated as quickly as it had pounced, leaving the boy genius spluttering and shuddering with disgust, coated with a light layer of clear-colored slime. Other than that and a bit of coughing, Archie seemed more or less all right.

"Stay with him!" Jake ordered Dani, running after the blob as it zoomed away down the long corridor of the art gallery and out across the entrance hall.

"Get back here!" His eyes blazed as he chased it. Nobody, living or dead, attacked his best mate and got away with it.

The Boneless glanced back at him, but swept on, leaving a few of the kids staring after it.

Only Jake chased.

As he ran, a shocking thought occurred to him. For all he knew, that bizarre creature might be the Dark Druids' *real* spy!

The night's playful spy-hunting mission had just turned possibly dead serious—and real.

"Come back here, you...thing!" Jake tore after it as it sped into a shadowy corridor that branched off the far side of the entrance hall.

Like many palaces of its era, the main block of Merlin Hall had been built as a massive quadrangle, with a grassy courtyard in the center, and two large wings branching off the sides.

The whole structure easily covered several acres, offering an endless row of formal parlors, dining rooms, music rooms, studies, meeting rooms, lecture halls, ballrooms, and all manner of gilded staterooms for large gatherings. There was even a theatre and concert hall.

In short, the sprawling size and grandeur of the palace gave the Boneless plenty of room to run.

Or float, as the case might be.

As Jake raced into the dimly lit medieval corridor, a shout from behind told him that, thank goodness, Archie had recovered.

"Jake, wait up!" Dani yelled.

He glanced back and shook his head, then waved them toward the other side of the quadrangle. "You two go that way! We'll trap it in between us! Block it if it comes your way, but don't get too close!"

Dani bobbed her head, grabbed Archie, then the two dashed off in the opposite direction.

Jake continued running down the long corridor before him. To be sure, this night was turning out to be more interesting that he had anticipated.

First a strange animal in the river, then a headless Highlander, now the Boneless.

Whatever it was, it was fast. He could hardly keep pace with the floating blob. He could not imagine where the thing was going, hurrying on as if it had some important business to attend to.

Somehow, despite the day's draining ordeal, he found the strength to pour on another burst of speed, refusing to let the thing escape him. It turned the corner, but Jake kept after it, his jaw clenched with determination, his heart pounding from this unexpected exercise.

Suddenly, he heard a banging sound ahead, followed by a gleeful cackle that promptly sent chills down his spine.

He paused to listen, chest heaving, and heard a second, softer voice that was not quite crying, but definitely pleading for mercy. Jake's first thought was that the Boneless was about to attack another victim.

"Don't you dare!" he hollered after it, once more in motion, scrambling to catch up. He yelled ahead to warn the blob's would-be victim. "Look out up there! Don't let the blob thing near you, it's dangerous!"

But when he flung around the corner, to the rescue, he ran smack-dab into a mere slip of a girl and knocked her off her feet.

She went flying and landed with an indignant *"Ow!"*

Jake skidded to a halt. He glanced around; the Boneless was gone.

"Did it get you? Are you all—" When he turned to help the girl up, he interrupted himself in surprise. "You!"

It was none other than Nixella Valentine, the gloomy but brilliant young witch from today's Assessments.

She ignored his offered hand and climbed to her feet, scowling at him and brushing her black skirts neatly into place. "Watch where you're going, fool!"

"I-I'm sorry. I thought you were in danger!" he stammered, taken aback by her rudeness. He glanced around. "Did you see which way it went?"

"What are you talking about?"

"The Boneless. It was headed your way. Didn't you see it?"

"No."

"But...weren't you crying?"

"I don't cry," she said. "What's the matter with you, anyway, running about like a crazy person?"

"Sorry—I was chasing something," he said in confusion. "I'm not really sure what it was. Some sort of apparition. It attacked my cousin—"

"What?" she asked, not quite hiding her blanch.

"I don't think it really hurt him." Jake eyed her in suspicion. "It's just like a blob or a cloud of fog. Really strange. Are you sure you didn't see it? It was coming right this way."

She shrugged. "No. But why so surprised? We're at Merlin Hall. Everything is strange here. Especially the people," she added pointedly.

Jake ignored the barb, rather sure she was lying. "Well, if you do see it, I suggest you keep your distance. It might be dangerous. And sorry I knocked you down. It was an accident."

At that moment, Archie and Dani appeared at the other end of the corridor.

"Jake! Did you find it? Where did it go?" Archie yelled as they pounded closer.

"It disappeared!" he called back as they approached, then gestured at Nixella. "All I found was her."

As Archie skidded to a halt, his eyes widened behind his spectacles. "M-Miss Valentine?"

She frowned and drew back in wary disdain. "Do I know you?"

"Well, no, but I saw your Assessment today. Absolutely brilliant!"

The black-clad girl seemed genuinely shocked by his enthusiastic praise. Indeed, her tough veneer cracked ever so slightly. She ducked her head as though confused and a little tongue-tied at his compliment.

"Uh, thanks." She glanced at Jake. "Is this the cousin you claim got attacked?"

"Claim?" Jake echoed, offended.

She shrugged. "He looks all right to me."

Jake glanced at Archie. "I told her about the blob attack."

"Oh, no worries, I'm right as rain!" Archie said cheerfully. "Didn't hurt. Just a horrid, nasty, slimy thing, that's all." He shuddered for effect. "I'm Archie Bradford, by the way. That's Jake and that's Dani. I trust you two remember Miss Nixella Valentine?"

"Just Nixie," she muttered. "And yes, my mother must've hated me, giving me a name like that."

Dani bit back a giggle at her admission, but Archie frowned. "Aw, it's not so bad! How do you think I feel having the full name Archimedes?"

Archie proceeded to regale the black-clad witch with the tale of what had just occurred. Dani arched an eyebrow at Jake as they both realized the boy genius was attempting the impossible once more: he seemed determined to befriend the gloomy girl or at least draw her out of her somber shell.

Good luck with that, Jake thought. For his part, he began to ponder Miss Valentine's Assessment, now that Archie had mentioned it.

As the four of them stood in the shadowy stone hallway, he remembered her incredible show of power over the four elements, and a dark suspicion began taking shape in his mind.

He was *sure* that the Boneless had come this way. But when he got here, all he found was her. Why would she lie about such a thing?

Archie and Dani had seen it, so spotting it did not require psychic powers, as with ghosts. Did Nixie know something about it that she wasn't telling? Might she be connected to it somehow? Then Jake's eyes widened at an even more sinister possibility.

Maybe she had *made* the blob creature, just like she made the mud rabbit. What had Aunt Ramona called it—a golem? Aye, maybe she was controlling the Boneless. She was, after all, a witch, and witches could not always be trusted.

In fact...

Jake narrowed his eyes, homing in on her, though he was shocked by the drift of his own thoughts. If the Dark Druids had indeed sent a spy, who better to choose than an innocent-faced child whom no one would suspect? The Elders would never question a mere wisp of a girl who was all of maybe eleven.

But like Archie, Miss Valentine obviously possessed abilities far beyond her years.

The boy genius was still chattering away happily to the gloomy young prodigy. Arms folded, Nixie was studying him, in turn, like he was some strange creature that had crawled out of a swamp.

Dani glanced from the pair of them to Jake in curious amusement. He met her gaze with a discreet shrug, finally interrupting Archie's chipper monologue when the boy genius took a breath.

"So, Nixie," Jake spoke up. "What were you doing back here all by yourself, anyway?"

"Nothing," she said defensively with a gesture at the walls. "Just looking at the paintings."

He glanced over and was startled to find the Vesuvius painting hung there. "Huh?" He blinked. "Didn't we just see that in the art gallery?"

"They jump around," Nixie informed him.

"Really?"

"It is called the Enchanted Gallery for a reason," she said in a tone of thorny sarcasm.

Jake frowned. "Say, when I was headed this way, I could've sworn I heard a banging sound coming from back here. Were you banging on something?"

"I was stomping my feet," she replied.

"Why?"

"I had a stone in my shoe. Why?"

"Well, I also heard a nasty cackle, like an old hag laughing. Did you hear that, too?"

She shrugged her thin shoulders. "Nope. All I hear is the music coming from the ballroom."

Jake nodded, narrowing his eyes. He was no empath like Isabelle, but he felt quite certain she was lying. "Right."

Nixie glared at him. "What?" she demanded.

"Well! We should be on our way," Dani said brightly, hooking one hand through Archie's elbow, the other through Jake's. She started steering them away with great determination behind her forced smile. "C'mon, boys! We've taken up enough of Miss Valentine's time. Good evening, Nixie, so nice to meet you!"

"What are you doing?" Jake demanded under his breath, though he went along with her willingly enough. "We should stay and grill her! That girl might be the Dark Druid spy!"

"Exactly!" Dani whispered. "We don't need her reporting back to *them* about you! Let's get out of here before she turns us into pinecones 'cause that little witch is definitely hiding something."

Archie was oblivious. He seemed to be having a hard time dragging himself away. "Cheerio, Miss Valentine! Hope to see you around again!"

"Goodbye, Mr. Bradford," she replied somewhat more civilly to him.

"You can join us for breakfast at our table if you want!" he added over his shoulder. "The more, the merrier!"

"Shut *up!*" Jake scolded under his breath. "Blazes."

"What? What's wrong?" Archie asked.

"Come *on*," Dani insisted, pulling on his arm.

"Doesn't say much, does she?" Archie remarked once they were out of earshot. "Quite a puzzle of a girl."

Jake and Dani exchanged a dire look. They both knew how much he loved solving puzzles.

"Must be shy around strangers," Archie mused aloud as they rounded the corner. "I'll just have to keep trying."

"You'll do nothing of the kind!" Dani scolded. "Sheesh, never mind Maddox, *she's* the one who's weird."

"What? Ah, don't be daft. Nixie's just a little different, that's all. Different's good," Archie said. "I like her!"

"You would," Jake mumbled.

"Archie, that girl's dangerous," Dani informed him, but he just laughed heartily.

"She did call down lightning out of the sky," Jake reminded him.

"So? I could vaporize this whole palace with my Aether Blast Propulsion Cannon if I wanted to. But just because I *can* doesn't mean I ever *would*. Leave the poor girl alone. I think she must be lonely, spending the first night of the Gathering back here all by herself. It's not right!"

"Archie—"

"Enough! Honestly, you've got her all wrong! I'm quite sure of it," he said, pulling away from them.

"Archie!"

"No! If you don't trust her, trust me. You think I'm not smart enough to be able to tell if someone's good or evil? Give a chap some credit!"

Jake started to protest, but Archie wasn't through.

"Frankly, you're both being very unkind toward the poor girl. Very unkind!" he declared, then he gave his vest a slight, indignant tug, and marched off down the hall without them.

"Well," Dani murmured. "I guess he told us."

She and Jake exchanged a worried glance.

"He's a terrible judge of character," she added in a whisper.

"I know," Jake said wryly. "He sees the best in everyone. Awful habit."

Dani snorted. "Let's hope it doesn't get him killed."

Nixie was relieved they had finally left. And just in time, too.

"My, my, what a gallant little gentleman!" Jenny Greenteeth floated back out of the large, gilt-framed mirror where she had been hiding the whole time. Boneless slithered down the wall from behind the candle-sconce and hovered before Nixie, gloating at the mischief it had caused.

She glared at it. "That boy was right. You *are* a nasty, horrid, slimy thing."

The blob puffed up, as though pleased by the compliment.

The hag cackled, showing off her algae-covered fangs. "Flattery won't get you anywhere with us, my dove," she taunted. "So, who are your new friends?"

"They're not my friends!" she protested automatically.

"Oh, but that dear, chivalrous gent in the bowtie. He seemed to like you well. When's the wedding, dear heart?"

"I said they're not my friends! I'm the one you're after! Just leave them alone!"

"Well, it *is* true that you are the one who must be punished," the watery hag conceded. "Just remember, after what you did to *our* friends, we warned you what would happen to any of yours."

"But I don't even know them!" she insisted in a panic.

"Are you sure?"

"You have eyes! You saw what happened. The blond boy and the red-haired girl didn't even like me. The three of them are clearly thick as thieves. That Archie fellow is never going to go against those two for my sake. All it'll take is one conversation and he won't like me anymore. Believe me, they are not my friends. I don't *have* any friends."

"Good," Jenny Greenteeth said in cold satisfaction. "See that it stays that way, unless you wish them dead. You're alone, little witch, and you always will be."

Then the hag disappeared back into the mirror, and this time, the Boneless followed, granting Nixie a temporary reprieve.

She stood there, trembling for a moment, and then wrapped her arms around herself. She shut her eyes briefly, so very, very tired. Letting out a long sigh, she wandered on through the shadowed corridors alone.

At length she came to the art gallery and drifted through it with little interest, until she came to the painting on the end.

How beautiful.

She stopped and stared longingly at the farm landscape in Provence. The golden field of sunflowers, the cloud shapes in the lazy blue sky. A peaceful summer's day.

A day without shadows. A safe place, where nobody was haunted by evil apparitions...

Or their own secret deeds.

Nixie sat down slowly on the bench across from the painting. She put her feet up on it, wrapped her arms around her bent legs, and rested her chin on her knee.

She gazed at the picture for she knew not how long, only wishing she could escape there somehow. Just disappear into that peaceful, sun-kissed landscape.

And sleep for a year.

PART II

CHAPTER ELEVEN
Born on Beltane

Beltane dawned, and as the first sunbeams of May stretched across the green hills, Jake awoke and rose onto his elbows, his first thought: *my birthday!*

Then he noticed the riotous birdsong filling the air, and a slight, rascally smile curved his lips. Maybe they were singing him happy birthday. Rubbing the sleep out of his eyes, he rose from the unfamiliar bed and went over to the window alcove, still in his pajamas.

The occasion felt momentous.

It was no small thing to wake up knowing in advance for the first time in his life which day of the year marked the date of his birth. *Thirteen...*

He wondered if the age would prove unlucky.

Then he noticed the girls in white dresses walking around outside with wreaths on their heads. He watched them collecting the Beltane dew in little glass vials, bending blades of grass or the leaves of trees or flowers to capture the precious droplets.

"Jake!" a scratchy voice greeted him from the other twin bed.

Still at the window, he glanced over his shoulder. "Morning, Arch."

His cousin sat up rubbing his eyes. "Happy birthday, coz!"

"Thanks. Shh!" He signaled for quiet, for Henry was still asleep. Since the chamber only had two beds, the shapeshifting tutor had curled up on an extra quilt in the corner in his wolf form.

"You're up early," Archie whispered loudly from across the room. "What are you doing over there?"

Jake flashed a smile. "Lookin' at some girls." He turned back to the window.

Archie reached for his spectacles and put them on, then climbed out of bed and curiously shuffled over to the window beside him. He glanced at all the pretty girls wandering around in the growing light of sunrise and shook his head. "Daft what they'll do for beauty, eh?"

"Better them than us."

Archie laughed and clapped him on the back. "Come on, then, let's get this birthday started!"

* * *

Jake had warned them all not to make a fuss over him.

Fortunately, with everything else going on for day two of the Gathering, his relatives restrained themselves to an elegant birthday brunch in the sitting room of their suite, where they showered him with gifts.

Archie gave him a telescope fitted with special gadgetry he'd made himself. "Since you're always borrowing mine."

Jake marveled at the optional night vision lens he had fashioned. All you had to do was click it into place.

"I modeled it on the glass from the Vampire Monocle, remember? It's also got a side compartment here, where you can store matches or other small items useful on an adventure."

"It's brilliant. Thank you so much!"

Archie grinned and blushed a bit.

Isabelle returned and put a victor's wreath that she had made on his head like a crown. She then gave him her present: an exceedingly fine pair of riding gloves.

"Very grown-up," Lady Bradford said in approval.

Henry soon emerged from the boys' chamber in a neat tweed jacket (in human form by now). He gave Jake a book about the fall of the Roman Empire, which seemed more like an assignment than a gift, but Jake thanked him nonetheless.

The tutor had to dash out quickly, however, to prepare to receive the group of shapeshifter children he and Helena were to be managing today.

Miss Helena had promised her twin that she would join him soon to host the group. She was running behind on account of chaperoning Isabelle in the ritual of collecting the Beltane dew.

The shape-shifting governess made sure to give Jake her present, too, before she left to join her brother: a magical neck-cloth that could tie itself in three different styles of knots, since he found it simply impossible to tie his own.

He smiled at her with gratitude. He had grown extremely fond of her, not just because Derek loved her, but because in Wales, she had saved his life in her black leopard form. She rumpled his hair affectionately, then hurried off after her twin.

Moments later, Aunt Ramona arrived from her private quarters in the Elders' wing of Merlin Hall. She sat down at the table, accepted a cup of tea, and then presented Jake with his very first yew wand in a long, velvet-lined box.

"Use it wisely, dear nephew, and only in emergencies."

"Thank you, ma'am," he said, though in truth, he planned to use it as little as possible. Telekinesis and his psychic ability were enough to manage, heaven knew.

The gifts continued.

As his present legal guardians, Lord and Lady Bradford gave him tokens of his deceased parents.

Uncle Richard, his mother's younger brother, presented him with a chunky signet ring that he'd had made for him in London. It bore the Griffon coat of arms.

"Your father would have wanted you to have this now that you're becoming a young man. See? You wear it on your pinky finger." Uncle Richard, who held the title of Baron Bradford, held up his hand to show him how a lord wore his family's insignia.

"Thank you, sir." Jake duly put it on; the heavy metal ring felt odd on his hand. He hoped it would not interfere with his telekinesis—not that he intended to use his ability any time soon after yesterday's ordeal.

Aunt Claire gave him an old, china doll that had belonged to Jake's mother. "Keep it on a shelf," she said gently, "and one day, you might have a daughter of your own who will play with it."

"Yes, ma'am, thank you," Jake forced out, finding it exceedingly odd for anyone to give a boy a doll for his thirteenth birthday. Even more bizarre was the thought of himself ever being a parent. All the same, he was genuinely touched by their thoughtfulness.

In truth, his aunt and uncle barely knew him, but they were doing their best to serve as stand-in parents when they were not traveling on their diplomatic missions for the Order.

Dani gave Jake her two gifts last. First, she set a whole Roly-Poly

Pudding down in front of him and grinned.

"You don't even have to share it," she said.

But to everybody's shock, he wanted to, so maybe he really was starting to grow up. Startled but pleased, Dani dished it out so everyone could taste it and see why it was Jake's favorite food.

But the carrot-head saved her more important gift for later, after the others had left the table and more or less gone on about their business. "Here." She put a homely sketchbook in front of him, its pages bound together with a ribbon. "I made this for you."

"What is it?"

She shrugged shyly. "Look inside and see."

He opened the booklet and found it filled with colorful drawings she had made, depicting his adventures. They weren't very good, in truth; he knew she had been getting drawing lessons from Miss Helena. Along with room and board, receiving a lady's education was the main part of Dani's pay as Izzy's hired companion.

Nevertheless, as he turned the pages, his heart ached at the care she had put into each misshapen, adorable picture. Him flying on the Gryphon, with Gladwin speeding along by his shoulder. Him and Derek fighting Uncle Waldrick's henchmen. Fionnula Coralbroom in her hideous Kraken form. He laughed at the picture of Archie in his flying machine, the Mighty Pigeon. The next one showed the four of them running away from the yetis...

And there were the living gingerbread men he had rescued at Christmas...

The two of them getting captured by the pixies...

Him meeting the Norse giants...

All four of them with the dwarves in the mine...

"That's Emrys and that's Ufudd," Dani said, tapping the smaller dwarf with a large white beard.

"I would've guessed that," Jake said, nodding.

"Well?" She glanced at him, her emerald eyes full of hope. "Do you like it?"

"No," Jake blurted out, "I love it." And to the surprise of them both, he impulsively leaned near and gave her a peck on her forehead. "You're a right plum lass, you are, Dani O'Dell," he mumbled, immediately embarrassed by his own show of affection.

Astonished, Dani jumped to her feet, her cheeks turning red between her freckles. Though she seemed too shocked to speak, she managed to utter the same-old reply she always gave to his same-old compliment: "I know!"

Then she dashed off into the girls' bedroom without explanation.

Jake smiled ruefully and looked again at the sketchbook, where all his daring deeds were so carefully recorded. He might never be chosen for a Lightrider, but at least there was one person in this world who already saw him as a hero.

CHAPTER TWELVE
Sorted

By midmorning, they had sampled some of the May Day festivities. Dani, for her part, had been mesmerized watching the fairies dance around the maypole, each holding a long, colorful ribbon as they wove back and forth. But all too soon, it was time to get on with the business of the day.

Sir Peter Quince came out and took charge once more, dividing all the magical children up into their groups to attend special sessions with an adult expert in their field.

Dani stood awkwardly beside Archie, watching Isabelle go off with the Empaths and Healers into one of the meeting rooms inside Merlin Hall, while Jake hooted with glee at being summoned to attend the Lightriders' session.

The young Guardians, including Maddox St. Trinian, joined Derek and a fierce, muscular, female Guardian in the nearby field.

Henry and Helena led the shapeshifter children off for a chat, including the three horrid skunkies who had tortured her during yesterday's Assessments. Dani saw the twins exchange a worried glance, experienced enough as teachers to realize they were in serious trouble with the three little horrors.

When even Her Ladyship, Jake's Great-Great Aunt Ramona, had retreated into another meeting room to speak to the young witches and wizards, Dani let out a glum sigh.

She wished she had somewhere to go, some way to participate. She usually didn't mind being an ordinary person, but at the moment, she just felt so inadequate, even unwanted. Must she be left out of everything?

"Ah, don't look so glum, Dani, ol' girl," Archie drawled, slinging his arm around her shoulders. "You've still got me! C'mon, I'll show you the library. It's really something."

"Very well," she said with another heavy sigh. She loved books, but spending a brilliant, sunny May Day in a silent crypt of a library sounded all wrong.

Ah, well, it was better than being alone.

Of course, being around Archie when he was working out equations or doing research was just the same as being alone, anyway. On such occasions, he went off into his own mental world of deep thoughts and advanced mathematics, where only other geniuses could follow. All the same, it was kind of him to invite her.

Dani shuffled after him as he marched down the hallway. But just then, she heard someone call her name.

A lady's prim voice echoed down the corridor. "Daniela Catherine O'Dell?"

Dani whipped around in surprise.

The lady was still searching the hallway. "Is there a Miss O'Dell here somewhere, please? I say, where is Daniela Catherine?"

She shot her hand up into the air. "I'm here! That's me! Archie, wait up!"

A lady in a long, slim, gray skirt was standing in the doorway of one of the meeting rooms with a clipboard in her hand and spectacles resting on her nose. "Miss O'Dell?"

She sprinted breathlessly to her. "Yes, ma'am! Can I help you? I'm Dani O'Dell!"

Archie followed, looking on in mild curiosity.

The lady tapped her clipboard with a pen. "I have your name down here, if you'd care to join us, dear."

"Me? But...there must be some mistake. I have no powers," Dani admitted with some embarrassment.

"No, of course, my dear. Neither do I," the lady said with a wink. "I'm Sir Peter Quince's wife, and my session is called Managing Magic Folk. It is exclusively for those of us ordinary souls charged with looking after our, er, *unusual* friends and loved ones. If you wish to participate, please don't dally, Miss O'Dell. Her Majesty is waiting."

Dani gasped. "Queen Victoria is in there? Oh! Oh, my goodness! Yes, of course. Thank you! Gotta go, Arch!"

"No worries, have fun!" he called.

Dani felt seven feet tall to find herself included—and in the

Queen's own group, no less! No doubt Queen Victoria, as the human ruler of the Order, had to deal with all sorts of questions regarding the many magical subjects in her Realm.

When Dani stepped into the stately chamber, she curtsied to the short, stout, black-clad Queen, then quickly took a seat on the end of the first row of chairs, feeling very important, indeed.

The lady with the clipboard walked to the front of the room and took off her spectacles, letting them hang by the slim chain around her neck. "Good morning, everybody. Your Majesty." She curtsied to the Queen. "Welcome to Managing Magic-Folk. Being married to an Elder wizard, I have years of experience, as you may well imagine, in dealing with all sorts of magic folk and the, shall we say, interesting situations they tend to generate. I do hope that my insights can provide some guidance to others who may find themselves now and then, in a position to aid a gifted friend or family member with their unique struggles.

"Never forget that our ordinary human bonds with our magical loved ones are an absolutely vital part of keeping them on friendly terms with the mortal world, rather than turning against humanity and joining the dreaded You-Know-Who's.

"I know we sometimes feel unimportant compared to the magical folk in our lives, but trust me, they need us. The worst fate that can befall any magical individual is to become alienated and alone, for then they become easy pickings for the dark side. In time, their talents could be used against our world and all that we hold dear.

"In short, even though we possess no powers of our own beyond our hearts and strength of character, there are times when *our* love and loyalty are all that stands between our magical friends choosing darkness over light. And *that* is no small responsibility."

Dani pondered this in awe.

"So! Let us begin. Today we will discuss Common Problems in dealing with the magical, top Do's and Don'ts, and any other questions you may have..."

With a great sense of duty, Dani picked up the pencil and paper provided and started taking notes on everything the lady said.

* * *

In the session for Empaths and Healers down the hallway, Isabelle sat at the end of the long table, paying no attention whatsoever. She was daydreaming, elbow propped on the desk, cheek resting in her hand, gazing out the window at the sunny fields where the Guardians had gathered.

They were too far away to tell who was who, but one of them was That Boy, so she kept watching, waiting, just in case she caught a glimpse...

She stifled a sudden yawn, her eyes watering with fatigue. Lud, between going to bed late after the Floralia and rising before dawn to collect the Beltane dew, she was dog-tired. It didn't help that crazed nervous energy had coursed through her veins from the first moment she had laid eyes on Maddox St. Trinian, but thankfully, it had started to run out.

Still, she could not stop thinking about him, not for one minute; it was utterly annoying. Especially since Dani had reported that he said he "had no time" for young ladies. Typical Guardian!

Well, be that way, then, Isabelle thought with a slight sulk. The way he had looked at her when he had seen her in her beautiful, first-ever ball gown had made her hope he might be interested in her, too.

Obviously not.

Instead of coming to the ball so they might talk and get to know each other, the mysterious young warrior had gone out to a blacksmith's forge, of all things, to weld something or whatever. Honestly, a girl could be insulted! Was he that indifferent to the lure of dancing that he'd rather be alone and make a *knife?*

For possibly the first time in her fifteen years, Isabelle found herself pouting a bit.

But then, she considered, maybe he had *wanted* to go to the ball. Maybe he just didn't own a tuxedo. Maybe he was poor...

She sighed again, still completely bewildered as to why she could not read him with her powers. Not one bit. It was like he was a blank.

It was a tad alarming, actually. As an empath, she had never experienced this sort of block from someone before, but there had to be an explanation.

Most likely, she had not been standing close enough to him to sense his feelings, she reasoned. Or maybe it was because she got so flustered around him that she couldn't even think, just stood there tongue-tied and blushing like a cake-head.

Maybe there was something wrong with her—or was something

wrong with him? Why was this young warrior so very cool-nerved, anyway? He seemed to be so expertly in control of his emotions that his energy was calm, calm, calm, in a way that she, as an empath, had rarely encountered, especially not in anyone so young. He was different.

She was so used to being overwhelmed by the surging storms of other people's emotions around her, backing away from all the noise and chaos they generated simply to protect herself. She did not know what to make of the deep, soothing quiet around this boy, whether it meant something good or something bad. That he was a blank alarmed her almost as much as his handsome face and dark, soulful eyes drew her in. She had to get to the bottom of it.

But on the other hand...no.

If he was not interested in her, she might as well forget about Maddox St. Trinian now. Feeling this way was awful, anyhow, all tied up in knots over somebody who barely even knew she existed.

Besides, if he was poor and lowborn, her parents would likely never approve. She would make her debut in Society next Season, and probably be married off to some loudmouth duke in his twenties who owned a large chunk of England.

Ugh.

Ah, well. She had been raised from birth knowing that a good girl of her station, a good daughter, married whom her father said—and Isabelle, if nothing else, had always been *very* good.

Besides, Guardians were not supposed to get caught up in romantic entanglements, anyway. Affairs of the heart were the sort of distraction that could get the Order's warriors killed.

She sighed again, feeling rather like a tragic heroine—until she remembered Jake teasing her about that very thing. Then she frowned wryly and wondered how the birthday rascal was faring in the Lightrider group.

* * *

Meanwhile, in the next room, Nixie sat in the group for young Witches and Wizards, hanging on their session leader's every word.

The Elder witch, Ramona, Dowager Baroness Bradford, was a legend with a whiff of tragedy in her past that Nixie could well relate to, though she did not know the details.

Nobody did. It was one of the best-kept secrets of the Order, though everyone had heard the whispers about how she no longer quite trusted magic.

It comforted Nixie to know that even a great witch like Lady Bradford could make a mistake in using her powers. It made her own blunder seem less awful. Like maybe there was hope, if only she could learn the right spell—something, anything, to rid herself of the Bugganes.

She dared not ask the Elder witch for help outright, of course, but if anyone could give her a clue about how to banish those dreadful apparitions and all their torment, it was the wise old witch.

"And so," Lady Bradford continued, "we must always consider the danger of unintended consequences when using magic and take steps to protect ourselves when working any spell. Can any of you tell me what the strongest protection that we have at our disposal is?"

Eager to impress her, the more confident kids raised their hands and shouted out answers.

"Oh, I know! Salt!"

"Holy water!"

"No and no," she answered.

"Sage? Lavender?"

"I know! Primrose oil!"

"Hardly," said the Elder. "Miss Valentine? You look very thoughtful. Care to share your guess?"

Nixie hesitated. The others all turned around to look at her, eyeing her with various degrees of jealousy.

Yes, she was well aware she'd shown them up terribly with her Assessment yesterday. There were adult magic-workers who couldn't do such things.

She shook her head. "I don't know."

"Very well. I will tell you, children. The success of any magic lies in the purity of your intentions," she said in a grave tone. "There is little you can do to protect yourself if you are using your powers for selfish purposes. Eventually, that ulterior motive will catch up with you and there will be a price to pay. Sometimes a dreadful price. But if your intention is pure, mainly for the good of others, then you'll find there is protection automatically built in. Your *reasons* for using magic in any given situation matter just as much as how efficaciously you perform the spell."

Now Nixie raised her hand. "But, Your Ladyship," she asked, "what if your reasons are mixed? Some pure, some selfish?"

"Then your results will be mixed, too. Good mixed with bad, benefit with danger, blessing with curse."

They pondered this for a long moment, then the bell rang, ending their session.

The kids started filing out, but Lady Bradford called to Nixie. "Miss Valentine, would you stay behind, please? I should like a moment of your time."

"Yes, Your Ladyship." Nixie automatically wondered if she was in trouble—if, somehow, the Elder witch had looked into a crystal ball or something and found out what had happened in Scotland. She swallowed hard as she walked up to the front of the room, where Lady Bradford still sat at the writing desk.

A few of the other kids sneered at Nixie for being singled out. Two stuck their tongues out at her as they left, no doubt hoping she was in the suds.

When the room had emptied, the Elder witch turned to her with a fond gaze and searched her eyes. "I saw your Assessment yesterday, Miss Valentine, and I must say, you are doing work far beyond your years. You do know that, don't you?"

"Yes, ma'am. I practice all day, every day, p-pretty much."

"And who is your teacher?"

"Um, I am mainly self-taught, my lady," she said in embarrassment. "I inherited my grandmother's grimoire a couple of years ago. That's how I got started. More recently, I received some training from the gypsies who took me in when I had to leave my home. Madam Zordova is especially strong in fortunetelling."

"I see. May I ask why you had to leave your home?"

Nixie lowered her gaze. "My stepfather hates magic. He's an ordinary mortal. My mother never really took to it, either, you see. It was more my grandmother's art. Mother was always embarrassed about it. So, she never told him about the gift that runs in her side of the family.

"Then the Kinderveil lifted off me when I was only nine, and she told me to hide it. I tried the best I could, but for a while, I couldn't control it at all. Odd things, magical things, kept happening around me whether I wanted them to or not, until finally, my stepfather got fed up with all my mishaps and said I must be cursed."

"Oh, dear," Lady Bradford murmured.

"I finally made Mother explain to him about our magical bloodlines, and that only made him fly into a rage. He said he wouldn't have married her if he had known, and I got so cross at him for making her cry that I sort of accidentally made a ladder fall on him.

"He almost walked out on her entirely, but Mama pleaded with him to stay. He said he would, but only on one condition: no magic. He said he wouldn't have it in the house, so Mama made me promise. Honestly, I tried! But I-I can't help it. It just comes out of me. I couldn't hide it forever! It's who I am!"

"Believe me, I understand," she said softly. "Go on."

"I decided to convince my stepfather it was safe. That I could use my abilities to make their lives easier. They both work so hard, so I made some servitors to do Mama's chores around the house for her and help him in his shop. I was only trying to help. But when he saw them, he flew into a rage again and called me devil's spawn."

"Ah," Lady Bradford said with a faint wince. "That is most unfair. Take comfort in knowing that countless great witches before you have been called the same thing—and worse. So, then he threw you out?"

"No, he sent for the priest to do an exorcism on me. As soon as they left me alone, I packed my things and ran away."

"Poor child. You were fortunate to be taken in by these gypsies you mentioned. I am surprised they knew to bring you here."

"Well...no," Nixie conceded. "They kicked me out, too, about a month ago. I brought too much attention to their caravan. I really can't blame them. They have enough problems as it is, you know, traveling around all the time, getting kicked off of other people's fields. When a farmer or a town is kind enough to let them camp out for a few weeks, the last thing they needed was me ruining everything with my, er, magical experiments."

Actually, it was the creatures haunting her that had ruined everything, plaguing the gypsies with their poltergeist activity, but at this point, it seemed like semantics.

Right then, Nixie was sorely tempted to tell Lady Bradford about the Bugganes, but she didn't dare. No doubt it would only lead to greater torment.

The Elder witch frowned, studying her. "Well, if you can't return to the gypsies, where will you go when the Gathering is over?"

"Um..." Nixie turned red with shame and dropped her gaze. "I haven't quite figured that out yet—oh, but I'm sure I'll be fine. I'm like a cat, ma'am. Always land on my feet."

Lady Bradford harrumphed. "This will not do. It will not do at all!"

Nixie looked up as Lady Bradford rose. "Sorry?"

"Something must be done with you, Miss Valentine! A young witch of your talent cannot be left to her own devices. Not if I have anything to say about it. T'isn't safe! Come."

Nixie backed away a little. "Ma'am?"

"We must get you sorted with some training and a stable home environment. To be sure, you've made astounding progress on your own, but you will never achieve your full potential without the proper guidance. It would be folly to leave you out there unprotected. We can't have the Dark Druids claiming you, now, can we?"

"No, ma'am," she answered with a gulp.

"Leave this to me," the Elder witch ordered. "Trust me, dear Nixella. We will fix your situation and get you the training you so richly deserve."

"But, my lady, I have no means of paying for it—"

"Pish, not a word. Follow me."

Nixie's heart pounded as Lady Bradford marched out of the room into the crowded hallway, where the other classes were also letting out. Jostled every which way by the throng of people milling around in the corridor, Nixie hurried to keep up.

"Where are we going, my lady?"

"After all you've endured, I daresay you could do with the chance to make a few friends who aren't mages and thus won't be jealous of your abilities."

Lady Bradford strode ahead, her spine erect, her chin high, the crowd parting for her, everyone greeting her with respect that bordered on awe. She lifted a willowy arm and beckoned to get the attention of someone in the hall.

"Isabelle, darling! Over here! Bring Daniela, too. Miss O'Dell! Come along, gels. There's someone I wish you to meet."

When the two girls came over, Nixie recognized the ginger-haired Irish lass, Dani, who had been palling around with the Griffon heir and the amusing Archie Bradford last night during their uncomfortable meeting. The older girl she did not know, however, until the old woman introduced them.

Miss Isabelle Bradford was golden-haired and ridiculously pretty, and Nixie was intrigued to discover, upon hearing her last name, that she was Archie's older sister. She seemed absurdly nice, but Nixie eyed her warily. She had her reasons to avoid making friends.

Isabelle was smiling at Nixie as though she were a lovely, colored egg she had found in the midst of an Easter egg hunt. The redhead, however, looked a bit more skeptical.

Nixie frowned at both of them and backed away with an uneasy stare. Jenny Greenteeth had meant it when she said she wasn't allowed to have any friends. The horrible, fanged hag had even killed poor Midnight, Nixie's black cat. Every witch was supposed to have a cat, but the Bugganes had murdered hers. When they said "no friends," she knew they meant it.

But if Isabelle's beaming smile wasn't bad enough, Nixie nearly choked when Lady Bradford mentioned that her niece was an empath.

Holy Hecate! The last thing Nixie needed was some angel-faced do-gooder trying to read her emotions and wanting to help—or worse, using empath powers to pry into her thoughts and find out what she was hiding.

I've got to get out of here. Get away from these two!

"Now then," Her Ladyship concluded, "I'll leave you girls to enjoy the day's festivities. I'm off to make a few inquiries on Miss Valentine's behalf. Nixella, I will be in contact with you as soon as I have news."

"Thank you so much, my lady," she mumbled.

"You are very welcome, child," the Elder witch replied, then left them.

The empath turned to her. "Miss Valentine, do you wish to take a walk with us? We're off to go and watch the Morris dancers. We'd be very pleased if you'd care to join us."

Her gentle tone made Nixie's suspicious scowl deepen. Was this girl for real? Nobody was that sweet. The redhead looked askance at Isabelle, but Nixie was already backing away.

"No, thank you, Miss Bradford," she said in a prickly tone. "I have some studying I have to do before supper."

"Oh, you sound like my brother," she said with a chuckle. "Always buried in his books! Well, as you wish. But if you see us in the dining hall later, do come and join us at our table. You have to meet my brother, Archie, and my cousin, Jake. The boys are always entertaining."

"Thanks." *But no thanks,* she did not add aloud.

With naught but a vague nod, Nixie hurried away.

* * *

Dani nudged Isabelle. "What'd you go inviting her to dine with us for? Crikey, you're as bad as your brother." She pulled Isabelle's arm down to stop her from waving goodbye to the gloomy grump of a witch.

Isabelle turned to her in surprise. "Why ever not?"

"One, because she's mean," Dani said, ticking the reasons off on her fingers. "Two, because she's shifty. She met the boys last night and didn't even mention it just now. And three, most of all, because Jake thinks she might be the Dark Druids' spy."

"What?" Isabelle started laughing. "Oh, Dani, don't be absurd. She's not a spy. She's just a little thing."

"How do you know? Did you read her? Are you sure?"

"Well, no…"

"Did you sense *anything* from her?" Dani persisted.

"She sped off so fast I didn't think to try. Now, what's this about the boys meeting her?"

"I was there, too. We found her creeping around the hallways last night while you were at the ball, and we saw this grayish blob thing. It attacked Archie, and then it disappeared—"

"What? Something attacked my brother—?"

"Don't worry, it didn't hurt him. It just slimed him. We warned him not to touch it, but you know he had to try. Then it ran away—well, floated, I should say—so we chased it. But instead of finding it, we found her instead. Don't you think that's an awfully strange coincidence?"

"Hmm," Isabelle said. She thought it over, then shrugged. "Aunt Ramona is nobody's fool. Whose word are you going to take, that of an Elder witch or a boy who's suspicious of everybody?" She shook her head as they ambled down the hallway. "I can't believe he took you spy-hunting. He's quite mad."

Dani frowned. "Then why is she so grumpy?"

"I don't know. Maybe she's got cares of her own. I'll try to read her next time we meet. What did Archie think of her? He's usually a good judge of character."

"Oh, Isabelle, you know your brother. Archie gets along with everybody. Just because *he* doesn't have a mean bone in his body, he thinks everyone else must be the same. Actually, though, he especially liked Miss Valentine."

"Oh, really?" Isabelle turned to her in surprise.

Dani nodded with a grin. "Mm-hmm. I think he fancies her. He even got offended when me and Jake said she might be the spy. He got all chivalrous and came to her defense."

"Oh, that is so cute!" Isabelle laughed merrily. "Archie's sweet on Nixie?"

"Seemed like it," Dani said.

"Oh, I can't wait to torment him. It's my duty as his sister to tease him, especially after he made fun of me yesterday about Maddox! Where did he say he was going? To the library?"

Dani nodded.

Izzy grabbed her hand. "Let's go get him! Jake's session should be letting out soon, then we can all go watch the Morris dancers together. Come on!"

Hand in hand, the girls ran off, giggling, to find the boy genius.

* * *

Archie peered over the edge of a thick tome of writings by Ptolemy, irked by the noise some inconsiderate soul was making.

Until a few minutes ago, he had had the whole place to himself, save for the ancient librarian who was snoozing at his desk. Then the front door had squeaked, and great, shuffling footfalls had thumped into the studious silence of the magnificent, medieval library, echoing every which way under the vaulted ceiling.

"Shh!" the old librarian had scolded, jolted from his nap.

"Urgh," came the reply.

How very glib, thought Archie, annoyed. But when he looked up with a frown to see who was making all the noise, his eyebrow quirked. It was quite the last person he ever would have expected to see here: Troll Boy.

Ogden Trumbull, Dr. Plantagenet's seven-foot-tall, artificially made helper from the zoo.

Hmm! Never would've even guessed he could read.

But on second thought, maybe he couldn't, Archie mused, watching the hybrid discreetly. Og just sort of wandered around, blankly staring at the books along the top shelves. Archie, who had yet to hit his growth spurt, had often wondered what was on those shelves.

He ducked behind his physics tome when Og looked his way, a pugnacious pucker on his snout.

Crikey, the beast boy really looked a fright, ugly enough to crack a mirror. Of course, that wasn't Og's fault, Archie quickly amended.

The half-troll glared at him for a second as he passed the table where Archie sat studying. As Og moved on, Archie sat up in his chair and followed the brute's progress with intense curiosity.

Og did not seem too clear on what the whole idea of a library actually was. He ripped some of the books off the shelves, held them up to his nose, and sniffed them, licking a few as he wandered among the aisles, so massively muscled that he barely fit.

It suddenly dawned on Archie why Og was here. Like himself, the troll boy did not fit into any of the groups.

Then Archie felt rather sorry for him. It was hard to remember, looking at the formidable, monster-sized brute, that he was really just a kid. He watched the big, lonely oaf shuffle into the aisle of children's books. Og had some difficulty pulling the book he wanted off the shelf with his big, clumsy ham-hands.

Fine motor skills: poor.

Observing him as a scientist, Archie wondered what sort of tests had been run on the creature. Had they measured his intelligence? His ability to communicate?

Somehow he doubted it. Indeed, he suspected that the wizard-scientist who had brewed up Og in the lab had only cared about testing his strength, considering he had created him to be nothing but a slave.

Ghastly. Archie felt the chivalry in him stirring up for the sake of the poor, sad monster boy.

Og chose a book and shuffled out to the center rotunda of the library, where he plopped down on the floor like a giant toddler.

A moment later, Archie could hear him reading the simple words aloud to himself, lifting the book all the way up to his face to stare at the pictures and occasionally sniffing it.

Look at him, Archie thought with compassion. *Poor thing.* Human enough to want to read a story to comfort him when he felt the sting of being an outcast, and yet still so much of a brute that his clumsy, three-fingered hands could barely separate the delicate pages to turn them. The dexterity needed for this simple maneuver soon had frustration building on Og's misshapen boulder of a face.

Archie felt a tug of sympathy on his kindly heart. His parents were diplomats, the peacemakers of the Order, while his empath sister had certainly influenced him to have a great deal more compassion for others than many scientists possessed.

As for himself, other people might be afraid of Ogden Trumbull, but the Honorable Archimedes James Bradford was a young man of Reason. He was also dashed curious to get a closer look.

Setting his physics book aside, he rose from his chair and approached Og without fear, hands in pockets.

"I say!" he greeted him in a friendly tone.

Dr. Plantagenet's tactful warning about keeping a distance flitted through his mind, but Archie shrugged it off in self-assurance. Yes, yes, rock trolls were nasty, violent, and brutish, but Og *was* half-human, as well. Besides, Archie trusted he could outsmart the big oaf if there was any trouble.

"What's that you're reading? Ah, *A Little Pretty Pocket-Book* by Mr. John Newbery. Jolly good! You know," he said with the utmost tact, "I do find the pages sometimes stick together, such a bother. Perhaps I could lend a hand?" Cautiously, he bent down, reached out, and turned the page for the troll boy. "There you are. I'm Archie, by the way," he said with a wide, reassuring smile, "how d'ye do?"

For a second, Og stared at the newly revealed picture of a bunny rabbit on the next page. Then the troll boy turned to him—not with gratitude, to Archie's surprise, but with a glare.

Offended pride shone in Og's deep-set, piggy eyes, followed by a low, belligerent *"Uuurgh."*

"Oh, dear," Archie uttered mildly, drawing back.

Realizing his mistake, he shot to his feet and tried to back away. But alas, Archie's reflexes were not as quick as his mind. And certainly not fast enough to escape a troll.

Or even a half-troll, as it turned out.

CHAPTER THIRTEEN
Lightriding 101

M eanwhile, Jake and the five other kids who had been invited to attend the exclusive Lightriders session hung on their expert's every word.

His name was Finnderool, and though the tall, princely wood elf didn't smile much, as an experienced Lightrider, Jake found him terribly impressive.

"Now, then. The mysteries of the Worldwide Ley Line Grid are some of the most closely guarded secrets of the Order."

Dressed in a gray velvet coat with intricate embroidery around the edges, Finnderool paced back and forth across the front of the room at a graceful glide, his long-fingered hands folded behind his back.

He had already warned them in stern tones that their presence here did not mean they were anywhere close to being officially chosen for the long and rigorous Lightrider training. They were all too young. But he admitted that the Elders had taken notice of them and each of them was under consideration.

Jake could hardly stand the excitement. Determined to make the cut someday, he absorbed Finnderool's words like a sponge.

"Indeed," the wood elf continued, "if you ever hear the ley lines discussed out there in the profane world, you are to scoff, as with most magical matters, and call it all bunk. Later in your lives, of course, if you are selected, you will have many advanced classes in esoteric subjects to build the foundation for your daily work as an agent in the field. Courses such as: Sacred Geometry, including both the Platonic and the Archimedean Solids, the Golden Mean and the Fibonacci sequence, with a whole term dedicated to the study of Mandalas."

Staring, Jake wished he had some faint idea of what the chap was talking about. Sacred geometry? He'd never heard of it.

"In year two, you will learn the Seven Great Hermetic Principles in almost as much depth as the Magic-workers' group must. Of course, you will also study all the usual subjects: mathematics, chemistry, including all the various types of aethers, and the principles of electromagnetism. A very important subject.

"How, now, why all these young faces full of dismay?" Finnderool remarked with a wry glance around at his captive audience. "You thought it was all swashbuckling adventures out there, didn't you? Hardly. A Lightrider must have the mind of a scientist, the silver tongue of a diplomat, and the instincts of a warrior. But for now, my young, would-be heroes and heroines, today's lesson is but a brief introduction to what the Grid is, as best we understand it so far, and a Lightrider's role in interacting with it.

"After I've laid the groundwork, one of my colleagues will join us to discuss the everyday life of an agent in the field. If he ever gets here," Finnderool added under his breath, glancing at the clock in disapproval. "So, let us begin."

Jake leaned forward in his seat.

"As I trust you are well aware, boys and girls, the earth has two magnetic poles, the North Pole and the South. Electromagnetic energy continuously circulates between them, but it does not simply churn round and round from the top to the bottom of the planet and back again. No. Our dear Mother Earth is more complex than that.

"For reasons we still don't understand, the circulating energy of our planet branches out into intricate geometric patterns and travels in straight lines over vast distances. As it spreads, it forms a grand, magnificent spiderweb of electromagnetic energy that covers the whole of the earth.

"Some view these lines as a kind of river system running through the planet, carrying subtle earth energies rather than water. Others say the ley lines are like the planet's veins, flowing not with blood, but with Mother Earth's own invisible life force. Our Chinese brethren refer to it as chi energy, the Indians as prana.

"Now, the ancient philosopher, Plato, was the first to theorize that as these energy lines spread out, they naturally form themselves into a gigantic geometric shape—a polygon, called an icosahedron." He picked up a piece of chalk and started drawing one on the blackboard at the front of the lecture hall. "An icosahedron is made up of twenty identical triangles, with thirty edges and twelve vertices where the angles intersect."

He completed his drawing, then pointed with the chalk. "And like the confluence of two mighty rivers, the energy flows that crash together in those spots can cause all sorts of wild cross-currents, like a whirlpool or a vortex. Which is why one of the first sayings we teach our Lightrider students is, *'Vortex at the vertex.'* That way, they'll always remember the dangers in such spots.

"You see, the concentration of energies at the vertices of the largest ley lines create mysterious places of intense power, complete with electromagnetic anomalies, such as ball lightning or compasses not working properly.

"Another example of this energy overflow would be manifestations of what *looks* like poltergeist activity, when no ghost is actually present. It's all caused by energy. The electromagnetic fields in these areas are unstable, chaotic, even dangerous.

"One of the trickiest vertices we know of, for example, lies in the ocean off the island of Bermuda. History has lost count of all the ships that have sunk there since the days of Christopher Columbus. Storms pop up out of nowhere. Compasses start spinning. We've even lost a couple of Lightriders there over the years. Heaven only knows where they might have ended up...but I digress."

Blimey, thought Jake.

"I mentioned that the lines can span great distances." He nodded, setting down his chalk to resume pacing. "This is true. And the longer they run, the more powerful they usually are. For example, the great Saint Michael Ley Line, which many of your parents stayed up all night at the Floralia to honor, runs across the width of southern England.

"The longest ley line ever recorded is called the Apollo line, stretching some 2,500 miles and ending at the ancient site of the Delphic oracle in Greece.

"That should not surprise you," he added. "Even the least sensitive of human beings over the centuries have noticed the powerful effects around the vertices. Many cultures have built great structures on those spots to try to channel the energy there for their own uses, from prehistoric earthen mounds and megaliths to ancient pyramids and temples, Druidic henges, cathedrals, even capital cities.

"Suffice to say that if you find yourself in a place where you can feel a particular, indescribable energy in the air, you're probably standing on a ley line. And if it's really powerful, it could be an intersection of two of them.

"Now, if you would like to try to sense a ley line for yourself, boys and girls, here's a tip. Because of their electromagnetic qualities, ley lines react on a daily rhythm to the energy of the sun. They are weakest at night, and the strongest time to feel them is just before sunrise. When the light starts flooding back in, it charges up the ley lines, and you can really feel the energy come roaring back. It can be pretty dramatic."

Must try that, thought Jake.

Finnderool took a sip of water and glanced again at the clock, looking slightly annoyed that there was still no sign of his colleague.

"Now, then," the wood elf continued. "The Lightrider's role. As you may or may not know, the ley lines have long been used as great energy highways for ethereal beings. In Ireland, for example, they are called the fairy paths. In the Orient, they are known as dragon lines. Other places call them spirit roads.

"Lightriders, then, are the chosen few who are authorized to travel nigh instantaneously through the Grid on the Order's business. Basically it's a form of teleportation.

"Within seconds, a Lightrider can travel from Stongehenge to the Great Pyramids of Giza, from Notre Dame Cathedral in France to the Taj Mahal in India, just to use a few, famous examples. Only a Lightrider has the ability and the authority to open up the portals or gateways into the Grid, and then, after being physically transmuted into the form of light, they can travel through it instantly, sending themselves like a message whisking through pneumatic tubes."

For a long moment, the children were dead-silent, pondering this unimaginable mystery.

At length, a girl with braids raised her hand. "Does it hurt, sir, being changed into light?"

He smiled wryly. "No, I wouldn't say it hurts. Tingles a bit, like when your foot falls asleep. Only, it's your whole body. Very well, it stings. Certainly it's disorienting, having all your molecules scrambled and put back together again in a few seconds' time."

"I should think so!" said another amazed boy.

"The new recruits usually get queasy on their first few jumps, but you get used to it. The ones who fare the worst are the VIPs a Lightrider is occasionally asked to escort through the Grid on some mission for the Order."

"You mean, you don't have to be a Lightrider to enter the Grid?" a bushy-haired boy in the next row asked.

Finnderool shook his golden head. "Lightriders can take along anyone they choose, though this is not done lightly. They often take Guardians with them, for example, when they need extra security on their assignments. *But,* here's the key: nobody else can enter the Grid *without* a Lightrider. Those who've tried usually end up getting vaporized by the planet's energy. This is one of Gaia's own natural defense mechanisms. The Lightrider, being personally connected to the Grid, must be present—aha, speak of the devil! Here's one now." Finnderool turned toward the door as it opened and arched a brow, with a meaningful glance at the clock as if to say, *You're late.*

"Howdy, y'all."

To the delight of all the kids, the expert chosen to speak to their group about the daily life of a Lightrider in the field was none other than the pincushion cowboy, sans arrows. He took off his ten-gallon hat as he stepped into the room and nodded warily to the group.

"Ladies and gentlemen," said Finnderool, "allow me to present one of the Order's finest, Mr. Josephus Munroe."

"Call me Tex," he said.

The wood elf ignored this improper request. "Mr. Munroe serves in President Grant's division of the Order of the Yew Tree in America."

Jake was startled to hear this. He had not even been aware they *had* magical creatures to contend with "across the Pond."

Finnderool bowed, closing his portion of the presentation, then retreated to the side of the room.

Tex tossed his hat and bloodstained duster coat on a nearby chair, then sauntered to the front, sat on the desk, and asked, chewing a toothpick, "So what do you young'uns wanna know?"

The kids stared at him in surprise.

To be sure, Tex was no ordinary teacher. He propped his feet up on a wooden chair, putting his magnificent, though dusty, alligator boots on display. Jake wondered if he had caught the alligator himself. Probably so. He also wore a flannel shirt and an unusual type of trousers made of dark blue canvas, faded around the knees and reinforced here and there with metal rivets.

Some strange sort of American pants, Jake supposed as he studied him, happy to see that the rugged individual had survived his brush with death. No doubt thanks to the same magical doctors who had fixed *him* after his Assessment.

Since all the other kids seemed too shy or perhaps too confuzzled by the American to start, Jake raised his hand.

Tex nodded at him. "Son?"

"When you arrived yesterday, sir, how come all those Indians were chasing you?"

"Heh. Now thar's a yarn worth a-tellin'...."

He proceeded to regale them with the tale of how he had been stalking something called a chupacabra through the deserts of the Southwest.

"But what's a chupacabra, Mr. Munroe?" another boy asked immediately, barely pronouncing the word.

"Nasty little varmint," Tex replied in his slow, deadpan drawl, still chewing on his toothpick, a glint of wild humor in his eyes so that nobody could tell if he was serious or joking. "Also known as a goatsucker. Preys on herds o' whatever it can git. You'd think them Apaches woulda been grateful I was thar to catch the beast and remove it from their territory. Huh."

"Sir, they could've killed you!" the girl with braids exclaimed.

"Welllll, shoot, lil darlin'. I was on their land. Reckon I had it comin'. Tribe's been at war on and off with the U.S. Army for years. Probably thought I was some kind o' spy for the federales. But don't ya fret. Folks from Texas ain't too easy to kill." He flashed a sudden mad grin that surely would have terrified any poor outlaw who had to duel against him at high noon.

Jake was in awe.

"I didn't know the Yanks were connected with the Order, sir," one of the boys spoke up, at which, the other kids nodded.

"Yep. Got passed down to us from ya'll. Which ain't too surprisin', since we're real simpatico, your country and our'n."

"Simpatico? What does that mean?"

"Allies." Tex shrugged his broad shoulders. "Means y'all need help, we come. We need help, y'all come. Ain't too hard to figure out. Gotta have friends you can count on in this here vale o' tears."

Hear, hear, Jake thought with a grin spreading across his face.

"So, do you have lots of magical creatures in America, Mr. Munroe?"

"Quite a few. None you'd want to meet in a dark alley. Let's see...

Large number o' witches, good and bad, settled in New England long ago. Though, o' course, a lot o' them got burned. We got a Headless Horseman who's been terrorizing folks around the town of Sleepy Hollow for a couple hundred years now.

"Vampires down in New Orleans," he mused aloud, stroking his whiskered chin in thought. "Occasional outbreaks of zombies there, too, when the voodoo queens kick up. Very unpleasant creatures, zombies. You meet one o' them, you aim for the head, no mistakin'."

"What about ghosts?" Jake asked, entertained.

"Boy, half the South's filled with 'em!" he exclaimed, leaning back in his chair. "O' course, most of 'em's harmless. Chupacabras in the deserts, like I told ya. Some of the Injun tribes have shamans who are shapeshifters. Got to treat 'em with respect. Last thing ya want's an Injun curse, no sir. What else?

"We got wild, hairy ape-men livin' in the forests everywhere ya look. Cousin to the yetis, best that we can figger. Gold goblins livin' under Wall Street in New York. And you don't even want to *know* what's crawlin' around in our swamps down yonder. Everglades... Mississippi basin... Shoot. That stuff'll give ya nightmares."

"Not us, Mr. Munroe," Jake assured him boldly, glancing around at his fellow future Lightriders.

"Ha!" Instead of scolding him for bragging, Tex let out a short, loud laugh. "That's how ya do it, son."

The bell dinged, but nobody moved.

Even Tex ignored it, launching into another wild story full of unexpected tangents, until the kids glanced around at each other with uncertain smiles.

They were all starting to wonder if the cowboy's "stretchers" were merely Texas tall tales or true accounts of his adventures. Jake dearly hoped it was the latter.

It all sounded so exciting.

When the students finally filed out of the room, thanking Finnderool and saying their goodbyes to Tex, Jake vowed to visit America someday, especially the Wild West.

Of course, he'd have to bring Archie and his tool-bag along. The Wild West didn't sound like a place for young ladies, so they'd have to leave the girls at home, and that was just fine with him.

Eager to tell his cousin everything about the Lightrider session, Jake sprinted at top speed down the corridor, skidding to a halt and pausing only long enough to ask a gnome which way to the library.

The little fellow pointed to a door that led outside onto the grassy courtyard in the center of the palace's massive quadrangle.

Flush with dreams of heroic derring-do, he hurried out and strode across the courtyard. The library was housed in its own, chapel-like building, semi-attached to the back of the palace. It was very old, with medieval arches and intricate stone carvings around the heavy door.

Jake pulled it open. As he stepped into the dimly lit, high-ceilinged space, he saw thousands of books on tall, somber shelves. But instead of the quiet he expected, a ruckus of angry shouts, taunting, and yelling was coming from somewhere nearby. The distant echoes bounced around under the vaulted ceiling, though somehow the noise was not loud enough to wake the ancient librarian, who went on snoring away at his desk.

Jake frowned, cocking his head and listening. It sounded like some kind of fight was going on.

Then his stomach clenched as he recognized a few of the voices.

"Let him go, you brute!"

"Put my brother down!"

Dani? Isabelle?

Oh, no. What now?

CHAPTER FOURTEEN
The Trouble with Trolls

J ake dashed off, following the sound of the fight. Heart pounding, he looked in all the bookshelf aisles he passed, but there was no sign of them. The echoing quality of the ancient stone library made it hard to tell which way the sound was coming from.

"Leave my brother alone!"

That was definitely Isabelle, which meant it was Archie who was under threat. *Blast it, where are they?*

The yelling grew louder as he neared the back of the library, and came upon another large door. He shoved it open and found it was an exit onto the grounds of Merlin Hall.

As soon as he looked outside, his eyes narrowed. He had found them, all right.

Out on the green, the girls were yelling at the huge, ugly troll boy from Dr. Plantagenet's zoo. Ogden Trumbull had a hold of Archie and was dangling him upside-down, one oversized, stone-gray hand wrapped around his skinny ankles. Archie was doing his best to reason with the brute and to keep his spectacles from falling off.

Jake stepped outside in a fury. "Hey, ugly!" he shouted. "Put the genius down!"

"Jake!" Dani cried. "Thank gosh you're here!"

Og looked over as Jake marched toward them, glaring at the bully, his heart pounding in wrath.

"You want to pick on somebody, why don't you fight me?" he challenged.

"Uh-oh, you're in trouble now," Dani taunted the creature.

Og glanced over and scowled. "Who are you?" he grunted.

"I'm that kid's cousin, and if you don't let him go right now, I'm going to make you very sorry."

The hybrid sneered at him. "If you say so."

To Jake's horror, Og whipped Archie back like a ragdoll and threw him violently into the air, like you'd throw a stone.

The girls screamed and Archie shouted in terror as he went flying skyward in a wide arc, arms and legs pinwheeling frantically.

Just in time, Jake summoned up his telekinesis and caught Archie on a cushion of air as he started plummeting back to earth.

He checked his rage and, with a steady current of energy from his fingertips, lowered his friend safely to the ground.

"Thanks, coz," Archie said, sounding shaken.

At once, the girls rushed over to see to him, gathering up his papers and the contents of his trusty tool-bag, which were scattered all over the ground.

With his cousin safely out of the troll boy's grasp, Jake, still enraged, did not take his eyes off Ogden.

The brute turned to smirk at him.

"Are you all right, Arch?" Jake called in a taut voice.

"I-I think so."

"What happened?" he demanded.

"I made the mistake of trying to be nice to that...*thing*!" Archie burst out, pointing at his tormentor. "I was only trying to help him t-turn the pages of a baby book he was trying to read, and just like that, the brute attacked me. For no reason!"

"I don't need your help!" Ogden roared at Archie in his garbled voice. "I don't want your pity! You can go hang!"

"You see that? Honestly!" Archie spluttered, gesturing at Ogden. "Monstrous toad! They should lock you up in one of those zoo pens because, whatever you are, you aren't fit for civilized society!"

Og's reply was a huge bogey, which he spat on the ground, then grinned, as though proud to prove the truth of Archie's words.

The girls gagged.

"Oh, that's very nice," Archie scolded in disgust. He glanced at Jake. "I tried to run away, but this was as far as I got. He's faster than he looks."

"Apologize to my cousin, and then be on your way," Jake commanded the hulk in kingly tones.

"Don't tell me what to do, you twerp," Og rumbled.

"You're askin' for it," Jake warned, unconsciously beginning to sound like the rough street kid he used to be until a year ago.

The troll boy guffawed. "You're no bigger than a goose turd! What can you possibly do to me?"

Jake smiled coldly. "Well, if you insist. Let me show you." With another burst of angry power from his fingertips (and, admittedly, a slight pain in his head, for he was still not fully recovered from yesterday's ordeal), he did the same thing to Og via telekinesis that *he* had done to Archie by brute strength.

Grunting with effort, Jake lifted Og off the ground. Suspending him in midair was not quite enough, so with a wicked smile, Jake slowly turned Archie's tormentor upside-down.

It was amusing to see the half-troll struggle and flail. With nothing to push off against but empty air, Og could gain no leverage to escape.

Well, he brought it on himself, Jake thought in cold satisfaction. Living on the streets had taught him one thing about survival. You had to fight back viciously against bullies right away to make them get the point.

Bullies only attacked nice people because they seemed like easy prey. But when a *nice person* fought back like a demon unexpectedly— and even better, brought allies of his own—bullies usually ran away with their tails tucked between their legs and didn't come back.

That was the outcome Jake desired.

He hadn't the slightest interest in hearing Og's excuses as to *why* he had attacked Archie. No reason would have been good enough. A bully was a bully, and a troll was a troll, and that was all Jake really needed to know.

Dani understood this, too, having come from the rookery, London's own brick-and-mortar jungle. The sheltered Archie and Isabelle, however, exchanged a startled glance.

"Ha, ha! Not so scary now, are you, ugly?" the carrot-head yelled, pointing and jeering at Ogden while Jake hoisted him higher into the air.

Still, after the strain of lifting baby Stonehenge megaliths yesterday with his mind, Jake did not want to risk blacking out again and leaving his friends at Og's mercy.

Best to wrap up this little lesson.

"Put me down!" the brute roared.

"Ask me nicely," Jake taunted, but Ogden just growled.

Relenting, Jake lowered the upside-down troll until Og dangled in midair on about eye-level with him. Then he sauntered closer, careful to stay out of reach of Og's powerful, gangly arms.

"If you ever lay a finger on my cousin again or any of my friends, I'll pulverize ye. Savvy?" he asked, sounding as mean as he possibly could.

"Urrrgh," Og rumbled.

Confident he had made his point, Jake stepped back and released his telekinetic hold, feeling magnanimous for his mercy. Ogden tumbled onto the ground.

But what happened next was not what Jake had expected.

He had thought Og would slink away in shame at being bested, but instead, the hybrid suddenly sprang up off the ground and lunged at him.

It all happened so fast.

Jake only had time to get in one good move to try to ward off the attack; he leaped up and kicked Ogden in the stomach.

It was like kicking a boulder.

The next thing he knew, the hybrid's huge hand was wrapped around his throat. His feet dangled off the ground. He clutched the rocklike forearm, trying to peel away the iron fingers around his throat.

It didn't do much good.

With Troll Boy squeezing the life out him, Jake was vaguely aware of the girls screaming and Archie trying to find anything in his tool-bag that might be of use.

"Derek, help!" Dani's ear-splitting plea was Jake's first indication that the Guardians had come strolling onto the scene.

Well, hurrah for Guardian instincts, Jake thought, beginning to turn blue. Talk about good timing.

But when he looked over, Derek and Maddox St. Trinian were just watching curiously, arms folded, as though they wouldn't dream of stepping on his toes, if he wished to vanquish this enemy himself.

Aw, come on! Kicking his feet and pulling against the giant hand around his throat, Jake tried to turn his head to scowl impatiently at Derek.

"A little help?" he rasped.

Derek turned to Maddox. "Care to do the honors?"

The older boy nodded, crouched down briefly in a sprinter's stance, then exploded into action, racing across the lawn like an arrow shot from a bow.

Troll Boy didn't even see him coming.

In the next heartbeat, Maddox ran up the hulk's broad back and hooked his arm around Ogden's thick throat in a wrestler's move, cutting off his air.

"Let him go," he ordered in a menacing tone.

Bloody embarrassing, Jake thought, annoyed to find himself, the would-be hero, in need of a rescue. He kept kicking Ogden, at least, while Maddox tightened his hold.

Og waved his free hand around angrily behind him, trying to knock Maddox off his back.

"I said let him go," Maddox repeated.

"Can't...breathe!" Og choked out.

"Makes two of us," Jake wheezed. He sent Derek an impatient scowl. *Care to help here?*

The master Guardian arched a brow, watching with a look of amusement and pride.

"Last chance," Maddox warned Og through gritted teeth, while Jake started seeing black spots float across his field of vision.

Great. Now I get to faint like a little girl again in front of everyone.

"Get *off* me!" Ogden yowled.

"Wrong choice," said Maddox. Then he gave the troll a wrench with his arm, and Ogden's beady eyes rolled up into his head.

Og's grip on Jake's throat released as he crashed to the ground, out cold.

"Hooray, Maddox killed him!" Dani cried triumphantly as she came running over.

"Nah, he just fainted," the young Guardian said, dusting off his hands, while Jake crawled out of Ogden's reach, coughing and gasping for air. Then he sat on the grass, disgusted, and rubbed his half-strangled throat.

"Thanks," he croaked.

Maddox nodded, eyeing the distance between where Jake sat and the unconscious hybrid. "You might want to move farther back. He'll be awake again shortly."

"No worries," Derek interjected as he came strolling over. "Nice work, lad." Then he crouched down and waited the few seconds until Og woke up.

Thus, the first thing Troll Boy saw when he came-to was the steely eyed Guardian looming over him and looking none-too-pleased.

The difference between the boys' skill levels and his was that Derek did not have to say a word. Did not have to make a threat. Did not even have to make a *fist*.

He only had to stare for a long moment into the confused troll's eyes, his own slightly narrowed.

Og seemed to shrink several inches in size. He whimpered slightly and slid backward away from Derek, crab-walking on his hands.

The Guardian watched his every move, still silent.

Maddox stood a short distance behind Derek, clearly ready to attack again on his trainer's orders.

Isabelle had tiptoed over to stare at her idol, but Jake paid her little mind, loving every minute of seeing the oversized bully show his true cowardice.

A safe distance from Derek, Og jumped to his feet and knuckle-ran off in the direction of the zoo.

Dani started to jeer loudly after the fleeing brute, but Derek laid a finger over his lips and chided gently, "Shh. No need to heap coals on your enemy's head, my little Irish brawler."

"Sorry," Dani muttered. "But that was great!"

Archie, marched over to Jake and offered him a hand up; Jake clasped it, and his cousin pulled him up off the grass.

"Quite a day we're having, what?"

"I'll say," Jake agreed, his voice still sounding froggy from semi-strangulation.

Archie then turned to Maddox. "You were brilliant!"

Jake's pride could hardly endure his being rescued by his rival, but as Archie proceeded to laud the older boy, Dani made matters even worse by running over to Jake and fussing over him like a mother hen.

"I'm fine!" he said, brushing her off while his cheeks flamed.

"Thanks to Maddox!" she retorted.

Jake scowled, but Derek chuckled.

"What's so funny?" he exclaimed.

"You are, Jake," Derek said with a knowing look.

"You wouldn't be laughing if you were here when that thing nearly killed Archie!" Jake huffed, desperate for a change of subject, anything other than his needing to be rescued by the Guardians like a blasted damsel in distress. "He should be kept in a cage if that's how he's going to act! Who ever thought it was a good idea to try to tame a rock troll, anyway? Vicious cannibals. We're lucky he didn't eat us."

"I'll bet he was thinking about it," Dani said with a nod.

"I say, could you perhaps teach me that trick you did to make him pass out?" Archie asked Maddox hopefully. "How'd you do it? Constrict the carotid artery?"

"Huh?" Maddox asked when Archie poked him in the arm. He had been gazing at Isabelle like he was in a trance.

"Will you show me how to do that?" Archie repeated.

"Oh, er, that's not going to be the best strategy for somebody your size. No offense. If I were you, I'd look to figure out what particular strengths *you* have to fight him with if he comes back." Maddox shrugged. "My approach won't necessarily help you 'cause everybody's different."

Isabelle actually sighed at his kindly advice to her brother.

Oh, please. Jake shook his head and looked off into the distance, trying to rein in his annoyance.

Maddox froze, wide-eyed, as she stepped closer to him. Something like a raging troll on the loose did not shake him in the least, but he looked almost terrified of delicate, gentle Isabelle. Jake shook his head.

"Thank you so much for saving my cousin, Mr. St. Trinian."

"Er—it was nothing, Miss Bradford," he forced out.

"It was to *me*," Jake chimed in with lavish sarcasm. "Hullo, strangulation?"

But even Dani ignored him this time. The carrot-head wore a grin from ear to ear, glancing from one smitten youth to the other.

Ugh, thought Jake. "Well! Now that that's over, can we get out of here, please?"

"That's actually what I came to talk to you about, Jakey, old boy," Derek spoke up, giving him an affectionate clap on the back. "I have a birthday present for you! And it's much better than nearly getting strangled by a troll."

"Half-troll," Archie reminded him.

"A present, you say?" Jake asked, mollified. "You didn't have to get me anything, Derek."

"Well, you don't turn thirteen every day, and besides, this one's special, since it's the first birthday in your whole life that you knew of in advance. I have to make the trip anyway, and I got permission for you to come along, thanks to certain connections of mine."

"A trip?" Jake echoed.

"Aye, but you have to do as I say the whole time—I mean it," he said sternly. "Understood? No exceptions. No running off. You follow orders. Those are my terms. Agree to that, and you can come along."

"Of course! Where are we going?" Jake asked eagerly.

"Romania. Come, follow me. *Tempus fugit,* boys." Derek started walking away.

"Romania?" Jake stood there for a moment in confusion. "What, right now? We're leaving in the middle of the Gathering?"

"No worries, we'll be back in time for supper," Derek said over his shoulder.

Jake's eyes widened. He suddenly gasped. "Derek! Hold on!" He ran after him in amazement. "Do you mean—?"

The big warrior paused and turned around with a warm smile. "That's right, Jake. I'm taking you into the Grid. Like a real Lightrider. Special treat for your birthday."

"Yes!" He hugged the big man like a crazed sports fan and went mad with rejoicing for several seconds, jumping around like the winner of the London lottery. Then he had a hundred questions. "Are you *serious*? But why Romania? We can go anywhere, right? Why are we going there?"

Derek finally confessed the rest of his surprise. "There's been an outbreak of the dragon pox among the dracosaurs up in the mountains there."

"Dracosaurs?" Dani breathed, for the others had followed, listening to everything.

"A very important species, very ancient," Derek said. "The forest-dwelling *Dracosaurus silvanus* is believed to be the missing link between dragons and dinosaurs."

"Whoa," Archie breathed.

"They're protected in a huge remote valley the Order owns in Eastern Europe. Unfortunately, we just received word that one of the females is showing signs of dragon pox. It can be very contagious. As rare as this ancient species is, Dr. Plantagenet wants to go right away to treat the infected reptile, before the pox spreads to the rest of the colony. He's asked for extra protection since Green Men have no defenses against fire. Fire-breathing dragons…kind of a phobia with Green Men. So a couple of us are accompanying the good doctor on the trip for protection." He looked at Jake. "Thought you'd like to tag along."

He nodded eagerly, but his friends started whining.

"Aw, why does he get to go and not us?" Archie protested.

"Settle down! It's his birthday," Derek said. "Maybe you can go some other time."

"Well, it sounds a little dangerous, anyway," Dani mumbled.

"Dracosaurs are relatively peaceful in the daytime. Besides, the doctor has stinkberry bracelets for all of us to wear once we get there. All dragon species hate the smell and stay away from it."

"Dragon repellent?" Archie asked.

"Precisely. Dragons know the berries are poisonous to them. Wearing some of the dried berries makes it safe to work around them— though it does smell awful. So, what do you think, Jake? You want to go?"

"Yes!"

Archie heaved a sigh. "Have fun, coz."

"And don't get eaten," Dani added with a pout.

Isabelle smiled. "Come back in one piece."

"Hold on!" Archie said suddenly, reaching into his tool-bag. "Why don't you take some pictures of the dragons for us?" He pulled out his miniature subcompact camera, a newly invented gadget normally used by real-life spies and private investigators.

It had worked well on their trip to Giant Land. Archie had managed to snap amazing pictures of the Norse giants and their village.

Jake accepted the camera with a nod and tucked it into his coat. "I'll try to get some good ones."

"Right, then! Come along, you two," Derek ordered. "Let's get moving. Best not to deal with *any* breed of dragons after dark."

You two? Jake wondered, but then he realized Maddox was following Derek, too. His jaw dropped for a second. *Oh, you have got to be joking!*

Hurrying ahead of the Guardian-in-training, Jake caught up to Derek and walked alongside him, keeping his voice low. "Derek, why does he have to come?"

The warrior sent him a quick frown. "I think he earned it just now, don't you?"

"Hey, I know how it looked, but trust me, I had it under control!" Jake insisted.

Derek chuckled. "Not so easy without Red to help you, is it?"

He scowled. "Fine. So the kid saved my neck. Still, it's *my* birthday!"

"And you are being granted a special privilege because of it. Listen, just like you are being considered for the Lightrider program and would do well to get your first look at the Grid, Maddox also needs to join us as part of his apprenticeship in learning how to protect a Lightrider on a mission."

Jake scoffed rather violently. "I don't need protection," he muttered, ignoring the troll incident, which he told himself was obviously an exception and didn't count.

Derek shrugged. "Someday you might."

"Yes, but that's why I've got you. Isn't it?"

"For now, of course," he replied. "But one day, I'll be old and decrepit and too slow to keep up with you. If they make you a Lightrider, protocol requires you to have a Guardian accompany you on your more dangerous missions. You know that. It's better to get familiar with a particular Guardian or two. It makes the missions go smoother."

Jake stopped walking. "Wait a second." Archie's words from last night after they had left the blacksmith's forge echoed in his ears. He had suggested exactly what Derek was all but saying now. "Don't even tell me the Order is thinking of assigning St. Trinian to me. Like, permanently?"

"Well, I could tell you that, Jake. But then I would be lying."

"*Oh,* you *cannot* be serious! I don't want that kid shadowing me! I don't even know him! He's way too full of himself! Plus, he's boring!"

"I can hear every word you're saying, you know," Maddox spoke up from a few yards behind them.

Jake looked back at him with only a smidgeon of regret.

The older boy tapped his ear, looking amused by his rude protests. "Extra-sharp Guardian senses, remember?"

He heaved an irked sigh. "Sorry," he forced out.

Derek chuckled and then rumpled Jake's hair. "Come along, my brave young heroes!" he said wryly. "Let's go see some dragons. Do try not to kill each other along the way, hmm?" He strode off ahead of them.

Jake glanced at Maddox in annoyance and followed.

CHAPTER FIFTEEN
There Be Dragons

Considering it was his birthday and that he *was* about to have the experience of a lifetime, Jake decided not to ruin it for himself by being in a bad mood over Maddox coming along. The Guardian kid *had* saved him from the troll boy, after all, as much as it galled him to admit it. So, he gave up his vexation and found he felt better immediately.

As Derek led the boys out to the same green expanse of lawn where the portal had appeared yesterday, Jake was delighted to spot the tall, lanky cowboy waiting for them there, hands in pockets, chewing on his toothpick.

Tex looked decidedly intimidating as he stood there in stillness, his face shadowed under the brim of his hat, his duster coat blowing ominously in the wind.

Dr. Plantagenet was with him, dressed in his white lab coat, with his black doctor bag in hand, and a curious pile of equipment gathered into a large sack made of rope netting on the ground beside him. The Green Man looked nervous as the breeze rippled through the twigs on his head.

Seeing the zookeeper reminded Jake to report the troll boy's vicious behavior; after all, Dr. Plantagenet seemed to have charge over Ogden. But as they approached, Maddox caught Jake's eye and shook his head in a discreet request not to bring it up, at least not yet. Jake frowned at him uncertainly.

Tex tipped his hat as they joined him. "Stone. Boys. Y'all ready to go?"

"Ready? We may have trouble holding them back," Derek replied as he greeted Tex with a hearty handshake. "Good to see you on your feet."

"Healers fixed me up right quick."

"You two know each other?" Jake remarked in surprise, glancing from one man to the other.

"Aw, we go way back," the cowboy said.

"Appreciate you doing this for the boy," Derek said.

Tex nodded and sent Jake a wink. "Kid's old man was my friend, too."

"You knew my father, Mr. Munroe?" Jake echoed in amazement.

"And your ma. We were in the same graduatin' class."

Jake absorbed this in shock while Maddox introduced himself to Dr. Plantagenet. Jake and the Green Man had already met, of course, but he jarred himself out of his daze in time to say hello.

He made no mention of Troll Boy's attack—but not because Maddox said so. It was obvious the Green Man was already on edge about having to go and give medical treatment to fearsome dracosaurs.

Jake nodded to him. "Thanks for letting me come along, Dr. Plantagenet."

"I'm not sure your Gryphon would approve," the veterinarian answered with a rueful smile.

Jake grinned. "Red hates dragons."

"And that, my boy, makes two of us," the Green Man said in a taut voice. "At least this time, I don't have to give them any shots."

"Blimey!" Jake couldn't even imagine how the dracosaurs' caretakers managed *that*.

"Hey, Stone, you wanna get that bag for the doc?"

"Sure." Derek picked it up and slung the rope sack over his shoulder. "I'll go first."

"Yep. Stone first. You, Guardian kid, you go second."

"Yes, sir. Maddox St. Trinian. Pleased to meet you."

"Likewise. Greenie goes third. Then Jakey boy. I'll go last to close the door after us." As Tex spoke, he pulled up his left sleeve, exposing once more the strange tattoo on the inside of his brawny forearm—an intricate geometrical shape rather like a sunflower with layered petals, but inscribed with all manner of arcane sigils.

On the points of the tattoo, tiny bits of glass or crystal glowed like buttons on one of Archie's gadgets.

"*What* is that?" Jake exclaimed.

Not looking over, Tex began punching in particular chips of the glass with the pointer finger of his opposite hand. He'd seen him do it yesterday. "Didn't that dad-gum wood elf teach you young'uns nuthin?"

"He didn't mention a tattoo!"

"*Tattoo?*" Tex turned to him indignantly. "Boy, my sweet ol' mamma would whup my behind if I ever got a tattoo. This here's a navigational device."

"Device?"

"That's right." Tex held out his arm and showed him. "Go on. Feel it. Your daddy had one just like it. But don't touch none of them shiny buttons or we might end up in Timbuktu."

Jake eyed him warily, then stepped closer to ogle the four-inch disk embedded under the skin of Tex's forearm.

When he lifted a hand and cautiously touched it, he felt a bump under the skin—the rounded edge of a hard circle about four inches wide, implanted in the Lightrider's arm.

He drew back with a blanch. "That's disgusting."

He laughed. "Beg yer pardon."

"I, er, w-were you born with that, o-or did they put it in your arm by surgery or something?"

"What do you think?" Amused at Jake's confused revulsion, Tex sent Derek a glance, his wild blue eyes dancing. "Kid's a hoot. Just like his daddy, ain't he?"

"I know," said Derek.

"After a student has gone through all the Lightrider trainin', the final step is the surgery. And you have to think hard about it 'cuz it's a lifetime commitment and it can't be undone. They knock ya out, then go ahead and embed one o' these doodads under the skin. That way, nobody can steal it."

"Looks painful," he said with a grimace.

"Ain't too comfortable, you're right."

"What is it?"

"It's called the Flower o' Life. A Lightrider's 'open sesame' into the Grid. It's a flat, two-dimensional representation of the Grid's icosahedron. The wood elf at least mentioned that much?"

Jake nodded, staring at it. "What's it made of? Stone?"

"Mainly iron pyrite."

"Fool's gold," Dr. Plantagenet informed him.

"Fool's gold?" Jake echoed in surprise.

The Green Man nodded. "Iron pyrite has very special paramagnetic properties. It is then encased in the same Preseli bluestone from Wales used in Stonehenge."

"Really?" Jake murmured.

"Indeed," the doctor said. "Something about the crystalline structure of that particular rock deposit resonates with the frequencies of the Grid. Why else would the ancestors bother carrying all those gigantic boulders over two hundred miles, from Wales to the Salisbury Plain?"

"Yep," Tex concurred, nodding. "That's how it works. So, when I need to open up a portal, I just punch in my destination on these here buttons—chips of quartz crystal, by the way."

"Mysterious stone, quartz," the Green Man remarked. "It's been revered since ancient times, but we're only just beginning to discover the range of its properties. It, too, resonates in harmony with the frequencies of the Grid, and we're beginning to find that, in fact, quartz stores all kinds of information."

"How can a stone store information?" Jake asked.

"No idea," said Tex. "I gen'rally leave the technical parts to the wizards. They're the ones who figured out how to make the thing an implant. In the old days, see, Lightriders used to wear the Flower on a chain, like a locket or a fob watch. But bad folks was always trying to steal 'em."

Derek nodded at Jake. "The Dark Druids would love to get into the Grid and subvert it for their own purposes."

"I'll bet they would," Maddox murmured.

"So now, by a blend of science and magic," the Green Man said, "they've figured out how to embed the Flower under the skin, instead. The body accepts it almost like another organ, when the Lightrider dies, the Flower dies, too. Then it's of use to no one."

"They could still try to steal it," Maddox pointed out, glancing at Tex. "Capture you and carve the device out of your arm."

"Our wizards thought of that and took measures against it," Dr. Plantagenet told him. "Pyrite and the poison arsenic often form together in nature, which is handy. If anyone tries to surgically remove the implant, a flood of arsenic seeps out of the pyrite and straight into the bloodstream, killing the Lightrider within moments. As soon as he or she dies, the Flower of Life dies, too. The device becomes unusable."

"The Dark Druids wouldn't be able to fix it?" Maddox asked skeptically. "I hear they have some of the most talented warlocks on

Earth among their number."

"Don't matter," Tex said. "The Grid knows her Lightriders like her own kin. She don't let nobody else come a-callin'. You don't have a Lightrider with you, you ain't gettin' in."

"You make it sound as though the Grid is alive," Jake remarked.

Tex hooted, and the Green Man chuckled, looking askance at him.

"It's not as though you can have a conversation with her, Jake, but of *course* she is alive," Dr. Plantagenet said.

"She?" he echoed in surprise.

"My people have always worshipped her as Mother Earth," the Green Man added with a reverent bow of his leafy head.

"'Course, y'all are pagans," Tex said in a philosophical tone. "Well, y'are! No offense."

The Green Man huffed. "Colonials."

"Anyhoo, the Flower o' Life is a flattened representation of what actually exists out there in three or more dimensions. The Grid itself, in miniature. Right here in my dad-gum arm," Tex said. "Can't never get rid of it, neither, like I said. Once it's in there, you die if it's removed. It's a security measure."

Maddox was still pondering various enemy moves. "But what if they left you alive and simply cut your arm off? Might the Flower still work then?"

Tex turned to him in astonishment. "Well, ain't you a ray o' sunshine, boy! I don't partick'ly care to try it and find out. Shoot! Where'd you find this one, Stone?" Tex grinned. "He's mean, ain't he?"

"I told you he was good," Derek said proudly.

Maddox arched a brow at him, pleased.

"Well, suffice to say, nobody can open the Grid but a Lightrider, and let's just leave it at that." Tex punched a final button embedded in his arm, still chuckling. "Heh. Wouldn't wanna make an enemy outta you, boy."

Maddox smiled coolly.

Jake changed the subject before everybody started talking about how great Maddox was again. Between Archie, Dani, and, above all, Isabelle singing the older boy's praises, he was a little *tired* of that subject.

"So you can go anywhere you want with that thing?" he asked Tex, nodding at the Flower. "Just tell it where to go and it takes you there?"

"Long as your end point's pegged to one of these here waypoints."

Tex tapped the toe of his boot on a circular brass plaque sunk into the ground, like a poor man's gravestone.

Jake hadn't even noticed it there, overgrown with grass around the edges. Even if he had, though, he never would've thought it had anything to do with the Grid. It looked like a part of the palace grounds' waterworks system, like an ordinary metal cap over an underground pipe where the gardener could hook in a hose.

"Waypoints like this one here are sunk deep in the ground at regular points around the globe, anywhere we want to have quick access to. At ground level, you barely notice 'em, but y'see, these pegs run some twenty feet deep into the earth. The metal in them collects the Grid's energy."

"Like an underground lightning rod," Dr. Plantagenet offered.

"Ohh," Jake murmured in wonder.

Tex nodded. "That's what generates the gateway when I call for one. All right now, folks. If y'all done jawin', we should be ready to jump. We got sick dracosaurs to tend. So stand back and hold on to yer hats—and yer molecules. Portal should be poppin' open right about...*now*."

Tex certainly knew his business, for as soon as he finished speaking, a sudden flash of light blinded them, heralding the opening of the Grid.

Jake winced and tried to shield his eyes, but the burst of brilliance was gone as quickly as it appeared. When his vision readjusted, he saw once again, as yesterday, a pulsating circle of thick, clear, almost liquid-looking energy before them, like a hole in the fabric of reality, shimmering with delicate colors, as if to beckon them in.

Perfectly round, the portal reminded Jake of a manmade pond filled with very pure water, little waves and ripples playing across its surface—except that it stood upright rather than lying flat.

Through this watery window, a strange silver tunnel opened up. Beyond it, he could just make out a rugged landscape of misty mountains and forests waiting for them.

The Green Man peered over Derek's shoulder into the portal. "See any dragons basking near our landing point?"

"Don't worry," the Guardian replied, "there's a barrier around the waypoint to keep them off."

"They're still dragons," the veterinarian muttered.

"Aw, settle your branches, Doc. We'll be fine."

"So what do we do?" Jake asked Tex.

"Just step in. She won't hurt ya, long as you're with me."

Derek shrugged the sack of equipment higher onto his shoulder, then stepped up to the portal. "See you on the other side, boys."

Jake watched, heart pounding, as Derek's body blurred into streaks and disappeared in the twinkling of an eye as he went shooting off through the Grid.

Maddox and Jake glanced at each other in alarm.

Jake stepped back. "You're next, not me."

"Go on, kid. Time's a-wastin'," said Tex.

"Yes, sir." Maddox visibly braced himself, then went up to the portal.

Cautiously, he poked his finger into the swirling energy field to test it. But with a sudden yelp, Maddox went flying into the tunnel, as though the Grid itself had caught him by the arm and thrown him down the ley line's energy highway.

Tex just chuckled as Maddox blurred and whizzed off into the distance.

Jake turned anxiously to the Lightrider. "Is he going to be all right?"

"'Course he is. Doc, you go next."

The Green Man let out a large sigh and gazed at the portal for a moment. "Go easy on me, Gaia." Clutching his doctor bag, he closed his eyes, stepped into the circle, and swiftly vanished like the others had.

"Your turn, kid."

"Er, all right." Heart thumping, Jake stepped up nervously to the pulsating circle of energy. "That's all I have to do, then? Step in?"

"I gen'rally find it helps to yell *'Yee-haw.'*"

"Why? What does that mean?"

"No idea."

"Is it a spell?" he asked hopefully.

"Naw, it's just fun to say. Now go on, boy! Quit stallin'. You'll be there in two shakes of an armadillo's tail. Go on, now, make yer daddy proud."

"Right," Jake forced out, but still, he could not force himself to go. Odd to find himself so terrified. This was, after all, a foretaste of his greatest dream in life. Yet his very knees were shaking.

What if something went wrong?

He cleared his throat. "Yee-haw," he attempted, his voice barely a whisper, dry-mouthed as he was with mingled fear and excitement.

"Whatcha waiting for, son, the Rapture?"

"Huh?"

Tex's shrewd stare homed in on him. "Now, I ain't one to criticize. But I'd go, if I were you. Otherwise, that other kid, he's gonna think yer yella."

Jake slanted him a sharp look. Tex grinned.

Oh, that canny Lightrider knew just what to say. But maybe it was good to have a rival because, without further hesitation, he kicked his fear away and leaped at the portal, yelling out the words the cowboy had suggested.

"Yeeeee..."

To his confusion, time slowed down to an inchworm's crawl just inside the tunnel, and silence blotted out the birdsong.

No, not silence, Jake realized as he floated in mid-jump. He could hear a deep hum, a pulsating rhythm of energy like a heartbeat. The very frequencies of the planet.

In that first sliver of delayed non-time, even his own voice came out slow and distorted.

But it didn't last. Time snapped back on itself; his molecules blurred into long colored streaks, as did the grounds of Merlin Hall behind him.

Then—*whoosh!*

The Grid sent him careening headlong at the speed of light nearly to the other side of the Continent.

"...*haaaaaw!*"

He was still shouting the cowboy's silly phrase when he tumbled out of the Grid onto a desolate hilltop in Romania. He rolled across the rocky ground and stopped himself a few feet from the waypoint sunk into the earth.

The others were there, too, but Jake was too much in shock to pay them any mind. He felt foggy-headed and shaken as Derek picked him up by one arm and moved him out of the way.

"D-do I have all my m-molecules?" Jake mumbled, glancing down at himself. Two arms, two legs. All his bits seemed to have arrived in the right place, properly connected.

He noted that his companions were likewise intact when the nausea suddenly caught up with him. Perhaps his stomach had been the last to arrive, for it revolted without warning. He stumbled a few feet away from the others and vomited into the underbrush.

Belatedly, he remembered what Finnderool had said about the first few jumps making someone queasy.

Happy birthday to me, Jake thought, then puked again.

It was somewhat mollifying, though, to notice that Maddox was leaning on a nearby boulder, also retching his guts out. *Ha. Not so tough now, are you, Mr. Invincible?* Still, Jake couldn't help seeing a certain humor in them both being sick.

"You knew we'd puke, didn't you?" he accused Derek a few minutes later, after he had recovered and rejoined their party.

"It's nothing to be embarrassed about," he answered. "Most people do."

Dr. Plantagenet offered the boys a piece of candied ginger. "Here. It'll help to settle your stomachs."

"Thanks." Maddox and he both took a piece.

Then Tex arrived, stepping out of the watery-wavy circle as smoothly as you please. He pulled up his sleeve again and punched a quartz crystal button in the middle of the Flower of Life implant, closing the portal behind them. "So, how'd we all do? You boys look a little green around the gills."

They muttered that they were all right, though Jake still felt woozy and discombobulated.

"You git used to it," Tex assured them. "That's just your molecules settling down again where they're supposed to be. So, what's the plan, Doc?"

"The dragon pox is highly contagious," the Green Man said as he untied the top of his big rope-netting bag. "And I regret to say, it tends to make a dragon very grumpy. Not that they need any help in that department."

"This virus, it doesn't spread to people, does it?" Maddox asked.

"Not a virus, a bacterium. If this were a virus—in a lizard species—we'd be in real trouble. And no, it doesn't."

"Bacterium?" Jake echoed. He recalled Archie rambling on in his laboratory back home about some newfangled "germ" theory of disease.

It was hard to believe that people in hospital could get sick enough to die from something as insignificant as surgeons not washing their hands between patients. But that was the latest, shocking claim by the scientists.

"The only thing worse than an especially grumpy dragon," the Green Man said as he passed out stinkberry bracelets, "is a whole colony of them."

Jake put it on but winced at the smell.

"So," the veterinarian continued, "we need to scout them out and quarantine the infected beasts to stop the pox from spreading to the rest. Because if *that* happens...ho, ho." He shuddered with dread. "There'll be dragons attacking villages all along the edges of these forests faster than you can say St. George. Here, everybody take one of these, too." He pulled a stack of round shields out of the rope sack. "They're fireproof."

Derek nodded to the boys, who each accepted a shield, just in case. As for himself, he was starting to look a little concerned. "Don't dragons usually crawl into one of their caves or retreats and hide when they're feeling ill?"

"Normally, yes," Dr. Plantagenet replied while Maddox practiced lifting the shield, getting a feel for its weight. "But, er...this particular infection also tends to stimulate the appetite."

"What?" Tex turned to him and stared. "Now he tells us! Extra-hungry dragons on the loose? Aw, that's real nice, Doc." The Lightrider waved off the offered shield with a scowl. "You coulda told us that before we brought these boys along, ya overgrown broccoli! I should turn around and take these two young'uns back now."

"No! Please!" said Jake. "It's my birthday!"

"You wanna live to see the next one?" Tex retorted.

"Don't worry, Munroe, they're not getting anywhere near the dragons," Derek assured him. "That's what you and I are here for. The boys will stay back. You and I can assist the doctor."

"Huh." Tex still frowned and looked from Derek to the boys. He rested his hands on his hips, pushing back his long coat just enough to reveal the gleaming pair of Colt revolvers holstered at his hips.

Of course, the pistols wouldn't do him much good against a dragon, Jake supposed. He had seen one before, in Giant Land. Even the giants had been afraid of Old Smokey.

Nevertheless.

"If Derek says we're safe, then I'm sure we are. He's saved my life loads of times," Jake assured the frowning cowboy.

And himself.

Derek nodded. "I'm not worried. The dracosaurs *are* one of the tamer dragon species, and the colony here is used to seeing people from the Order moving through."

"Well, you don't have to worry about me," Maddox said coolly. "I can take care of myself."

"Me, too!" Jake chimed in. "I've already dealt with giants, after all. And Loki, a crazy Norse god, and his fire wolf, who was as big as a building! And Gar—" He almost mentioned Garnock, but caught himself at the last moment, remembering that nobody outside their main group was supposed to know about his recent battle against the founder of the Dark Druids.

The long-dead (sort of) alchemist had almost made it back from the grave with the help of some unholy black magic.

"Never mind," Jake mumbled, dropping the subject.

Derek looked at Tex. "With reasonable precautions, I'm confident the boys will be quite safe."

"Well, it's your call, Stone. They're your charges."

"And the dracosaurs are mine, and I must see to them. Come. Time is of the essence," said the doctor. "We mustn't waste the light."

"He's right," Derek said. "We've got a lot of forest to cover. Let's go find our patients."

With that, he picked up the rope-sack again, slung it over his shoulder, and marched out past the dragon-proof barrier.

Maddox immediately followed him down the mountain into the forest. Jake clutched his fireproof shield, heart pounding, and hurried after them.

It was time to hunt for dragons.

CHAPTER SIXTEEN
The Tower

The trail wound down the mountainside, back and forth among the gnarled trees and wind-whipped pines. They walked single file, carrying their shields and equipment. Jake scanned the woods constantly for the dracosaurs, his nerves jangling with a mix of dread and eagerness.

Dr. Plantagenet had said the colony spent most of their daylight hours sunning themselves and dozing on the rocks around the river that ran down the middle of the valley.

Lazy in the daytime, the dracosaurs preferred to hunt at night and fed mostly on the forest animals, deer and such, although they were also known to eat fish and even turtles. But they must have picked off lost peasants once upon a time because the villagers for miles around had stopped coming into this valley centuries ago, according to Dr. Plantagenet. Local lore warned that death lurked in that valley between the two mountains.

Pondering all this as he walked deeper into the valley in question, Jake felt a surge of terror quickening his heartbeat. *What am I doing? This is insane.*

Thankfully, Maddox spoke up before his imagination ran away with him. "Guardian Stone? Question on procedure."

"Aye?"

"Is it correct to say that, in the event of an emergency—say, if the dragons charged us—we're to make Mr. Munroe our top priority?"

Derek glanced back at him with a curious smile. "You tell me."

"I believe that's the case. After all, if Mr. Munroe gets eaten, the rest of the party is stuck here."

"You are correct," Derek said in approval, while Tex let out a short bark of laughter.

The Green Man instantly scolded him. "Shh! We're trying to sneak up on these animals, remember?"

"So? I like the way this kid thinks," Tex drawled, grinning at Maddox. "Yep, save the Lightrider first. That'd be my vote."

Derek snorted, then glanced back wryly at Maddox. "Since some Lightriders are more prone to trouble than others, you'll want to stick close to the one you're assigned to, whatever the mission. The fact that your Lightrider happens to be your ride home is merely added incentive to keep him or her alive."

The veterinarian huffed. "And I thought you were here to protect *me*."

"Aw, don't ya fret, thar, leafy boy." Tex was clearly enjoying all this, even though the tall, slightly crazy gunslinger looked well able to take care of himself. "If things get hot, at least *you* can make like a tree and leave. Get it? Heh, heh."

"Whoa! What is *that*?" Jake stopped and pointed at a knee-high, brown, stinking mass on the side of the trail ahead.

Maddox looked at him. "You're joking, right?"

Jake held his nose as his nausea from the Grid jump threatened to return. He started gagging.

"Figure it out yet?" Derek asked. Even he winced at the stench.

"Dragon poop," Jake said in a nasally voice, still holding his nose. "Ugh, get me out of here."

Eyes watering, he hurried past the huge mound of scat and only breathed normally again once they had emerged from the woods a hundred yards or so away.

The path now led them out along a precarious stretch, with a steep rock face on their right and a sharp drop-off into the valley on their left. Jake gratefully inhaled the fresh wind that blew through his hair and paused to marvel at the dramatic mountain view. The others did the same, scanning the landscape for dragons.

Everybody shouted in surprise when they suddenly saw one jump from hilltop to hilltop in the distance and disappear again into the trees.

"Not one of the dracosaurs," the Green Man said. "That looked like one of the larger, winged species around here."

"Maybe a Leaping Blue?" Derek asked.

The veterinarian nodded his leafy head and set his equipment on the ground to rest for a moment. "Could be."

Then Maddox pointed at the sky, where another dragon with a slim body and a very wide wingspan was soaring high above the ground like an eagle riding the currents of air.

"Look at that!"

"Ah, beautiful, isn't he?" Derek said with a smile. "The Feathered Falcondrake is one of my favorites. I always wished I could've had one for a pet when I was a boy."

Jake grinned at him. He had long since noticed that the Guardian was quite the dragon enthusiast.

"I didn't realize there were so many kinds of dragons around here," Maddox said.

"Hope they all hate these god-awful stinkberries," Tex muttered.

"They do," Dr. Plantagenet assured him. "They've learned over time that the whole plant is very toxic to them. But don't worry. We're in the dracosaurs' territory. The other breeds should keep their distance."

"Are they scared of them?" Jake asked. "I thought you said the dracosaurs were relatively peaceful."

"Yes, but all dragons are highly territorial," Derek answered. "Most know to stay off each other's land unless they want a fight. They usually save the fire-breathing routine for other dragons who challenge them."

"Well, that's good to know," Jake murmured. Then, searching the vista before him for more dragons, he spotted a formidable stone tower whose hulking silhouette poked above the trees on the mountain across from them. "Hey, there's a castle or something over there!" He pointed it out to the others. "I wonder if they've noticed they're, er, living in a dragon-infested forest."

"You'd think," Maddox agreed. "Why would anybody choose to live there? It seems awfully dangerous."

"Oh ho, my boy, the people in there aren't going anywhere soon," said the Green Man. "That's no ordinary castle, but one of the Order's most formidable dungeons."

"Really?" Jake said in surprise, looking at it again. "A jail?"

"Housing only the Order's most dangerous prisoners. The warden keeps an eye on the dragon population for me," Dr. Plantagenet added. "After all, the beasts *are* a calculated part of the tower defenses—a great deterrent to those who might otherwise try to escape. Prisoners don't even bother trying to get out, considering it means crossing dragon country, on foot and alone, after dark."

"I should think so," Jake murmured.

"The warden of that dungeon is actually the one who sent me the Inkbug this morning about one of the dracosaur females showing signs of the dragon pox," the doctor said. "You can imagine the disaster we'd have on our hands if it spread to other breeds."

"On that note, we should go," Derek said grimly. "The sooner you treat your scaly patient, the safer they'll all be. Let's press on."

Something in his voice made Jake glance over at him. "Is something wrong?"

"No. Let's keep moving."

Guardians weren't very good liars. Jake looked again at the tower, and, suddenly, understanding dawned. "Wait a second... Is that the jail where Uncle Waldrick's locked up?"

"Come on, Jake," Derek said in a low tone, turning away.

Instead of following him, Jake stared out across the valley with an icy sensation creeping down his limbs. He did not like thinking about his murderous uncle, but he belatedly recalled hearing about a year ago that the villain had been locked up in dragon country somewhere after his crimes had been exposed. There had been a trial in the Yew Court and everything, but Great-Great Aunt Ramona had shielded Jake from all the unpleasantness at the time.

At least now Jake had seen the great, green maze and met the Old Yew, who had been Uncle Waldrick's judge at his trial before the Elders. *They must have used the open space of the Field of Challenge as the courtroom,* he thought, recalling Sir Peter Quince's instant magical renovations. The Elders could probably change the setting of the field to serve as any sort of space they needed.

"You might as well admit it!" Jake prompted, catching up to Derek. "I know that's the place."

Derek paused and sent him a dark glance that showed the master Guardian did not like recalling those days any more than he did. "Aye. That's the place."

"I knew it!" Jake murmured, then he stared at the bleak, distant tower with cold memories of hatred rumbling through his soul like thunderclouds.

Jake had managed not to think about how his uncle had ruined his life in quite a while, getting used to his new existence, reunited with his relatives.

It had been a drastic change, to be sure, going from a penniless, orphaned pickpocket to a boy-earl. But his distraction during this period of adjustment did not mean he had forgotten any of the wrongs done to him. Any of the pain. Any of the loss. Like the fact that he never even would have *been* an orphan if it hadn't been for Uncle Waldrick and his greed.

And now, there the man was once more, just across the valley. Jake couldn't believe he was looking at the very jail where his horrible excuse for a kinsman was incarcerated. How he used to strut around London like a master of the Earth. Oh, how the mighty had fallen!

He gritted his teeth with rage at the memory of Uncle Waldrick's haughty face, with its constant expression of sneering superiority. The man had *loved* being the Earl of Griffon for those eleven years when Jake, the rightful heir, was missing—before Derek had tracked him down on the streets of London.

It had been a very narrow rescue, too. Waldrick's plans for Jake had been pretty straightforward, considering he had ordered his henchmen to cut his throat.

Jake turned to the Guardian who had saved his life that awful day. "I want to see him," he said coldly. "Take me over there when we're done with the dragons."

"No."

"Why not?" he demanded.

Derek looked at him, visibly striving for patience. "It's probably bad enough that I've brought you into dragon country, Jake. I'm not taking a kid into a prison."

He scoffed. "I've been to jail before, remember? Or did you forget the time we both got thrown into Newgate?"

Maddox glanced from him to Derek in surprise.

"Forget? Hardly," the big man muttered.

Thankfully, Jake's telekinesis had proved pretty handy at getting them both out of a jail cell.

"Why in the world would you even want to see him?" Derek asked, nodding toward the tower.

"Just to spit in his face. And see him behind bars. And tell him how much I despise him. And how much I'm enjoying the life he tried to steal from me!"

Derek shook his head. "Not going to happen. Come on. Let it go for now. We've got work to do."

"Derek!"

"Jake. You wanted to know what it's like to be a Lightrider. That's your birthday present. Coming on this mission with us. Not seeing your uncle. So, no, we're not going over to see him. Come on. We've got to carry out our mission and get out of here before it starts getting dark. You want us all to get eaten?"

He heaved a disgruntled sigh, but gave up the argument and followed. "Fine."

Dr. Plantagenet lifted the medicine sprayer back up onto his shoulder. Tex, bringing up the rear, scowled at the tower in the distance, mumbling under his moustache about lowdown, no-account rattlesnakes.

The path ahead led into another section of the forest.

As they continued down the sloping trail, Maddox fell back to walk beside Jake. "So what's all this about? What did your uncle do to land in a godforsaken Order prison?"

"He killed my parents and tried to murder me," Jake muttered, still upset. "He would've succeeded, too, if it weren't for Derek arriving just in time."

"He killed your parents?" he echoed in shock.

"Aye, fratricide. My father was Uncle Waldrick's elder brother."

"Why on earth did he kill his own brother? To get the title?"

"In part." Jake heaved a sigh. There was nothing else to do on their hike through the woods, so he told Maddox the story in the briefest possible terms. "My father had telekinesis. That's where I get it from. But Waldrick inherited a related talent called pyrokinesis—the fire gift."

"Whew," said Maddox. Everyone knew that pyrokinesis was one of the most formidable abilities anyone could have.

"I know," Jake agreed. "Only, Waldrick was too immature to handle it. The Kinderveil had barely lifted when he fried a local village with it by accident."

Maddox winced.

"He was only my age and was terrified by what he had done, even though it wasn't on purpose. To protect him, his big brother—my father—agreed to help Waldrick cover up his involvement in the fire on one condition: Waldrick had to agree to let my father perform the Extraction Spell on him. My father promised him he could have his power back when he was older and better able to control it.

"Waldrick agreed to this. He felt bad about the peasants he had burnt. Maybe at age twelve, he wasn't so far gone. When my dad performed the Extraction Spell on him, his ability was distilled into a magical vial and stored in a great vault beneath our family castle. I've tried to find the vault," Jake added, "but it's too well-hidden by enchantments. Not even the castle ghosts can show me where it is.

"Anyway, the two boys stored it there until such time as Waldrick would be old enough to handle that huge responsibility. Thing is, he never got mature, at least, not in my father's eyes. Waldrick grew up to be rotten and selfish and corrupt, and my father knew that if his brother ever got his power back, he would hurt more people and certainly use it for evil.

"So he destroyed the vial to stop Waldrick from ever reclaiming his pyrokinesis. That's why Waldrick killed him, and my mother, as well, and even tried to kill me, though I was just a baby. For revenge."

"How did you survive?" Maddox asked, marveling.

"My father was already shot, but somehow kept fighting, at least long enough to buy my mother enough time to run. Waldrick shot her in the back like the coward that he is, but at the last minute before she died, she was able to hand me off to the water nymphs in the brook nearby."

"Water nymphs!" he murmured.

Jake nodded. "They were supposed to keep me safe, but they lost me. I ended up floating off down the Thames, and nobody knew where to find me because of the Kinderveil masking my location. You know, how it's there to keep the Dark Druids from hunting us down when we're small? Well, apparently, it also stops the Elders from being able to locate us, too. So that's how I grew up in an orphanage. At least until I ran away," he added.

Maddox pondered all this for a long moment. "I can't believe they didn't hang him."

Jake shrugged. "They couldn't convict him on the murders. Everything I just told you? Nobody could prove it. I found out most of this from the ghost of the man he used as his scapegoat. The poor fool who got blamed for my parents' murders."

"And you believe this ghost was telling the truth?"

"Oh, yes. He got to cross over after he helped me figure it all out, so there's proof that he was clean, right? Waldrick was the one behind it, along with his helper, Fionnula Coralbroom."

"Sea-witch, right? I think I've heard of her. Pretty nefarious reputation. You do know how to make enemies, don't you? Isn't she the one who tried to overthrow King Oceanus of the mermaids?"

Jake nodded. "That's her. When she got banished to the land for that, my uncle found her and they joined forces. Fionnula's in jail now, too, somewhere at the bottom of the ocean. They both got put away on charges of kidnapping, which I guess is better than nothing."

"Kidnapping you?"

"Me, Gladwin the royal garden fairy, and my Gryphon, and some other magical creatures they were using for experiments, trying to steal their different powers. Gladwin almost escaped, too," he added, "but Waldrick caught her and cut her wings off! We used one of my Gryphon's magical healing feathers afterward to help her sprout new ones, though, so it all worked out."

Maddox furrowed his brow. "What about the other magical creatures?"

"I rescued them," Jake informed him rather proudly. "I just hope I don't run into that grumpy cherub any time soon."

"What?" Maddox looked askance at him.

"Oh, never mind," he said wryly.

Charlie the sarcastic, cigar-smoking cherub had promised (or threatened?) to help Jake win any girl he wanted for his sweetheart in the future—a token of his thanks for freeing him from Uncle Waldrick's cage.

Of course, Jake's reaction to the thought of a girlfriend had been about the same as his reaction to the dragon poop.

But Charlie the Cherub, laughing at him, had promised he was setting aside one of his silver love arrows anyway to help Jake win his chosen lady when the time came.

The time most definitely had not come yet, but the thought of all that disgusting love stuff made him send Maddox a shrewd, sideways glance. "So you have no interest in my cousin, Isabelle, eh? Could've fooled me."

Maddox colored, but he was saved from having to answer by a sudden outburst from the back of the line.

"Whoa, Nelly! Would ya look at that!"

Everyone stopped and turned to find Tex marching off the path toward a large tree. On the branches, some twelve feet above the ground, hung a torn length of shed reptilian skin with orange-colored scales. A few more pieces with discolored scales littered the ground around the bottom of the trunk.

"Don't touch those!" Dr. Plantagenet called. "That orange color signifies the dragon pox! Obviously, we're getting close. The infected dracosaur must have rubbed against the tree trunk to try to get some relief. The pox can make them itchy—like the chicken pox for your kind."

"This sickness turns them orange?" Jake asked as Tex returned to the path.

"In places, yes. The dragon pox presents as blistering spots, and rusty orange patches of discoloration, as you can see in those shed scales. It's quite painful for them."

"No wonder they get grumpy," Jake mumbled. He'd had the chicken pox himself when he was little.

"Fortunately, the disease doesn't usually kill them," the doctor said. "But when aggressive predators like dragons are uncomfortable, they're more likely to get into fights with others in their colony, and that can lead to needless dragon deaths. We're almost at the lookout point with a view of their main basking area," he added. "Once we reach it, I'll tell you all how we shall proceed."

"Sounds good," Tex said. "You boys holdin' up all right?"

Before they could answer, a ferocious roar blasted out from a peak in the distance and echoed down the valley.

Jake gulped. Even Maddox flinched at the sound.

The Green Man froze with a terror-stricken stare and started to go into motionless tree mode—a natural defense—but Derek turned and continued down the trail, fearless as ever.

"Gentlemen," he summoned them.

Maddox quickly followed. Striding after them, Jake glanced back to make sure the other two were coming. He saw Tex poke the Green Man in the arm, then point toward the path.

Dr. Plantagenet's barky camouflage quickly softened back into his usual brownish skin. Tex clapped him on the shoulder, and the veterinarian nodded, gathering his nerve.

Then they all hiked on into ever-deepening wilderness.

CHAPTER SEVENTEEN
Great Minds Think Alike

Meanwhile back at Merlin Hall, Archie hoped Jake remembered to take pictures.

The girls had gone off to watch the Morris dancers, but Archie, still bothered by the unprovoked attack from Ogden Trumbull, found himself brooding on Maddox St. Trinian's advice.

Maddox was right. A bully like Ogden Trumbull would be back. And if he didn't bother Archie, next time he'd simply go and bother someone else. The brute was dangerous.

Something had to be done.

Archie knew that, obviously, he didn't have Maddox's physical prowess with which to face the threat, but he *did* have an oversized brain, and that he resolved to put to work on the task for the rest of the afternoon.

There had to be some sort of useful invention to keep the half-troll in line...

Though it was scary, he forced himself to go back into the library where he had been attacked. He had to do some research there to develop the idea brewing in his head. Plus, he simply refused to cower and hide, refused to be chased off from a place that he thought of as *his* territory. After all, Derek's glare had run Troll Boy back to the zoo where he belonged, at least for now.

Nevertheless, Archie felt nervous, jumping at any small sound in the library around him. He wasn't used to having enemies. He did his best to get along with everyone and treat others the same way he wanted to be treated.

Ah, well. He collected a few useful reference books and then sat down to consult them at a table with a good view of the door. If the half-troll came back, he wanted fair warning.

Then he got to work, sketching his plans bit by bit on a notebook as he figured out the specs for his device.

Soon he was engrossed—until the library door banged as somebody came in. He jumped again, jolted out of his concentration. Then he looked up from his work and drew in his breath.

Nixie Valentine!

She padded past the snoozing librarian's desk without noticing Archie, moving as silently as a little black cat.

Archie tucked his pencil behind his ear and watched her disappear into one of the aisles. A moment later, she reemerged, glancing left and right and looking every bit as suspicious as before. Without a sound, she climbed over the chain that was supposed to stop unauthorized persons from going up the spiral staircase to the gallery above.

It housed the restricted section of the library.

Well, well. Archie lifted an eyebrow. What wouldn't that girl try? She was ever so amusing, but he still thought Jake was daft to think she was a spy.

Of course, she *was* sneaking now...

He watched her scale the clunky metal staircase without a sound. When she reached the top, she glanced over her shoulder to make sure the librarian was still comatose, then stole into the aisle marked "Grimoires."

Archie was usually pretty content in life to follow the rules; breaking them was Jake's territory. Still, curiosity about this puzzle of a girl made him get up from his chair and stroll casually after her.

There were dangerous books up there, and if she really was a spy for the wicked Dark Druids, someone probably ought to stop her before she did something rash. Besides, after all the unpleasantness with Ogden Trumbull today, the prospect of chatting with the intriguing witch prodigy again already had him feeling more cheerful.

Archie found he was not as good at sneaking as Nixie was. The spiral stairs creaked halfway up, and he paused, wincing. But the librarian merely snorted in his sleep.

Whew. He tiptoed on. A moment later, he arrived in the forbidden gallery, his heart pounding over this act of rebellion.

He stepped into the "Grimoires" aisle and saw Nixie, kneeling on the floor, poring over a couple of huge, ancient books she had lying open. One leaned against the shelf, another on her knee, another on the floor; she was leafing through the pages, obviously looking for something in particular.

"You're not supposed to be up here," Archie whispered with a grin.

She glanced up, then blinked when she saw him. "Oh. It's you again."

"Just me." Hands in pockets, he sauntered over. "You'd better hurry before the librarian wakes up. What are you looking for?"

She hesitated, fear flickering in her night-dark eyes. "None of your business."

"Maybe I can help," he said, crouching down to her eye-level.

She eyed him warily. "No, thanks. You should go."

"You're trying to find a spell, right? What's the name of it? Don't worry, I know Latin." Latin was the favored language of many of the old spells—*and* most of the antique works of early science. Many times both topics occurred in the same books! Wizards and the scientist-philosophers of old were frequently one and the same.

Nixie let out a sigh when she saw that he wasn't going away. "Thanks, Mr. Bradford, but I don't even know what I'm looking for."

"Please call me Archie."

She frowned at him uncertainly, and then continued flipping through the pages. "What are you doing here, anyway? Shouldn't you be outside with everyone else?"

"I'm working on something," he said.

"I heard you got beat up by the troll kid," she said glancing at him.

Archie winced. "Does everybody know?"

She sent him a regretful look.

He scowled to hear that his humiliation by Ogden Trumbull was now the talk of the Gathering. She must think he was a weakling. "Well, he'll be sorry."

"You're not hiding from him in here, are you?"

"Certainly not! I'm working on an invention to put him in his place."

"Really?" This got her attention. "How?"

"Mind your own business," he replied, giving her back her own prickly words. "Besides, it's technical. I wouldn't want to bore you."

"You just assume it's too hard for me to understand?"

"Do you think I'd understand your advanced spells?"

She looked at him. "Ah."

"Let's just hope it works before that monster attacks somebody else," Archie said.

"Are you all right? I hope he didn't hurt you."

Archie sighed. "I'm fine. Just a little embarrassed to have to be rescued yet again by my cousin, Jake."

"Oh, this might work!" she whispered all of a sudden as she turned a page.

Archie looked down and read the name of the spell in Latin: *Vindico*. "What's it for?"

"Pest removal," she muttered. Nixie took a piece of paper and a pencil stub out of her pocket and quickly started copying it down. "Would you put those other two books back on the shelf for me?" she whispered, writing at top speed.

"Sure. Nixie?"

"Hold on...I have to get this spell down exactly right."

His frown deepened, for he had read the Latin title of the spell. "Nixie, I know perfectly well that *vindico* means to liberate, avenge, punish, or deliver—which would make that some sort of protection spell," he persisted. "What do you need protection from?"

He could see that his question startled her. She turned to him with an unguarded stare, a sudden rush of tears flooding into her eyes.

"It's all right," he offered. "You can tell me."

"No. I can't," she said in a taut voice, turning away. "I really can't."

"Nixie, if somebody's bothering you—"

"It's nothing I can't handle! Leave me alone!" she said fiercely. Finished copying the spell, she jumped to her feet and dashed off, leaving him to put away the book she had been using.

He glanced at the page with the *Vindico* spell again, but there was no time to lose. Nixie was already pattering down the spiral stairs.

Archie closed the heavy grimoire and slid it back up onto the shelf before hurrying after her. "Nixie, come back!" he insisted in a loud whisper. "Tell me what's wrong. Maybe I can help you."

"Just leave me alone, Archie! It's for your own good." She braced her hand on the banister and jumped over the chain at the bottom of the steps to escape him.

"Nixie! Protection from what? Or whom?"

"Good*bye!*" she said angrily. Then she ran to the heavy front door of the library and used all her strength to haul it open.

He jogged after her. "Nixie, please—wait!"

"Shh!" the librarian scolded him, finally waking from his nap.

Archie stopped and looked at the glaring old man, then lowered his head.

"Sorry," he mumbled, both worried and confused.

He hated being confused, and girls were possibly the most confusing thing on earth.

Pushing his spectacles back up onto the bridge of his nose, he lifted his head and looked at the door again, his gaze troubled.

With every fiber of his chivalrous nature, he wanted to help this mysterious damsel in distress; Jake wasn't the only one, after all, who dreamed, deep down, of being a hero.

But the girl herself had said flat-out that it was none of his business, so what was he to do?

He blew out a long sigh. Well, she was pretty dashed good at magic. Maybe the *Vindico* spell would free her from whatever pests in her life needed removing.

He hoped she'd be all right.

Wish Jake was here, he thought. No doubt his cousin would've had some idea about how to help her. Well, provided Jake was not still convinced she was a spy.

Of course, even Archie could admit that her behavior just now had seemed slightly suspicious. But try as he might, he could not think ill of her. Nixie was obviously in some sort of trouble. He just wished he could help.

He resolved to speak to Jake about the matter when he returned from dragon country. For now, his chief worry was taming Ogden Trumbull.

With that, Archie went back to his table and continued working on his new invention.

He was soon engrossed in his figuring once more, calculating and recalculating the amperage, checking his work against Ohm's Law, looking up different types of conductive materials in his reference books to make sure he wasn't missing anything. The gadget was coming along well.

He resolved to call it the Bully Buzzer, and it might well change the world for weaklings everywhere.

With a draft of his design plans complete, at least on paper, it was time to focus on step two: building his crafty little device.

A short while later, Archie left the library with ink smudges on his fingers and a mischievous gleam in his eyes. He couldn't wait to get down to the fine work of wiring up the circuitry.

Long ago, King David had beaten Goliath with five stones and a slingshot. Their mismatched sizes were roughly equal to his and Ogden's, but Archie's weapon of choice for slaying *his* giant would be a few thousand volts of electrical current delivered through a couple of brass nodes.

Indeed, once his Bully Buzzer was ready, Ogden Trumbull had *such* a surprise in store. Make that, a shock.

Literally.

Archie smiled.

Brains beat brawn every time.

CHAPTER EIGHTEEN
Dracosaurus Silvanus

"Ooo-weee! Look at 'em down there. Sunnin' like a bunch o' gators," Tex whispered as they all peered down from the rocky lookout point.

Jake's heart pounded as he, too, stared, motionless and sweating from his hike. Halfway down the mountain, a rocky outcrop overlooked a secluded bend in the peaceful river that wound through the valley.

On the flat rocks beside the water, he beheld the magnificent but terrifying sight of a dozen dinosaur-like dragons lounging in the sunshine, relics of primordial history.

The visitors crouched down behind the boulders, staring at them.

"Whatever we gotta do, let's try not to wake 'em up from their siesta."

"Agreed," Dr. Plantagenet murmured.

"Incredible, aren't they?" Derek glanced at Jake, grinning. He had always been an ardent dragon enthusiast.

Jake nodded in reply, hoping that his dread of the giant reptiles didn't show on his face. Then he looked again at the clan of beasts below.

The dracosaurs were a dark olive-greenish color for the most part. Some had a dappling of brown or gray spots along their backs— camouflage, no doubt, to help them blend into the forest better.

All sported nubby horns on their heads and twitchy, stand-up ears. They had yellow eyes and sinister large fangs. The stumpy, vestigial wings on their backs, however, lent them a comical air at odds with their wicked crocodile smiles. The dracosaurs were a non-flying species of proto-dragon. The wings, Dr. Plantagenet had explained, were only used to help them with balance, for they were swift runners and long leapers.

Jake was glad to see they were nowhere near as large or terrifying as Old Smokey, the gigantic, solitary, treasure-hording black dragon Jake had seen in Giant Land. The largest dracosaur, by contrast, was about the size of a draft horse, a bit taller at the withers than the top of Jake's head.

Aye, he told himself in relief, *these beasties aren't very scary at all.*

Of course, it wasn't nighttime yet, when the dracosaurs hunted in packs...

But for now, they were placid.

Jake pulled Archie's subcompact camera out of his waistcoat and started taking pictures for his friends, as promised.

By the light of the afternoon sun, the dragons were clearly off-duty from terrorizing the forest animals. A few of the dragons slept contentedly, flopped down on their bellies on the flat, sun-warmed stone, twitching away an insect now and then with a flick of a too-small wing.

Some lay on their backs like huge, dozing dogs, legs sprawled, stubby forearms in the air, their stumpy wings spread out beneath them. One let its tail trail lazily in the water while it gnawed its front claws, sharpening them. Another had curled up like a sleeping cat, puffs of smoke rising from its nostrils with every snore.

Jake smiled to see a baby one the size of a Great Dane splash into the water and catch a fish, swallowing it whole in one gulp.

But one dracosaur had separated itself from this idyllic group, taking shelter in a large clump of underbrush. From inside the bushes came a miserable groan.

"I think that's your patient," Derek whispered to the Green Man.

The baby dragon in the river, concerned about its relative's sorrowful moan, bounded over to the one hiding in the bushes.

It made a funny little sound and nosed the edge of the underbrush, as if to say, *Are you all right in there?*

But the dracosaur in the bushes was in no mood for curious youngsters or for sympathy. It thrust its head out of the bushes and roared, snapping its fangs to scare the little one away.

The baby screeched and ran to the smoke-snoring dragon— apparently its mother—and curled down beside her, still cowering.

"I see what you mean about the pox making them grumpy," Maddox remarked.

"She's a feisty one, all right," Tex drawled.

Dr. Plantagenet nodded. "Definitely our patient. Did you notice the patch of orange scales on her cheek?"

"How can you tell it's a she?" Jake asked.

"The females have the spots. Males have a row of blunt dorsal spikes from the top of the head to the tip of the tail, like that one over there. I didn't see any spikes on our unhappy friend. It's just as well she's telling the others to leave her alone," he added. "That way, they might not catch it. Still, we'll quarantine her for a few days just to make sure the others stay healthy."

"And how are we going to do that, exactly?" Maddox inquired with a skeptical look.

Dr. Plantagenet studied the dragons' immediate territory. "They'll panic if we put her too far away from them. They are group animals, after all. If we can just herd her over into that second basking area... You see those flat rocks farther down the river?"

"*Herd* her? Sounds like an excellent way to get eaten," Jake muttered.

The Green Man ignored him. "That should keep her away from the others and still give her access to the river for drinking water and fish to eat. The trick is convincing her to go there so we can set up a barrier between her and the others."

"*Well,*" Tex said slowly, scratching his chin, "I can lasso the ol' gal. Git her movin' in the right direction."

Derek nodded. "I'll help you. Once we get her into the quarantine area, Munroe can keep her distracted. I'll calm her down with an old trick I know that works on all sorts of reptiles, then Dr. Plantagenet can give her the medicine."

"What sort of trick?" Jake asked, furrowing his brow.

"There's a simple way to activate a natural response in lizards that puts them into a trance. You'll see. I could explain it, but you won't believe it until you see it with your eyes, anyway."

He tilted his head curiously. *How bizarre.*

"Once she's out, you'll have about half an hour to administer the medicine," Derek told the doctor.

"Please don't tell me you have to give that thing a shot?" Jake said.

"Fortunately, no," the Green Man said with a slight shudder. The thought alone made him look like he might go into tree mode again, but he shook it off with a will. "It's a topical ointment. A five-percent carbolic acid solution, mixed with a little powdered calendula—an excellent antiseptic herb. I'll have to spray the medicine on all her affected scales with this."

He reached into the rope-sack and pulled out a strange contraption that looked like an oversized plant mister. It had a copper nozzle and pump fixed atop a thick glass jar. The medicine was inside. The sprayer sat in a leather holder with a sturdy strap, which Dr. Plantagenet put over his shoulder.

"What can I do to help?" Maddox asked.

"You boys will be in charge of setting up the barrier behind the dragon once we've moved her into the quarantine spot. Find two good strong trees to tie the rope netting to. That's what I brought this for."

Dr. Plantagenet removed the last few items from the sack, then he untied a couple of key knots in the rope netting. Once they were freed, he showed them how it could be unrolled like a very large, sturdy swath of fisherman's net, perfectly suitable for using as a barrier.

"That's clever," Jake said.

"Are you sure this rope is strong enough to hold back a dragon?" Maddox asked.

"Can't you smell it? I soaked it overnight in stinkberry juice, same as our bracelets. An old trick from medieval days. Besides, I don't think the others will really want to go near her with her acting so hostile. They can usually tell when something's wrong with one of their own."

"Now, listen up, you young'uns." Tex tipped his hat back and stared sternly at Jake and Maddox. "When you boys go down there, you keep your shields in hand in case one of Miss Grumpy's cousins takes an interest."

"Yes, sir," said Maddox, but Jake was only just absorbing the fact that the adults actually wanted him to go down there.

Near the dragons.

"Um, I'd like to live to see my fourteenth birthday," he said gingerly.

"Ah, they won't bother you. You can see how inactive they are in the daytime," Derek said. "They feed at night."

"But you said they're very territorial."

"We're not dragons," Derek said. "Besides, these fellows are pretty well used to people from the Order coming through."

The Green Man nodded thoughtfully. "I daresay they can probably sense we're here to help their ailing pack member. Even I will admit that dragons do seem to have an ancient wisdom all their own."

"When they're not biting your legs off," Jake said under his breath.

"I can put up the barrier myself if you're afraid," Maddox offered.

Jake scowled at him, cheeks flushing. "I'm not *scared*. I was only...joking."

Derek smiled and looked away.

"If anyone's gonna get eaten, it's gonna be me," Tex declared as he stood up. "In which case, she better like spicy foods 'cause I take Tabasco sauce in my coffee."

"Yee-haw," Jake encouraged him, ignoring Maddox.

Tex rumpled his hair in reply.

"Be careful, Munroe," Derek advised. "Don't do anything crazy. Like the boy said, you're our ride home."

"Don't do anything crazy, he says!" The cowboy scoffed. "I'm about to lasso a danged dragon here! Shoot. You just back me up quick with that weird lizard trick o' your'n."

"Absolutely."

Tex took a deep breath, pulled his hat down lower over his narrowed eyes. He eased the loop of rope off his belt and sneaked down off the ledge.

"He's insane," Jake whispered.

"That's a Lightrider for you," Dr. Plantagenet remarked as they all looked on.

Derek took off his coat while he waited, and the boys picked up their shields. Maddox took the bundle of rope netting with a nod to Jake; their task would require them to work together. Dr. Plantagenet pumped the nozzle of his medicine sprayer to make sure that it, too, was ready to go when the moment came.

Below, Tex crept down the slope as silent as a sidewinder snake. Alligator boots planted firmly in the dust, step by step, he cleared the area where the other dragons were relaxing and started closing in on the underbrush.

He shifted the rope in his hands, then started twirling the knotted loop in his right.

They heard him let out a low whistle. "Come on outta thar, lil lady." He kicked the edge of the underbrush, startling the grumpy dragon.

It rose upright on its hind legs out of the thorns and shrubberies and promptly roared at him.

Jake stared, riveted, in disbelief as Tex threw the rope.

It landed across the dragon's snout.

One blast of fiery breath would have burnt the rope to cinders, but Tex tugged and whipped it somehow, snapping the dragon's mouth shut.

The tall, scaly beast blinked, looking more astonished than even Jake was.

Then three things happened all at once: The dragon turned tail and fled toward the basking area; Tex held onto the rope with a wild *"Yee-haw!"*; and Derek leaped off the ledge and chased after them.

As he ran past, all the other dragons looked on with lazy curiosity.

Jake's heart thumped in his chest.

"Let's go," Dr. Plantagenet whispered. He and the boys hurried down the slope, praying none of the other dragons decided they were in the mood for lunch.

Thankfully, they cleared the main area without incident. As they rushed past, the dracosaurs glanced over, but only the baby had the energy to come bounding after them to find out what they were up to.

"What about these two trees here?" Maddox asked quickly, pointing. "Do they look strong enough?"

The Green Man nodded. "Put up the netting and then come round on this side of it, please!"

"Gladly," said Jake.

He took one end of the rope and Maddox took the other. They ran toward opposite trees, rolling out the netting between them to block the wide, well-worn path the dracosaurs had made traipsing back and forth between their basking areas. Though the rope netting easily spanned the width, the boys had to climb up the trees to tie the fifteen-foot-high barrier in place.

The rope smelled awful, but if that was what it took to keep the colony clear of their infected sister, Jake was glad to hold his breath.

"Make sure you tie the knots tight enough!" Maddox ordered.

Jake sent him a sharp glance. *Don't tell me what to do.*

Meanwhile, in the quarantine area, Tex had his hands full keeping the large, scaly patient from slashing him to bits with her claws. The sick dracosaur was clearly in no humor for this nonsense.

When Jake had tied the last knot securely into place, he started climbing down, but stopped and gaped when he saw the positively mad thing that Derek Stone did.

While Tex fought with the lassoed dragon from the front, Derek vaulted up onto the creature's back. Only the battle prowess of a master Guardian allowed him to keep his balance on the bucking dragon.

"Now!" Derek yelled.

Standing back at a cautious distance, the Green Man tossed Derek's coat up to him. The Guardian caught it in one hand, then ran up the dragon's back and threw his coat over the animal's head, covering her eyes.

She didn't like that.

At once, she started thrashing back and forth, but instead of flying off, Derek launched himself at her head, holding on in a sort of bear hug. He wrapped his legs around the dragon's neck to hold on better and placed his hands over her bulging lizard eyeballs beneath the coat. He started rubbing her eyes gently.

What the—?

As the boys scrambled down and hurried around to the safer side of the barrier, they could hear Derek speaking soothingly to the creature.

"Calm down, girl. Easy now, you're all right. You'll be fine. Atta girl..."

Maddox shook his head.

Jake's mouth was hanging open as he stared.

To both boys' shock, the dragon started settling down as Derek pressed on her eyeballs.

"That's right, nice and easy now..."

A moment later, the dragon sank downward, then flopped onto her belly with a groan, out cold.

Tex started laughing, sweat pouring down his face. "Nice work, Stone. You're up, Doc. You boys get that barrier tied up good?"

"Yes, sir."

"Then come on over here! Y'all stay close."

They went running over to the cowboy.

"That was brilliant," Jake said.

Tex grinned. Derek smiled but held his position straddling the dragon, still massaging the comatose creature's eyeballs.

"That's the response you mentioned? She's in a trance now?"

"As long as I keep applying pressure to her eyes." Derek nodded toward the Green Man. "See if Doc needs a hand."

The boys hurried over to Dr. Plantagenet, who had begun squirting the medicine on all the different places on the dragon's body where her scales had turned rust-orange. In the worst spots, a few scales had fallen off, with blisters on the skin underneath.

"Poor thing." The Green Man winced sympathetically as he doused the sore spots with the antiseptic solution. "Keep a hold on those eyeballs, Stone. This medicine may sting for a minute. The pain could wake her up."

"Oh, I think she'll be out for a while," he replied, but he did as the doctor asked.

Thankfully, the dracosaur remained inert.

"Anything we can do to help?" Maddox offered.

"If you could lift the tail up for me here, she's got a bad patch that looks like it wraps all the way around it."

Maddox looked a little startled by this request, but hurried to assist the veterinarian. Jake watched, bemused, as the serious young Guardian bent down and gingerly lifted the unconscious dragon's limp, heavy tail up off the ground. The tip still sagged a few yards away, but Dr. Plantagenet got right to work squirting the sore patch with the medicine.

Jake decided to go make sure that the barrier was holding and the other dragons were keeping their distance.

All seemed well, but blimey, the dracosaurs looked so much bigger from the ground level than they had from the lookout point up on the ledge. Jake glanced around uneasily, wondering if there was another path they could take back to the waypoint. Nocturnal or not, waltzing past all those lounging monsters really seemed like tempting fate.

Satisfied that the net was in good order, he turned around and was heading back toward the others when he suddenly felt a tingle of awareness at his nape and had the strangest sensation of being watched.

He whipped around—and startled the creature studying him.

It dove off its perch atop a nearby boulder with a small "eek!" and disappeared, but not before Jake had glimpsed it.

What?! It can't be...

That was certainly no dragon.

He dashed over to the boulder for a closer look. But the spider— hairy, white-spotted, and the size of a dinner plate—had vanished.

I know that spider...

"Malwort?" Jake was quite sure he had heard the thing say *"Eek."* Generally spiders were not supposed to talk, but there was one species he knew of that did: the arachno-sapiens.

Very rare.

Indeed, his Uncle Waldrick was the only person Jake had ever met who had owned one as a pet.

"Malwort?" he repeated slowly. "Is that you?"

"Uh-oh," said a clinkety, arachnid voice from somewhere in the weeds behind the boulder. "N-no Malwort here. The Jake is scary. He will squish me."

Jake's mouth tilted. He folded his arms across his chest. "I'm not going to hurt you. Come out now. What are you doing out here in the middle of nowhere?"

Silently, Malwort crept out of the weeds. At first, his ten beady eyes peered over the edge of the boulder fearfully.

Jake just stood there, waiting.

Moving with caution, Malwort scuttled atop the rock, but looked around nervously, ready to leap to safety at any moment.

"Well? What are you doing here?" Jake repeated.

"Malwort follow Master to the dungeon. Most bravest adventurings. Very, very far."

"Well, you'd better be getting back to him," Jake said stiffly. "Give him my regards."

"Malwort doesn't wants to go back!" the spider burst out, sounding slightly hysterical. "Malwort doesn't loves Master anymore! Master baaaad."

"Oh, you finally figured that out, did you?"

Blimey, Uncle, Jake thought. *Even your weird little pet can't stand you anymore.*

"Bad Master is mean. He called Malwort bad for not bringing him the shiny key hanging on the nail when the guard-man go sleepy-sleepy. But Malwort doesn't wants Master to escape from his cage!"

"Why not?"

"Because! If Master stays in his cell, then Malwort can have Master all to himself. Be together forever, happy-happy. But Master is *baaad*," Malwort said, shaking his odd head.

"Why? What did he do now?"

"Yell. Scream, 'Give me the key!' Even tried to squish me! So Malwort ran away very, very fast, right through the bars and out of the dungeon, into the woods. Malwort never go back to bad Master. Malwort good spider! Not deserve to get squished!"

A smile of satisfaction spread across Jake's face at the thought of Uncle Waldrick tormented by the prospect of escape—and then the obstinate spider refusing to assist. No wonder he'd wanted to squish him.

"Malwort, you made the right decision," Jake declared. "It would have been very wrong to steal the warden's key for him. You're right, he is bad, and he should stay in his cage for the rest of his miserable life."

"But what about Malwort? Can Malwort come with the Jake away from dragon land? Then the Jake will be Malwort's new master!"

"Uh, no. That would never work," Jake said.

"But Malwort *lonely*!" The spider burst into tears. "Malwort good spider, but nobody love Malwort!"

"Oh, there, there, don't cry. Sheesh, I didn't realize you were such an emotional bug."

"Bug?!" He looked utterly offended and continued weeping even more piteously. "Spiders are an arachnid. Malwort been through a lot! The Jake don't understand. Malwort needs a new home!"

"Hey, you tried to eat my friend Gladwin, remember?"

"Oooh, fairy blood is fizzy-sweet! Like root-beer," he crooned, soothed only briefly by the reminder of this delicacy before he started crying again. "Malwort hate dragon land. Malwort is *lost* here! Big dragon feet everywhere to squish me. It's terrible!"

"All right, all right!" Jake exclaimed. He wouldn't want to get stuck out here, either.

Poor Malwort had got used to living in a mansion with the previous Earl of Griffon. He'd never survive out here in the wild. "Maybe you can go back to the magical menagerie with Dr. Plantagenet, the Green Man over there. He's very nice. He runs a zoo at Merlin Hall full of, er, unusual creatures like yourself. There's lots of new friends for you there."

The tearful spider perked up. "Friendses?"

"Aye, I think you'd have a lot in common with the Fairy Stinger, actually. He's a sort of scorpion."

"Ooh! Scorpions is my cousinses!"

"Well, hang on a minute. I'll go ask him for you. Don't disappear again," Jake advised. "We'll be leaving in a moment."

He hurried over to ask the Green Man if there was room in his zoo for one more.

"Arachno-sapiens? Why, I would be honored," the veterinarian said when Jake explained the situation and pointed at Malwort waiting nervously atop the boulder.

Once the veterinarian finished treating the dragon, he gathered up his things and then went and greeted the spider. Malwort seemed pleased to meet someone who understood how very rare he was. Dr. Plantagenet opened his black doctor bag and offered it to Malwort.

Hesitantly, Malwort glanced at Jake, all ten eyes full of uncertainty.

"Go on, you can trust him," Jake said, and Malwort crawled into the doctor bag and snuggled himself down.

Jake and the Green Man headed back to the unconscious dragon's side, where Derek was still putting pressure on her eyeballs through the coat. Likewise, Tex was still holding onto the rope in case she woke up. Maddox stood by waiting to help wherever he was needed.

"Right, then," Dr. Plantagenet said. "If everyone's ready, we can take the restraints off our patient and head back to the waypoint. I certainly want to be out of these woods before it starts getting dark."

Tex nodded toward the trees on their left. "Noticed another trail over yonder. Should loop back up to the main path. Might as well avoid goin' past the rest of the colony if we have a choice."

Everyone agreed.

"You all go on ahead in case the drac wakes up faster than expected," Derek said. "She should be groggy for another fifteen minutes, but I want everybody clear before I take this coat off her eyes. I'll catch up."

"You sure you don't want me to stay and hold the rope in case she gets feisty?" Tex offered. "Greenie can lead the boys back up to the main trail."

"No, I'll be fine," Derek answered. "You can untie your lasso now."

Tex shrugged. "You're the dragon expert." He untied the knot and tugged his rope clear of the dragon's snout.

"Be careful, Derek," Jake urged.

"No worries. I'll be right behind you."

Taking leave of him, they marched into the woods single file, moving quickly to put a safe distance between themselves and the soon-to-be-woken dracosaur.

CHAPTER NINETEEN
Jealousy

The path the Green Man found through the forest, guided here and there by his brother trees, quickly proved to be a shortcut. They had to scale a steep hill, but once they reached the top, it put them right back onto the main trail, heading for the waypoint.

Behind them, things were quiet. Derek, with his keen Guardian senses, should have no trouble tracking them.

Jake heaved a sigh of relief that it all had gone smoothly. His first mission was a success. Now that their task was complete, he could finally feel the tension easing from him. *So this is the life of a Lightrider.*

The trip through the Grid had been a magnificent birthday present, but he doubted Derek had asked Aunt Ramona if it was all right to bring him here. The Elder witch probably would have been aghast at the suggestion. Even lazy dragons could be dangerous, after all. Not to mention the fact that Archie and he had almost been murdered by a half-troll today.

The thought reminded him of his question for Maddox. He paused on the trail to wait for the Guardian lad to catch up.

"Wanted to ask you something," he said as Maddox reached his side. He kept his voice low to avoid the adults' overhearing. "Why didn't you want me to tell Dr. Plantagenet about the troll boy attacking everybody?"

Maddox shrugged. "All's well that ends well."

"Easy for you to say! He could've killed somebody."

"Luckily for you, I saved your arse."

Jake scowled at the reminder.

"Look, I've heard some things about Ogden Trumbull that you might not be aware of. I think there's a chance that if you were to tell on him..." Maddox hesitated.

"What?"

"Well, from what I've heard, some of the Elders wanted him put down ever since he was a baby. This could be enough to seal his fate. I didn't think you'd want to be responsible for that, at least not without knowing about it in advance."

"Put down? You mean killed?"

"Yes. Though I'm sure they'd try to do it humanely, but..."

"Why on earth would they kill him?" Jake asked in shock. The Elders were hardly known for ordering people's deaths.

"Because he never should've been created. Wizards aren't allowed to tamper with Nature like that, taking bits of different species and patching them into one. It's considered a crime against nature."

"He is pretty grotesque," Jake admitted. "Still, it seems a bit much to order his death for something like that. I'm glad you warned me." He brooded on this a moment longer as they walked up the trail. "Can't they just train him?"

"They're trying."

"At least they could keep him in a cage."

Maddox shrugged. "He's committed no real crime."

"Attempted murder?"

Maddox laughed. "All kids fight, don't they? But unlike the zoo creatures, see, Ogden Trumbull's half-human. That means he has certain rights, like not being locked up for no cause. He can think to some extent, you know. He's somewhat self-aware. Can you imagine how it must feel knowing you are literally a freak of nature? A monster?" Maddox shook his head with a surprising look of compassion for the beastly being he had trounced. "I feel sorry for him. The older he gets, the more he understands his fate. He's got cause to be angry. He never asked for this."

"Well, attacking people isn't going to help his case. I can't imagine why he went after Archie, of all people. He's probably the most pleasant person on the whole planet. Gets along with everyone."

"It is strange. Og's not usually that aggressive." Maddox shrugged. "Maybe something about your cousin set him off."

"Don't blame Archie—"

"I'm not. Just trying to figure it out. Og probably felt bad about not being included in any of the groups earlier today."

Jake rolled his eyes. "You sound like Isabelle, always making excuses for everyone to try to be nice. It's annoying." Jake elbowed him. "Maybe you *would* make a good beau for her. I could put in a good word for you with her father. Of course, then you'd owe me."

"It's you who owe me, since I saved your neck. But I'm not interested, anyway." Maddox stared straight ahead, though he looked a little wistful. "Guardians don't have time for girls."

"Really? Tell it to the lovebirds, Derek and Miss Helena."

"That's different. Derek's a master-level Guardian. At this point, he can do whatever he wants. He's earned the right. Besides, the Order needs him too much. Me...they can drop."

"You do like her, though."

"No, I don't."

"You're a terrible liar."

"Well, I'm not as good at it as a former thief," he retorted.

Jake stopped walking. *Low blow!* "Was I supposed to starve?"

"None of my business," Maddox replied with a slightly judgmental look as he continued up the trail.

"Sorry if everybody can't be as perfect as the great Maddox St. Trinian," Jake muttered.

"I'm not perfect. I just train harder than you do. I have a work ethic. Discipline. And I don't expect everything to be simply handed to me because of my bloodlines...Your Lordship."

Jake's jaw dropped.

Maddox swaggered up the trail without looking back.

"Pompous often?" Jake fairly shouted as soon as he recovered from his shock. "So is that your problem with me—my title?"

"*My* problem with *you*?" Maddox retorted, turning around. "You're the one who's been giving me dirty looks from the moment Derek introduced us!"

"Have not!"

"Oh, yes, you have," Maddox said with a piercing stare. "And I think we both know why."

"Uh, excuse me?"

"Do I have to say it? Fine. You're jealous of me. Because you're used to being the center of attention, and you can't stand it that I can do certain things better than you. You don't have to be like that, all right? We're not in competition. You're just a little kid to me."

"*Little kid?*"

Infuriated, Jake watched him strut away. Unfortunately for

Maddox, at that moment, he happened to be walking past the giant pile of dragon poop.

A wicked grin spread across Jake's face. He was no glorious Guardian, but he did have telekinesis. A well-timed flick of his fingers from a distance was all it took to spatter the great, pompous Maddox St. Trinian with dragon poop.

The older boy froze in his tracks while Jake laughed heartily.

"If Isabelle could see you now! Oh ho, what's that smell?"

Maddox looked down at himself in astonishment, his clothes speckled with stinky dragon doo.

Unbeknownst to Jake, Isabelle had guessed right about the reason why Maddox had not gone to the ball; he didn't own a tuxedo. In fact, the clothes on his back were nearly all he had brought and among the best he had. Thus, Jake did not expect the reaction he got in answer to his prank.

The dragons they had left behind were nowhere near as terrifying as Maddox St. Trinian when he turned around, fury burning in his coal-black eyes.

Jake abruptly stopped laughing.

Indeed, he would not have been entirely surprised if Maddox had breathed out flames of fury at him.

Instead, the oh-so-controlled Guardian lad wiped a small splash of brown off his cheek. Caught in the young warrior's blazing stare, Jake took a step backward, all signs of a grin wilting off his face.

Gulp.

What was he thinking, picking a fight with a Guardian-in-training who casually talked about cutting people's arms off?

Jake's hands fisted at his sides. "I-it was only a joke," he stammered.

"Hilarious," Maddox murmured in an icy tone, then he charged him.

In the split second as Maddox came tearing down the path, Jake froze. *What do I do? Defend myself? Apologize?* He didn't really want to fight him.

"Aw, come on! I was just messin' aroun—"

He never did get to finish the sentence. The Guardian's hard shoulder collided with him, knocking the wind out of him and sending him sailing six feet off the trail.

Fortunately, the cushion of leaves on the forest floor gave him a soft landing.

Unfortunately, Maddox wasn't done punishing him yet. He yanked him up off the ground while Jake was still trying to catch his breath.

"You spoiled brat." Tossing him onto his feet, Maddox wrestled Jake's right hand behind his back—obviously, to stop him from using his telekinesis. "I'm sick of watching you get away with everything. It's time somebody put you in your place, you little runt." Maddox was shoving and marching him toward the dragon poo.

"Hey! Leave me alone! What's wrong with you?" Jake protested, finally managing to breathe again. "Can't you take a joke? Let me go! You can't push me around! I outrank you, you know!"

"You think your fancy title makes you better than me?" Maddox shot back in outrage.

Still keeping Jake's right hand immobilized, Maddox knocked his feet out from under him with a sideways kick. The young Guardian grabbed him by his legs, and the next thing Jake knew, he was dangling over the mound of dragon doo, headfirst.

"Noooo!" Jake pleaded, his eyes watering at the stench. This was a much closer look at the disgusting droppings than anyone could ever want. He winced, he grimaced, he pleaded, and Maddox darkly laughed.

"Tex! Help me! Dr. P!"

The Green Man shot a worried look at the cowboy. "Munroe, do something!"

"Aw, wouldn't dream of it, Greenie. Boys got to sort it out 'emselves. Just a part o' growin' up." Tex lit a cheroot and watched the proceedings with a chuckle.

"You're barmy!" Jake yelled at him. "Useless Lightrider."

"The Guardians have a saying," Maddox informed him, panting with exertion as he held him over the dragon poo. "You hit me, I hit back twice as hard. You flick that stuff on me, I toss you in it. What do you say? Whew, my arms are getting tired," he taunted.

"Don't you dare!" Jake bellowed, upside-down, the blood rushing to his head, the tips of his blond forelock almost touching the giant turd as Maddox lowered him another inch closer to it.

"They're too much alike, that's the problem," Dr. Plantagenet mused aloud.

"No, we're not!" both boys answered vehemently.

The Green Man arched a leafy brow.

"You'd better let me go—now!—or I swear my Gryphon will rip your guts out as soon as he's done molting!"

"I'm not afraid of your big, bald Gryphon! But your little red-haired wife, she seems pretty scary."

"That does it!" Jake bellowed in utter fury.

Better to be dropped in the poop than accused of being married to Dani O'Dell.

Although it did occur to Jake just then that he *had* kissed her on the forehead earlier today. Ugh, what the deuce had he been thinking? Must have been temporary birthday insanity.

"I demand to be released this moment!" he ordered, folding his arms across his chest as he hung upside down, and trying to sound very lordly and intimidating. Which was rather difficult under the circumstances. Nevertheless. "You do *not* want to go to war with me, St. Trinian!"

"What are you going to do, sic your ghosts on me?" Now it was Maddox's turn to laugh at him. "But very well. I suppose if you *really* want me to let you go..."

"That's not what I meant, no!" Jake flailed again, feeling the older boy's grip on his ankles starting to loosen. "Don't drop me, please!"

"Maddox St. Trinian!" a deep voice roared all of a sudden from farther down the path. "What do you think you're doing?"

Suddenly, Derek was there.

"Sir." Blanching, Maddox whisked Jake away from the giant turd and immediately set him on the ground.

Jake jumped to his feet, red-faced and scowling, brushing leaves off his clothes. "He tried to kill me!"

"Don't be absurd," Maddox muttered.

"What is wrong with you two?" Derek boomed with an angry glance from one to the other. "I turn my back for one minute and you two are at each other's throats!" He stepped between them, moving protectively in front of Jake and glowering at Maddox.

The older boy dropped his gaze. "He started it," he mumbled.

"And you lost your temper. That is a luxury a Guardian cannot afford. Besides, blast it, you're the older one, Maddox! You're supposed to be an example!"

Maddox started to object, then bit his tongue. "Quite right, sir. I apologize."

"O' course, there was the small matter of some dragon turds bein' flung in your protégé's direction, courtesy of our birthday boy," Tex drawled, taking another thoughtful puff on his cheroot.

"You cannot be serious." Derek glanced at Tex, then looked at Jake in disbelief. "What did you do?"

Jake cast about, trying to look innocent, but Derek scanned Maddox and read the true story in the flecks of dragon dung all over his clothes.

"He was being pompous!" Jake insisted.

Derek rolled his eyes, then growled under his breath in frustration and seized them both by the backs of their coat collars. "Come on!"

He thrust them forward on the path, grumbling and lecturing them by turns all the way back to the waypoint.

Look what you've done now! Maddox's angry glance seemed to say.

Jake made a face at him. Perhaps he was acting a little immature, but he couldn't seem to help it.

The worst part came when Derek ordered them both to apologize and shake hands while Tex punched in the coordinates to take them back to Merlin Hall. Neither boy wanted to lower himself to a truce; they just glared at each other. This impulsive quarrel seemed to have taken on a life of its own, and Jake didn't know how to back out of it. Plus, his pride wouldn't let him.

Maddox was staring at him like he thought him a spoiled baby. *You're just a little kid to me.*

How insulting! And yet, now he couldn't stop acting like one.

"Apologize!" Derek ordered while Dr. Plantagenet collected his things and jumped into the waiting portal.

"It was just a joke!" Jake exclaimed.

"You're not going into the Grid before you say you're sorry. You want to be treated like an adult? Act like one!"

Jake stifled his rage and ground out, "Sorry!"

"Maddox?" Derek prompted.

"Yes, sir." Jake seethed as the Guardian-in-training made a great show of his vaunted self-discipline. Even in apologizing, he was showing off.

"Terribly sorry," Maddox said in a flat monotone. "Just a misunderstanding, I'm sure."

His stare seemed to say, *See? I can even apologize better than you.*

Jake could have howled with frustration at his rival's hardheadedness. He just wanted to get back to civilization and end this vexing excursion. It was *his* birthday. Maddox never should have been invited.

"Now shake on it," Derek commanded.

"No way! I'm not touching him," Jake said. "He's got dragon doo on him."

"And whose fault is that?" Derek roared.

Maddox thrust out his hand, eager to prove himself the bigger man once again.

Oh, I can't stand you, Jake thought, but two could play that game. Aye, Jake took it even a step further, summoning up an Uncle Waldrick-like smile as he shook Maddox's hand.

They parted sharply.

"You. In," Derek ordered Jake, nodding at the portal. "And when you get there, go straight to your room."

"Fine." Without any hesitation this time, Jake jumped in and went whooshing through the Grid, still too angry to care much about all the wonder of it and so forth.

But then, a few minutes later, fate gave him one last, sweet twist of revenge.

Jake was standing on the lawn, getting over his queasiness, when Isabelle came running over with a bunch of pretty older girls—the same ones with whom she'd gone out collecting the Beltane dew. And that stuff must *work* because they all looked awfully pretty to him.

"Jake! How was it?" Isabelle greeted him, eager to hear about his adventures on the other side of the Grid. Jake eyed her friends with interest.

Brimming with curiosity, the girls had gathered around the portal when, suddenly, Maddox St. Trinian came tumbling out, rolling across the grass and landing at Isabelle's feet.

Still covered in dried dragon poop.

Innocent, pure-hearted as she was, even Isabelle couldn't help herself, automatically wincing and clamping her fingers over her nose with a low, "Ew." All the other pretty girls laughed and did the same.

Maddox squeezed his eyes shut and thumped his head on the grass in wordless humiliation.

Now *we're even*, Jake thought in satisfaction. And his roguish grin returned.

It didn't last, however.

When Derek stepped through the portal, he swept the scene before him in a glance, then offered Maddox a hand up.

He pulled him onto his feet, clapped him on the back, and said, "Good work back there. Dismissed. As for you, Jake, your behavior was atrocious. Go to your room!"

With all the lovely young ladies looking on, Jake withered slightly, his usual defiance rearing up. "Hey, it's my birthday, I want to—"

"I SAID GO!" Derek thundered so loudly it was a wonder that the towers of Merlin Hall didn't crack and fall down like the bloody walls of Jericho.

All the girls jumped and went absolutely silent.

Jake was very sure he shrank to the size of the dwarves they had recently visited in Wales. His voice was gone. His cheeks glowed like red-hot coals.

Maddox glanced back over his shoulder with a sly smile as he marched off across the grass alone.

Jake looked at Derek helplessly, then dropped his gaze, and without another word, did as he was told.

But he sure didn't like it.

CHAPTER TWENTY
Smoke on the Wind

"I hate this place," Jake grumbled at Red that night, having sneaked off to have a grand sulk in the company of his Gryphon. "I hate dragons. I hate that kid. I tried to get along with him, but he's a pompous fool! Derek and he can have each other, I don't care!"

"Becaw," his peach-fuzzed pet said sympathetically.

"Why is the whole world against me? Oh, yeah—and I hate that troll kid, too. Frankly, I hate everybody. Except for you, Red. And Gladwin. And Archie, I guess, and maybe Dani, too. I want to go home."

"Becaw?"

"Fine! I don't hate Isabelle, either, but she's been *really* annoying ever since she met Mr. Saint Perfect," he said vehemently. "Or as I prefer to call him, Mr. Poop-Stink. Heh."

"Caw," Red said with a bit of a frown about the edges of his beak.

"Hey, I can be mad if I want to. It's my birthday! At least for a few more hours. Some birthday." He let out a sigh, ignoring the fact that he was alone at his pity party.

Then a sudden, worried thought occurred to him. He glanced at the dark woods around the Gryphon's nest. "Red, make sure you warn me if you see that hideous troll coming this way. I think he lives in a cave or a hole around here somewhere. I swear, if he bothers me again, this time, I'll levitate him into the Venemous Tython's cage. See how he fares then!"

Night had fallen, and he didn't even care that he was in the zoo after dark. How dangerous could it really be after spending the day with dragons in the wild? The menagerie was kind of peaceful after dark, actually.

The Dreaming Sheep were bouncing high into the sky with the winged sheepdog chasing after them. He could hear the Venemous Tython snarling in its cage below, but he was confident the thing couldn't get out. Near the entrance, the climbing fish were chirping in the mud while Malwort was chatting away down in the Fairy Stinger's cage, getting to know his green, hairy, oversized "cousin."

On his way to Red's nest, Jake had stopped to see how the two were getting on. The arachno-sapiens had been babbling nonstop in his weird little voice, and the Fairy Stinger answered, humming its equally strange tunes.

Quite a pair they made.

He had also spotted Ogden Trumbull bedding down for the night. The half-troll hybrid had tucked himself into a long, low indentation among the rocks in the hillside.

"I sure won't miss him when we leave," he mused aloud. "I can't believe I've got to stay here for—how many more days?"

Red rested his beak on Jake's knee, but did not answer.

Comforted by his big pet's presence, Jake stroked the Gryphon's head. Baby-chick type feathers had started popping up all over Red's scalp, shoulders, and wings.

"You're looking a lot better than yesterday, you know."

"Becaw."

Jake took that to mean that Red was feeling a good deal better, too. But, for himself, his restless thoughts kept on churning.

"I mean, who does that kid think he is, anyway?" he burst out. "Where does he even come from? I wish Derek never tried to foist him off on us. He wants us to be *friends*. Isabelle insulted him today by accident. It was pretty hilarious. She wasn't trying to be mean—it just slipped out—but that should get rid of him now. I almost felt sorry for the glocky bloomin' mumper. *Almost*. Do you realize if he became her beau he would always be lurking around us? Ugh."

"Becaw?" Red asked, as if to say, *Is he really that bad?*

Jake ignored the question. "I just want to go back to Griffon Castle, don't you? This Gathering's a bore. Can you believe that troll kid nearly killed Archie and me today?"

Red growled sympathetically. "Caw!"

"No, that's all right, boy. Don't worry, we handled it. But thanks, though. All's well that ends well," he added, wryly echoing Maddox's conclusion about the debacle. He shook his head in resentment, hating the fact that he'd had to be rescued.

It did not sit well with his male pride at all.

"You know what it is?" he admitted to Red in frustration after a moment. "It's knowing I'll never be as good as that kid. It's not just skills, I mean—his character. He's as strong as Derek, and as chivalrous as Archie, and it's completely annoying, because then there's me. Truth be told, he kind of terrifies me. How am I ever supposed to live up to *that*?

"I feel like I'm walking on eggshells half the time, making it up as I go along. And you realize nobody's ever going to let me live it down that I used to be a thief. Maddox threw it in my face today, and I just... I don't know, Red. I just wanted to shake him up. Show him he's not so perfect, either. That's why I made the dragon poo fly up on him, I guess. To get a reaction. It wasn't very nice, I know, but at the time, I just wanted to get under his skin the way he gets under mine. Give him a taste of his own medicine."

"Becaw," Red answered wearily.

Jake heaved a sigh. "I know. I'm an idiot. Derek was right. I acted immature." He paused. "Maybe I *am* still just an annoying little kid. Maybe I always will be. Red, growing up is rotten."

He sat there, brooding in philosophical silence for a moment, and then absently, he noticed that one of the downy feathers on Red's shoulder looked a strange color in the lantern's glow. Not the usual scarlet, but gold.

Weird.

He smoothed the golden bud of a feather, still distracted by his thoughts. "I can't wait for Maddox to see you once you're all better," he remarked. "That glock-wit actually claimed he wasn't afraid of you. Ha! We'll see about that once you're back on your feet. Will you scare him for me? Not for serious, just for a joke."

Red didn't answer either way, serenely enjoying Jake's attention.

"Oh, and I almost forgot to tell you about this girl. Nixella Valentine—how's that for a name? She's really bizarre, but I think Archie likes her. Actually, I've had my suspicions she might be a spy for the Dark Druids."

"Caw?" Red lifted his head and looked at Jake in astonishment. His golden eyes blinked.

"She's just a young girl, Dani's age, and that would be unlikely, right? But on the other hand, doesn't it make sense that they'd send a spy nobody would suspect? I mean, she's incredibly talented as a witch. Really smart and powerful. Even Aunt Ramona was impressed." Jake shrugged. "Why not? She could be the one."

"Becaw," Red chided.

"That's true... Fooling Archie is one thing, but not too many people can fool Aunt Ramona. Say, what's that?" Jake pointed at the sky, where the winged sheepdog suddenly started barking.

Wings pumping, it raced past the moon, chasing some flying creature away from one of its bouncing sheep.

Jake had brought along the telescope Archie had given him for his birthday. Even if he wasn't allowed to talk to anybody until tomorrow, banished to solitude per Derek's orders, he could still observe others from a distance and maybe keep watch for the spy while he spent time with Red. He quickly took the telescope out of his waistcoat, unfolded the cylinder, and lifted the lens to his eye.

The dog was definitely chasing something, but it was too dark to see well. Jake flipped the special lens clockwise, clicking the night setting into place. *That's better.*

Once he found his target, he was startled to see the dog chasing away a giant black bat that was trying to bite one of the sheep.

The big, fluffy dog snarled and snapped at it, going on the attack, until the bat gave up and flapped away.

Jake shuddered at the sight of its four-foot wingspan, watching its every move. "That thing had better not come this way."

The great bat descended in swooping spirals toward the ground. But what happened next was even stranger. Following its progress through the telescope, Jake gasped aloud, for as it neared the ground, the bat turned magically into a person.

It jumped down onto the grass, a man.

He smoothed his black clothes with an elegant gesture, then strode toward the entrance of Merlin Hall, barely missing a stride.

Jake stared in disbelief, gooseflesh prickling down his arms. He barely dared blink as he watched the bat-gentleman through the telescope.

The shapeshifter or whatever he was moved at a gliding gait. He had longish, dark hair that hung past his shoulders in a sleek queue. As he neared the lanterns that glowed around the palace entrance, the people loitering there to enjoy the night air stopped and stared at him.

He did not acknowledge them but kept his sights fixed on the front doors: a man on a mission.

Why on earth would he try to bite the Dreaming Sheep? Jake wondered, watching in bewilderment.

Then he gasped and shot to his feet.

A vampire?!

He had never seen one before, but he felt very sure he was looking at one now.

But here? How? Merlin Hall was protected from evil forces, and from all that Jake had heard, the vampire race definitely fell into that category.

Guardians came running from all directions, and Jake's heart thudded to see Derek at the forefront.

The vampire (if such he was) stopped before the iron-muscled row of Guardians that closed ranks a few feet before him; he cast a sidelong glance at the others closing in on both flanks.

Derek held up his hand in a signal to belay his fellow warriors, then the master Guardian took a step forward and said something to the intruder.

Jake trained his telescope on Derek's face.

Even when his beloved mentor had been furious at him today, Jake had not seen anything approximating the rage that now hardened Derek Stone's face.

He had scolded Maddox for losing his temper this afternoon; tonight, it was his turn.

When the warrior spoke, Jake strained to try to read his lips. He was fairly sure Derek's words were something like: *"How dare you show yourself here?"*

The vampire gave an answer that did what Jake had, until that moment, thought impossible: It made Derek lose control.

Wrath broke from him.

With a fury the warrior had never before displayed, even on the day he had saved Jake from Uncle Waldrick's henchmen, Derek charged the vampire, tackled him, and slammed him to the ground. Other Guardians closed in to assist, but he snarled at them over his shoulder, loudly enough to be heard from this distance: *"Stay back! This one's mine!"*

Derek whipped a knife out of an ankle sheath hidden beneath his trouser leg.

Vampire, all right, Jake thought, his eyes widening as the new arrival sprouted fangs and vicious fingernails to protect himself. But the creature did not strike.

Nor did Derek stab him, though he held the blade up for the blow.

Instead, the two stared at each other; and when the vampire's fangs receded, Jake realized that the two men shared some sort of history.

Aunt Ramona came whisking out the palace doors just then, looked at them in alarm, and gave Derek a command.

Still glaring, Derek slowly withdrew and rose to his feet, his chest heaving with barely restrained fury.

The vampire lifted upright onto his feet with an unnatural magic, not even having to bend his knees.

Definitely a vampire, Jake concluded, amazed. But that still didn't explain what this smooth-faced monster was doing here.

The vampire eyed Derek with smug caution as the Guardian stepped back and let him pass. He followed Aunt Ramona, and they disappeared inside. Jake noticed the Elder witch had taken her wand out, just in case. That, in itself, was very rare. He had never seen his aunt utilize serious magic.

When they had gone, Derek pivoted and stalked off into the night by himself.

Well, well, Jake thought as he sat down again, astonished by what he had witnessed. *Looks like they found the spy, after all.*

* * *

In another wing of the palace, Nixie was finding out the hard way that the Vindico spell wasn't strong enough to banish Jenny Greenteeth.

Though it flattened Boneless temporarily, all it really succeeded in doing was enraging the hag. She got tangled up for a moment in the black cloak Nixie had draped over the looking glass to try to keep her out.

With a screech, she tore it off her head, then began chasing Nixie through the chamber, making glass shatter and chairs whirl violently around the room.

"Thought you could get rid of me, eh?" she cackled.

Nixie darted toward the door, passing Boneless, who floated in midair like a dried-out pancake, struggling to pop back into his three-dimensional blob form.

"Where do you really think you're going to go, stupid girl?" the hag taunted. "There's no escaping us!"

Sure enough, the moment Nixie flung out into the hallway, she heard the dire footfalls and bagpipe strains of the Headless Highlander.

"Oh, no," she whispered. She spun around just in time to see the kilted figure at the far end of the hallway exchange his bagpipes for his deadly claymore.

She drew in her breath as the Scottish warrior charged at her.

With a small shriek, she backed into her chamber and pulled the door shut with both hands; a second later, the claymore's blade chopped through her chamber door like an axe.

Lifting her hands to shield her head and eyes from the unholy whirlwind of her possessions flying around the room, she inadvertently bumped into Boneless. Half of him was dry and crispy, but the half she ran into was as cold and slimy as ever. She shied away in revulsion, then realized Jenny Greenteeth was right behind her.

"Back so soon?" the hag asked sweetly, green algae dripping off her fangs as she smiled in Nixie's face.

The Highlander kept chopping at the door.

Utter chaos overwhelmed Nixie. No longer could she hold back her screams.

"Help! Help! Somebody, help me!"

"Shut up!" Jenny Greenteeth knocked her off her feet with a small but powerful and foul-smelling whirlwind.

The next thing she knew, the witch was dangling her out the window by her wrist.

"That's enough of that! Are you trying to wake the dead, girl? Perhaps you'd like to join them?"

"No! Please, please, no—I'm sorry." Nixie flailed in terror as she saw the ground three stories below. "Put me back inside!"

"That spell of yours stung, you ungrateful brat. Try something like that again, and it's nighty-night for you."

"Just drop me if you're going to kill me. Do it and get it over with!" Nixie wrenched out.

"Oh, but this is so much more fun. Nuckalavee, fetch!" The demonic witch swung Nixie with all her might and hurled her out into the darkness.

Nixie screamed so loud the Dreaming Sheep scattered in fear above her, but the real nightmare came galumphing across the lawn below to catch her.

Skinless, blood-red Nuckalavee, a bogey-beast of Scottish children's nightmares, galloped across the lawn and leaped up, opening his gigantic mouth.

Nixie saw his gaping maw beneath her with its protruding bottom tusks and felt sure the monster would swallow her in one bite.

Instead, Nuckalavee caught her by the arm, holding fast to her with his rubbery lips rather than his razor-sharp teeth. The beast tossed her roughly onto the grass, breaking her fall rather than letting her die.

No, death would have been too easy.

The Bugganes had made it clear that they wanted her alive so they could continue toying with her like a mouse captured by a cat. How they relished tormenting her at their leisure for her "crimes."

After throwing her aside like a rag-doll, Nuckalavee galloped on into the woods, where he had been lurking, Nixie suspected, in the naiads' brook.

Through half-hysterical tears, she glanced back up at her chamber window and marveled at how high it was, how far she had fallen. But the hag had disappeared from the window. It seemed the Bugganes had had their fun with her for now. She finally remembered to breathe, though her exhalation came out sounding like a jerky, panicked sob.

She swallowed hard, trying not to cry. Sitting in the tall grass, she struggled to calm herself and make yet another plan that was sure to fail, when suddenly, the winged sheepdog flew down to her and licked her cheek like she was a hurt lamb he was supposed to be minding.

The big, fluffy dog's show of tender concern was more than she could bear. Nixie broke down crying and pushed him away. "Don't be kind to me, stupid dog, whatever you do. They'll kill you. Go away! Leave me alone."

The dog whined and sat, but Nixie curled up and wept in despair, hiding in the tall grass with her arms wrapped around her bony frame. The Bugganes had promised they wouldn't stop until they broke her spirit.

As of tonight, Nixie felt they had succeeded.

Maybe the Dark Druids were right about everything. Maybe the darkness really was stronger than the light.

Outnumbered and alone, hanging by a thread, she barely cared what happened to her anymore. Whatever light she possessed was flickering. Indeed, it was all but extinguished. And she was beginning to wonder if joining the dark side was the only hope she had for making her suffering stop.

* * *

You do your best all the time and it's still not good enough, Maddox thought, brooding as he walked across the dark meadow.

Lights flickered in the colorful lanterns ahead, and he stepped cautiously past the ring of toadstools marking the boundary of the fairy market.

It was said anything you might want could be bought here—for a price. After his humiliation today at the feet of Miss Isabelle Bradford, Maddox was wondering what *his* price was.

Perhaps, he mused, it was better to be rich and feared for his strength rather than penniless and deliberately noble for honor's sake. What good was it being so handy in a fight if he was constantly required to hold himself back? How was that fair?

It was tiresome, especially when he was left looking a fool, like today, thanks to that brat, the Order's precious golden boy.

Jake didn't seem to realize not everybody owned a bloody goldmine.

Maddox sighed as he ambled through the market. Ah, well. At least he didn't end up having to waste what little money he possessed on a set of new clothes.

He could not imagine what sort of nasty acids dragon dung contained, but as it turned out, the stuff stained. He'd spent most of the afternoon shivering on his knees beside the brook, trying to scrub it out of his clothes by hand. He had washed and rinsed his beloved black jacket and ruined twill trousers numerous times, until he had spotted a strange, hulking, blood-red creature in the brook.

Astonished, he had reached for his sword and stood to fight it in his long johns; but then a few beautiful water nymphs had swum by, giggling and pointing at him, as if he needed to be humiliated one more time today in front of females—with or without scales.

By the time the water nymphs had disappeared, so had the scarlet creature in the water. Well, there was no telling what manner of beasts might inhabit the woods around Merlin Hall.

He had gone back to the task of trying to salvage his clothes and was starting to wonder if he'd have to attend the rest of the Gathering naked, when the gnomes from his Assessment had brought him a fresh set of new clothes, nicer than the old.

He had been quite taken aback by this unexpected gift. He did not know where the gnomes had got the clothes from, perhaps they had sewn them for him themselves, but they fit. He had thanked the little fellows uncertainly for the gift, but they'd just stood there, staring up at him.

Gnomes, he had found out, really didn't say much.

But then, neither did Guardians. So, Maddox had mumbled his thanks and put them on, relieved that he wouldn't have to squander a chunk of his meager savings all because of Jake Everton's prank. After all, he'd already sent most of the money he'd earned back home to his adoptive parents.

The notion, however, of spending a little bit of his money as he pleased had got him thinking...and so, he had come to the fairy market.

He didn't really want anything for himself, but after his embarrassment today in front of Isabelle, he burned to get some of his pride back. He thought it might help him regain a measure of dignity in her eyes...those beautiful blue eyes...if he gave her some little gift.

Why he cared what the rich girl thought of him, he couldn't say. He didn't even know her. He couldn't understand why he felt so drawn to her. He only knew that her father was a lord and would never approve of him.

And besides, of course, future Guardians were not supposed to get bogged down in silly, lovesick sentiments.

And yet he could not get her out of his mind.

Probably it was pointless, he thought as he strolled among the vendors' carts and tents. What could you really buy for a girl whose wealthy father already gave her everything her heart desired? And if she already had unicorns, for heaven's sake, what else could she want?

Probably nothing he could afford.

He only knew he didn't want her to pity him, and he feared she did after his embarrassment today. By now, she probably saw him either as pathetic or a joke, but the right sort of gift might show her he was neither.

Still, Maddox was unsure if he should even be here. He knew about the dangers of buying objects from fae-folk.

On his guard, he wandered through the market, wary but fascinated by all the magical items on display. There were wands and potions; magic robes; magic pets in cages—homing pigeons, spying falcons, horned owls; magic mirrors; magic slippers; magic necklaces of all kinds; crystal balls; other glowing spheres whose purpose he could not guess; flying carpets; extraordinary clockwork gadgets; fully-trained Inkbugs; and a complete set of servitors for sale that changed from silverware into footmen and maids as needed. There were small pouches of fairy dust, exorbitantly priced, and tools of the trade for all the different varieties of talents in the Order.

As a Guardian, of course, Maddox homed in on the enchanted weapons and stopped to salivate over the highly prized Giant Silkworm body armor. Very rare, it was feather-light but impenetrable to bullets.

He tested an elven sword that could be made to glow in the dark when needed and serve as a torch; a crossbow that shot exploding arrows; a dart gun that never missed; and a shiny pistol with silver bullets expressly made for killing werewolves.

Amid the vendor stalls, fortune-tellers would read your palm for a shilling. There were many performers: strolling musicians, creepy clowns with trained animals, and grotesquely triple-jointed acrobats. Carnival games and contests drew in people everywhere; others stood around, laughing, as they watched.

Maddox waved off a barker who tried to coax him over to test his strength with a sledgehammer game. Instead, he wandered by a tanner's stall, where he stopped and looked at the array of leather knife sheaths, gun belts and holsters, saddles, tack, and various types of bags.

The leatherworker's fare looked pretty straightforward.

"So none of this is magical?" he asked.

"Most of it, no," said the mysterious, pointy-eared merchant. "But you can always take it over to the witch across the way if you want a spell put on."

Maddox nodded and continued perusing the goods, then whistled at the sky-high price on a tiny leather coin bag.

"Ah, you've an excellent eye, young master!" the merchant praised him, sidling closer. "You've found the most valuable piece in my whole collection."

"Really? This little thing?" He picked it up and looked at it. "Why? What's so special about it?"

The merchant lowered his voice. "That's a Thief's Purse, my brave lad. It comes with ten enchanted gold coins. Likely all the money you'll ever need for the rest of your days!"

Maddox furrowed his brow. "How's that?"

"The coins magically return to the purse twenty-four hours after you use them. Whoever you bought from is none the wiser."

"Isn't that stealing?"

Poof!

The Thief's Purse vanished, disappearing right out of his hand. Maddox stretched out his fingers in confusion. "Where did it...?"

The merchant pulled the purse out of his robe's capacious pocket and gave Maddox a sly smile. "Never mind, then. I can see something like this isn't for you."

"But how did it—"

"Sorry," the merchant interrupted. "It doesn't like you."

Maddox frowned, shook his head, and moved on. It wasn't as though Isabelle would want the Thief's Purse, anyway. Her cousin, the ex-thief, might have enjoyed it, but when a lad owned a goldmine, there was probably no point. *Humph.*

He sought out a more girly gift for her across the aisle, where an array of sparkly things on offer caught his eye.

Fairy jewelry.

He picked up an opal brooch on a short, choker-style ribbon, the sort the ladies liked to wear these days. The mottled pastel hues of the polished stone would have looked perfect on Isabelle: the white of her skin, the pink of her cheek, the sky-blue of her eyes.

"Something for a special lady, my brave young knight?" a wheedling female voice asked nearby.

He sent the witch selling the baubles a wary glance. "What does this one do?"

"The wearer can walk through walls or locked doors. Just press on the stone. An excellent choice for a young lady who'd like to have secret trysts with her beau and no chaperone, perhaps? Only twenty quid."

"Twenty quid!" He put it back at once as if it had burned his fingers.

"Ohh, not to her taste, dearie?"

Maddox scoffed. "Honestly. Do I look like I have twenty quid to you?"

"Well, no," the witch admitted. "But...you could barter with me for something else that you possess."

"Like what?" he demanded.

"Oh, a favor...using your particular skills, perhaps? I can tell by your bearing you are a Guardian, though not perhaps of age yet."

Maddox eyed her suspiciously. "What sort of favor?"

Slight fangs showed when she smiled. "Kill somebody for me."

"What? Daft old woman! Don't be insane."

"Very well...perhaps a bit steep. But you could maim him in exchange for the necklace. No? Would you at least beat him to the point of unconsciousness—merely leave him at death's door? Look at these muscles! It would be easy for you..."

Maddox scowled and pulled away when the creepy old thing tried to squeeze his biceps. "Good evening, madam." Bristling, he walked on, shaking his head and leaving the necklace for Isabelle behind.

What am I doing here? This place and even Isabelle herself were temptations he could not afford. Especially not now.

No, now was a time when a lad in his position had to be more conscientious than ever. Purity was strength for his kind, going all the way back to the first Guardian, Sir Lancelot, charged with keeping King Arthur out of trouble.

And that hadn't gone very well, on account of Guinevere.

Gazing at the flame of a nearby torch, Maddox could still feel the uneasiness churning deep inside him. All the Guardians had been feeling it of late.

Their deepest instincts whispered that something bad was coming. In fact, it was already here. But it wasn't a person, no...

It was bigger than that. Darker than any one individual. A shadow slowly creeping over the whole world.

He stopped walking and closed his eyes to search within himself as he had been trained to do. All he saw in his mind's eye was flames, and all he heard was the deep, ominous beating of drums. He lifted his hand to his forehead with a vague wince of pain.

When he opened his eyes again, he prayed he was wrong—he was only an apprentice, after all—but deep down, he knew he was right.

The fight was coming whether they liked it or not. It was only a matter of time, and somehow that impossible boy-earl, Jake, was going to be at the center of it all.

Derek must have felt it, too, which was why he had told Maddox to guard the Griffon heir with his life.

No one could pinpoint when it might begin, but Maddox knew deep in his bones...that there was going to be a war.

On a scale the Order hadn't seen since the Old Yew was a sapling.

Evil was rising just beyond the horizon, and someday soon, together, like it or not, they all would have to *stand*.

PART III

CHAPTER TWENTY-ONE
A Shocking Accusation

The next morning, as the four friends sat around the breakfast table, Archie showed them his finished Bully Buzzer and explained his plot to attach the nodes to Ogden's back from a safe distance via blow-gun, if only he could get his hands on one.

If all else failed, he could always make one, he mused aloud, although he still had to work out the proper adhesive to make sure the nodes stuck to Og's back. Then he described his plan to stalk the troll while he was at his chores in the zoo. The big lug was so thick-skinned that if he felt the sting of the blow-gun at all, he'd probably assume he had been bitten by a horsefly.

Then Jake described the vampire's arrival, and though he was riveted by the capture of the possible "spy," nobody else seemed to grasp the importance of this thrilling turn of events. Especially the girls. Dani wondered aloud what they were going to do for fun today while Isabelle sat silently with curlers in her hair.

In the midst of all this chatter, the door to the Bradford suite opened from the hallway beyond, and Henry stepped into the sitting room.

"Ah! Jake, good, you're dressed," he said. "I need you to come with me, chop-chop. The Old Yew wants to see you."

"What? Why?"

"Don't ask me. All I know is I've been told to bring you into the maze, post-haste." Walking over to the table, Henry grabbed a pastry off the tiered silver platter. "Why the curlers, Izzy?"

"Royal audience today," she said with a look of dread. "All the upcoming debs are to be presented to Queen Victoria this afternoon. Mother's making me go."

"Why does the Old Yew want to see me?" Jake repeated, barely knowing what to make of it.

"Only one way to find out. So let's go." He took a large bite.

Dani gasped. "Oh! I'll bet I know what it is, Jake!" She leaped out of her seat and gripped his forearm in excitement. "I'll bet they've decided they want you for the Lightrider training!" She started jumping up and down.

"Really?" He drew in his breath. "Do you think so?" His stomach flip-flopped. "Blimey. Do I look all right?" He dashed over to the mirror to make sure his neck cloth was straight and his hair wasn't sticking up in all directions.

"Er, I'm not entirely sure that's it," Henry said as he finished chewing.

"But it could be, right?" Jake asked breathlessly.

"I suppose."

"We're coming with you!" Archie vowed, already shouldering his tool-bag.

"The summons was for him alone," Henry said.

"But we can come as far as the entrance to the maze, can't we? Please?" Dani begged.

"Oh, as long as you hurry! A summons to the Yew Court is not the time to dawdle. Spit-spot!" Henry said.

So they went. Only Isabelle stayed behind on account of her curlers. "Good luck, Jake!" she called as they hurried out.

"You, too, with the Queen."

"Don't remind me," she mumbled.

Soon, they were striding out into the morning air. Heart pounding, Jake mentally rehearsed a very gracious acceptance speech, if indeed the Old Yew had called him down to inform him he had been chosen to follow in his parents' footsteps. He was really rather shocked. Not even *he* had expected his dream to come to fruition so soon.

He walked with his fingers crossed with hope, his pulse pounding with nerve-wracked exhilaration. When they reached the opening of the maze, Archie and Dani saw him off with encouraging pats on the back.

"I'm so excited for you!" she said.

"When you come back, we'll have a proper celebration," Archie promised.

"Wouldn't plan the party just yet," Henry murmured.

Right, Jake thought. *They might have a list of improvements I need to make before I'll be considered...*

No matter. He'd do *anything* to become a Lightrider, even have surgery to get one of those Flower of Life thingamabobs implanted in his arm.

"This way." Henry led the way through the maze, which was fortunate. Dizzying hope and churning worry had so muddled Jake's senses that he would never have found his way through the labyrinth alone.

At last, they came to the Yew Court. It looked much smaller today than when it had been transformed into the Field of Challenge. The Old Yew's eldest offspring, great towering trees themselves, each several centuries old, had crowded round the central courtyard, throwing long shadows across the grassy inner square.

Unlike during the Assessments, this time, they had come close enough that Jake could see the wizened faces in *their* trunks, too.

It was really rather disconcerting, in truth, having a ring of huge trees looming around, staring at him with their weird, gnarled, woody faces.

Jake gulped discreetly. He imagined this was how the Yew Court must have looked when Uncle Waldrick had been put on trial here, with the Elders for a jury and the Old Yew for his judge. A few Elders were on hand now, too: the affable Sir Peter Quince, the unpleasant Lord Badgerton, and the mysterious Dame Oriel.

Their aloof stares and the absence of any Lightriders present suddenly made Jake wonder if Dani's theory was all wrong. Not even Sir Peter was smiling, and nobody else looked inclined to congratulate Jake on a great accomplishment.

Quite the opposite. The realization sunk in slowly. *Aw, cheese it. What have I done now?*

Henry halted at a respectful distance. Jake followed suit, his heart pounding. His tutor bowed. "Greetings, Your Serene Leafiness. I've brought the boy, as requested."

"Thank you, Mr. DuVal."

Jake offered a formal bow, in turn. "You, er, wished to see me, sire?"

"Come closer, Lord Griffon," the Old Yew ordered in his wheezy, raspy, old-man voice.

Jake obeyed, careful once again not to step on the gnarled roots. His palms sweated as he waited to find out if he was in trouble for something or what.

"Now, then, boy," the ancient tree said. "If there's anything you'd like to tell us, now would be the time to speak up."

Jake stood in baffled silence for a moment. "You mean about my trip through the Grid yesterday, sir?"

"No, no, nothing to do with that," Dame Oriel interrupted sharply.

Jake glanced at her, startled and alarmed. "Sorry, I'm confused."

"Indeed." Whiskers twitching with disapproval, Lord Badgerton rose from his chair. "Let me help get you started then, Lord Griffon. Aside from being a former thief, you are known as something of a prankster, are you not?"

Jake glanced at Henry in bewilderment. There was no possible way of answering such a question without making himself look bad.

Was this about his throwing the dragon poop on Maddox yesterday? Had the big, bad Guardian kid told on him like a little crybaby? But he had apologized for that.

"Your Honors, perhaps if you could give us some idea of why we're here...?" Henry asked on his behalf, seeing Jake was genuinely baffled.

"Do you know where your charge was last night, DuVal?" Sir Peter asked, loosely interlocking his fingers.

"Yes, of course. Jake was confined to his chamber all evening on account of, er, a disagreement he had yesterday with Guardian Stone."

"And are you *quite* sure he remained in his chamber, as ordered, hmm?" Badgerton asked in his annoying, supercilious way.

"I believe so. Why?" Henry looked at Jake in confusion.

Jake's shoulders slumped as he let out a sigh.

Henry stared at him in astonishment. "You sneaked out?"

"Only to visit Red!" he admitted, glancing at the Elders. "My Gryphon. He's molting, you know. It's very unpleasant for him. I had to make sure he was all right."

"So you ignored the punishment Guardian Stone gave you," said Sir Peter.

"Oh, Jake," Henry whispered in exasperation.

"I didn't think anyone would really care!" Jake floundered, cheeks flushing. "It was my birthday! It didn't seem fair to get sent off to my room by myself!"

Dame Oriel spoke up again. "We understand you came back from your Grid adventure very angry with one of your companions on the trip. A young man you treated most unjustly."

"Unjustly?" Jake echoed with a knot forming in the pit of his stomach. This was bad. All he could think was that Maddox, the hero everybody loved, must have indeed told on him.

Of course, there had been a cluster of girls with Isabelle, and any one of them might have blabbed about the story to the rest of the Gathering, he supposed. Still...

Dame Oriel shook her head, tsk-tsking. "Ignoring your punishments. Fighting with other children. You seem to have been in quite a troublemaking mood yesterday, Jacob."

Sir Peter nodded. "We heard about your altercation with Ogden Trumbull yesterday afternoon, as well. How you used your telekinesis to turn the poor creature upside-down."

"Poor creature?" he exclaimed. In the nick of time, he stopped himself from telling them what Og had done to Archie. Recalling the whole euthanasia conversation, however, he kept his mouth shut. He was no fan of Troll Boy, but he didn't want to be responsible for getting the brute killed.

"I'm sorry," he said again, striving for patience. "I really don't understand what all this is about."

Finally, they came to the heart of it.

Lord Badgerton enunciated every word with scathing precision: "Did you or did you not steal the royal standard?"

Jake blinked. "Wait, *what*?"

"The Queen's flag, boy!" The rodent-man jabbed an angry finger in the direction of the palace. "The one flying over Merlin Hall—at least until yesterday! Today it's somehow disappeared! But I don't suppose *you* would know anything about that?"

"N-no, I-I don't!" he stammered at this news. "Sorry—why would I?"

"Cheeky!" Dame Oriel huffed.

"Now, Jake," Sir Peter said in a rather more soothing tone, "I'm sure you and your companions are young enough to find this kind of prank *most* entertaining, but we cannot have Her Majesty treated with this kind of disrespect, not at Merlin Hall. It shows the entire magical community in a very unflattering light. You realize our continued safety as the Queen's loyal subjects rests on her royal favor. And this could be taken as a pretty serious insult."

"What Sir Peter is trying to say," Dame Oriel continued, "is that we need you to return the royal flag immediately before the Queen finds out."

"Or face the consequences," Lord Badgerton said.

Jake stared at them in open-mouthed shock.

"Jake?" Henry murmured.

"You really think I did this? I don't know anything about it!" he burst out when he'd recovered from his astonishment, feeling wronged in the extreme. "Why the devil would you all automatically jump to blaming *me*?"

"Let's just say your reputation precedes you," Lord Badgerton answered with a sneer.

So. It was all because of his past as a thief. Jake was so offended he could hardly speak.

Henry turned to him. "Jake, if you had anything to do with this—"

"Henry! It never even occurred to me to steal the Queen's stupid flag! Why would I do such a thing? I only stole in the old days so I could eat! Besides, I like Her Majesty! She's my godmother, anyway!"

"All the more reason for you to think that you could get away with it, hmm?" Lord Badgerton prompted.

Jake looked around at him and the others in disbelief. They were really serious about this. He strove for calm, even as crushing disappointment flooded him. He struggled to make them understand, appealing to the Old Yew.

"Your Leafiness, Elders, I promise on my honor that I had nothing to do with this. But I assure you, I will find out who did—and make you eat your words!" he burst out angrily, red-faced and quite unable to contain himself.

"Jake!" Henry scolded him, aghast.

But he wasn't listening, outraged at their unjust accusation, not to mention his tutor's willingness to believe them. Livid, he pivoted and stormed out of the Yew Court, and the towering green walls of the magical labyrinth receded to form a straight corridor before him.

Apparently, the maze was as happy to get rid of him as he was to escape. He stalked out, too angry to care that his rude response had probably just ruined his chances of ever becoming a Lightrider.

They were never going to choose him, anyway. So this was what they really thought of him. And it hurt like the blazes. They would never let him live down his past as a thief.

But he'd show them.

He'd find out who *had* stolen the Queen's flag, and when he got it back, why, he'd shove it down their throats!

Even better, he had a feeling he knew just where to start—and as it turned out, he didn't have to look far. As luck would have it, Maddox St. Trinian was the first person he saw when he stepped out of the maze. Aye, the Guardian lad had probably planned it that way. So he could gloat.

"You." Jake narrowed his eyes as he homed in on Maddox, who was chatting with Archie and Dani on the lawn. "Get away from my friends, you traitor!" he yelled, striding toward them.

Maddox looked over at him curiously. "What's your problem?"

"You are." Well aware of how dangerous Maddox could be, Jake knocked him down by telekinesis when he was still several feet away.

Dani and Archie cried out in shock as Maddox went flying off his feet and landed flat on his back in the grass, as if an invisible giant had kicked him.

Jake smiled coldly. Rage flooded Maddox's face. He started to perform some acrobatic trick for jumping to his feet, but Jake anticipated that, having seen Derek's group practicing such moves. He used his powers to hold Maddox pinned down and immobilized; that way, he could get some answers.

"You set me up," he accused him, moving closer to loom over him.

"What are you talking about?" Maddox asked through gritted teeth.

"What's that old Guardian saying you quoted for me yesterday? 'You hit me, I strike back twice as hard?' Well, you got me. Nice try, St. Trinian. But it isn't going to work. Now where'd you hide the flag?"

"Jake, what is going on?" Archie cried, finally finding his tongue. "Let Maddox up!"

"Not until he tells me where he put the Queen's flag!"

"The Queen's flag?" Dani echoed.

"He stole it, knowing I'd be the one they'd all blame!"

She furrowed her brow and looked at Maddox, then him. "But why would he want to do that?"

"To get me back for yesterday," Jake said bitterly. "I embarrassed him in front of Isabelle, and now, true to Guardian form, he's hit back twice as hard by *ruining* my chances of ever becoming a Lightrider!"

She drew in her breath. "Oh, Jake..."

"How could you do this to me?" he shouted in the older boy's face. "This is taking it too far!"

"I have no idea what you are talking about!" Maddox boomed back.

"Yes, you do. Throwing dragon dirt on you was just a prank, but this was my whole future and now you've ruined it!"

Maddox shook his head, looking baffled, which only made Jake seethe more. He grabbed him by his lapel. "Don't play innocent with me. I know it was you. Who else could it be? We all saw your Assessment. We all know how well you can climb. Not just anyone could do it, climbing up onto the palace roof and stealing the Queen's flag right off the flagpole. Oh, but for a mighty Guardian like Maddox St. Trinian, it would be easy! Wouldn't it?" he yelled in his face.

Henry suddenly grabbed him by the shoulder and hauled him back. "Let him go!" Jake hadn't even noticed the tutor coming out of the maze, so absorbed he had been with his foe. "You are not helping your own cause here!"

"He's the one behind this, Henry, I just know it!"

"Don't be absurd." The moment Jake's telekinetic hold was broken, Maddox jumped to his feet. "How dare you accuse me of such dishonor? I'll break you in half."

"Whoa!" Dani stepped into his path, her hands up, as Maddox moved toward Jake.

"Get out of my way, little girl. This is between me and the thief."

At that comment, Henry had to hold Jake back, too. "Let me at him!"

"I'm sure this is all just a misunderstanding," Archie attempted in his most tactful tone.

"Guardians don't steal!" Maddox bellowed, pointing at Jake. "That's your expertise!"

"Well, pardon me!" Jake flung back. "But have *you* ever tried starving? Being homeless? No? Then don't preach to me about how virtuous you are, you pompous arse!"

"Insult me again, and I'll give you a thrashing you'll never forget."

"Oh, I'm terrified," Jake drawled.

"Both of you, that's enough!" Henry ordered. "Maddox, must I send for Guardian Stone?"

"I'm leaving," he growled, and then he stalked off, bristling with anger.

"What the deuce is going on?" Archie exclaimed.

Jake was stone-cold silent, his chest heaving with the aftermath of rage.

Dani looked at him, then grimaced at Henry. "I take it they didn't call him down to the Yew Court to give him a spot in the Lightrider program."

"Not exactly." Henry quickly explained to the other two what had just transpired in the maze. Jake was still too furious to recount the tale himself.

His friends paled when they heard the news.

"Oh, no..."

They looked at the roof of Merlin Hall, confirming that the flagpole indeed stood bare.

"We have to find it! Right away!" Dani said anxiously.

"Well, I don't think Maddox had anything to do with this," Archie declared.

Dani nodded. "I agree. Guardians are honest to a fault."

Jake scowled and dropped his gaze to the ground. He hated to admit it, but in hindsight, recalling Maddox's shocked reaction to the charge, he believed him, too.

He heaved a sigh. "So where does that leave me?"

"Well, obviously, it must have been somebody else," Archie said in a calm, reasonable tone.

"But who?" Jake cried, feeling rather sick to his stomach. There were hundreds of people at the Gathering. Where would he even *begin* to find out who was really responsible for the misdeed that had been, naturally, blamed on him? He dragged his hand through his hair.

Dani patted him on the shoulder. "Don't worry, Jake. We'll clear your name. We'll find the flag, unmask whoever took it, and prove it wasn't you."

"How?"

"I could turn wolf and try to track the flag down by scent," Henry offered, looking apologetic for having doubted him.

"Thanks, Henry," he mumbled. "No hard feelings."

"I'll go fetch my sister!" Archie said. "Isabelle could use her empath powers to try to sense the guilty party, while I start a proper investigation. I might even be able to scrounge up a dusting kit for taking fingerprints."

"And I'll go talk to Gladwin," Dani chimed in. "She has the Queen's ear. She can let Her Majesty know that you had nothing to do with this, in case anybody tries to say you did. You don't want your royal godmother getting angry at you, after all. Oh—and maybe Gladwin can help us search for the flag, too! A fairy can cover a lot of ground faster than we can."

"All well and good, but what am I supposed to do in the meantime?" Jake asked, too upset over the whole debacle to think straight.

"Why don't you go and talk to a few of the castle ghosts and interview them," Dani suggested. "You always say the ghosts that haunt a place tend to see everything that goes on, remember?"

"That's not a bad idea, actually," he muttered.

She shrugged. "We've got to start somewhere. Don't worry, Jake." Her smile of reassurance helped to calm him down. "Somebody out there has this thing, and we're going to find it. No matter what." She nodded at Archie, indicating they all were behind him. "We're your friends, and we're not going to let them take your dream away from you."

He stared at her for a second. "Thanks, carrot."

She nodded. "C'mon, Arch."

Then they parted ways to pursue their separate tasks.

As Jake strode back into Merlin Hall, he tried to focus on figuring out where to find the ghosts from his Assessment. Whether they would cooperate was another matter. Cheery, larger-than-life Constanzio, King of the Tenors, seemed the best one to start with, but Merlin Hall was huge. *If I were an opera ghost, where would I haunt?*

"Excuse me, isn't there a theatre somewhere in here?" he asked a gnome in the entrance hall.

The wizened, knee-high fellow pointed him down the corridor past the art gallery.

Jake nodded. "Thanks."

As he strode down the hallway, he couldn't help feeling like everyone was looking at him, thinking, *Stop, thief!* But he realized he was probably being absurd. It was just his embarrassment coloring his perception of everyone and everything. Anxious to prove his innocence, he hurried on, down the seemingly endless stone corridor before him.

He passed the main entrance to the art gallery and wove through the streams of people coming and going from the dining hall and pausing to chat with friends. The farther he went down the corridor, the more the stream of guests thinned out to a trickle.

He passed a worried man checking his fob watch, as if he were late to breakfast with someone, and a dwarf couple arguing as they trudged toward the dining hall.

The hallway stretched ahead, completely deserted now.

As he neared the second doorway that marked the far end of the art gallery, he heard a clamor coming from inside it and paused.

There was a thudding bang and a shrill cry of pain, followed by a nasty cackle of laughter.

"Wake up, little witch! Dear me, looks like you're going to miss breakfast!"

"Ow! Let me go!" someone pleaded.

What the deuce? Jake thought. Instinctively, he put his plan to find the King of the Tenors on hold and went to investigate the commotion.

Sneaking up to the doorway, he peered into the long gallery, with its red walls and white marble floor.

It was empty.

As he recalled from the other night, there were several such long galleries joined together to house the whole collection.

The echoing noises sounded like they were coming from the next chamber, so he advanced in that direction.

The paintings seemed to watch him as he crept across the first gallery, following the sound. With every step, the situation seemed more apparent. Somebody in the next room was clearly under attack.

Whether the Elders ever picked him as a Lightrider or not, he was still honor-bound to help.

"Please! Why must you torment me?"

A girl's voice. It sounded familiar.

"You know why, my dear. You brought this on yourself."

Jake peered silently around the corner. He furrowed his brow, shocked to see Nixella Valentine pinned up against the gallery wall, some ten feet off the ground.

She hung there between two paintings like a living work of art, a girl-shaped sculpture on display.

The wand she was so good with had fallen to the floor, out of reach, leaving her defenseless. She was crying, which startled Jake. Not that anyone could blame her, for, much to his shock, three horrid spirits were absorbed in the game of torturing her. What a motley crew of monsters!

Two of them, Jake had seen before. High up on the wall where she hung, the Boneless amoeba creature was floating in front of her, taunting her with its cold (according to Archie) and slimy touch.

But that wasn't all. On the ground of the gallery, waiting for her to fall down, stood the terrifying spirit he had met the other night in the woods. The Headless Highlander, glowing grayish-blue. He swung his claymore menacingly, like a warrior warming up before a battle. He didn't need a face to make his feelings clear: He couldn't wait to chop Nixie up into little bits.

Jake saw that Boneless and Headless were only the henchmen of the third figure there, running the show: a slim, spectral hag with long stringy gray hair, great fangs like a tiger, and a green ghostly glow all around her.

She was the one doing the cackling, and she was holding Nixie on the wall by a green current of energy like a lightning bolt.

Jake stared with a chill down his spine. He had never seen a ghost work magic before.

No, this was something else. *What on earth are they,* he wondered, *and why are they doing this to Nixie?*

There was no time to ponder his questions. He had to help her—for Archie's sake, if nothing else. Lord knew the skinny little witch had been nothing but rude to *him.*

It didn't matter.

Any boy as bent on being a hero as he could not do otherwise than Jake did at that moment, even though he really had no idea what he was getting into.

Ready to join the fray, he stepped into view around the corner and bellowed at the spirits: *"Put her down!"*

* * *

Nixie looked over, aghast. *No, no, don't interfere! Meddlesome boy!*

"Stop!" she tried to warn him, thinking of her curse, but the young Earl of Griffon paid no mind.

With a wild swing of his hand, he sent the nearest bench flying through the air to smite the Headless Highlander.

But the kilted apparition promptly vanished, leaving the bench to crash into the wall, knocking down a painting. Meanwhile, Boneless began floating in Jake's direction, swelling in size like a malicious fog trying to engulf him.

Nixie grimaced with impatience as Archie's bullheaded cousin quickly learned that his telekinesis was of no use against a creature made of cold, slimy mist.

Even when Jake caused a bolt of energy to rend Boneless in two, both halves kept coming. Not that there was much the blob could do to anybody, other than render them disgusted.

The *really* dangerous one, of course, was Jenny Greenteeth. She hissed as she turned toward the intruder, baring her green, algae-dripping fangs.

"Crikey," the young would-be hero muttered, dashing and weaving past Boneless.

"And who is this fine young knight come to rescue the damsel in distress?" the hag wheedled.

Jake ignored the question. "Let her go!" He brought up both hands and sent a double shot of telekinetic energy at the hag.

Nixie held her breath.

Even though Jenny Greenteeth was not a fully material being, the energetic blow was enough to make her molecules ripple, unsettled.

Nixie was impressed. Except that the moment the hag's concentration was broken, *she* went plummeting to the floor.

A sharp cry escaped her. Her teeth knocked together and a jarring pain shot up her leg the moment she landed. "Ow!"

"Nixie!" Jake ran over, crouching down beside her. "Let's get out of here!"

"I think I sprained my ankle," she forced out through clenched teeth, while the pain brought smarting tears to her eyes. "Quick, here she comes—my wand!"

Jake twisted around and dove for it, even as a nasty cackle heralded Jenny Greenteeth's swift return to full strength. "Well, me, what a talented boy! You'll pay for that."

"Quickly!" Nixie cried.

Jake snatched her wand from the floor where she had dropped it and handed it to her just in time for Nixie to deflect a nasty, green, crackling bolt of magic that the crone sent his way.

She drove it up into the ceiling, where it left a small, charred hole.

Jake looked up at it with a low curse, finally starting to ask himself, it seemed, what he had rushed into here.

"Foolish boy, thinking you're strong enough to help this useless little witch. Against me?" the hag taunted. "You've thrown your life away for nothing."

He took an angry step toward the threat. "Leave her alone! Who are you? You have no right to attack her, especially not inside the walls of Merlin Hall! This place is protected—whoa!"

He shut up abruptly and rolled out of the way to escape another drippy, green bolt of magic, pulling Nixie with him to safety.

She landed on her stomach on the floor, whimpering a bit at the throbbing in her ankle.

"Got some fangs on her, don't she?" Jake muttered under his breath while the green lightning blasted a smoking pockmark in the wall behind the spot where they had just been.

Nixie swallowed hard. "That's for ripping people's throats out, either before or after she drowns them."

He lifted his eyebrows and looked askance at her. "You don't say! That's pleasant. Well, get ready to run."

"I can't."

"Lean on me." Brow furrowed, Jake angrily zapped the hag with his telekinesis again and jumped to his feet, hauling Nixie upright as if she weighed nothing. He slung her arm across the back of his neck and half-dragged, half-carried her a few steps; leaning on his shoulder, she hobbled on her good leg, but kept an eye behind them with her wand at the ready.

Jenny Greenteeth shimmered, fighting the energy blast Jake had used on her, trying to hold her molecules together by dint of will. Likely, he had only made her angry.

"Come on, we've got to hurry!" her would-be rescuer urged, taking her toward the corner where he had first appeared.

Nixie wasn't sure she saw the point. "It's nice of you to help me, but she'll only follow us or reappear later. You should go now while you can."

He ignored the suggestion. "Why is she after you? Hey!"

He didn't wait to hear her answer as Boneless swept ahead of them and began stretching itself as tall and wide as possible, forming a thin barrier to block their escape until its mistress could rematerialize. "Move aside, you thing! What is this thing?" Jake demanded.

"It's just called the Boneless. Don't you have them in England?"

He looked at her impatiently as they kept trying to duck and weave past the creature. "You act like it's an everyday thing! Blimey! Boneless, Headless?"

"Be glad you haven't met the skinless one," she mumbled.

"Tell me you are joking!"

She sent him a dark glance.

"What the devil are they?"

"They're called Bugganes. The Scottish version of bogarts. Well, the skinless one, Nuckalavee, is technically a bogey-beast. The point is, I can't get rid of them!"

"So that's why you've been acting so mysterious," he said. "You're being hunted."

"And haunted," she said under her breath.

"You don't sound Scottish," Jake remarked.

"I'm not from there, I was only passing through." As he pulled her along, Nixie limped as quickly as possible to keep up.

"So what do they want with you?"

She shook her head, unwilling to share her deep, dark secrets with somebody she barely knew. "It's a long story."

"Right. Well, you can tell me all about it later. For now, this blob thing isn't strong enough to stop *me*." He nodded at the Boneless. "It's just a stupid cloud with a face. We can run right through it. C'mon!"

He started to pull her onward, but Nixie resisted.

"Bad idea, Jake! You saw what happened to your cousin, didn't you? The touch of the Boneless is so revolting, we'll be temporarily immobilized, and then Jenny Greenteeth will get us!"

"Got any better ideas?" he cried.

"Why, *I* do, children!" the hag cut in, reappearing with a vengeance and whooshing up behind them with a wild cackle. "The two of you can *die!*"

Before they could react, the crone hit them with a jagged green explosion that slammed them forward and sent them flying off their feet. They passed right through the slimy mist layer of the Boneless. Ahead, the hard wall waited for their crash, another fine painting slated for destruction—to say nothing of their skulls.

Nixie feared she was about to get a broken neck to match her sprained ankle. She had to do something! In that split-second, time slowed to a crawl. Jake shouted in mid-flight beside her and threw up his arms in front of his head to break his fall; but Nixie—casting about desperately for a spell to soften their landing—aimed her wand at the gallery wall and shouted, *"Culcita actutum!"*

Alas, the spell went seriously wonky.

Perhaps it was due to the clash of the hag's magic sparking off her own, on top of all the deep layers of age-old enchantment that made up Merlin Hall. Whatever the cause, a most unexpected thing happened.

Instead of crashing headlong against the wall, she and the Griffon boy went flying *into* the painting.

CHAPTER TWENTY-TWO
The Enchanted Gallery

They tumbled onto soft, damp, emerald turf and rolled, still shuddering with disgust at having passed through the Boneless. *Ugh!* Jake felt covered in cold slime.

No expert in magic, he had no idea what had just happened, but it reminded him of falling out of the portal in Romania.

As soon as he caught himself, he immediately shook his head to clear it, fully expecting another magical assault from the green-fanged hag at their backs.

Aware of Nixie on the ground beside him, Jake looked up to meet the next attack, tossing his forelock out of his blazing eyes. To his astonishment, however, he saw the hag's face pressed against a bizarre sort of window that hung in midair. *What the devil?*

With Boneless hovering behind her, she banged furiously on the window with her fist, but her curses at them were muffled by the strange invisible barrier.

Jake calmed down a bit as he realized she could not get in. Nixie had also recovered from their fall, but as she pushed up onto her knees, Jake heard a sound of dismay escape her lips.

"Oh, no..."

He did not take his eyes off the hag, just in case she got through that weird window. "Did you hurt yourself again?"

"My wand!" When she lifted it, paling, he saw that it was badly cracked, the upper part hanging off the base like a broken arm.

"Not going to do much magic with that," he said tautly.

"What am I going to do?" she cried. "I'm useless without it! Jenny Greenteeth's out there! Now I'm defenseless!"

Jake frowned at her. "Now, now. There's no need to be so

melodramatic. She can't get in, look." He pointed at the window, then glanced around uneasily. "Where are we, anyway? What did you do? Wish us away somewhere?"

Nixie looked at him, as though startled that he hadn't figured it out.

"I don't do magic! What?"

"Um, Jake... I think...we're in the painting."

He stared at her as if *she* had gone mad. "How can we be in a painting?"

Before she could reply, Jenny Greenteeth punched the window angrily.

"I'm pretty sure that's the picture frame," Nixie said, nodding toward it.

He squinted at it in confusion. "Nah..."

"You may be safe in there for the moment, little witch, but don't worry," the horrid hag wheedled. "You have to come out sometime, and when you do, I'll be waiting. For both of you!" Then she spun around with a creepy, unnatural motion and zoomed away, dragging Boneless with her.

Nixie gulped.

Jake looked askance at her. "You've got interesting taste in enemies. Whew! Dashed lucky I came along."

Instead of thanking him, she huffed. "Don't you ever stop bragging?"

"What? I'm not bragging. I just saved you!"

"Actually, I saved *you*," she retorted. "Without my spell just now, we'd both have fractured our skulls, as was her intent."

Jake stared at her, taken aback. "Talk about ungrateful."

"You shouldn't have interfered!" Nixie yelled at him. "You had no business barging in like that. Now they're going to kill you, too!"

"Ha. No, they're not." He frowned at her, then jumped to his feet. "They can try, but trust me, I've already dealt with worse. Hey, did you see that?" he asked all of a sudden, turning quickly.

"See what?" Nixie mumbled, still cross at him.

"Not sure... Barely glimpsed it out of the corner of my eye. It just went running by the edge of the pasture. There, along the stone fence. An animal of some kind, I think."

She straightened up. "Did it look dangerous?"

"No, I think it was just maybe a...dog or something."

"Oh," she said uneasily.

Jake was surprised by how timid the usually-tough girl was acting now that her wand was broken. She really seemed to think herself helpless without it. So, this was why Aunt Ramona always warned against anyone becoming overly dependent on magic.

He shrugged off her problems. She could easily buy a new wand from the fairy market. He had problems of his own. Ghosts to interview. A reputation to save. And how the deuce were they to get out of here?

Hands on his hips, Jake glanced around at the rural autumn landscape they had somehow landed in. A pretty boring picture, in his view. Not much of interest to look at, just a typical English pasture in the countryside, with squat stone fences and thorny hedgerows, their leaves reddened with the season. A babbling brook meandered past nearby, and a grove of brilliant-hued trees filled the dip between hills.

Still, he was surprised at how convincing the world inside the painting was. He could smell the unmistakable scent of autumn on the crisp, chilly air: a mix of homey hearth fires burning in the distance and the pleasant pungency of decaying vegetation.

"Huh," he grunted philosophically after a minute. "Can't say I've ever been in a painting before. Didn't even know they had a spell for that." He looked at Nixie. "Do you do this often, then? Go flying into paintings?"

"No, of course not!" She gave him a withering look, as though she could not fathom the thick-headedness of boys.

"Touchy!" he chided, taken aback.

"Well, I didn't know this would happen! I can only guess it was all of the magic combined that landed us here."

"Fine, never mind, then. Let's figure a way out and get you to a doctor." He reached down to help her up, but she knocked his offered hand aside.

"I don't need your help! Not now, not ever! Don't you get it?"

"Blimey," Jake muttered. *Girls are so moody.* He gave her a reproachful frown, for really, that was no way for a damsel to talk to her rescuer.

On the other hand, she *was* a witch, he remembered. They weren't really known for being friendly.

Shrugging off her ingratitude, he turned his attention to getting out of the painting and started toward the strange window hanging in midair at about chest level.

Nixie let out a huge sigh as he walked away. "Jake? Jake!" she repeated insistently.

"What?" He stopped and turned around with an impatient look.

"Sorry—I don't mean to be so cross. It's just I'm so monstrously tired because of the Bugganes. Beyond all toleration. They're trying to drive me insane by depriving me of sleep."

"Oh." That would explain the dark circles under her eyes.

She flopped onto her back on the grass and shut her eyes as though she could fall asleep right there. "They threw me out of my bedroom window last night, three stories up."

His jaw dropped. *"What?"*

"I thought I was going to die. I almost wished I would've."

He went back to her in shock and crouched down to be nearer to her eyelevel. "They *threw* you out a window? Are you serious?"

"No, I'm joking," she snapped, sitting up again and shooting him another look of annoyance. "I'm just telling you what happened."

"How did you survive?"

"Nuckalavee caught me outside before I hit the ground. The skinless one I mentioned. He's the worst one of the lot. He's horrible. Thankfully, he doesn't come inside much 'cause he's a bogey-beast."

"What does he look like?" Jake asked in concern.

She shrugged. "Nuckalevee's sometimes called a water-horse, but he's not the nice kind—he's a monster. He's blood-red 'cause all his muscles and tissues are showing on account of his having no skin."

Jake stared at her, aghast. "I think I've seen that thing lolling in the stream where the naiads like to swim. Will he hurt them?"

She shook her head. "He might if they get too close, but as a water bogey, he'd at least have some respect for them."

"No skin... He sounds disgusting."

"Try having him grab you in his mouth." She sighed, looking exhausted and small. "Last night, when I finally got away from them, I went into the art gallery to look at the paintings for a while 'cause it makes me feel better. But as tired as I've been, what with them tormenting me every night, I fell asleep right there on the bench. That's where they found me this morning, a little before you did. They started right back in where they left off, pushing me around."

"How long have they been torturing you like this?" Jake asked angrily.

"Months."

"Have you told anybody to try to get some help? Like the Elders?"

"I can't! Jenny Greenteeth put me under a curse!" she burst out. "Anyone who tries to help me gets killed! Don't you understand? That includes you now! That's why I got so angry at you. You can pretend to be as cocky as you like, but trust me, you're no match for them in the end. I thought *I* was, but now, look at me. I'm a wreck!" Her coal-black eyes filled with tears, and the protest on the tip of Jake's tongue dissolved.

Yes, he was a thoroughgoing blockhead when it came to girls' emotions, but even he could see she just needed to talk. Get her troubles off her chest.

Nixie shook her head, turned aside, and quickly wiped away her tears, though he had already seen them. "I've been trying so hard to keep my problems to myself. But then you came barging in, pretending you're a hero."

Well, I am. Jake frowned indignantly. At least, he was trying.

"And now you're going to get murdered, the Order's golden boy, and it'll be all my fault. I'll probably get banished from Merlin Hall for this, thank you very much. Why didn't you listen? I told you to stay out of it. I told you to leave me alone, but you ignored me. So don't blame me when the Bugganes pick their time and place and come to kill you. When you're a ghost yourself, maybe then you'll learn to mind your own business!"

Crikey. Jake took a moment to absorb all this while Nixie looked away and strove to get her understandably frazzled emotions under control. Though it took all of his considerable bravado, he ignored a vague twinge of alarm at her dire words.

"I am not going to get murdered, I promise you," he said calmly, doing his best to sound as fearless as Derek.

"They've done it before. They killed my cat! Poor Midnight."

Jake was taken aback. "I'm sorry, that's terrible."

Nixie sniffled. "Jenny Greenteeth drowned her."

"Well," he said after a moment, "I am not a cat. I'm a person."

"They almost killed my friend, Amelia, too. I had to pick a fight with her for no reason and tell her I didn't want to be friends with her anymore before they'd leave her alone. They made her get pneumonia!"

"Nevertheless." Jake gave her a stern look. "I'm helping you and that's final. Got it?"

"Jake—"

"Did it ever occur to you that the reason they beat you up so badly is because you're trying to take them on alone? There's always strength in numbers, Nixie. You'd be surprised at how well me and my friends manage against all sorts of unpleasant entities. We've dealt with giants, gargoyles and—other things." He stopped himself from mentioning Garnock.

Instead, he counted off his other victories on his fingers to assure her (and himself) that he knew what he was doing. "A sea-witch, my uncle's insane servitor henchmen, a number of dangerous ghosts, a dragon—oh, did I happen to mention an angry Norse god?"

She rolled her eyes and looked bored at his accomplishments.

Jake scowled. "Point is, we are hardly going to be intimidated by that sorry lot out there, so you might as well accept our help."

"It's bad enough that you're already a part of it, but don't drag Archie into this," she finally said after a long, weary pause.

"Aha, so you *do* like him!" Jake grinned from ear to ear.

The vampire-pale girl blushed to an almost-normal flesh-tone color. "If you care about your friends, you mustn't risk their necks. That's all I'm saying!"

"First of all, they'd be furious with me if I didn't bring them in on this. They're not cowards. They love adventures nearly as much I do. Second, a genius is an awfully good chap to have on your side. You'll see." He grinned at her again, gloating with his knowledge of her interest in his brainy cousin.

She might be as ornery as a little green garden snake, but if she fancied Archie, then at least the chit was an excellent judge of character.

"Now, let's get out of here," he said firmly, feeling very much the man in charge (and loving it). "I reckon we climb out this way. First, let me make sure they're gone."

She continued muttering about his stubbornness under her breath, but now that he understood the truth about her mean façade, he found it rather amusing. She had fooled everyone—well, except for Archie—into thinking she was nasty and cold, a typical, sharp-edged witch.

In light of his present understanding, Jake found he actually admired Nixie for her bravery and her good intentions about protecting others from her curse. It was sad to realize she only acted like a gloomy grump to drive away anyone who tried to befriend her.

Well, the poor girl had been through enough. He vowed to himself that he and his friends would see her freed from this curse, and those horrid Bugganes stopped and punished. If only Red were back in fighting shape...

As Jake marched to the picture frame window, another thought occurred to him. *What about everybody thinking I'm a thief? When will I figure out who took the Queen's flag?*

But he shrugged the matter off as unworthy of the sort of selfless hero he desired to be one day. This was more important. Better he should lose his reputation than poor little Nixie lose her life.

He hid a wry smile as he thought of how much the tough girl would hate being called *"poor little Nixie."*

Arriving before the window, his first order of business was to check and make sure the Bugganes had indeed vacated the gallery and were not lurking out there, waiting for them to emerge so they could renew their attack.

Peering through the thick, glass-like pane, Jake could see the bench he had overturned and the portrait he had knocked off the wall. He winced, hoping it wasn't too badly damaged. But when he leaned closer, trying to get a better view down the long gallery, he bumped his forehead on the same invisible barrier that had kept the Bugganes from getting in. He rubbed his brow, scowling.

That was his first inkling, however, that getting *out* of the painting might present more of a problem than either he or Nixie had anticipated.

A sudden wave of uneasiness washed through him. He slowly turned around and looked at Nixie's broken wand. It had got them *into* the painting somehow, but cracked into its broken-arm shape, he doubted it was fit for duty now.

No, magic had got them in, but it clearly wasn't going to get them out of this. Turning back to the gilded frame, he examined it, running his hands over the carved wood, knocking on the glass. It seemed solid.

"I hope nobody's out there strolling around the art gallery and sees us climbing out of the painting," Nixie remarked wryly. "That would be pretty funny."

"Aye, and if anyone sees us, we'll probably get in trouble for this, too—and some of us can't really afford it at the moment." As he spoke, Jake continued trying to figure out the trick of the picture-frame window. He took hold of the bottom and strove to lift it open like a regular window, but it wouldn't budge.

"I'm cold."

"Uh, Nixie? I think...we've got a problem."

"What?" She was lying on the grass again, half-asleep and shivering a little in the autumn chill.

"How do we get out of here?"

She didn't move. "How should I know?"

"Well, you better help me figure it out because I am beginning to think we might be trapped."

"Trapped?" She sat up, furrowing her brow. "Here, let me take a look." She struggled to her feet, wincing with pain, (he didn't dare offer to help her stand up), and limped over to investigate the matter herself.

She repeated the same motions he had performed, knocking on the pane, then tracing the joints with her fingertips, searching for a latch.

"It doesn't want to open," she admitted.

"That's what I told you. Face it," he added darkly, "we're stuck inside this painting."

She scoffed, refusing to accept it. "There's got to be a way out."

"Maybe I should break the glass. I'll go find a rock from that stream to smash it with—"

"Absolutely not!" She put an arm out to stop him. "We can't risk breaking the da Vinci barrier."

"Huh?"

"I mean, even if you *could* physically shatter this thick, magical glass, which I doubt, it'd ruin the whole purpose of the collection. The Elders would lock us up and throw away the key! They don't call it the Enchanted Gallery for nothing, you know. We're going to have to find another way."

"I didn't know they call it the Enchanted Gallery, and what's a da Vinci barrier?" Jake muttered.

She stared at him. "You didn't read the plaque?"

"What plaque?"

"The big brass one by the entrance! That tells the history of what all this is about?"

Jake pressed his lips together.

"I'll bet Archie read it," she said reproachfully.

Aye, I think he did. As Jake recalled, *he* hadn't been listening while his cousin had nattered on about the paintings.

234   E.G. FOLEY

Blast.

"I'm not really the plaque-reading sort," he admitted in chagrin. "Mind giving a quick summary?"

She rolled her eyes. "Very well. This whole collection was recently donated to the Order by a wealthy Jewish family who acquired the art over several centuries, starting from the days of Leonardo da Vinci. He was a family friend of their original ancestor in France—and a great mage himself. Leonardo invented many things, as Archie could probably tell you."

"Aye." Inventor of the original flying machine, Leonardo da Vinci was one of his cousin's top heroes.

"Well, one of Leonardo's secret discoveries was a formula for some magical varnish or shellac that lets people travel into paintings, like we just did. According to legend, Leonardo originally used it to hide his Jewish friends when the agents of the Inquisition came to arrest them unjustly. The churchmen were going to force them either to convert or face torture and burning at the stake—along with the town's witches, gypsies, and other Magic-folk."

Jake winced.

"Leonardo saved many by these means," Nixie continued. "The Inquisition suspected something supernatural was going on and destroyed several of his paintings. They would've killed him, too, if he weren't so famous. But Leonardo realized the danger. If one of his paintings was destroyed with his friends inside it, he knew they could die. So somehow he fiddled with the formula again and was able to connect several pieces of artwork by magic. This way, the people hiding inside could escape from one painting to another in case the Inquisition got hold of the one where they were hiding.

"Once he transported his paintings with the fugitives inside to a safe location, he let them out and gave the paintings to them so they could use them again anytime another persecution broke out. He also taught them the formula for the shellac so they could apply it to more artwork if the need ever arose again in the future. And, of course, it did.

"The size the collection has grown to proves how often fresh rounds of persecution have broken out against the Jews throughout Europe, poor souls." She glanced pensively at the window frame. "I have no idea how my spell penetrated Leonardo's protective magical barrier, but maybe the Enchanted Gallery took us in, since Jenny

Greenteeth meant to destroy us. Maybe it somehow sensed that we were in mortal danger, just like the people for whom it was originally created."

"Just when I thought my day couldn't get any stranger," Jake mumbled. "Paintings that look back at you."

Nixie shrugged. "For all I know, some of the fugitives might still be hiding somewhere in the collection."

"Medieval folk? Wouldn't they be dead now?"

"I should think time works differently in here, Jake. We're not in the regular world anymore."

"You can say that again. Well, if they're in here somewhere, maybe we can find them and they'll show us the way out."

"Good thinking. But—wait. There's something else you need to know about these paintings."

"What's that?"

"The Inquisition captured a witch who had once hidden inside the collection. They tortured her until she gave up the secret of how to get in and how the paintings were connected. Measures had to be taken. From that point on, the fugitives added all sorts of obstacles and booby-traps into the paintings to stop any intruders."

"Really?" He looked around. "I don't see anything dangerous-looking here. That dog ran by a few minutes ago, but it showed no interest in us. We've seen nothing since."

She shrugged. "From what I've heard, only one of the paintings is truly safe—the beautiful farm landscape on the end. Did you see it?"

"The sunshiny one? With all the sunflowers? Aye, I know it." Jake smiled at the thought of getting to go there in semi-real life.

Nixie let out a wistful sigh. "It looks so peaceful. That's the one I fell asleep staring at," she added. "It's supposedly a painting of the original family's home in Provence."

"Leonardo painted them a picture of their home where they could take refuge? That was goodhearted of him."

"Actually, the farm scene was by a much later artist. I don't know his name. Point is, if anybody's still hiding in the collection, that's probably where we'll find them. I vote we make our way there."

This could be fun, trekking from painting to painting, thought Jake. It was a little like being a Lightrider going through portals, only in miniature. Good practice, anyway—and after being accused of stealing the Queen's flag, this might be as close as he'd ever get to living his dream, so he might as well enjoy it.

He shrugged off the depressing thought. "Well, we'd better get walking. Er, *can* you walk on that ankle?"

"Not very well, and not for the distance I have a feeling we're going to have to go." She looked down at her feet, encased in the black, lace-up boots that all witches seemed to love. "Good thing I had my boots laced tight, or I might've wound up with a break instead of a sprain."

"You want to soak it in the stream before we go?"

"No, let me try a healing spell." She sat down with her broken wand and tried to straighten it out without snapping the floppy end off; Jake heard her mumbling under her breath that it might still have a little bit of power left in it, since the tip hadn't broken off entirely.

While she concentrated on her ankle, he studied the autumn scenery around him, looking for any clue about hidden dangers or which way they should go. The green, distant ridge was empty. He looked for a path among the grove of gorgeous trees, to no avail.

"Nixie," he remarked, looking around in all directions, "did you happen to notice what sort of painting we flew into? It all happened so fast, I didn't even have time to look."

"No, I didn't dare take my eyes off Jenny Greenteeth."

"Hmm." There was not so much as a sheep in the field with them. It might make sense to follow the brook that meandered through the pastures...

But when he started scanning the squat stone fence around the field, he suddenly stopped on the rustic, weathered stile built over the thorny hedgerow.

In the old tradition of common-use land laws, quaint stepladders like that could be found all over the English countryside, allowing health-minded walkers easy passage over farmers' fences. Since many country ramblers also loved to take their dogs along on their hikes, many stiles even had a pull-up chute called a dog door.

But *this* stile, Jake thought, had to be unique in all of England— namely, because one of the ladder's wooden uprights was shaped like a giant paintbrush.

It was as good as an arrow pointing to the exit.

"Think I've found our way out." A wry smile crooked his lips as he tapped Nixie on the shoulder. "Lookie there. I reckon we go that way."

She followed his gesture, spotted the strange stile over the hedgerow, then turned and actually smiled at him. "Clever. I guess we'll just have to follow the paintbrushes."

He nodded. "Did the wand work at all?"

"A little, I think—" she started, when a strange sound in the distance cut off her words.

Two deep, brassy, musical notes floated to them on the brisk air and then were instantly repeated.

Nixie turned to Jake in alarm. "What was that?"

"Dash me, it sounded like a horn," he said, confused.

But the next noise gave them their answer: a clamor of wild barking.

They looked at each other and gasped in mutual realization of the kind of painting they were in.

The foxhunting scene!

"That creature you saw a little while ago—that must have been the fox!"

Jake pulled Nixie to her feet. "Come on. We've got to move or they'll trample us! Look at all the riders coming over the ridge! They're heading straight for us!"

"Never mind the riders, look at all those dogs!" Nixie gulped. "Jake, we've got to go. They're on the hunt, they've scented blood! If they find us instead of their quarry, they'll tear us apart, just like they do to the poor fox when they finally catch it!"

He clenched his jaw. "Hold onto me." He grabbed her elbow to support her on the side where she was hurt. Then he hurried her along across the uneven field, while the baying of dozens of bloodthirsty hounds grew louder, and the ground began to shake with the hoofbeats of the riders bearing down on them.

The red-coated sportsmen flew over fences, water ditches, and fallen logs on their gleaming Thoroughbreds. The dogs streamed through the dog gates of two distant stiles.

All of them, men and dogs alike, had gleaming red eyes.

The hunting horn sounded again.

"Tallyho, lads! There's our quarry!" boomed the master of the hunt.

"Hurry up!" Jake pulled Nixie up the rungs of the stile.

The pack's furious barking grew deafening, and the thunder of the horses' hooves swelled as the riders began leaping over the hedgerow on the far side of the field.

The hounds would be upon them in seconds.

"We'll never outrun them!" Nixie cried, looking over her shoulder.

But when Jake reached the top of the stile, he stared down at the other side in confusion. Instead of solid ground, the bottom rung gave way to empty air. He caught a whiff of salt breeze from somewhere far below.

Before he could show Nixie his dilemma, she pushed him forward, not realizing he was standing on a ledge. "Go, hurry up, they're coming!"

"Wait, no—*ahhhhh!*" Jake lost his balance at her shove.

He fell off the stile, arms flailing, and screamed as he plummeted like a stone through the clouds below.

CHAPTER TWENTY-THREE
The Queen's Flag

"Don't worry, this won't take long," Dani assured their captive.
"I know you're nervous about meeting Queen Victoria, but it's hours until teatime and Jake needs our help!" Archie chimed in.

The two of them had only just succeeded in dragging Isabelle out of the Bradford suite, now that her hair was curled and coiffed to perfection.

"I still don't see what you need me for," she protested halfheartedly as they pulled her down the hallway, each holding fast to one of her wrists so she didn't try to escape. "Where is our cousin, anyway?"

"Oh, he's interviewing some ghosts to find out if they saw anything last night," Archie said. "He'll be back soon, I should think."

"We just want you to walk around the crowd with us and try to sense who the *real* thief is, since we know it wasn't Jake who stole the Queen's flag," Dani explained.

"Oh, is that all? Pick an unknown thief out of the crowd?" Isabelle asked dryly. "I thought I had my Assessment two years ago."

"Won't you at least try for a few minutes, please?" her brother insisted, but Dani took a roundabout tack.

"You know, Izzy, Jake blamed Maddox for the theft. If you help us find the real culprit, you'll be clearing Maddox, too."

She let out a glum sigh. "Very well. But you can quit harping on about him. Mr. St. Trinian has made his feelings clear."

"If you believe him," Dani said with a shrug.

"Guardians don't lie, remember? Oh, never mind. Let me concentrate." Isabelle yanked her hands free as the three of them arrived at the top of the staircase above the entrance hall. "Hmm."

She sauntered down the steps, perusing the throng of excited youngsters waiting to participate in the games that had been organized for them that day.

Dani and Archie exchanged an eager glance.

By the front doors of Merlin Hall, the centaur lady in charge of arranging the day's entertainments for the children clapped her hands to get everyone's attention, and when that failed, she banged the marble floor with her front hoof. "Quiet, now! Everybody, please! Let us begin!"

Her fairy helpers buzzed over the children's heads, shushing them. "Listen up for your instructions!"

Isabelle walked casually along the back wall, scanning the crowd. Dani pursed her lips in thought, then leaned toward Archie.

"What if it wasn't a kid who took the flag?" she whispered.

He shrugged. "What sort of adult would bother?"

"Good point."

Someone in the crowd seemed to have got Isabelle's attention. She stopped, tilted her head, gazing into the middle of the throng. She took a few steps closer, paused again, glanced around, and then walked back to the two of them.

Dani and Archie went down to the bottom step to hear her results just as the centaur lady finished explaining the rules of the treasure hunt to all the children gathered in the entrance hall. The doors opened, and the kids poured out noisily into the sunshine and rushed off to participate in the game.

"I think I've got something," Isabelle said.

"Who? Hurry, they're all leaving!"

Isabelle turned, quickly scanned the crowd, and then pointed. "There. Those three. They are definitely up to something."

Dani let out a startled huff when she saw the children Isabelle was pointing to—two boys, one girl. "The skunkies!"

"You know them?" Archie asked.

"They're the shapeshifter children who kept pestering me during the Assessments! Remember? They were sitting right by us. Triplets. Henry had to growl at them for me."

"Oh, right!" Archie said, nodding. "You know, shapeshifters are usually born in multiples like their animal counterparts are born in litters. That's why Henry and Helena are twins."

"Well, those three are definitely up to no good," Isabelle said, staring at the suspects. "Actually...I think they might be Lord

Badgerton's niece and nephews."

"Who's that?" Dani asked.

"An Elder," Archie said.

"Uh-oh," said Dani.

"Well, I have to go," Isabelle announced. "I did as you asked. I'm sure you two can handle it from here. I am not traipsing around the woods with you in my tea gown and risking getting dirty before the royal audience."

"That's all right, sis, you don't have to. We can manage from here. Good luck with the Queen."

"Thanks, Izzy!" Dani called, waving, as the older girl left them to their own devices.

Archie turned to her. "Come on, we mustn't let those wily shapeshifters get away."

"Aye, we're not going to let them pin their misdeeds on Jake."

They rushed across the entrance hall, blending in with the crowd of rowdy children.

"Too bad you didn't make some extra Bully Buzzers. Take it from me, those three are pests," Dani said as they hurried out into the brilliant spring sunshine.

"I wonder why they'd even want to take the Queen's flag."

"Same reason they bothered me—just to be annoying! Little stinkers."

"Yes, but how do you suppose they got up there? Standing on each other's shoulders, what?"

"I don't know!" Dani said impatiently. "Let's just find out if they have it with them or if they've hidden it somewhere." She seized hold of his arm and pulled him into a run.

The skunkies were among the flood of children pouring into the woods on the treasure hunt. The kids spread out, searching for prizes in small teams of two or three.

Archie and Dani kept their eyes on their quarry and proceeded to follow them onto the forest path. They pretended to be participating in the game, but all the while, were keeping their targets under surveillance.

The skunkies made their way through the green underbrush, and soon had led Archie and Dani quite a ways from the majority of the treasure-hunters.

"I wonder where they're taking us," Archie murmured. "They do seem like shifty little things, don't they?"

The triplets giggled and snickered amongst themselves and were constantly glancing over their shoulders with an air of furtive glee.

"They're certainly acting pleased with themselves. Like they just got away with something big."

"Do you really think they framed Jake on purpose?"

"Oh, I don't know. They probably just liked the pretty colors on the flag," Dani said wryly. Then she let out a gasp as one of the boy skunkies glanced over his shoulder and spotted her. "Oh, drat! They've seen us! Duck!" She pulled Archie behind a tree, but he brushed her off.

"No, if they've already seen us, they're going to run. We can't afford to lose them. Come on!"

He was right. The boy had already told his siblings they were being followed, and now all three of them began running away as fast as the forest's uneven ground and layer of knee-high ferns would permit.

"I say!" Archie called as Dani and he hurried after them. "A word with you three, please!"

"They're not going to listen to reason, Archie, not those three," she muttered. But they might respond to more of a rookery approach. "'Oy! You lot! Get back 'ere before I crack ye!"

It didn't work. The fleeing shapeshifters were no more impressed with her bellicose shouts than they were with Archie's plea for civility. They just did whatever the devil they wanted, Dani thought in frustration as she tripped, unable to see her footing amid the ferns.

Archie righted her before she fell and they kept on, but a moment later, the skunkies disappeared into the sun-dappled thicket ahead.

"Blast, where'd they go?" the boy genius exclaimed, panting with exertion.

"I don't know." Dani turned, looking around in all directions. Some of the branches ahead were vibrating from their passing. "That way!"

They chased again.

"Quit runnin' away, cowards!" Dani taunted.

"Why'd you steal the Queen's flag?" Archie yelled when they caught sight of them again.

"Aye! We want it back!"

The other skunkie brother pulled a folded, colorful length of silk out from under his shirt and waved it rudely at them, grinning.

"Hey! That's it! They've got the Queen's flag!" Dani said in shock.

"Look at them! Have you ever seen such little horrors?"

"Audacious," Archie said in disapproval. "If they're stealing royal property at this age, imagine what they'll do by the time they're twelve. Come on, Dani. We've got to be the adults here."

"I just want to throttle 'em."

Once more, the skunkies ducked them. It was no fun trying to catch a shapeshifter. Sir Peter's wife hadn't given any tips on how to do that in her class.

They shoved on through the woods, getting scratched by branches and bitten by insects for their pains, but although they could not see their quarry, the skunkies could not have got far yet. They knew the triplets could still hear them, so they kept trying to engage them—or, at least, provoke a reaction.

The sound of tittering gave away the shapeshifters' position in a dense thicket about twenty yards to the right. Archie pointed at it, Dani nodded, and they immediately closed in.

"I say, we just want to talk you!" Archie yelled into the woods as they approached. But he peered through the branches, confused. "Did they give us the slip again? Why can't we see them?"

"Maybe they changed form," Dani said worriedly, then raised her voice once more to a shout, "You'd better not turn yourselves into skunks out here, or we're stealing your clothes and then what will you do when it's time to walk back to Merlin Hall and the three of you are starkers, eh? Not too clever, are you?"

But the moment they burst into the thicket where they expected to find the trio, they realized—too late—that they had walked into a trap.

Skunks sprayed them full-blast from three directions at close range. Even worse, they were so startled by this veritable chemical attack that they shrieked in revulsion, only to learn the hard way that the very worst thing you can do during a skunk attack is to open your mouth.

They dropped to the ground, gagging on the taste as well as the overpowering odor of skunk.

Roaring with laughter, the skunkies turned themselves back into the rotten human children that they were, waving the Queen's flag in their faces again. At least, Dani was fairly sure it was the flag. All she could see were the bright royal colors as tears poured down her cheeks from the eye-watering smell.

"I'll get you for this!" she vowed amid her retching coughs.

One of the skunkies nudged her rudely with a toe in response—not quite a kick, but almost. "Next time, mind your own business!" It was the girl shapeshifter, speaking with belligerence worthy of the rookery.

"Archie, are you all right?" Dani wheezed.

"Horrible!" he gasped out. "Humiliating!"

Indeed, they had been bested.

The thieves got away.

* * *

Meanwhile, Jake continued falling through the sky.

Nixie had shrieked when she realized she had just pushed him off the edge of the world—at least, the world of the foxhunt painting.

But then, she, too, grasped that the only way to escape the pack of hounds and riders bearing down on them was to jump off the stile, and so she did.

Both of them went crashing through thin air, but the wispy top layer of clouds soon gave way to dark woolly thunderheads. They fell into a chaotic, highly charged stratum of storm winds that buffeted them and whirled them around like autumn leaves.

Falling and falling through the tempest, they were pummeled by rain and hail and very nearly zapped by lightning. Nevertheless, they were better off than the sailors below, as it turned out.

Jake first realized which painting they had entered when he heard a great, cracking groan of splitting wood below and a chorus of distant male screams. He wrenched his neck looking over to locate Nixie, and caught a glimpse of the sinking tall ship from the corner of his eye, its sails torn to ribbons by the gales.

The next thing he knew, he plunged into the storm-tossed sea, twenty-foot waves crashing over him. Oh, yes, *this* famous painting he remembered. He recalled admiring all its drama and danger.

'Twas a fine thing to look at, but he had never counted on *visiting* the Turner shipwreck scene from the inside. He kicked his legs and clawed wildly at the water with his arms, struggling upward through the swells.

Just when he thought his lungs would burst, his head popped up above the waves. Sucking in huge lungfuls of air, he immediately looked around for Nixie.

Since she was so light-framed a girl and had leaped a few seconds after he did, she was still falling. He heard her shrieking as she approached and looked up. Treading water for all he was worth, he winced when she hit the water. He hoped she had not hurt her ankle even worse.

He swam in the direction where she had landed. It took several terrifying minutes of screaming each other's names, but at last, they managed to find one another.

"Are you all right?" Jake demanded, pushing his soaked hair out of his eyes while the bitter cold of the sea seeped into his hands and feet.

Nixie looked even worse off. "I'm alive."

In the distance, the great sailing ship had all but broken in two, and now the burning halves were sinking slowly into the waves.

Note to self, Jake thought. *Don't join Royal Navy.* True, they had steamships now.

Still.

"Jake, I saw an island while I was falling," Nixie said, pointing. "It's that way! We should swim for it."

He nodded. "I saw it, too. Let's go. If we get separated, we'll meet up somewhere on the beach, yes?"

Nixie nodded, and then they both headed for the island, swimming side by side and taking care not to get separated.

The powder stores aboard the vessel must have exploded in the wreck, and as a result, much of the grand old frigate was on fire, its doomed masts burning like great candles in the night. By the orange glare of this giant bonfire, Jake could just make out the shape of the island in the distance, but it was difficult to tell how far away it was. He just prayed they could stay alive long enough to reach it.

It was their only hope.

Again and again the waves dunked him underwater, but he refused to be drowned and did his best to look after Nixie and keep the girl alive. Her face was a pale oval in the darkness.

Whether she had done worse injury to her ankle, he could only guess. If she had, she did not complain. Of course, this was no time for conversation. Every precious ounce of air had to be preserved for breathing as the waves arced under them and threw them forward and clawed them back again and again.

After what seemed like hours of swimming for their lives, they finally reached the gentle surf around the island and stumbled through the shallows, staggering up onto the beach amid the litter from the shipwreck.

Wooden planks, barrels, everyday items, and other bits of wreckage (including a few dead sailors that Jake hoped Nixie didn't see) were already washing up onto the beach, drifting sadly back and forth as the waves rolled in.

Jake gained his feet in the shallows and spared Nixie the effort of walking, pulling her through the waist-high water like a tugboat. A length of wood that he thought was a broken yardarm from the ship floated in their way, but as he pushed it aside, he realized it was actually the paintbrush marking the boundary into the next picture.

He pointed it out to Nixie. "We're entering a new painting," he croaked, his voice raspy, his throat sore from having nearly drowned in saltwater.

She acknowledged his comment with the barest of nods.

Ahead, the island loomed, the black spiky leaves of tropical palm trees silhouetted against the predawn gray.

There was no sign of the sailors who had tried to escape the sinking ship in their rowboats. But as Jake recalled, the point of the Turner painting was to honor a tragedy in which there had been no survivors.

Or something like that.

At last, the two of them staggered up onto the empty beach and collapsed on the sand in sheer physical exhaustion. For a long time, they lay without moving, half-dead, bedraggled castaways.

Jake could barely move his body. But gradually, it occurred to him that, if all of the paintings had been booby-trapped with dangers and obstacles, then they could not afford to wallow on the beach like a pair of wounded seals.

The sun had climbed up over the horizon and had started to dry their clothes. It was really very pleasant, but for how long?

For all he knew, there could be headhunters living on this island.

He glanced over at his waifish, black-clad companion. The little witch had fallen fast asleep, and he hated to wake her.

Still, out here on this beach, they were exposed, easily seen by anyone else who might be on the island. It would be safer to at least move farther up the strand into the shadows of the trees.

"Nixie."

She didn't stir, and he found he didn't have the heart to insist right away. Truth be told, he felt dashed sorry for her. If only he were as insightful as Archie, maybe he would've realized from the start that the poor little mite was in need of help instead of letting his offended pride get in the way.

He gave her a few minutes longer to rest while he sat up and took off his shoes. He squeezed as much of the dampness as he could out of his socks, then lay them on the sand to let them dry a bit more, and rolled up the bottoms of his trousers.

His stomach grumbled, which brought another ominous thought. What were they supposed to eat? If they got lost in these paintings for any significant length of time, might they starve to death?

Frowning, Jake visored his eyes with his hand and looked out to sea. There was no sign of the sinking ship anymore. Even the wreckage was gone, including the dead sailors.

The beach was pristine. All he could think was that Nixie and he must have crossed fully into the next painting.

Whatever that might entail...

Strange sounds were coming out of the jungle at their backs. Jake looked warily over his shoulder and stared, amazed, at a showy, jewel-colored bird that swooped along the treeline. *Maybe a parrot?*

Many bird calls and insect chirps emanated from the trees, but when a lizard flicked among some rocks nearby, Jake had had enough. He was a city boy, accustomed to the hubbub of London, and this tropical paradise was giving him the creeps.

He shook Nixie by her shoulder. "Wake up. We've got to get going."

She groaned, refusing to open her eyes. "Leave me be."

"I know you want to sleep, but it isn't safe here. Come on, open your eyes and take a look round. What painting are we in?"

"I hardly memorized all the pictures in the Enchanted Gallery, Jake." Lying on her stomach, she heaved herself up onto her elbows and looked around, squinting in the brilliant sunshine. "I suppose, if I had to guess...I'd say we've arrived on Prospero's island."

"Is that good or bad?"

"Prospero's island? As in Shakespeare's *The Tempest*?" She stared meaningfully at him. "Sound familiar?"

Jake pressed his lips shut.

She sighed. "You really are an ignoramus, aren't you?"

"An ignoramus who just saved your life *again*," he grumbled. "Can you walk or not?"

"What choice do I have?" she asked grimly, and climbing to her feet, to his relief, she found she could stand.

It was difficult for her to walk in the deep, soft sand, however, so once more, Jake gave her his arm to steady her. "Come on, we've got to find the next paintbrush. Is this Prospero fellow somebody we're going to have to worry about?"

"No, not *him*. Prospero was the sorcerer in the story and the heroine's father." She paused, glancing around warily at the jungle. "It's Caliban that worries me."

"Caliban?"

"A monster Prospero created to be his servant."

Jake immediately thought of Ogden Trumbull, and turned to her, wide-eyed. "What sort of monster?"

"Hard to say. In the theatre, they always show him with like...horns and a hump. He's supposed to be very ugly and walk with a limp. I always imagined him like a minotaur, I guess."

"Oh, perfect," Jake muttered.

"Let's just hope we don't run into him before we find the paintbrush."

Somehow, he doubted they would be so lucky.

* * *

Isabelle fidgeted in her chair, her hands folded in her lap, her palms sweating with anxiety.

Eleven debutantes dressed in their very smartest daytime finery sat in the marble anteroom, waiting in varying states of dread for the great honor of being summoned in as a group to see the Queen.

The chamberlain was expected at any moment to usher them in and present them to Her Majesty and her royal daughters, who had just joined their mother in the opulent stateroom a few minutes ago.

Isabelle decided that Queen Victoria had too many daughters to keep track of properly, but it would be nice to meet them, anyway.

Everyone was rather terrified. One could have cut the tension in the air with a cake-knife. Last-minute adjustments were discreetly made to gowns. Final flyaway hairs were smashed down by the girls' hovering chaperones, governesses, and mothers.

The grown ladies all seemed a little distraught that their charges would be going in for their royal inspections without them, but those were the rules.

Her Majesty wished to see for herself what the girls were made of, who they really were, without their minders signaling to them what they ought to say.

The rumor was Her Majesty had a certain interest in adding a magical family member to her considerable brood by way of marriage.

Contrary to fairytales, however, none of the girls in the anteroom were keen to marry one of the Queen's many younger sons. (The future king was already spoken for, of course.) Still, if the Queen wished to have any one of them for a future daughter-in-law, she got first dibs and it wasn't like the chosen girl could say no.

Her Majesty clearly relished the task of choosing brides and grooms for her large brood of marriageable offspring.

Isabelle prayed she would not be noticed. She didn't even want to *think* about how some spoiled royal husband might expect her to use her gift to help him politically or in other, less-than-ethical ways.

Truly, being an empath was a road fraught with perils.

Even now, she was all too aware of the undercurrents of hostility coming from three of the girls, who had decided at the Gathering two years ago that they didn't like her. They had been making fun of her behind her back (as if this were possible) ever since.

Ah, well. Everyone has their detractors, she thought, trying to ignore them. But surely this was proof that it didn't matter how nice you were to people, how perfect you tried to be; there were always those who would find fault with you and delight in hurting your feelings, just because.

Frankly, Isabelle was feeling rather weary of trying to be perfect all the time, especially since she had failed to impress Maddox St. Trinian. Impress him—gracious, she couldn't even read his emotions with her gift! She still did not understand why and was afraid to ask one of the older empaths, who might have had an explanation.

Across the room, meanwhile, her critics—two witches and a horse shapeshifter girl—were whispering about her behind their hands, laughing at her and at some of the other girls, too. As if they all needed something like that to make them even more nervous.

She frowned a little and looked away, and it was then that she heard low-toned arguing coming from beyond the doorway, out by the colonnade.

She leaned forward in her chair so she could see past the row of marble columns. *Hmm.* The Queen's uniformed chamberlain was trying to soothe the anger of a tall, elegant, black-clad man.

"Now, look here! Gather the Elders and let me in to see the Queen."

"In due time, Your Highness, you will have the royal audience—"

"Don't feed me that tripe! Do you not understand how I've risked my bloody undead life, coming here to bring them this warning? And now I'm told to wait and cool my heels while these insipid little misses waltz in to chat with Her Majesty about what, the weather? Sweet Artemis, you people! How many more insults must I withstand?

"Your hospitality, by the way, is atrocious," he added. "I have not been offered a single drop to drink since I arrived last night. On the contrary! I have been attacked, interrogated, locked up, scanned, probed, insulted—not to mention knocked around by certain barbaric Guardians in Her Majesty's employ." He cast scornful glances at the two large, looming bodyguards flanking him.

Neither of them was Maddox.

"Truly, my abject apologies, Prince Janos! Please bear with us. I implore your patience." The chamberlain shook his head in apparent sympathy, but Isabelle could sense that he was terrified of the stranger. "If there's anything I can do to make up for how poorly you've been treated—"

Prince Janos waved off the niceties. "I do not desire your blandishments, lackey. I merely want to see Her Majesty today, as I was promised, and be on my way. So tell me, good chamberlain. Exactly how much longer must I wait?"

"It will be but a-a short delay. I'm so sorry for this inconvenience, truly, but if you'd kindly follow me into the sitting room just here and make yourself comfortable, I shall make absolutely certain that you are next in line to see Her Majesty."

"Very well." The prince leaned closer to the little man. "But I must warn you. Do you know what I will do to you if you are lying to me, hmm?"

The chamberlain gulped; the Guardians moved closer.

"Not to worry, Your Highness," the chamberlain replied with admirable calm. "If you could find it in your heart to be patient just a short while longer. Truly, we mean no disrespect, but Her Majesty's schedule is set months in advance. If we veer from it at the last moment, all would quickly turn to chaos." The chamberlain laughed weakly, as though pleading for him to understand, but the stranger just stared.

"You want to see chaos? Then keep wasting time while the Dark Druids prepare," he replied.

"Please, sir, not in front of the young ladies!" the chamberlain begged him, aghast at the supposed harm to their delicate female sensibilities. "This way. I'm afraid I must insist."

The bristling Guardians stepped up to each side of the stranger to escort him into the nearby sitting room. The prince scowled at them.

From this safe distance, Isabelle looked on, riveted. By now, she had realized who the undead stranger was—obviously the vampire Jake had seen arrive last night.

She shuddered, never having seen one of the bloodsucking creatures before. But, recalling her cousin's urgency about figuring out why one of his kind would dare come to Merlin Hall, she knew what she had to do. Jake was right. It had to be something vitally important.

Something the adults would never tell mere children.

Dark Druids...preparing for what? she wondered.

And so, determined to find out what he was hiding, she closed her eyes and concentrated, summoning up all of her ability, reaching deep within her own heart and mind, to where she made empathic connections with her subjects.

She ignored the fleeting warning that it might not be wise to try to connect her awareness with that of an undead creature of the night.

The vampire prince was such a large personality that she found his pulsating presence in the etheric realm at once—but drew in a breath when she did.

His inner world was a very strange and frightening place. Her mind swam to meet his through a cold, surging sea of instinct and fear, power and loss, sadness and hate, all of it emanating from him. She felt him protecting someone...

Why are you here? her mind whispered to his.

She quickly found an answer lurking in the enigma of his cloaked thoughts, though it wasn't complete. He had indeed brought the Elders some sort of warning, as he had mentioned to the chamberlain, but it didn't come for free.

Oh, no...he wanted something in return. Something big. And he didn't mean to budge.

She detected in him a bittersweet sense of loyalty however, as if perhaps he once had belonged here...

All of a sudden, the connection was cut off as crisply as though someone had sliced it with a sword. And a terrifying voice came back to her—from inside her head.

Who's there?

She flicked her eyes open to find that the vampire had stopped walking away. She shrank down in her chair as he slowly turned around.

A chill ran down her spine, and she clasped her hands more tightly in her lap, staring, wide-eyed, at him, willing him to take no notice of her.

It didn't work. He saw her.

And he knew.

He raised a brow, anger in his blazing eyes and a faint, bitter twist on his lips. Then she nearly screamed when she heard his voice in her mind again. Mocking her.

Such a nosy girl! It isn't nice trying to pry into other people's thoughts. How would you like it if someone did it to you? His smile fell away, and an icy threat emanated from him. *Mind your own business,* he ordered her without a single word spoken aloud.

No one else even knew they had communicated.

The big, burly Guardian by his side gave the visitor a nudge. "Come along, Your Highness," he ordered.

Isabelle held perfectly still, her heart pounding, as the vampire released her from his telepathic hold, pivoted on his heel with an elegant motion, and allowed the warriors to escort him out.

"Goodness, are you all right, dear?" one of the chaperones asked, turning and noticing the look on her face just then. "You're so pale! There, there, now, don't be frightened." With a chuckle, the kindly woman put her arm around Isabelle's shoulders and gave her a squeeze. "Her Majesty knows you girls are nervous. But don't worry, she has no wish to terrify you. It's just a pre-debut formality. You'll do fine."

Somehow Isabelle forced a smile, hiding the true cause of her apprehension, but as she dropped her gaze, murmuring her thanks, she feared she had just made a very powerful enemy.

CHAPTER TWENTY-FOUR
Art Appreciation

The tropical sun was starting to get hot. The constant breeze was nice, but Lord only knew what waited for them in the jungle ahead.

Jake trudged through the deep sand with Nixie, the gentle surf washing the beach at their backs. She was trying to remember details about Caliban from the Shakespeare play—just in case.

"He's sort of a wild mutant. In the play, his mother was a witch and his father was the devil."

"Sounds charming."

"Um, that's not the worst part."

He turned to her, wiping a bead of sweat off his brow.

She hesitated. "Shakespeare supposedly came up with the name Caliban by rearranging the word *cannibal*. So..."

"I see. So we might end up as supper. Is that the fastest you can walk?"

She made a sound of frustration. "It's slow-going on this sand. Every step makes me twist my ankle again. I can't believe I broke my wand or I'd have already fixed myself."

Jake nodded. "Come 'ere, I'll carry you. Get on my back."

"What? No!"

He stepped in front of her and ignored her huffy, I-don't-need-anybody protests, until she relented and climbed onto his back for a piggyback ride.

She hardly weighed a thing. "You need to eat more."

"This really isn't necessary," she muttered, clasping her wrist in front of his neck to hold on.

"Beg to differ," Jake said as he trudged through the deep sand. "I've got more meat on my bones than you. He'll eat me first. So pardon if I seem eager to get out of here." He paused when he reached the edge of the jungle, looking up at the spiky, soughing trees on their long, slim stems. "Never seen a jungle before. Except the Palm Room under glass at Kew Botanical Gardens."

"Neither have I. Oh, look at the parrots and cockatiels! Such bright colors," she said, marveling at the gaudy-plumaged birds swooping overhead, though their squawks were surprisingly ungraceful for such magnificent specimens.

"Hey, look, a path," he said suddenly. "Our next paintbrush might be that way."

She nodded, and he continued carrying her deeper into the jungle of Prospero's island. The ground was more packed down here, making it possible for Nixie to walk again—though Jake warned her to be careful of the tiny crabs scuttling back and forth across the path. One crunched underfoot when he put her down; Nixie winced, but it was impossible not to step on them.

They hadn't gone far when they heard a weird snuffling noise amid the trees, twigs crackling and the low mumbling of someone talking to himself in some primitive, guttural language.

They froze, then quickly crouched down.

Through the screen of brilliant emerald vegetation, they could just make out a large, somewhat human-shape. It was hunched to one side and had horns. They could hear its odd gait as it dragged a foot behind it with each step.

They looked at each other, wide-eyed.

Caliban.

They could hear him sniffing the air rapidly. "Visitors have come! Yum-yum..."

Jake blanched. With nothing but a few leaves between the two of them and a wild, cannibalistic monster, he cast about for a distraction. He spotted a cluster of coconuts on a palm tree some distance away. Clearing his mind, he used his telekinesis to shake them off the tree.

Caliban whirled to face the noise. "Dinner is served!" He bounded off in the direction of the sound, his lame foot not enough to slow him down.

"Look!" Nixie mouthed the word, pointing to a little mossy cave off the path. It had water trickling down one side and a wooden bar across the cave entrance—in the shape of a paintbrush.

Thank gosh, Jake thought. They crept toward it as speedily and silently as possible. Jake kept Nixie ahead of him so he could use his telekinesis to push Caliban back if he returned to pursue them.

Moments later, an angry roar a few hundred yards away suggested the beast had discovered the coconut ruse.

"Hurry up, he's coming back!" Jake breathed.

"I am, it's just these vines—" Nixie suddenly shrieked when one of the hanging vines she smacked aside proved not to be a vine at all, but a cold, clammy snake. Descending from the odd-looking tree above, it coiled back at her and hissed.

As it bared its fangs to strike, Jake blasted the snake with his telekinesis. It flew backward into the jungle, and they ran toward the cave, Nixie limping worse than Caliban.

Jake glanced over his shoulder. The monster was bearing down on them with long, uneven strides, snarling as he came.

"Go!" Jake yelled.

Nixie flung herself toward the paintbrush, threw it aside, and tripped into the cave, while Jake paused to stare for another second at the monster, barely able to believe his eyes.

Horned, muscle-bound, and hideous, Caliban really did resemble a minotaur. When the creature leaped toward him, he bolted to the paintbrush, while Nixie screamed, *"Come on!"*

The moment the paintbrush swung back into position behind him like a door closing, the world went dark.

Prospero's island disappeared—and thankfully, so had Caliban.

They paused in the pitch-black cave for a moment to catch their breath.

"You all right?" he asked, panting.

"Ew, I touched a snake."

"Thought witches like snakes."

"Some witches. Not me. Ick, ick, ick."

He heard her wiping her hands on her skirt. Glancing around, he could just make out a glimmer of flat gray light outlining the rectangle shape of an ordinary door ahead.

"You ready?" he asked.

She stood up with an unsteady motion, bumping against him. "I'd better be, since we don't have much choice."

"Don't suppose you remember which painting comes next?"

"I don't think they're connected in any particular order."

"So we have no idea where we'll end up. Well," he said with a wry gesture toward the door, "ladies first."

"Thanks a lot." Bravely, Nixie stepped up to the door ahead and felt around until she found a doorknob.

When she opened it, they both poked their heads out and looked around. They found themselves peering out of a closet inside a narrow, wooden house painted in somber shades.

"So far, no monsters," Nixie whispered.

Jake caught a whiff of baking bread and onions frying in butter. He could hear the busy back-and-forth footsteps of someone working in the kitchen down the hallway, and the pleasing, homey rhythm of someone chopping vegetables on a wooden cutting board.

"Food!" His mouth instantly watering, he stepped out of the closet built under the staircase. "I was worried we might starve to death in here!"

"I hardly think we can invite ourselves to dinner," Nixie warned as they started creeping down the hallway.

"Why not?"

"Jake!"

Within a few paces, they arrived at a modest foyer with a coat-tree in the corner. A muddy pair of floppy, old-fashioned boots with fold-over tops sat drying on a mat by the wall.

Nixie signaled Jake to wait while she silently opened the front door and peeked out. "Canals! I think we're in Amsterdam. Oh...I see. We must be in a culinary still-life by one of the Dutch masters! Maybe even a Rembrandt."

"Huh?"

"The Dutch masters were always painting things like bowls of fruit or the ingredients for rabbit stew."

That got his attention. "Rabbit stew?" His eyes glazing over, Jake glanced longingly toward the kitchen. "Think they'd give us some?"

Nixie closed the front door of the house and frowned at him, but Jake shrugged. "Better to eat dinner than *be* dinner."

"Shh! I think there's somebody in there!" Nixie pointed to the open doorway of the room on the other side of the foyer.

At once, Jake tiptoed past her to investigate, and, indeed, as he approached, he could hear small clanking and scribbling noises, a crinkle of paper as someone turned a page.

"What are you doing?" Nixie breathed in exasperation.

He waved her off impatiently. "If it's one of the Enchanted Gallery's fugitives, we should try to talk to him about how to get out of here."

"What if it's not?"

He ignored the question and drew upon his ex-pickpocket's stealth to sneak a peek around the corner.

A man in an odd, rather squarish, black velvet hat was counting coins on the table and doing figures in his ledger book.

"I think it's the owner of the house," he reported back to Nixie a moment later.

"Hmm." She tilted her head. "As I recall, a lot of the Old Masters used to support themselves in their starving artist days by painting portraits of the town's merchants or local gentry."

Starving artists? No wonder they painted food, Jake thought. "Well, he doesn't look like he intends to bother us. He's caught up in counting his gold." He stole another glance into the room, but froze when the merchant noticed him there—and mistook him for a servant.

"Is dinner ready yet?"

"Er, almost, sir," Jake replied on cue.

"Tell Cook to hurry. I have a meeting with the new shipmaster at the docks within the hour."

"Yes, sir. I'll go tell her right away." *Ha.* Having been given the perfect excuse to enter the kitchen and try to wheedle the cook into giving him a bite to eat, Jake flashed a mischievous smile at Nixie, then headed past her to go relay the message.

"You can't—Jake! Wait up!"

As Nixie hurried after him, he continued marching toward the kitchen. Passing through the hallway, he glanced at a small painting on the wall and stopped short, startled to find that, in fact, it was not a painting, but a picture-frame window, like the one they had seen in the foxhunt landscape.

This one looked out into a bedchamber in Merlin Hall, and to Jake's amazement, he saw Constanzio, King of the Tenors, practicing scales.

"La, la, la, la, la, la!" the deep, perfectly modulated voice boomed. *"La, la, la, la, LA, la, laaaa!"*

The portly, affable ghost was the only person present.

Jake rushed over to the picture-frame window and began banging on it. "Constanzio! Hullo? *Signore!* In here! Help! Can you hear me?"

Nixie tried to shush Jake as he banged louder on the glass. "What are you doing? There's nobody there!"

"Yes, there is—a ghost. Hey, Constanzio! *Signore!*"

"La, la—oh!" Constanzio stopped abruptly, noticing them there at last. At once, a broad smile of surprise broke out across his expressive face. "Why, if it isn't my young friend, Lord Griffon! *Buongiorno, ragazzo!* I say, what are you doing in that painting?"

"We're stuck," Jake said, then in an aside to Nixie, "Why does he call me *ragazzo*?"

"It means boy in Italian."

"Does it? Say, how'd you get so smart?" She just shrugged. Jake returned his attention to Constanzio. "Sir, you have to help us. I need you to go and tell my cousin, Archie Bradford..." Jake's words faded in mid-sentence as he realized the obvious fault in his logic.

His cousin couldn't see ghosts. None of his friends could.

"Have the ghost tell Dame Oriel we're in here," Nixie suggested, but Jake shook his head.

"I'm already in enough trouble with the Elders as it is."

"Ha, ha! I knew you were a rascal when I met you." Constanzio braced his hands on his waist and let out a laugh at this confession. "What did you do, *ragazzo*?"

"Actually, I didn't. They accused me of stealing the Queen's flag off the roof of the palace last night."

"What?" Nixie exclaimed.

"You didn't happen to see who took it, did you?" he asked the ghost.

"Last night? Heavens, no! I had a huge performance singing for all the earthbound spirits in St. Petersburg! Another triumph, if I say so myself."

"Congratulations."

Constanzio bowed in thanks with a courtly flourish.

"Maybe you could ask some of the other castle ghosts if they saw who took the flag and let me know?" Jake requested, but before Constanzio could answer, a big-framed servant woman carrying an armload of folded towels suddenly stepped around the corner into the hallway and let out a scream when she saw Nixie and Jake.

"Who are you? What are you doing in my master's house?" she demanded.

Apparently, the old Dutch masters had not set much store in making everyone they painted look beautiful. This one had a face like a shovel.

"Er, we work here," he said quickly, since the master himself had mistaken him for the kitchen boy or something.

"No, you don't!" she retorted, then glanced at Nixie. "And neither do you! What are you, intruders?"

"Nothing like that!" they assured her as they began backing away.

"Got to go!" Jake told the ghost.

Constanzio laughed again. "*Ciao, ragazzo!* Don't worry, I have every confidence in your ability to get yourself out of any scrape."

"*Grazie,*" Jake muttered under his breath, which was about all the Italian he knew.

Since the glaring, wide-shouldered maid was blocking the way to the front door and their route to freedom, they had no choice but to keep backing up toward the kitchen.

"Ma'am, we can explain," Nixie started.

"Save your breath! Malou, I found these two lurking in the hallway!" the maid hollered to the cook, who was still bustling about the kitchen at the back of the merchant's house.

The cook turned, kitchen knife in hand, as Jake and Nixie unwillingly retreated into her domain. At once, she looked outraged at their intrusion. "What's this? Who are you? Burglars?"

"No, ma'am!"

"We're simply lost, you see," Nixie attempted, but Jake could not help glancing at the food on the table.

The cook saw him look at it, and her eyes narrowed to angry slashes. She pointed at him with the knife. "Don't even think about it, you!"

"We'll be happy to go—but could you spare some food for two poor children?" he suggested.

"Oh, beggars, are you? Humph. You want charity, try the church. Now, shoo, off with you, before I call the constabulary! Pesky little brats!" She hurled a turnip at him, as much to drive him off as to feed him.

As if any beggar kid would be grateful for a raw, stinking turnip.

"Thanks a lot." Jake smirked as Nixie tugged him out the back door.

The brawny maid tromped after them to glare from the doorway. "And don't come back!"

Nixie pulled him by his arm through the little, enclosed yard off the back of the merchant's house. "Let's go find the next paintbrush before you get us arrested, shall we?"

They pushed through a wooden gate and found themselves in the mews behind the row of houses. Horses munching hay looked out from their stalls as Jake and Nixie hurried down the private alleyway.

Anyone in his right mind hated turnips, but Jake took a tentative bite of this, the only food they had, only to discover that it was made of plaster.

He spit it out in disgust, spewing chalky bits off his tongue. "Ugh! Painted food made for painted people."

Nixie shook her head, limping fast to keep up with him on her sprained ankle. "Would you quit fooling around?"

"Fooling around?" He wiped off his plaster-powdered mouth with a grimace. "Did it ever occur to you we could starve to death in here? At the very least, we're going to need water. Archie says people *die* in three days if they don't have anything to drink. What are we supposed to drink inside a blasted painting, Nixie? Linseed oil? Turpentine?"

"Now, now. Maybe we'll end up in a *water*color painting." She sent him a sly grin.

He was taken aback to see the little witch actually smiling, but he gave her a sardonic look in answer.

At the end of the alley, they reached an ordinary side street. There was no sign of any paintbrush, so they followed the cobbled street down to a bustling thoroughfare that ran alongside the busy canal full of boat traffic.

Nixie gasped, pointing to the nearest bridge. "There!"

Jake saw it at once: a huge paintbrush disguised as one of the beams supporting the bridge over the canal. "I guess we go over that bridge."

They crossed the street and walked across the bridge, but nothing happened. They were still in seventeenth-century Flanders.

Jake threw up his hands. "What now?"

"Maybe we go under it."

He snapped his fingers. "Right! Come on, let's grab a boat."

They hurried down the quayside steps to the water's edge, where Nixie was lucky to be in the company of a skilled ex-thief. Jake knew just how to make his theft look casual as he ordered her into one of the rowboats tied up there, then stepped in, sat down, and picked up the oars.

"Hey! You there! Stop!" Some fellow in a neck ruff standing on the street above spotted them and came running. "That's my boat!"

But he was too late. Jake was already rowing at top speed for the bridge. It wasn't far.

"Sorry!" Nixie called back.

"What are you apologizing for? These people aren't real. Like the turnip."

"I still don't want them to catch us!"

"Don't worry, they won't," Jake said grimly, putting more muscle into every stroke.

The yelling man had got the attention of a boat full of rugged fishermen at work out on the water, and they rushed to help apprehend the boat-thieves.

But as soon as Nixie and he glided under the rattling bridge, horses clip-clopping and carriages rumbling overhead, the whole scene disappeared.

As they came out on the other side, Nixie looked back in shock, but noisy, crowded Amsterdam had vanished behind them. Instead of a canal, they were now drifting peacefully down a babbling brook that wound through a sun-dappled forest.

Heart pounding, Jake took a slight break to catch his breath, and then rowed on.

At length, it occurred to him that the woods seemed a little too perfect.

Even Nixie noticed. "It's so beautiful here."

Aye, not a leaf out of place. He stared in suspicion at a cuddly bunny rabbit that gazed at them from the side of the stream as they went gliding by. The breeze blew just so; the birds tweeted in harmony; and a golden sunbeam slanted in between the branches like a warm caress.

Whichever artist had created this picture was obviously obsessed with sweet, nearly cloying prettiness.

"Do you think we've arrived at the edge of the farm landscape? The one where it's safe?"

"I don't know," he said uneasily, scanning the idyllic forest as he rowed. "Somehow I doubt it. Keep your eyes open."

"And your ears," she said suddenly. "Do you hear that?"

Jake stilled the oars and listened intently. Over the merry gurgle of the stream and the chirping of the birds, he heard music in the distance.

Laughter...

Giddy voices of men and women having a grand time, all set to an elegant sonata full of fast, dizzying trills on a harpsichord, paired with a lilting flute.

"Where the deuce are we?" he murmured, even as the boat glided out of the perfect woodland into the outer reaches of a vast formal garden with a palace in the distance.

An ornate fountain sat in the middle, a crown of water jets shooting out around a muscled bronze god driving a chariot pulled by porpoises.

"Oh, Lord," Nixie said, her lip curling in disdain. "French Baroque. That explains a lot. What on earth are those courtiers doing over there?"

"Oh, I dunno. Just being French?" he jested.

Nixie sent him a sardonic glance. With her gloomy demeanor and somber black clothes, the little witch could not have looked more out of place than in this exquisite land of pretty-pretty-prettiness.

They both stared at the painted adults having their elegant country picnic, mystified by their giddy behavior—not to mention their antique clothes.

Ladies with huge belled pannier skirts, tall white wigs, and dark satin beauty marks glued to their powder-whitened faces pranced around the garden, giggling as they were pursued by amorous gents in jewel-toned frock coats and long, curly wigs, with rouged cheeks and lips.

They were the silliest lot Jake had ever seen.

"At least they don't look dangerous," Nixie said at last.

"No, but he does!" Jake pointed at the sky.

A chubby cupid, flapping his stubby wings to stay aloft, zigzagged out from behind a stand of trees, armed and dangerous with his bow and arrows. Fluttering above the heads of the silly courtiers, he laughed maniacally, firing his golden arrows at will.

And it seemed he never missed.

"Blimey, let's get out of here! I'll bet you he's the one causing all the trouble." Wasting no time, Jake rowed over to the opposite side of the brook, away from the gardens and the courtiers.

"Let's just hope the paintbrush doorway is on this side," he muttered, tossing the rowboat's anchor overboard.

He used the oars to hold the boat steady while Nixie climbed ashore. Placing her weight gingerly on her sprained ankle, she hobbled up onto the grassy bank. Jake jumped out after her. At once, they started hurrying up the dainty path through the woods—but they were not fast enough to escape the roving eyes of the horrible Cupid.

Nixie gasped. "He's coming!"

"Come on!" Jake cried as the diaper-clad menace swooped after them.

Nixie hung onto his arm for support, but quickly gave up. "Save yourself, I can't go any faster!"

"Don't be daft. We can take cover among the trees. Get off the path. This way!"

Cupid buzzed along the path just as they took shelter in the woods. "No one can hide from me forever, *mes amis!*" he taunted as he nocked another arrow.

They ducked behind a perfectly formed elm tree as the Cupid opened fire.

The first arrow missed, whizzing off among the leaves, but their winged pursuer was undaunted. He drew another out of his quiver and circled back, whistling a love song that sounded slightly sinister.

Jake peered out from behind the tree, his jaw clenched. "Stay behind me," he said grimly. "I'll use my telekinesis to knock the arrow aside."

But Cupid did soon find them, and when Jake stepped out to zap the dart off course, he promptly learned that telekinesis did not have the slightest power to deflect a weapon of this magnitude.

"Ow!"

Nixie gasped; Cupid laughed in triumph and flew away; and Jake looked down in disbelief at the golden arrow sticking out of his thigh.

Immediately, he grasped the shaft to pull it out, but the whole thing crumbled in his hand, dissolving *into* his leg in a puff of sparkling, golden powder, sifting through his fingers like Gladwin's fairy dust.

"Where'd it go?"

He stared down at his leg, then looked, aghast, at Nixie. "Uh-oh."

"Jake?"

Her voice grew distant; her face went fuzzy for a minute. He felt a pleasant buzzing sensation in his head, a tingle down his arms and legs, and a weird warmth glowing in his chest.

Nixie grasped him by the shoulder and shook him. "Answer me!

Are you all right? Jake, can you hear me?"

He blinked until her face came back into focus, then he gazed at her, awestruck by her unimaginable beauty. How on earth had he not seen it before?

"What?" she asked in alarm.

A dazed laugh escaped him. He gazed breathlessly at her, marveling, as though he had never seen a girl before.

Nixie furrowed her brow, looking all the more adorable. She had the loveliest dark eyes, like a starry night sky...

She punched him in the arm. "Jake! Can you walk? We have to go."

"Ahh," was all he said, mesmerized by her.

"What is wrong with you?" she demanded.

"Nothing. I've never been better. I feel...wonderful, Nixie. Nixie...Valentine. Valentine! Hearts and flowers..."

She began backing away, staring at him like he had sprouted two heads. "Come on, then. Let's get going. We have to find the paintbrush."

He leaned against the tree, unable to tear his eyes off her. "Maybe we should just stay here and talk. I hardly know anything about you. Do you realize that? We've never really *talked.*"

Nixie stared at him with a sudden grimace of revulsion. "Oh, *God.*" She rolled her eyes and then started limping away rather indignantly.

"Come back, my love!" Jake called, prancing after her. He could not stop smiling and felt like he was floating.

"Would you be serious, please? This is just repulsive."

"Please! Tell me more about yourself! I must know everything!"

"Focus, idiot. We have to find the paintbrush door, remember?"

But he just laughed, charmed at how adorable she was when she was annoyed. "I don't care if you call me an idiot. I call you an angel."

"Oh, if only my wand worked," she muttered, keeping to the path.

"Why do you always wear black, little Valentine? You'd look even more beautiful if you wore some colors. But if you must wear black for your own mysterious reasons, then I shall wear it, too! Always."

"Would you snap out of it, please? You're not yourself!"

"I'm not, am I?" he agreed, considering his soaring emotions. "I've never felt so happy in all my life, actually. I'm not even hungry anymore! Maybe music really *is* the food of love. Hmm. Nixie!"

"What?" she retorted when he grasped her wrist.

"Look!" He pointed into the woods. "Let's go pet those bunny rabbits together! Maybe they'll let us hold them. They look so soft. Hullo, birdie." He held out his finger and a bluebird hopped onto it and started tweeting.

Somehow he understood every word.

"Goodbye, little friend!" he called as the bluebird flitted off into the pretty-pretty woods.

Nixie stopped hobbling down the path and turned to him.

In truth, she looked like she wanted to punch him, but instead, she pressed her lips together for a moment, perhaps holding back an exasperated curse word. "Jake."

He gazed rapturously at her. "Yes, my love?"

* * *

Nixie didn't know whether to laugh or to scream. But she saw the glazed look in Jake's blue eyes and the vacant smile on his lips, and knew perfectly well what had happened. It wasn't his fault, of course, that he was suddenly in love—with *love*, not with her, though at the moment he couldn't tell the difference.

Her first-ever suitor waited with bated breath for her to speak.

She almost started to reason with him but then gave up on that idea. There was no point in it, since she was dealing with a boy under a spell.

"If you love me," she said calmly and slowly, as though she were speaking to either a very young child or a very thick dunce, "you will help me find the paintbrush door. Do you understand what I am saying to you?"

A crestfallen look came over his admittedly handsome face. He was cute, she'd give him that. But she still liked Archie better. "Well, yes," he said, "but...why do you want to go so soon? I never want to leave this wonderful place." She jolted when he took both of her hands and held them with an earnest look. "I want to stay here forever, my darling! With you."

"Oh, puke." She scowled, thought about how that feisty little red-haired girl would want to punch her lights out for this, and yanked her hands free. Nixie strove for patience. "But, Jake, if you really loved me, you'd want to make me happy. Wouldn't you?"

"Oh..." He considered this and still looked a little disappointed, but to Nixie's relief, he must have seen she had a point and resigned himself to it. "Right! A mission for my lady. You stay here, my love, where you're safe. Rest your poor hurt ankle. I will find it for you. Leave this to me! For I am your servant!"

With that, he raced off, the golden boy of the Order, careening through the woods to do her bidding.

Nixie rolled her eyes and shook her head, but couldn't help laughing silently in relief. She leaned against a tree while he did the work.

"Found it!" he yelled several minutes later.

He ran back and helped to steady her, showing her the way up the path, solicitous over her every step. She kept her amusement to herself, but vowed she was never going to let him live this down.

"Here it is!" He presented the paintbrush doorway to her with a proud flourish. This one appeared as a rustic country gate leading into a sheep pasture on the far side of the woods.

"Ah! Good boy." She reached to give him an ironic pat on the head, but to her surprise, he captured her hand and kissed her knuckles like some sort of revolting charmer.

"I deserve a reward, don't I? Give us a kiss!" He started to pull her toward him, but she planted her feet with the stubbornness of a mule.

"Get away from me!" She arched back with a grimace as he leaned toward her, lips puckered.

Nixie shoved the idiot aside and bolted through the door.

"Come back, my princess!" he called after her, distraught, but thanks to his dart-induced infatuation, he followed.

And much to her amusement, the spell wore off as soon as he had walked a few steps into the next painting: a dim room.

Nixie glanced back over her shoulder at the sound of his mortified groan.

"Uh...what just happened?" Jake mumbled. "I don't feel so good."

She stopped and turned around. He was standing a few feet behind her, holding his head in confusion. She folded her arms across her chest, amused. "You don't remember?"

"A little." It seemed he could not bring himself to look at her. "Enough." Another pained moan of embarrassment escaped him. "I am...so sorry about that. Please don't tell anybody."

"What, that you love me until death?" she asked pleasantly.

"But I don't!" He glanced up, wide-eyed, and looked a little panicked. "I would never! Not when Archie—" He stopped himself abruptly.

Nixie arched an eyebrow. "Archie what?"

Jake lowered his head again, his forelock falling over his eyes. "Never mind. Not my place to say."

Nixie felt a bit as if she had been grazed by a love arrow herself to think that Archie might have said something nice about her to his cousin. He really was the most interesting boy, and he looked so cute in a bowtie.

For now, she chuckled at Jake's discomfiture. "Don't worry, I know full well it was just the Cupid arrow talking."

"Thanks," he mumbled, then cleared his throat and struggled to regain his dignity, glancing around in a businesslike manner. The poor lad was obviously desperate to change the subject. "Right. So where are we now?"

"No idea," Nixie said, but when she turned around and saw the scene on the other side of the large room, she quickly signaled for silence, a finger over her lips. She pointed across the dark background to where a richly dressed court dwarf and a royal lapdog in a jeweled collar were having their portrait painted.

They were both holding very still—and both looking very annoyed at the tediousness of this assignment.

Jake saw them, too, and nodded. Then they proceeded to tiptoe past, heading for the paintbrush lever on the far side of the room.

* * *

Isabelle did not know what made her glance up just then at one of the many masterworks hung around the stately parlor where the Queen received them. But the last thing she expected to see was her cousin and Nixella Valentine tiptoeing through the background of the painting.

In the presence of the Queen, the royal daughters, and the other nervous debutantes, she let out a small shriek of astonishment and sloshed her tea on herself.

Every pair of eyes in the room turned to her in startled annoyance.

"What is the matter with you, gel?" Her Majesty demanded in her no-nonsense way.

The royal princesses barely held back scornful titters, and the other debs gloated, seeing they had just moved ahead of her in

Society's great pecking order.

Isabelle gulped and looked down at her tea-stained gown. "Um," she said haltingly, "I'm so sorry. I seem to have made, er, a little spill."

Royal Victoria rolled her eyes. "Honestly, Miss Bradford, I fear that any gel who cannot manage a teacup may not be ready to join Society for some time yet."

"No, Ma'am," Isabelle agreed, lowering her head. "Sorry, Your Majesty."

"Humph. Go." The queen waved her off with a flick of her chubby, jeweled hand. "Run along, then, and do try to steady your nerves. You are excused."

"Thank you, Ma'am. Sorry again," she mumbled.

An attendant glided over and took Isabelle's half-empty teacup and dripping saucer from her, handing her a napkin in exchange.

"Er, thank you."

The other girls smirked as Isabelle dabbed at her ruined pastel skirts in dismay, then popped up to her feet, sketched a curtsy, and started backing out. One did not turn one's back on the monarch. At least she managed to remember that much.

As she walked backward slowly toward the door, trying not to trip and ruin whatever dignity she had left, she ran a furtive gaze over the art on the walls and held her breath when she spotted her cousin again.

How on earth had he got inside the paintings?

Oh, Jake, what have you done now?

He and Nixie had somehow found their way out of the background of the dwarf's portrait and were now slogging with obvious difficulty across the gooey ground of a blurry, swirly, riverbank scene, in that radical new style known as Impressionism.

But dread filled Isabelle when she saw where they were heading next. *No, don't go that way!*

She had no idea how they were traveling from one picture to the next, but the painting dead ahead of the river scene—the one they'd reach as soon as they turned the corner—was the giant, twenty-foot mural labeled *The Last Day of Pompeii.*

It showed the legendary catastrophe of Mt. Vesuvius erupting, spewing lava all over the Mediterranean like an ancient doomsday.

As she bumped up against the door, Isabelle had no way of signaling her cousin not to go there. Somehow at that very moment,

Jake glanced into the parlor and spotted her there.

At once, he ran up to the frame of the picture and began waving his arms to make sure he'd got her attention. Oh, she saw him, all right, and the look of distress on his face told her he was desperate to get out.

She tried not to stare, worried that somebody else might notice her shocked gaze and also see him. There was no telling what sort of trouble he might get into with the Elders if they found out he was traipsing around inside the palace art collection. She did not know how to help him.

When the attendant opened the parlor door for her to leave, looking at her with a mix of pity and disdain for her blunder a moment ago, there was nothing she could do. She offered a hapless smile and stepped out; the door closed in her face.

She whirled around. *I have to find the others.*

Isabelle dared not waste any time trying to reason with adults right now. She had to tell Archie and Dani that Jake and Nixie were stuck inside the Enchanted Gallery. Her brilliant brother would surely dream up some notion of how to get their cousin and the witch out of the magical paintings.

Sneaking past the room where the chaperones waited for their girls to return, she slipped down the opposite hallway. Unfortunately, this meant she had to go by the room where the vampire was pacing back and forth, waiting for his turn to see the Queen.

He pivoted on his heel and pinned her with his unnerving stare, letting out a small hiss as she hurried by. Isabelle met his gaze for a fleeting second as she fled, but fortunately, he made no move to follow her—not with two large Guardians posted by the door.

One could never be too careful with a vampire.

It wasn't long before she rushed back into her family's suite on the upper floor in Merlin Hall, bursting to tell the other two about Jake's latest scrape.

"Archie? Dani?" she called as soon as she stepped into the apartment.

"In here!" Dani hollered back.

Isabelle rushed toward the girls' room, opened the door—and screamed at the site of Dani O'Dell sitting in a bathtub full of blood.

"Calm down, it's just tomato juice!" Dani said. "We got skunked."

"What?" Isabelle clutched her chest and leaned against the

doorframe, having been scared half to death. Lud, crossing paths with that vampire must have given her thoughts of blood on the brain. "You're all right?" she forced out, trying to recover.

"Aye, just really stinky," Dani said in disgust. "Archie said the only way to get rid of skunk smell is to take a soak in tomato puree. The gnomes gave us every can from the pantry. He's in there, by the way." She pointed toward the boys' room. "Don't have a conniption when you see him, though, he's fine! We both are. And we figured out who took the Queen's flag. You were right. It was the skunkies."

"Lord Badgerton's niece and nephews?" she clarified, still rattled as she went to check on her brother.

"That's right, sis," Archie drawled, his tone sounding unconcerned, but his appearance quite ghastly, in her view, as he sat up to his chest in blood-red tomato puree.

It was plastered in his dark hair and streaked across his freckled face, and the sight of it made Isabelle cringe.

"Afraid they got us good," he admitted. "We were ambushed. But this isn't over, believe me. Once we're de-skunked, we strike back."

"We just haven't figured out how yet!" Dani agreed from the other room. Isabelle could hear in her voice that she had definitely got her Irish up.

Isabelle shook her head to clear it. "Never mind that. We've got bigger problems. Jake and Nixie Valentine are stuck inside the Enchanted Gallery."

"*What?*" the two tomatoes shouted in unison.

"It gave me such a shock it made me spill my tea!" She explained what had happened and then rapidly concluded, "How they ended up in there, I have no idea, but we've got to get them out. Wash all that horrid red stuff off you and then we can start figuring out how to help them!"

They hurriedly agreed.

While the younger pair washed off the tomato puree with soap and water and then dried themselves and dressed in their separate rooms. Isabelle changed out of her fancy gown into a more ordinary walking dress, and then strove to rub the tea stain out of her skirt with some lemon juice before her governess saw it.

She had no idea what she was going to say to Miss Helena about the whole debacle—or to Mama, for that matter. At the moment, her social failure with the Queen seemed insignificant next to the problem of getting Jake and Nixie out of the palace artwork.

She hoped they were not getting turned into charred stone figures like those poor souls who had died so long ago in the famous ruin of Pompeii.

"Right, then. We need information," Archie said, striding out of his room, adjusting his lucky bowtie and looking neat and tidy once more, though he still smelled faintly of skunk. "I'll go to the library and dig up any clues I can on how to get someone out of the collection."

"Well, if you've got that under control," Dani said as she came out of the girls' room in the middle of braiding her hair in two pigtails, "*I'll* keep working on getting the Queen's flag back from the skunkies. Hopefully by now they haven't got rid of it to try to hide the evidence."

"What exactly do you mean to do?" Isabelle asked, reaching to help finish her braids.

"Steal it back from them," Dani declared, folding her arms across her chest while Isabelle worked on her hair.

"What if you get sprayed again?"

"I won't."

"You sound very sure."

"Because I am. I'm gonna get those three if it's the last thing I do. Disgusting little rats." Brushing off Isabelle's help, Dani finished tying the ribbon around her braid, then she set her fists resolutely on her waist.

It was then the rookery lass decided not to share with the genteel Bradfords the true extent of her Dark and Cunning Plan.

Namely, revenge.

Nobody skunk sprays me, Dani vowed to herself. *This is war.*

Those shapeshifter kids had made fools out of her and Archie by using their powers unfairly. She was sick and tired of being the only one around here with no magical abilities.

It was time to even the odds.

She knew just what she was going to do, too. She had thought it all out while sitting in the bathtub, and she was past caring if it brought her bad luck. She didn't dare tell Archie and Isabelle what she intended, because she knew they'd only try to stop her, and there were times when an O'Dell simply couldn't be stopped.

This was personal now.

Besides, she had promised Jake she'd help to clear his name, and Dani always kept a promise. She was *getting* that flag back, and then she was going to tell the Elders who the real thieves were.

Those skunkies were going to be sorry. This time, they had messed with the wrong redhead.

CHAPTER TWENTY-FIVE
Explosions

Jake and Nixie stumbled into the next painting and found themselves amid the end of the world. At least, that was what it looked like as Mt. Vesuvius belched fiery lava into the sky.

Hordes of fleeing people in togas raced past them, deafening them with their screams. Jake had never heard such a racket of men shouting, women weeping, babies crying, dogs barking. And all the while, the mountain rumbled in the distance like an angry, waking god.

Falling chunks of glowing-hot stone caught the buildings on fire as they punched through the roofs. Smoke lay as thick as the panic in the streets, choking Jake and Nixie as they tried to get their bearings. They were bumped and jostled to and fro, and had to hold onto each other to avoid being trampled or swept along with the stampede of evacuating townsfolk.

Shielding their mouths and noses to avoid breathing in the powdered ash that fell like snow, they struggled to figure out which way to go in the chaos.

"I think we're in Pompeii!" Nixie cried over the chaos.

Jake nodded, glancing around. This part of the doomed ancient city was a maze of narrow, twisting lanes; the smoke crept thickly through the streets like a great grey serpent looking for someone it could squeeze the life from. "We'd better get out of here, fast."

"We can't just leave, we need to find the next paintbrush! It's got to be here somewhere—" Nixie let out a sudden cry of pain as the surging crowd made her trip on her sprained ankle.

Jake caught her. Coughing a bit, he quickly helped her over to the side of the street, taking refuge in a sturdy spot between two houses. "Are you all right?"

She nodded, rubbing her leg, but he could see she was holding back tears of pain.

"Nixie, never mind the paintbrush for now. This city is doomed. We've got to evacuate while we can or we're going to get killed."

"All right." She steadied herself. "Maybe we could try to get away in one of those boats?"

She pointed down the stone street to the sea-port, where Roman galley ships were filling up with desperate people trying to escape the flaming missiles from the volcano. It seemed a dodgy solution at best. The sea churned with violent waves from earthquakes in the seabed, helping to prime the volcano's fury aboveground.

Even as Jake gazed at the port, weighing this option, one of the boats took a direct hit from a red-hot boulder, and everyone aboard it burst into flames.

"Maybe not." He shook his head, torn about which way to go.

"Jake, I know we have to get as far away from this place as we can, but what if the paintbrush doorway is right here *in* Pompeii?" Nixie spoke up. "When the last big blast from the volcano comes, everything in this city is going to be destroyed. If the paintbrush is somewhere in the town, that includes our only way out."

He gave her a grim glance. "Good point."

"You've got to find it. Go," she said. "I'll only slow you down."

"I'm not leaving you behind!"

"It's all right! Get to higher ground and see if you can spot it. The paintbrush, I mean. If you can see it somewhere in the town, at least then we'll know which way to go. If not, then we can evacuate. But we have to make sure. Hurry up and go. I'll wait here."

"Very well, but don't leave this spot. We can't afford to get separated. I'll be right back!"

She nodded. "Good luck."

Jake hated to leave her by herself in the middle of one of history's greatest emergencies, but she was right. If the paintbrush was here in Pompeii, it would soon be destroyed and then they might never get out of Ancient Rome.

He did not intend to die inside a painting. Ducking into the abandoned stucco house they had been leaning against, he dashed straight up the clay stairs, taking them two at a time.

A moment later, he reached the top floor and stepped out onto a rooftop patio with a view of the sea. Its canvas canopy was singed and smoking, but still intact. Potted lemon and fig trees and tubs of colorful flowers were placed here and there, along with a stone statue of some ancient Roman god. But the people who lived there must have fled in the middle of supper, in terror for their lives. Their abandoned meal was still sitting out on the mosaic-tiled table, under an ever-deepening layer of snowy ash.

Striding over to the edge, Jake stared at the hellish landscape of darkness and smoke before him. It sent a chill down his spine, knowing in advance that there was no hope for Pompeii or its neighbor, Herculaneum.

Scanning the city as best he could in the artificial twilight of the ash cloud, his eyes smarted from the smoke. He did not see any paintbrush in the chaotic streets around him nor in the surrounding countryside, with its olive orchards and huge, classical villas of the wealthy Roman aristocrats.

Blast it, where are you? He wished he had brought along his new telescope from Archie. The gadget's night vision lens would have come in handy.

Then, by the flare of a fireball that went arcing by overhead and slammed into the houses a block away, he spotted not the paintbrush door, but the window frame where he could look out into whichever room in Merlin Hall the Vesuvius painting was currently displayed.

Like all the rest that he had seen so far, the window hung weirdly suspended in midair, attached to nothing. It was huge, just sort of floating there, above another rooftop patio a few houses away.

Jake furrowed his brow, weighing his options.

Considering the gravity of their situation, he decided to go and try to get somebody's attention out there.

Nixie was already injured, and their situation, in all, was looking increasingly grim. He was not normally one to admit such a thing, but all vanity aside, the truth was, they needed help. At least Isabelle had seen them. He knew that she would fetch the others, and that his allies, especially Archie, would start to work immediately on figuring out how to free them. But how much longer could Nixie and he really afford to wait?

They were completely lost, without food or water, and if the volcano destroyed their only way out, they might need rescue from the outside somehow. Besides, although this was the most dangerous painting they had been in so far, what if the next one was worse?

If he could just flag down somebody's attention out there...

Knowing Nixie was waiting for him below, he set out across the rooftops. It wasn't his original mission—she expected him to try to find the paintbrush—but this wouldn't take long and it might just save their lives.

Fortunately, the houses in this part of the city were either connected by shared walls or had only narrow gaps between them, just a few feet wide. Going from roof to roof was a small thing for a former thief. So, off he went.

He jumped the gaps above a few passageways and climbed over a few wooden privacy fences, relieved that he did not cross paths with any of the residents in the midst of his trespassing. It seemed nobody was left to bother him. By now, everyone was long gone.

Please somebody be out there, he thought as he jogged across the patio toward the huge window. He climbed up onto a long table to get high enough to reach it.

As he crept up to the window, he moved with caution, unsure what he might find. The Bugganes might still be out there, hunting for him and Nixie. For all he knew, they might have figured a way to get in by now.

Instead, Jake was shocked to see that, after all the ground he'd thought they had covered, they had merely gone around the corner in the Queen's parlor—still in the same room!

Queen Victoria was sitting in her chair, but her daughters and all the debutantes had gone. There were others in the chamber now, older people. *Elders?* It looked like some sort of meeting in progress.

Jake knew full well that spying on the Queen's private conferences was forbidden. But when he peered around the room and saw who was speaking, he gasped in shock.

The vampire!

He paced restlessly back and forth across the chamber as he spoke. "Of course, I have certain demands in exchange for my information."

"And what might those be, Your Highness?"

That thing's a prince? Jake thought, ducking his head a bit to avoid being noticed, but he listened for all he was worth.

"Firstly, I want a seat in the magical parliament for my people. The vampire race deserves to have a voice among Magic-kind."

"That is never going to happen," a white-haired Elder wizard answered.

"Oh, but it will if you want to save your Lightriders," the vampire chided. "Secondly, I want the Order's help in finding a cure for the illness that afflicts my brides. You may think me cold, and no doubt, I am, but even I cannot bear to see the suffering of my wives and the withering of our hatchlings. There is some plague upon us, but I have confidence that your healing experts can help me find a cure."

The Elders exchanged guarded glances.

"We wish no harm upon your younglings, Prince Janos," an old wizard said. "This request is one we could consider. After all, it is not the vampire babes' fault that they are born of darkness."

"Born of darkness—?" the vampire sputtered, offended. "For your information, we are not *all* evil. Give me a little credit, old man! You know perfectly well I have used all my influence to keep the vampire race neutral in your ongoing spat with the Dark Druids. If not for my efforts, the vampires would have joined forces with your enemies years ago, and then where would you be?"

"Well, if you are here to help us as you claim, Prince Janos, the Dark Druids will know you've chosen sides. They will not easily forgive you," Dame Oriel warned.

"True." The vampire prince shrugged. "But as much as one might wish to be left alone to rest in peace in one's coffin, one cannot always stay out of a fight. And believe me, you've got a fight coming. Which leads me to my third demand."

"Let me guess." It was Sir Peter Quince who had spoken, Jake noticed in surprise. "You wish to be made back into a mortal, hmm? Resume your old post alongside Guardian Stone?"

"Hardly," the vampire said with a smirk that showed the tips of his fangs. "I want Urso the Shapeshifter released from the Order's dungeon in Romania."

"Absolutely not!" the old wizard huffed. "He was caught red-handed in the middle of last year's Gathering, spying for the Dark Druids!"

"Oh, he was not here to spy on anyone! Your Majesty, you have to believe me," the vampire said impatiently, taking a step toward Queen Victoria.

Two large Guardians instantly blocked his path.

He gave them a long-suffering look. "Urso came here for my sake, if you must know. I told him it was stupid, but if you knew the Bear, you'd understand. He only broke in to try to steal one of your healers' potions for my family."

"Who is he talking about, Sir Peter?" the Queen asked with a frown.

"A very large, very loud, German shapeshifter, Your Majesty. Very fond of beer, too, as I recall," Sir Peter said. "His animal form is that of a great Alpine bear. He followed the prince into exile."

"Urso's very loyal to me," Janos admitted with a shrug. "Which is why I demand his release if you want my information."

"Give us the information first in good faith, and we will consider what you ask."

"You will betray me!" he shot back.

"Like you betrayed us? No, Janos," Dame Oriel chided. "We keep our word, unlike your kind. Convince us first that your information is truthful, and we shall proceed from there."

Just then, a voice called to Jake from behind him on the rooftop.

"Jake! What are you *doing*?"

He shushed Nixie as she came limping over to stand beside the table with an angry glower, hands on hips. "Didn't you hear me calling you? I found the paintbrush."

"You did?" he asked in surprise.

"Come on, let's go!"

"Just a minute. Something big is happening in there," he whispered, gesturing to the room, where the vampire let out a world-weary sigh and shook his head.

"Very well. I shall be at your mercy, then, and my wives and children, too. But if that's the way you want it... The Order's always got to get its way, doesn't it? Some things never change."

Climbing up onto the table beside him, Nixie looked at Jake in astonishment when she saw Her Majesty in the parlor. "You can't eavesdrop on the Queen!" she whispered.

"Shut *up*," Jake breathed, straining with all his might to hear the vampire's guarded information above the din of the volcano and the screams of the populace below.

"I hear rumblings, you know, in my mountain stronghold in the Carpathians. Creatures of shadow often pass through my lands and bring us news. What I have heard is only a rumor as of now, but I would give it credence if I were you. Your Lightriders are in imminent danger."

"Which ones?" asked Sir Peter.

"All of them." Jake leaned closer as the vampire glanced around the room. "My creatures of the night—the bats, the wolves, the moths—they tell me the Dark Druids are preparing...for war."

The Elders reacted with shock all at once.

"What?"

"What's this?" they exploded.

"You lie!"

"Never trust a vampire, Your Majesty."

"The truce—!"

"Our treaty with the Dark Druids has been in place for fifty years!" Queen Victoria declared.

"It has been broken," the vampire informed her. Then he looked around at them. "Is it possible you really don't know what your long-lost golden boy has done?"

Silence fell.

Nixie turned to Jake, who turned white.

"What are you talking about?" the old wizard demanded.

"The Griffon heir, Jacob Everton," the vampire said. "You have him to thank for this."

Jake's jaw dropped as the Elders and the Queen protested in confusion.

"You cannot mean young Jacob. He's only a boy!"

"What's he got to do with this?"

"Perhaps you should ask Guardian Stone," the vampire said. "He's been keeping secrets, protecting him."

Jake's pulse pounded in his ears.

"I was told by a raven that, this past Samhain, a demon called Shemrazul—one of their foul servants, whom they often conjure—came forward among the Dark Druids. Shemrazul reported to his masters that Garnock the Sorcerer was woken from his tomb in Wales not long ago.

"Apparently, some Welsh coalmining company stumbled upon the cave where the Lightriders had buried Garnock alive centuries ago. Once the miners broke the seal on the tomb, the ancient binding spells the Lightriders used to trap him were broken, and his spirit escaped in wraith form.

"Young Lord Griffon happened to be on holiday in Wales at the time; his family has an estate there. Verify it for yourself. I am surprised that his aunt, the old witch, what's her name, Lady Bradford, did not share the story with you. But perhaps Her Ladyship is protecting him, as well."

The Elders glanced around at each other in shock.

The vampire shrugged off their stunned silence. "It seems Garnock was trying to regenerate his physical form using the Spell of a Hundred Souls. The boy spotted him preying on the locals. He has the gift of seeing spirits, does he not?"

From the corner of his eye, Jake noticed Nixie staring at him with her jaw hanging slack. She mouthed the words, *What did you do?*

Jake just looked at her, distraught.

"Nobody's quite sure how the boy did it," the vampire continued. "He might have had help from the Welsh dwarf clans who dwell in the Black Mountains there, though certainly they're not known for magic. The point is, by the time the boy and his gryphon left Wales, according to Shemrazul, Garnock the Sorcerer had been utterly destroyed."

Sir Peter was the first to recover from the shock of this news. "Oh, come, Prince Janos," he said with an uncomfortable little laugh. "You cannot mean for us to believe that a mere youngster could ever defeat the founder of the Dark Druids."

"Why don't you ask him yourselves?" the vampire replied with a subtle glance in the direction of the painting.

Jake and Nixie gasped and ducked lower, plunging out of sight. As they crouched below the bottom edge of the frame, Nixie looked at Jake in question, clearly wondering if the vampire could indeed really sense them—and if he intended to expose their presence.

Jake had no idea. His mind was in too much of an uproar for him to have any sort of opinion on the matter.

Nobody was to have found out that he had defeated Garnock, but he hadn't counted on word of his deed spreading in the underworld. Now it seemed like Derek and Helena, Gladwin, and even Aunt Ramona might all get into trouble for keeping his secret.

They had only done it to protect him.

"Well, I am only telling you what I have heard," the vampire said. "The important thing is, the Dark Druids have now heard this story from their demon, and they have vowed revenge. Let a mere boy crush their founding master? They cannot allow this blow to their prestige to stand. It would undermine their authority. Moreover, this gives them the excuse they've long watched and waited for: to make their play for power.

"You know it is their way to attack without warning," Prince Janos added. "That's why I am here. To give you all fair notice of what you're up against. Hopefully, my noble gallantry won't get me killed."

Someone scoffed.

"All I can tell you for now is that, according to them, the son of a Lightrider broke the truce and slew their master. Therefore, in their eyes, it's the Lightriders, all of them, who must be made to pay. None of them are safe now..."

Jake was in a daze, so horrified by all that he was hearing that he barely noticed the fireball that came screaming out of the sky straight at them. Without warning, Nixie pulled him off the picnic table, yelling at him to take cover. They dove behind the table as a large chunk of glowing stone slammed into the far corner of the roof that they were standing on.

The whole building shook; a corner of it exploded into a cloud of dust and crumbled away. The canvas sun-shade overhead caught fire. Black smoke billowed in the air above them.

"Come on, we've got to get out of here!" Nixie straightened up at once and limped as fast as she could toward the doorway.

Jake hesitated, glancing back toward the frame, desperate to hear more.

"Jake, come on, it's too dangerous! Besides, you can't do anything about this if we get stuck inside this painting!"

She was right. Another direct hit like that, and the whole building would collapse. They'd be buried in the rubble. Grimly, he tore himself away and caught up with her in a few strides.

They hurried back downstairs and out into the streets of Pompeii. The city seemed eerily abandoned now. Everyone who *could* take shelter already had, not that cowering in their cellars would do them any good. They could not hide from the toxic fumes nor the tidal wave of oven-hot volcanic matter that would soon come rushing down the mountainside.

For now, the ash was falling faster, swishing around their shins, light and powdery as snow.

"The paintbrush is this way," Nixie said urgently.

Jake followed her down the street, but could barely pay attention. His head was spinning. *I can't believe I've nearly started a war,* he just kept thinking, over and over again.

"Quit dawdling!" Nixie shouted, impatiently grabbing his arm and pulling him toward an ancient-style public well. The wooden handle was made in the shape of a paintbrush.

"Good find," Jake murmured, doubting he ever would have noticed it there. They moved closer, stepping up onto the platform around the well.

Jake tried to focus, though he was still numb with shock after that devastating news. "What do we do? Drink from it?"

"Dunno. Let me try pumping it."

But when Nixie pulled on the handle, it acted as a lever, opening a trapdoor under their feet. Instantly, the platform they were standing on gave way and dropped them into the well.

"Whoa!"

They fell into pure darkness, but instead of plunging straight down, they landed on their backsides and proceeded to whoosh and whiz down a long, twisting, stone slide. They both screamed most of the way down, until the dark tunnel dropped them out of the sky onto a haystack.

Jake landed with an *oof!* Nixie's cry was considerably sharper. He still couldn't see her, temporarily blinded by the dazzling sunshine.

"Did you land on your ankle?"

She groaned. "I think I'm all right."

As his vision started clearing, he sat up and glanced around anxiously, but there was no sign of Mt. Vesuvius—though their clothes still smelled of smoke. Other than that, it appeared that, once more, they had survived.

"Ugh." He fell onto his back in the hay and let himself relax for just a moment, striving for clarity. These leaps from one painting world to another were growing extremely disorienting.

"Jake!" Nixie uttered all of a sudden, looking around. "I know where we are!"

"You do?"

"It's the farmhouse painting! The safe one. Look! The old farmhouse in Provence!"

"Are you sure?"

"Look at this field around us! Don't you recognize the sunflowers?"

She was right.

"Sweet Pleiades! I think we're actually safe here." The young witch let out a sigh of relief and flopped onto the haystack, which was about the size of an elephant's back.

After the day they were having—and the news he had heard—Jake had a hard time believing they were actually safe.

"We should get out of the way in case anyone else drops in." He pointed at the opening of the tunnel weirdly hanging in the blue sky above them.

Though it dissolved even as they looked at it, one couldn't be too careful. "Hurry, let's get down. We're too visible up here. Who knows who might see us?"

"I suppose." Nixie didn't want to move, but she joined him in carefully sliding down to the ground.

He felt better when he had gained his feet. He looked over at Nixie to see if she was ready to continue and found her staring at him with a trace of awe.

"What?" he mumbled self-consciously.

"*You* killed Garnock the Sorcerer?"

He wasn't sure what to say; she had heard for herself what the vampire had reported. He heaved a sigh and finally admitted, "Sort of. He was technically dead when we met. But you're not allowed to tell anyone!"

"Don't worry, I won't. Sounds like they already know, anyway." She eyed him with lingering wonder.

"Would you stop looking at me like I'm a freak?"

She shrugged. "I just wouldn't have thought you had it in you, that's all."

He huffed.

"What I *mean* is that I wouldn't have thought somebody who wasn't even a wizard would have a chance against the original Dark Druid."

"Well, magic isn't everything, Nixie. Plus, Garnock nearly killed me in the process, if it makes you feel any better. And Isabelle, too, and a lot of other innocent people in Wales. Now let's go." He led the way into the field of sunflowers, rattled.

Broad, green leaves acted as flimsy doors, but he pushed them aside, stepping into one of the narrow rows between the towering plants.

The tough, fuzzy stalks reached several feet over their heads as Nixie followed. It was shady and green under the dense, emerald canopy of leaves, like walking through a sunflower forest. He felt as small as Gladwin. It was soothing and delightful, like everything in this painting was meant to be.

Still, all things considered, Jake was not yet fully convinced that something horrible would not pop out at them.

After several moments of hiking down the dirt furrow between the rows of flowers, Nixie spoke again in a thoughtful tone.

"Maybe you *are* meant to be a hero like they say."

Jake shook his head. "No, Nixie, I'm a menace to society," he mumbled.

"Can't believe I finally met somebody who's got worse problems than I do."

Jake sent her a thanks-a-lot look over his shoulder and kept walking.

"Wait." He stopped and turned around. "I mean...are you all right?" she asked cautiously, as though it was unfamiliar to her to let herself care.

"Of course I'm not all right!" he exclaimed. "I've gone and started a war! This is a lot worse than being accused of stealing the Queen's flag."

"There isn't any war yet! Maybe it won't happen."

He snorted. "Do you really believe that?"

She frowned, uncertainty written all over her snow-white face. "At least the vampire came and warned the Order so we can prepare."

He shook his head in disgust and resumed walking. "I don't want to talk about it. Come on."

"Where are we going, anyway?"

"To find the way out."

"We should rest. I'm exhausted."

"There was a grassy field beyond this one where you could lie down if you want. I'll keep looking for the exit."

"Can't we just stay here for a while? The Bugganes can't get us here. I need to rest before I'm ready to face them again."

"You can do as you please, but I've got to get out there and try to fix this."

"How are *you* supposed to fix this? You're just a kid. Let the adults handle it."

"You don't understand. This is all my fault!"

"No, it's not!" she insisted. "What were you supposed to do, let Garnock the Sorcerer bring himself back to life? You had to send him back to Hades with his beloved demons."

He paused. "You know about the demons?"

"He was famous for consorting with them. Jake, that's what black magic is." She shook her head. "I can't believe he even tried the Spell of a Hundred Souls. It's a pretty infamous spell, you know, among us mages."

He turned away. "Would you please stop talking about it now? I feel sick enough about it as it is. Either change the subject or just shut up for a while. Why do girls constantly have to be talking?"

"Pardon me, but you're not the only one who's ever got on the wrong side of the Dark Druids."

Jake pivoted to face her. "What do you mean by that?"

She clammed up and looked away.

"Nixie?" he asked sternly.

"Fine!" She rolled her eyes, then nervously met his gaze. "Those Bugganes?"

"Yes?"

"I banished them from Castle MacGool in Scotland. The castle and surrounding area had been their haunting spot for centuries. Over time, they had appointed themselves the protecting spirits of all members of the Clan MacGool. But the Laird MacGool and his family, Jake, they were horrible. Aristocrats," she said with a curl of her lip.

"Er, excuse me. Earl," he said, pointing to his person.

Nixie shrugged off his protest. "The MacGools made everybody's lives miserable in their county. Raised rents until the villagers were nearly bankrupt, held the people down with mad laws on every little thing. They owned the constable and the local judge, so they could have anyone arrested who tried to stand against them. No one could ever touch them because of the Bugganes acting as their supernatural helpers in everything. Any brave soul who went up to the castle to try to lay their complaint before the laird usually ended up running out screaming in terror—*if* they even got out alive.

"Well, when I used magic to banish the Bugganes from Castle MacGool and help the local villagers, I only meant to even the odds a bit."

Jake nodded, fully sympathetic. He would have done the same thing. "So what happened?"

She winced. "Once the villagers realized the MacGools were defenseless, they rose up and stormed the castle." She shook her head in dismay. "They got whipped up into a mob frenzy and decided to take revenge after all those years of being oppressed. They lynched the laird, tarred and feathered his heir, and ran the rest of his family out to sea. You don't push a Scot around forever." She paused. "I should have realized that a horrid, powerful clan like the MacGools would be in league with the Dark Druids. And you know the Dark Ones. They look after their own." A sorrowful expression stole into Nixie's eyes. "Three nights after the attack on the castle, on the full moon, a plague of fever and boils struck the town. Dozens of people died over the next few days. It was...an unnatural illness. They had been cursed.

"I know the Dark Druids sent the plague. But I never meant for those villagers to go on a rampage like that! They should have let it go and just enjoyed their freedom. But they had to get revenge. They brought it on themselves," she said bitterly.

Jake shrugged. "There's no helping some people."

"I'm not doing anything nice for anybody ever again," Nixie said.

Jake did not deign to point out that she had just saved his life back there in Pompeii. "Do the Dark Druids know you're the one who banished the Bugganes?"

"No. Thank goodness," she whispered with a worried look. "I always keep my magic fairly secret when I'm out in the world."

He could believe it. She was not the sort to want to draw attention to herself. He nodded in relief. "Good."

They continued walking.

"So that's why the Bugganes are haunting you," he remarked as he waved off a honeybee that flew past.

"Of course. I drove them out of their home," she replied. "But they also blame me for getting their nasty friends, the MacGools, killed. That's why they've vowed to kill anybody who makes friends with me."

"You might have mentioned that," he said dryly.

"I did. Remember? But you insisted on getting involved anyway."

"I'm only teasing. Besides, Archie would kill me if I had left you to your fate. We can help you, you know. The offer still stands. You can't face this alone. You're too outnumbered. We can take them on if we battle them together. Everyone needs allies."

Especially if there is to be a war.

Nixie was silent for a moment. "Maybe you *can* actually help me," she conceded in a low tone. "If you were good enough to beat Garnock..."

He glanced over his shoulder at her, a question still tugging at his mind. "Something about your story... The local people up in Scotland actually believed in these Bugganes?"

"They're the ones who invented them. At least, they invented Jenny Greenteeth."

Jake furrowed his brow. "How's that?"

"Jenny Greenteeth started out as a nursery bogey," Nixie explained. "There are many ponds and lochs and streams in the Scottish Highlands, y'see. So, a great long time ago, the parents invented Jenny Greenteeth to warn their little ones away from the water. They didn't want their toddlers falling in and drowning. So they told them, *'Don't go near the water or Jenny Greenteeth will get you.'* When enough children grew up believing in her and being terrified of her, she eventually became real."

"Became real?" He pushed aside a bent sunflower stalk that leaned across their path.

"That's how magic works. Things you believe in that intensely for a period of time have a funny way of coming into being."

"Like your mud-rabbit?"

"Yes, that's a form of it. A kind of golem. Unfortunately, I was too nervous to believe in him enough. Of course, I've always had trouble working with the earth element, too. The other three are a lot easier for me, don't know why."

"Hey, look! Here we are." Jake stepped out of the furrow, leaving the sunflower forest. Ahead, a sunny green meadow stretched before them, just like in the painting.

Nixie stepped up beside him. "Beautiful."

With the sunshine warming their faces and just enough of a breeze to stir the air, the cheerful tweeting of birds and the continuous song of cicadas to lull them to rest, it was the most supremely peaceful spot on which Jake had ever stood. Perhaps it wasn't as pretty as the spun-sugar fantasy of the French Baroque, but its humble, earthy simplicity made it seem that much more welcoming and cozy.

Nixie suddenly yawned. "I'm taking a nap." She walked a few steps ahead of him into the field and lay down, almost disappearing into the tall grass. A happy sigh came up from the spot. "Sleep! At last. How I've dreamed of this."

Jake didn't have the heart to tell her to get up. She had been a proper trooper all day, especially with a sprained ankle.

"And I don't need *you* anymore," she said, but Jake realized she was not talking to him, as her broken wand came flying up out of the tall grass where she had nested.

The wand fell to earth like any ordinary twig.

He smiled ruefully, but wondered how different their whole day might have turned out if her wand had not snapped in half right at the beginning of their adventure.

"Right, well. I'll try to find the exit."

"Why don't you go and see if there's somebody up at the farmhouse?" she suggested without getting up. "If some of the fugitives are still alive in here, maybe they'll tell us how to get out. Not that I'm in any hurry to go *now*. This feels wonderful."

Jake gazed off into the distance at the lovely French farmhouse, then shook his head. "Nah, the luck we're having, I'd just as soon keep my distance. If people are in there, they might not be too happy about having their sanctuary invaded by a couple of outsiders."

"But they might have real food. You said you were hungry."

"Not anymore." He still felt sick to his stomach after the horrifying news that he may have inadvertently started a war with the Dark Druids.

Unnerving memories surfaced of his final confrontation with Garnock, deep below the Black Mountains, there on the edge of the underworld. But he brushed them off with an angry glance around and focused his attention on getting out of here.

Scanning the golden French landscape in all its sun-kissed tranquility, he let out a weary sigh and wondered where to start his search for the next, and hopefully last, paintbrush. Or maybe it was some different mechanism here, considering the importance of this particular painting to the collection as a whole?

Only one way to find out. He turned once more to Nixie—or rather, to the grass where she was concealed. "Right, I'm off, then. But don't worry, I'll be back soon," he said.

The only answer was a snore.

CHAPTER TWENTY-SIX
Landscape with Monsters

"**E**ureka!" Archie whispered as twilight filtered in through the stained glass windows of the great library.

He had searched for hours, but when the stacks had yielded nothing, had finally taken a cue from Nixie, sneaking into the restricted section.

He knew he could get in serious trouble for this, but he had to help Jake and her find their way out of the Enchanted Gallery. Besides, he was twelve now, and someone who was twelve could not be realistically expected to follow the rules one hundred percent of the time. Even for Archie, it just wasn't possible.

Until that moment, the long day of scouring old books and folios had yielded nothing but eyestrain. Presently, he lifted a folded map out from between the pages of a thick tome about Merlin Hall. His heart began to pound as he unfolded it with care.

Yes! It was just what he had hoped to find—a clever diagram that showed how the paintings were connected. He quickly folded it up again and slid it into his waistcoat. *Jake, old boy, you must be a bad influence on me.*

Archie Bradford—stealing! What was the world coming to?

Well, he'd put it back just as soon as his friends were safe. Silently closing the book, he put it back on the shelf and made a mental note of where he had found it. Now all he had to do was slip out of here without getting caught and somehow get the map to Jake. Archie dusted off his hands, fought back a sneeze from the dust on the ancient shelves, then crept to the edge of the aisle and glanced around. No sign of the librarian or anybody else.

But of course not, he thought wryly. If it were raining, perhaps, but nobody in their right mind would want to spend a beautiful spring evening like this in a lonely old library.

Archie made no sound as he tiptoed down the narrow spiral of wrought-iron stairs. He climbed over the chain strung across the bottom step and headed for the exit.

All of a sudden, a thunderous "ha!" nearly made his heart stop. He gasped with shock as Ogden Trumbull leaped out from between the bookshelves and pointed an accusing finger at him. "You were up there!"

"Shh!"

"I saw you! You're gonna get in so much trouble! Nobody's allowed in the restricted section!"

"Would you be quiet? I had a good reason!" Archie hissed angrily.

"Don't matter, I'm gonna tell! I'm gonna tell on you!" The troll hybrid bounded off in the direction of the librarian's desk.

"Ogden! Ogden," Archie repeated in a sharper tone. "I'm warning you."

"What?" the creature flung back, pausing, to Archie's relief. "What are you gonna do, get your Guardian friends after me again? They're not here now. There's nobody here to protect you, puny little runt! I could squash you right now and no one would even know."

"No, you couldn't. You'd better try being nicer to me, Ogden," Archie said, sweat dampening his palms as he slipped his hand casually into his pocket.

The time had come to put his Bully Buzzer to the test. Good thing he'd got his hands on that blow-gun earlier today and secretly planted the brass nodes on Og's back. With Jake and Nixie stuck in the paintings, he could hardly spare the time for such nonsense. Unfortunately, he was well aware that, with Ogden lurking around, his own safety and that of all the other kids' at Merlin Hall was at stake. Somebody had to get the bully under control. And besides, this was personal.

"Ha, ha!" Og went on taunting him. "You gonna tell me what to do, gnat? I'm not afraid of you."

"Keep your distance."

"Or what?" His piggish eyes gleaming with belligerence, the towering brute took a step closer. "Why don't you make me—*ack*!"

Og suddenly fell to the floor, his big, gray body going rigid, his face contorting slightly from the electrical charge, though, in truth, it was hard to notice much difference, ugly as he was.

Looks like it works. Archie was altogether pleased.

"Something wrong, Ogden?" he asked in a casual tone, gazing down at his would-be tormentor.

"Help—me!"

"Help someone who was just threatening me? Why would I want to do that?" He did, however, let go of the button on the controller discreetly hidden in his pocket.

Ogden panted but made no effort to get up. He looked exceedingly confused.

Archie couldn't help gloating. "Now, Ogden, I would advise that you remember this feeling next time you want to start a fight with someone for no reason. You never know," he added, "the two might be related somehow—picking a fight and this seizure of yours. So much anger! It's really not healthy."

The troll hybrid stared at him in confusion.

"Au revoir," Archie said pleasantly. Then he simply walked around the lout, brimming with pride in his new gadget.

He punched the air in victory as soon as he stepped outside and took off running for the Enchanted Gallery.

He was surprised upon passing the ballroom to find another grand gala underway. More music, all the adults in finery again. Who could think about having another party at a time like this?

Of course, none of the adults were supposed to know about the two kids stuck in the painting, and Archie meant to keep it that way. He nodded politely at some friends of his parents going by and then strode hurriedly into the gallery.

Glancing around, he hoped he didn't cross paths with Boneless here again. Then he began running from painting to painting, checking them for any sign of Jake and Nixie.

He didn't know if they would be able to hear him in there, but he called their names at each picture as loudly as he dared. He ignored the fact that anyone witnessing this probably would have thought he was insane, going around talking to the artwork.

At last, he found Jake inside of the French farm landscape at the end of the gallery. He could see his cousin marching across the hill, but when he realized Nixie wasn't with him, Archie was terrified that something had happened to her.

"Jake! Jake!" He rapped on the surface of the painting and finally managed to get his cousin's attention.

He came running down the hill as fast as he could.

Archie waited, relieved to see his cousin in one piece, but Nixie's absence had put him in a state of dread. Jake arrived on the other side of the picture frame, panting from his sprint.

"Are you all right?" Archie asked at once, even as he noticed that his cousin didn't look so good. "What's happened? Where's Nixie?"

"Asleep." Jake's voice sounded muffled.

"Is she hurt?"

"Nah, she sprained her ankle, but she's fine."

Archie let out a sigh of relief. Then he reached into his vest and pulled out the map he had stolen and unfolded it. "I found you a way out. There's good news and bad news." For a second, Archie located the farmhouse painting in the diagram, then showed it to Jake, pressing the map up to the painting. "You are here." He tapped the spot.

Jake leaned closer, studying the map. "What's the good news? I could use some."

"There's an emergency exit in the silo next to that barn." Archie pointed to the farm on the hill. "You've only got to go through one more painting to get out."

"And what's the bad news?"

"Uh, it's the Hieronymus Bosch."

Jake stared at him. "Of course it is. That's just perfect."

"I tried to find another way out for you. There isn't one. It's this or nothing. My guess is that they put it last to stop enemies from trying to sneak into the farmhouse scene through the back way. Nobody would willingly cross a Bosch landscape unless they had no other choice. The fellow was a thorough, raving loon-bat."

"So what should I expect?"

"Oh, monsters, demons, scenes of eternal damnation. More or less."

"Got it," Jake said grimly, hands on hips.

Archie shook his head. "Be careful. Keep Nixie safe."

Jake nodded, visibly bracing himself for the final leg of their journey. "Thanks, Archie. I knew I could count on you."

"Of course. Good luck. I'll be waiting for you in the gallery at my end of the Bosch when you come out."

If you make it out alive.

A moment later, Archie watched his cousin trudge off to fetch Nixie for the end of their trek. His throat felt tight with anxiety as he folded the map up again, hid it in his vest, then allowed himself to wander off nervously, hands in pockets, only as far as the edge of the gallery.

Jake and Nixie would need a little time before they'd be in range, but Archie didn't intend to go far, just in case they needed him upon making their reentry.

Wandering restlessly back out to the entrance hall, he was startled to see his sister heading into the ballroom once more, wearing yet another fancy gown—and a morose look on her face.

He hurried over to tell her about the latest developments. "Isabelle, this is no time for you to be flitting off to another ball."

"Flitting? Do you think I want to do this? Mother's making me. She says it's imperative I make up for botching tea with the Queen today. Apparently running out of the room in the middle of a royal audience is rather frowned upon."

"Ah, I suppose it would be. Listen, I found a map of the paintings..." He quickly explained.

Isabelle was thrilled to hear they were safe so far. "Maybe I can get out of here early if I make a good impression this time," she said, nodding toward the ballroom.

"Well, if you can, I'll be waiting for them out here. So come as soon as you can."

"If I can't get away, will you let me know once they're out?"

"Will do. Hang in there, sis."

Just then, Gladwin buzzed over to them. "Hey-ho!" the wee fairy said cheerfully. "Has anyone seen Dani O'Dell? I have a wonderful surprise for her!"

"Haven't seen her in hours," Archie said.

"What sort of surprise?" Isabelle asked.

"I was able to get permission for her to come to the ball tonight as a special treat!" Gladwin clapped her hands in excitement and twirled in a spiral, trailing golden sparkles.

"Oh, good!" Isabelle exclaimed. "That'll make this thing more tolerable for me, too."

"So where is the lucky girl?" Gladwin asked, beaming, as she hovered in midair, hands on hips.

"She went out to the zoo to visit Red," Archie answered.

"Well, I'd better go find her, then! She needs to hurry and put on her best party frock! I didn't think you boys would be interested,"

Gladwin added, "so I didn't bother getting permission for you."

"No, no, that's quite all right," Archie assured her. "Jake won't mind, I'm sure."

"Where is that rascal, anyway? With Dani and Red?"

"Oh...he's around here somewhere," Archie said vaguely, brushing off a twinge of guilt for lying to Gladwin. What choice did he have? As a royal garden fairy, she'd be duty-bound to tell on Jake and Nixie for going in the paintings. He was not going to get his friends in trouble on top of everything else they had already been through. "I daresay he'll be along at any moment."

"Very well. See you in the ballroom, Izzy! I'm off to find Dani."

"See you soon!" Isabelle waved, but when Gladwin had gone, she turned to Archie and whispered, "Is Dani really visiting Red?"

He shrugged. "That's what she told me. Why do you ask?"

"You know I don't like eavesdropping on the emotions of friends and family, but I couldn't help but notice she was *really* angry all day about what happened with those shapeshifter brats."

Archie snorted. "So was I."

"You and I don't get angry in the same way Dani does." Isabelle shrugged. "Maybe it's the redhead temper or something, but I have this sneaking suspicion that she's planning something."

"Like what?" he asked in surprise.

"I don't know." Isabelle shook her head. "Revenge."

"Well, don't ask me, I was in the library all day. I'm sure it'll be fine."

Isabelle nodded after a moment. "Yes, you're probably right. She wouldn't do anything rash," she said, but she looked doubtful.

"You can ask her what's on her mind once Gladwin brings her to the ballroom. Oh, there's Miss Helena looking for you." He nodded toward the open doorway of the ballroom, where the elegantly dressed governess stood, beckoning to her charge.

Isabelle let out a sigh. "Here we go again."

"Better you than me, sis." Archie smiled ruefully, then sauntered back into the art gallery and began pacing back and forth, waiting for Jake and Nixie to emerge from the hideous Bosch painting.

* * *

Dani O'Dell had lied to her friends, knowing they could have no part of this.

In fact, she had not gone to visit Red. She had brooded on revenge all day, and now, under the cover of nightfall, the time had come to carry out her plan.

Though every drop of superstition in her Irish blood screamed at her not to do it, she dared step over the mushroom boundary into the fairy ring and was instantly engulfed in the hurly-burly of the infamous fairy market.

She stared all around her at the stalls, where non-human vendors were hawking their magical wares. Magical food was on offer, as well, but at least she knew enough not to take a bite or she might be trapped in fairyland forever as a slave or a changeling child, a fairy prisoner. Fairies, it was known, were very fond of children and would rather keep them small than let them suffer the pangs of growing up.

But Dani very much intended to grow up, and right now she had important things to do—clearing Jake's name, for starters. She would not permit anyone to falsely accuse her best friend of this crime, and even more importantly, she intended to get back at the skunkies. Oh, they were going to be sorry by the time she was through with them...

Magical swords on display in an armorer's stall whispered to passersby with soft, metallic voices, but Dani didn't want to kill her foes. That was a bit extreme. What she really wanted was a prank of some kind...equal in wickedness to what the skunkies had done to her and Archie today with their chemical attack.

"Pardon, sir. What's that?" she asked at the stall of a magical chemist. He had pointy ears and funny goggles and wore a white coat. He looked over the edge of his counter at her.

"Why, that's a jar of onion gas, love."

"What do you do with it?"

"You twist the lid open and let the gas out. It creates a magnificent stink. You could clear out a stadium with that."

"Hmm." It *would* be poetic justice, but it occurred to her that skunk shapeshifters were probably immune to bad smells. She shook her head and moved on.

"Hullo, dearie," said an old witch with a market stall full of potions.

Dani stared at her, instinctively afraid. The hunch-backed, wart-nosed crone in her hooded cape was not the sort of proud, patrician witch like old Lady Bradford. More the come-and-see-my-gingerbread-house-out-in-the-forest sort of hag. She gave Dani a toothless smile.

"And what is a clever little biscuit like yourself doing wandering 'round the fairy market, child?" the crone asked sweetly.

"Um, looking for a potion...or something?"

"Well, I have many magical solutions to everyday problems. Amulets and powders, spells for sale, too. You're welcome to come and take a look." She gestured at her countertop with a claw-like hand. "What sort of difficulty are you facing, might I ask?"

Dani took a hesitant step toward her. "Some shapeshifter children have been giving me and my friends a hard time."

"Shapeshifters, hmm. I believe I may have something here..."

"I don't really want to hurt them, per se," Dani hastened to explain as the witch bent down behind her counter and began searching for something. "I just want to make them leave me alone. Put them in their place." She paused, standing on her tiptoes, trying to see what the witch was doing. "It's not fair, you know? Being harassed by magical kids when I'm just an ordinary human."

"Are you, indeed?"

"Yes, ma'am," Dani said. "The only thing that's different about me is my ginger hair."

The witch peered over the edge "Do you want me to fix it for you? Would you rather be a blond? Brunette?"

"No!" Dani said in alarm, clasping her hair protectively. "It may be different...but it makes me who I am."

"Oh ho, and you like who you are?"

"I do!" Dani replied, only realizing it herself even as she said it. Even though she didn't have magical powers. She looked away while the witch continued searching for something, mumbling to herself. *What am I doing here?* she wondered. *This is probably a terrible idea...*

"Ah! Here we are." The witch placed a small silk pouch of something on the counter.

"What's this?"

"Sticking Powder. You use it like fairy dust."

"Throw it on a person?"

"Aye. If it's just a prank you want, this will do the trick. It'll keep those shapeshifters of yours stuck in between their human and animal form, which is always very embarrassing for their kind. They like being fully one or the other so they can blend in."

"It doesn't keep them like that permanently?"

"Only lasts an hour or two."

A grin spread across Dani's face. "I'll take it."

She paid for the Sticking Powder, though it cost her three weeks' wages, and thanked the witch profusely, but forgot to ask the most important question: *Does it have any side effects?*

Eager to get the skunkies back, she put it in the pocket of her pinafore and marched toward the edge of the fairy market. Just then, a familiar trail of golden sparkles appeared ahead, and Gladwin came zooming out of the darkness.

"Dani! There you are!"

"Hullo, Gladwin," she answered uncomfortably.

"What are you doing in here?" her fairy friend exclaimed. "I've been looking everywhere for you! You're not supposed to be here. Don't you know it isn't safe? Jake had better not be in here with you." Gladwin glanced around.

"No, he's not. Why were you looking for me?"

"Because...I got you invited to the ball tonight!" She twirled in an eager circle.

"You did? Really? I can go?"

"Yes! Hurry, run and put on your best party frock and then you can join Isabelle in the ballroom."

But, crestfallen, Dani halted her. "Thanks so much, but I'm sorry, I can't go."

"What?" Gladwin flew back to her, searching her face with a frown. "I thought that was all you wanted to do!"

"I did, but right now I have more important things to worry about."

"Like what?"

"I promised to help clear Jake's name for starters. I found out who stole the Queen's flag, but I can't take them on alone. They've got magical powers and I've none. So I came here to find something to help me even the odds a bit."

"Oh, Dani, you should know better than that. Who stole the flag, anyway?"

She explained everything to Gladwin, who was most indignant on her behalf and Archie's and Jake's.

"Let's go tell Lord Badgerton about this," the fairy said at once. "They're his niece and nephews. He can hand down their punishment himself."

"No, Gladwin! I'm not a baby, I don't want the adults solving all my problems for me. Don't you understand? It's bad enough that I always have to be the youngest. Doing that would only make me a tattletale, to boot."

"Well, what do you want to do, then?"

"I've got to handle this myself. But believe me, I've got a plan."

"Dani, what's on offer here is not the answer to your problems, trust me," Gladwin warned, gesturing at the vendors' stalls.

Dani just shrugged, but said nothing about having bought the Sticking Powder.

"Will you at least let me help you? As a friend?" Gladwin asked.

"All right, but we have to do it my way."

"Very well. What did you have in mind?"

"Come on," Dani said. "I'll show you."

* * *

A short while later, Dani pounded her fist boldly on the front door of the skunkies' suite. She was guessing their parents were at the same ball Isabelle had gone to, leaving the three little miscreants to their own devices.

Dani's plan was simple. She would distract the skunkies while Gladwin sneaked in through the window and stole the Queen's flag *back*. In truth, Dani would have liked to have done the stealing personally, but Gladwin was better suited for it, being a great deal smaller.

As soon as they had recovered the flag, they would bring it to the Elders and unmask the real culprits. Jake's name would be cleared, so by the time he escaped the Enchanted Gallery, he would be pleased as punch to hear how she had saved his reputation.

It felt good to know that she could rescue *him* sometimes, too. Heaven knew he had often done the same for her. Why, just this past Christmas at the North Pole, Jake had stopped a great, stinking yeti from biting her head off like a lollipop. This seemed the least she could do for him in return. *Besides*, she thought with vengeful glee, *I can't wait to use the Sticking Powder on the skunkies.*

Thankfully, Gladwin had never actually asked if she had *bought* any magical items at the market. Dani would not have wanted to lie to her. Gladwin would soon see the truth, but at least she could not technically accuse Dani of fibbing.

In any case, as Dani waited, heart pounding, she heard sneaky rustling sounds coming from behind the door, along with decidedly guilty whispers.

"Who's there?" one of the boy shapeshifters called from inside the suite.

"Our parents said not to open the door to strangers!" the girl chimed in.

"Oh, we've met before," Dani said in a hard tone.

The door swung open, and there they were.

"Well, well. Do you two smell something?" the girl drawled to her brothers, her nose twitching with hilarity at Dani's expense.

"Very funny."

"I see you finally made it back from the forest."

"Yes, and I came to say you're not going to get away with this."

"Aren't you brave?" one of the boys taunted. "Three against one."

"Foolhardy," his brother remarked.

"Stupid is more like it," said the girl. She seemed to be the ringleader, adept at causing trouble.

"I'm not afraid of you runts," Dani said. "But let's try to be mature about this, shall we? I came to talk to you like civilized people."

"That was your first mistake," the taller boy said.

"Why did you steal Queen Victoria's flag?" Dani demanded. "What are you planning to do with it?"

"I don't think that's any of your business," the girl said with a sneer.

"Are you going to sell it? It's probably worth a lot."

"Why? You want to buy it, Spot?" the shorter boy asked with a mocking leer at her freckles.

"No, Stripe," she replied to the skunk boy. "I'm just curious about how you pulled it off."

They glanced at each other and couldn't resist the chance to brag.

"It was pretty slick of us if we do say so ourselves..."

They all began talking at once, eager to show off and trying to outdo each other in describing their individual parts in scampering up to the roof of Merlin Hall, shimmying up the flagpole, keeping a lookout, and untying the ropes that had held the flag in place. Dani asked a few questions, pretending to admire them begrudgingly for their derring-do but really just keeping them talking and distracted.

Behind them, she could see Gladwin buzzing in through the open window and flying around the suite to find the Queen's flag.

"You know you're going to be in trouble if somebody finds out," Dani pointed out.

"So?" the taller boy asked.

"We don't get in trouble," the girl informed her.

That explains a lot, Dani thought. *Spoiled brats.*

"Unless you're going to be a baby and tell on us?" the shorter boy asked.

"I don't recommend it," the taller one said with a glower.

"I'm not a tattletale," Dani retorted.

"Good, because you wouldn't like what that would get you."

Dani scoffed. "Pfft, save your breath. You think I'm scared of your threats?"

"You should be. You don't even have any magical powers!"

Dani saw that Gladwin had disappeared with the Queen's flag out the window. "True...but I do have—*this!*"

All of a sudden, Dani pulled her fists out of her pockets and threw the Sticking Powder in their faces. The skunkies gasped in surprise, which only made them inhale more of the glistening dust.

It worked in seconds.

Their fluffy, skunk tails popped out. The girl turned in circles, trying to figure out how it had appeared, while the brothers wrestled with themselves in confusion—one with a skunk head atop a human body; the other, boy from the waist up, skunk from the waist down.

"What have you done to us?" they cried.

Dani backed away, laughing, jeering, and pointing. "Ha, ha, got you! Look at the freaks!"

But her triumph was short-lived.

There was a reason, after all, that people were advised not to buy things from the fairy market.

She felt a queer tingling sensation running all over her skin, and then two sharp pangs on the crown of her head and another fierce jolt at the base of her spine. Dani shrieked as a fiery burst of pain seared her face around her nose and she realized that now the skunkies were laughing at *her,* pointing and jeering.

"What?" she cried in alarm.

"You'd better go look in a mirror, cotton-tail," the half-skunk brother said.

"Before some*bunny* sees you like that," said the girl.

"Like what? W-what are you talking about?" In dread, Dani reached up to touch the twin spots on the top of her head where, just a moment ago, it had felt like somebody had driven two screwdrivers through her skull. She gasped as she felt long, velvety-soft protrusions coming up out of her head.

Ears?!

Then, at the bottom of her field of vision, she noticed something stuck to her face. She touched her cheek and was horrified to realize she had whiskers. She reached around and found a cottony puffball of some sort on the back of her dress.

She ran in a circle trying to see it, refusing to believe what she already, deep down, knew. "A tail. I have a *tail!*"

She stopped and stared at the half-skunk freaks. "What's happened to me?" she choked out.

The girl smirked, folding her arms across her chest. "Let's just say you're some*bunny* now."

Dani shrieked and leaped back from the door, covering a surprisingly wide distance. "The witch said it was temporary! *Gladwin, is Sticking Powder temporary?*"

She ran off, screaming for the fairy, racing so fast down the hallway that her strides turned into long, bounding hops.

* * *

The tumultuous swirl of three hundred people's emotions in the ballroom had quickly overwhelmed and exhausted Isabelle.

Add a tightly laced corset that she wasn't used to wearing, and the evening soon became a recipe for utter misery. She kept waiting for Dani to arrive, knowing her friend would cheer her up, but still, nothing. What the dash was taking them so long?

She glanced again at the long-case clock, hoping Dani hadn't got lost in the dark on her way to visit Red. One more thing to worry about, as if Jake and Nixie being stuck inside the Enchanted Gallery wasn't awful enough.

How she wished she weren't trapped in here, wasting time, but Mother had insisted.

Thankfully, the magical orchestra started up the next waltz, and her glamorous parents and their friends went off to dance. Relieved to the bottom of her soul for a few minutes free of the agony of making small talk, she watched the dancers whirling across the gleaming parquet floor for a moment, but when she could no longer stand the debutantes nearby snickering at her for her bumbling in front of the Queen, she withdrew to the terrace outside.

She went to the stone railing, casting a disgruntled perusal over the moonlit gardens. *I am so ready to go home.* She missed her unicorns.

"Well, if it isn't little miss nosy," said a low, silken voice from the shadows.

Isabelle whirled around to find the vampire sauntering toward her. "Stay away from me."

"Oh, but I have business with you, young lady. What were you about, prying into my thoughts like that today?"

"No, I—that's not true—I can't read people's thoughts." She backed away as he approached, wilting under his piercing stare. "I can only sense emotions," she admitted, praying he did not murder her. "I'm an empath, you see. Not a telepath, like you. I-I can only read the heart, not the head. I didn't learn anything, I promise!"

"No, I should think not, considering the heart in me stopped beating long ago." He smiled in cool amusement when Isabelle winced slightly at the notion of a dead, silent heart sitting in his chest like a lump of rotten meat.

She tried to hide her distaste. "What are you doing at Merlin Hall? I thought vampires weren't allowed at the Gathering."

"Maybe looking for my next bride, hmm? What do you say, girl? You look healthy enough. Look at this golden hair! You shine in the darkness."

"Get away from me!" She threw up her arm to block his hand reaching to touch a lock of her hair.

He gave her a droll look and lowered his arm to his side, and Isabelle realized he was only toying with her. "Ah, come, just because I drink blood, that doesn't make me a bad person."

"Actually, it does!" she said, shaken.

"Miss Bradford!" a harsh voice clipped out. "Is he bothering you?"

Isabelle drew in her breath as Maddox appeared at the top of the stone steps leading up from the gardens. Prince Janos turned and arched an eyebrow as Maddox marched toward them, his stare fixed on the vampire. Isabelle's heart pounded.

"What have we here? Oh, Stone's latest protégé. Noble Guardian!

Another cannon-fodder boy."

"Step away from Miss Bradford," he said. "I'm only going to warn you once."

"Indeed?" Prince Janos laughed. "Hold on! You look familiar to me. Do I know you?"

Isabelle slid to the side, escaping the focus of the vampire's attention as Maddox stepped between them. She stared, wide-eyed, at the prince from behind the broad-shouldered Guardian lad.

"Of course," Janos murmured, studying him. "You're Ravyn's pup. You have her eyes. And how is your lovely mother these days? Still cursing like a sailor and drinking like a fish, I hope?" A nostalgic smile skimmed the vampire's face. "Such times! Tell the lethal lady that I miss her. That girl could hit an enemy in the throat with a dagger at twenty paces. What a woman."

Isabelle could feel Maddox seething. "Unless you wish to test the skills that I inherited from her, I suggest you go away now, traitor."

"So that's how it is, eh? Very well. I shall not trouble you, for her sake. But be warned, lad. I was like you once. Young Guardian, head full of mush. Until I realized there's no future in it." The vampire flashed a smile that showed the tips of his fangs but did not reach his eyes. "On that day, I wised up, put away my little-boy dreams of heroics, and became—"

"A monster," Maddox said.

The vampire feigned hurt. "A realist, I was going to say."

Maddox held his stare. "If you go near Miss Bradford again, I will personally put a stake through your heart."

The humor in Prince Janos's eyes vanished. "You children bore me." He turned away, took a few angry strides toward the railing, changed into a bat, and flew off through the trees.

Her heart thumping, Isabelle was still holding her breath when Maddox turned to her.

"Are you all right, Miss Bradford?" he asked in a taut voice.

"I think so." She stared at him. "Thank you."

"Of course. Can I get you anything? A glass of punch? Er...smelling salts?"

Her lips twitched a little. "No—thank you. I am well."

He nodded like they were discussing military maneuvers. "You should go inside now."

She glanced toward the French doors to the ballroom and then shook her head with a sigh. "Honestly? I can't bear to. Not yet. There's just...too many people."

"I understand."

"You do?"

He hesitated. "I don't much care for crowds myself."

She gazed at him in wonder. He turned away, clearing his throat.

"Well, if you mean to stay out here, then I should keep watch. In case he comes back."

She hid her glee at the prospect of spending a few minutes with him. "If it's not too much trouble, I would...really appreciate that."

"No trouble. It's my duty," he replied, already glancing around, on the lookout for any sign of the vampire returning.

She tried not to stare at him. "It's lucky for me you came along," she ventured after a moment.

"Not luck. Instinct, Miss Bradford," he replied.

But then he seemed to realize what he had just admitted to. Everybody knew that a Guardian could only arrive in time to protect people with whom he felt some sort of bond.

"Oh. I see." She managed a decorous nod and feigned ignorance on this point to spare his feelings. Because, frankly, Maddox looked rather panicked that, for all intents and purposes, he had just accidentally admitted that he liked her.

Isabelle somehow held back a shout of joy and smiled at him politely. Maddox looked away, scanning the night, the trees, the roof, the garden, looking *anywhere* but at her. But it was no use. Even though she could not read him, the fact that he was standing here gave his feelings away.

* * *

"Ahhhhhhh!"

Jake and Nixie ran through the final painting, screaming their heads off. Nixie was too scared to pay the slightest attention to her sprained ankle. Speed was their only hope to escape the monsters everywhere.

Nightmare creatures peopled the underworld landscape of the insane Hieronymus Bosch, some so strange that Jake almost wanted to stop and stare at them in morbid fascination.

Bosch had clearly given great thought to the denizens of Hades:

devils and gargoyles, chimeras and grotesques of all kinds.

Part-shrimp, part-toad, part-cactus.

Torso-men with no proper heads, but weird, angry faces set into their bare chests. They carried spears and seemed to serve as the wardens of this underworld prison.

A huge, nautilus-shell creature flailed its long green tentacles about, grabbing prisoners every which way and pulling them into its round, saw-toothed mouth.

A wolf-like beast with horns and blue-black fur sat on a throne in the center of the scene, howling with bone-chilling laughter at the antics of the goblins.

The very air was fetid, thick with smoke and useless pleas for mercy. Continuous screams issued from the severed heads displayed on pikes along the path down which Jake and Nixie fled. Above, winged furies circled, their threshing sickles at the ready. Rat-like bird-lizards with beaks and claws sharp enough to tear flesh pecked out people's spleens while giant machines shaped like internal organs served as bizarre torture devices.

Their exit waited for them in the form of a window-like picture frame, set into the reddish stone wall of the underground world.

Just get from point A to point B, Jake kept telling himself, holding onto sanity for all he was worth.

It seemed to take forever to run the high stretch of path that hugged the cavern wall above the writhing scene, but by some miracle, they finally reached the rickety ladder that rose up to the picture-frame.

"Go! You first!" Jake stood guard at the bottom of the ladder while Nixie climbed. He used his telekinesis to zap away a pair of torso-men who approached to investigate.

At the top, Nixie dove through the picture frame. Jake scrambled up the rungs and followed.

Seconds later, he came flying out of the painting to sprawl on the gallery floor. When he realized he was back safe at Merlin Hall, he could've kissed the ground.

Panting, Jake looked over at Nixie. "You all right?"

"Um..." To his surprise, she had landed on top of Archie.

Jake realized his gentlemanly cousin must have tried, helpfully, to catch her when she came flying out. Instead, fueled by her terrorized momentum, Nixie had bowled him over and they both had landed on the floor. Judging by his beaming smile, Archie didn't seem to mind a bit.

"Sorry about that," Nixie mumbled, climbing to her feet.

"N-no worries," Archie answered as he did the same. Pushing his spectacles back up onto his nose, he came and gave Jake a hand. "You two all right?"

"That was terrifying," he whispered.

Nixie nodded, still looking shaken.

"Jake!" a familiar voice suddenly called.

He looked down the long gallery. "Dani!"

She came running toward them. "You're safe!"

"Just barely," he mumbled.

To his surprise, Dani threw her arms around him and gave him a big hug. Startled, Jake hugged her back rather gingerly.

"Great news!" she said at once, stepping back again. "Gladwin and I returned the Queen's flag for you! Your reputation is saved!"

"Really?"

"Of course, it wasn't easy, but never mind that," she said hastily. "The important thing is, your name's cleared and the evildoers are being punished as we speak."

Jake marveled at her news. "Who took it?"

"Those shapeshifter brats. But don't worry, Gladwin and I stole it back a little while ago and handed it over to the Queen's chamberlain. We told the Elders, too. Those skunkies are in so much trouble! Did you have fun in the paintings?"

He gave her a sardonic look. "Not exactly." Then he glanced around at the others. "Come on, everybody. We need to go talk to Red at once. We've got serious matters to discuss, and it's safer if we all stick together."

"Serious matters? Like what?" Archie asked in surprise.

"Like war," Jake murmured, glancing at Nixie.

She met his gaze with a somber nod.

Dani and Archie exchanged a look of concern.

"My Gryphon will know what to do," Jake assured them. "But first, where's Isabelle? I'll need her to translate Red's advice."

"She's in the ballroom," Archie replied, and they all hurried off to find her.

Since children were not allowed in through the ballroom doors, they ran around the palace and through the gardens, hoping to flag her down from the double doors along the back terrace.

When they arrived at the terrace, however, Isabelle was already there, sitting on a bench, with Maddox perched on the wide stone railing beside her.

Dani called out to her. "Izzy, look, Jake's back! He's all right! Nixie, too!"

"Oh, good." She made no move to get up.

"Something's going on, sis," Archie advised her. "You'd better come along."

"I'm busy," she protested, nodding discreetly at Maddox.

"He can come, too," Jake conceded with reluctance.

"You're assuming that I'd want to?" the older boy replied, staring at him.

Jake sighed and lowered his head. The last time he and Maddox had seen each other, it had erupted into a fight. A fight Jake had started, with accusations against the other boy's honor that he now knew were false.

"Look, I owe you an apology," Jake forced out. "I thought you set me up, but I know now you had nothing to do with stealing the Queen's flag. I should've realized that you, of all people, would never do something like that, no matter how annoyed you were at me. So, yes, I'm sorry that I accused you. Happy now?"

"And?" Maddox prompted, folding his arms across his chest.

"Sorry for throwing dragon dung on you," Jake mumbled.

The others glanced at him in surprise, but Maddox smiled wryly. "There. Was that so hard?"

"Are you coming with us or not?" he exclaimed. "Trust me, you're going to want to hear this."

More to the point, Jake already knew they had a fight ahead of them, and obviously, Maddox would be an excellent ally to have on their side.

"So? Spit it out."

"Not here," Jake said. "We're going to see my Gryphon. He'll know what to do. Isabelle, please come, even if he won't. We need you to translate what Red says."

"Very well." She glanced questioningly at Maddox.

He met her gaze and shrugged. "As you wish. I've never seen a gryphon before, anyway. Why not."

The older pair joined them, and they went.

PART IV

CHAPTER TWENTY-SEVEN
The Secret War Council

"This information is not to leave our circle," Jake told the others a short while later as they sat around the edges of Red's nest in the darkness.

It felt like a safe place there, atop the windy pillar of rock that the Gryphon had claimed for his aerie, with a ring of tall trees standing guard around them.

Being near Red made Jake feel calmer about all the terrible news he had learned. It also helped to know that the Gryphon would soon be back to his full strength—and his full plumage. The noble beast's feathers were filling in nicely, albeit with a few more gold ones sprinkled in among the scarlet. Jake had no idea what the golden feathers meant, but they winked in the dim glow of the lantern Archie had picked up along the way.

By its flickering light, Jake looked around at his friends' somber faces as they waited to hear what he had to say. "While Nixie and I were inside the paintings, I found out why the vampire came to Merlin Hall. The Dark Druids are preparing for war."

The others drew in their breath and listened tensely as he filled them in on what he had overheard while inside the Vesuvius painting. He almost couldn't bear to answer the question, though, when Archie asked what had set the Dark Druids off.

Jake lowered his head. "I'm pretty sure it's my fault. They found out I killed Garnock, and they've taken that as an act of war. They're preparing to come after the Order, starting with the Lightriders."

Dani and Archie looked at each other, wide-eyed.

Red nested his head on Jake's knee with a small, sympathetic groan. Isabelle exchanged a worried glance with Maddox, who did not look surprised in the least.

Nixie, meanwhile, having already heard the dreadful news, was distracted, anxiously watching the shadows for the return of the Bugganes. She froze at a flicker of motion in the weeds, a small scampering in the shadows.

It turned out to be Malwort.

"Oh!" she said, drawing back, startled, as the spider ventured nervously into view and said, "Good evenings, gentlemens and ladieses."

"What are you doing here?" Jake demanded, shooting to his feet. He immediately thought the arachno-sapiens was there to spy on them, just like Uncle Waldrick had often ordered his former pet to do in the past.

Malwort shot backward and cowered. "Malwort only being social! The Jake not be so mean! Fairy Stinger cousins's boring."

"Well, get out of here," Jake said in a hard tone, shooing him off.

Malwort whimpered, doing his best to look lonely and pathetic.

"Aw." Nixie reached out her hand toward him. "Can't he stay? I've heard about arachno-sapiens, but I've never seen one before. He's kind of cute."

"Malwort very cute!" he agreed, venturing toward the young witch. "Most uniquest spider anyplace."

"Ew," Isabelle mumbled, cringing slightly as Malwort stepped onto Nixie's hand.

But witches sometimes had very different reactions than other girls. Nixie giggled at the creature. "Your feet tickle!"

Encouraged by this unexpectedly warm reception, Malwort pranced about on her palm like a music hall performer, tittering in his weird little voice.

"Can't he stay?" Nixie asked.

Archie sent Jake a pleading look and nodded discreetly toward the poor girl, who had been through so much.

Jake rolled his eyes. "Oh, very well. But everything we say here is a secret, Malwort! If you're spying on us, mark my words, I'm gonna squash you good."

Malwort ignored him, gazing at Nixie with as close to a smile of delight as a spider could manage.

Maddox scowled and brought them back to the dire topic at hand. "Did the vampire say anything about the Dark Druids' time-frame?"

Jake shrugged. "No, he just said he believes they've got plans in motion against the Lightriders."

"What are your thoughts, Maddox?" Archie asked, since he was the only one with training in military matters. "Have you heard anything amongst the Guardians?"

"Not exactly. But..." He searched for the words. "I've been sensing something like this for a while now through the Guardian instinct. A lot of us have."

"Maybe that's what I was sensing in the ballroom tonight," Isabelle remarked. "I didn't think of it at the time, but in hindsight, there was a lot of tension coming from some of the adults. It was giving me a headache."

"I'd bet word is traveling fast, at least among the leaders of the Order," Jake said. "So far, only a few people know about it. Her Majesty and a few of the top Elders."

"I'm sure the Elders will want to keep it that way," Maddox said. "Secrecy gives us an advantage. The Dark Druids still think we're oblivious. Instead, when they make their move, now we can be ready for them. I should think they'll want to bring all the Lightriders in from the field so they can be briefed on the situation and their security increased. Especially those who think they can go whooshing around the earth with no Guardians for protection." Maddox gave Jake a pointed look.

He shook his head, still feeling sick to his stomach. "I can't believe I caused this."

"Don't blame yourself." Dani put her arm around his shoulders. "This isn't your fault."

"Oh, really? Then why do I feel so horrible?" he muttered, shrugging her off, unwilling to be comforted.

Stung by his dismissal, Dani scowled. "What were you supposed to do? Let Garnock go free to keep feeding on innocent people's souls until he recomposed his body and returned as the leader of the Dark Druids? You had no choice."

"That's what I said," Nixie agreed.

"And hullo," Dani added, "Garnock was going to sacrifice Isabelle to a demon to try to weasel out of his deal with the devil!"

"*What?*" Maddox uttered, turning to her in shock.

Isabelle smiled dryly. "What can I say? Evil beings love me. I'm such a lucky girl."

Nixie chuckled.

"What surprises me most about all this is that the vampire came forward to do the right thing," Isabelle remarked.

"Are we sure we can believe him?" Archie asked.

Everyone pondered this, a very good question.

"Well," Maddox ventured, "vampires are known as master manipulators, but Janos used to be a Guardian and Guardians don't lie. Perhaps some of that is left in him."

"I hope he's lying," Archie muttered.

"I don't think he is," Isabelle said.

They all fell silent for a moment, until Dani spoke up with her famous practicality, shaking her head.

"Even if it is true and there is to be a war, I don't see what *we're* supposed to do about it. We're just kids, after all. This is up to the Elders to handle. They're the adults and the leaders. We have to trust them to take care of us, trust that they know what they're doing. I don't think we have much choice."

Maddox smiled fondly at Dani. The others started nodding, and even Jake could not deny the wisdom of her words.

"She's right," he said. Being just a kid, able to do nothing in the face of this disaster, was the worst part to him.

So much for being a hero.

But perhaps it's for the best, he thought. Because it seemed like, instead of solving problems, all he did was cause them.

He dropped his gaze, his brow furrowed. If he rushed in trying to help, he'd probably only make it worse.

"There's nothing we can do about the war, except maybe Maddox, and you're still not officially a Guardian yet anyway," Jake said in a low tone. "But as it turns out, that's not the only fight we're facing. If we work together, I think there is something we can do—to help Nixie." He glanced at the witch, then looked around at the others. "Nixie's being haunted."

They turned to her in surprise.

"I say!" Archie burst out.

"And not by any ordinary ghosts, either," Jake added. "Remember that Boneless thing we saw in the art gallery and chased down the hallway? That's just one of four creatures who've been tormenting her for months."

He told the others all about the Bugganes and their determination to make Nixie's young life a living torment.

"How awful!" Dani murmured.

"I knew it!" Archie said. "I knew there was something wrong, that you couldn't be that gloomy on purpose."

Nixie gazed ruefully at him, but Malwort marched up onto her shoulder and sat there, guarding her, and scanning the darkness with his ten beady eyes. Jake believed the spider actually growled a little. How was *that* possible?

"Anyway, she was trying to keep everyone at arm's length because these Bugganes, as they're called, have promised to murder anyone who tries to help her."

"Sweet Galileo!" Archie murmured.

"But if we unite against them, they haven't got a chance," Jake declared. "I promised Nixie we would help her. She saved my life today inside the paintings, after all."

"If you don't want to get involved, I fully understand," Nixie hastened to tell them. "You barely know me, you shouldn't risk your lives—"

"Nonsense!" Archie said.

"We've risked our lives for less, believe me," Dani mumbled.

"Of course we want to help you," Maddox informed her.

"It won't be easy," Jake warned. "I've seen three of these creatures so far myself, and Nixie says the one I haven't seen yet is the worst."

"Nuckalavee, the water-horse—or water bull, as some call him. He's a great, horrid beast with no skin."

"I think I saw him in the water nymphs' stream," Jake said.

"Hey, I saw that, too," said Maddox. "Red in color, pointy ears?"

"That's him," Nixie said.

"I thought I had imagined it," he murmured.

"But I thought water-horses... Wasn't there a legend that they can only be in seawater?" Dani spoke up. "My granny spoke of them in Ireland. They'd come up onto the shore during a storm, rising from the foam of the waves. If one chased you, the only way to escape him was to cross to the other side of a freshwater stream or pond. Then he couldn't come across. But this one's bathing in freshwater? That's weird."

"Oh, that's the part that's weird?" Archie mumbled.

"No, these Bugganes followed me from Scotland," explained Nixie, "and in Scotland, the water-horses can live in the lochs or the ocean."

"Ohh," Dani said.

"That Headless Highlander ghost I saw in the woods that night when we were walking around—he's one of them, too," Jake told the others.

Nixie turned to him in surprise. "You didn't tell me you saw him! While you were alone? You're lucky to be alive." She turned to the others and explained. "If the Headless Highlander comes across somebody who's alone, then he attacks. He's killed countless travelers that way. He picks a stretch of road and sets up shop there. Any solitary soul who comes along, he pretty much chops them into bits with his claymore. But, if you come upon him when you're with at least one other person, he disappears without a fight."

An eerie silence fell as they pondered this.

"It probably has something to do with the way that he died," Nixie added, "but he'll never let himself be outnumbered."

"See? You're lucky we were there," Archie told Jake, who nodded heartily.

"One other thing about Headless, he has to stay in the shadows. He prefers the night, but he can move about in the daytime, as long as he keeps out of sunlight."

"Good to know," Maddox murmured.

Jake furrowed his brow. "But Nixie, you were on your own in the art gallery this morning when I found them tormenting you. But Headless didn't kill you."

"Jenny Greenteeth won't let him," she said bitterly. "The hag enjoys tormenting me too much."

"Jenny Greenteeth?" Isabelle echoed.

Jake explained to his puzzled friends who Jenny Greenteeth was, the leader of the Bugganes. He also repeated Nixie's information about how the hag had started her existence as nothing more than a scary tale told by nervous mothers to keep their tots away from local streams and ponds so they didn't stumble in and drown.

"Yes," Nixie said with a shudder, "over time she became all too real. Now her favorite hobby is drowning people. Or cats."

"And the Boneless creature?" Archie persisted. "What the devil is that thing?"

She shrugged. "It's just called a Boneless. More annoying than dangerous, really."

Archie, however, was mystified. "An unknown species! Maybe I could catch it and study it for science..."

"Would you be serious?" Dani scolded him.

"I am being serious! It could be my presentation at the next Invention Convention!"

"What about your submarine?"

"It's not ready yet."

"Oh, you," Dani said, waving him off. She glanced around a trifle uneasily at the dark woods around them, then turned to Nixie. "You don't think they'd come after you while we're out here, do you?"

"Not with the Gryphon present. They wouldn't dare," Nixie said. "Not even Nuckalavee would risk going near him."

"Good thing the Bugganes don't know Red's not up to his full strength yet. But you will be soon, won't you, boy?" Jake patted his pet on the head.

"Caw, caw, becaw."

Jake looked expectantly at Isabelle, awaiting translation.

She smiled. "Basically, he said, *'You can do this.'* He'll help us if we need him, but he trusts we can handle the Bugganes without him."

"Caw!"

"Yes, Red," Isabelle amended, then she added his extra message: "If we all work together."

"Hear, hear," Archie said.

Red snorted and tossed his head in approval. "Caw!"

"Oh," Isabelle murmured, gazing at the Gryphon.

"Well?" Dani asked the older girl, smiling.

Isabelle hesitated.

"What did he say?" Jake prompted.

"Um, he says it'll be good practice for us. Before the Dark Druids come."

Everyone fell silent, chilled to the marrow by Red's statement, even though he had intended it as encouragement.

Maddox folded his arms across his chest and looked at Jake, his face stoic in the dim lamplight. "So how do you want to handle this?"

"Divide and conquer," Jake said.

Archie nodded. "Let's take them in order, easiest to hardest? That's how I work out my equations."

"The Highlander's the hardest?" Maddox asked Nixie.

"Certainly, he's the most skilled warrior. I believe he was a champion of the MacGool clan ages ago. The thing is, how to fight him?

If you face him alone, it's certain death. But if you go up against him with friends, he simply disappears and comes back later...when you're alone."

"Very tricky," Maddox murmured.

"As for Nuckalavee, he's just brute animal strength," she continued, "but he'll eat you as quick as any bear. Boneless is the least vicious of the lot, but a prankster and extremely persistent. It seems to think it's funny to pester people until they break down. It can go through walls, so if it wants to harass you, there's no way to escape it."

"What about the hag?" Dani asked.

"She can travel magically between bodies of water or by mirrors, since a mirror has the same reflective properties as a lake or pond," Nixie said.

"She can also hurl these green balls of energy at people," Jake reported. "That's how we ended up stuck in the paintings today."

"Hmm, very interesting," Archie said, intrigued.

They began discussing strategies for how they might separate and defeat each of these foes, when all of a sudden, a branch cracked loudly in the woods below.

A clumsy rustle came from the underbrush.

Dani shrieked and flew behind Red, already spooked by all the talk of the Bugganes. Jake and Maddox leaped to their feet while Archie pulled Nixie behind him, automatically assuming that the Bugganes had tracked her down.

Jake's heart pounded as he scanned the darkness, bracing himself for the attack and already summoning up his telekinesis. Maybe the Bugganes weren't so afraid of the Gryphon after all or could somehow tell that Red wasn't up to his full power...

Maddox braced a foot on a boulder at the edge of the precipice, his fists clenched. "Who's there?"

"Show yourself!" Jake ordered, not to be outdone.

The Gryphon sniffed the air, then turned to Isabelle. "Becaw, caw."

"Are you sure, boy?" She peered over the edge of the rocky precipice. "Red says it's only Ogden Trumbull."

"Ogden Trumbull?" Dani cried.

"Are you serious?" Archie cried, letting out a huff of angry disgust. "Go away, troll!"

Realizing he had been found out, Ogden leaped up from the bottom of the rock-pile and vaulted into their midst with a ferocious roar. Everyone cowered to varying degrees—except for Archie, who simply reached into his pocket and pressed a button, unseen by the rest.

Og let out a yelp of pain, lost his balance, and long arms flailing, tumbled right back off the rocky precipice. He went crashing onto his back some thirty feet below and landed in the darkness with a *thunk*.

"You all right down there?" Archie called politely, peering over the edge, while Maddox and Nixie marveled.

"What's wrong with him? Why did he fall down like that?" Nixie asked.

"No idea," the boy genius said mildly, a devilish curve on his lips.

Jake sent his cousin a pointed smile. *Glad to see the Bully Buzzer works.*

"Archie's decided to teach the troll some manners," Dani informed her.

"How?" Nixie asked.

"He made a gizmo," Jake said.

At Nixie's questioning glance, Archie discreetly pulled the controller for the Bully Buzzer out of his pocket to let her in on the secret.

She lifted her eyebrows. "Is that magic?"

"Science, my dear."

When Nixie's eyes widened with admiration, Archie seemed to grow at least two inches taller right before their eyes. He cleared his throat in mild embarrassment and looked over the ledge once more. "I say, what do you want this time, troll? Why are you bothering us again?"

"He's a half-troll, Archie," Isabelle chided. "Show a little kindness."

"I am showing kindness! If I wanted to be cruel, I'd have doubled the voltage, sis. Trust me, he's a savage."

"And a snoop," Jake said, feeling much more prepared to deal with Ogden Trumbull now that Archie had the situation well in hand. "Why are you lurking around here spying on us?"

"You're plotting and planning! I'm gonna tell!" Ogden rumbled, climbing to his feet below, a bit dazed but none the worse for wear.

Trolls were very hardy.

Jake held out the lantern and could just make out the pugnacious glower stamped on the hybrid's ugly face. "You'll do nothing of the kind."

"Oh, yes, I will! Unless...unless you let me help, too!" Ogden burst out.

"Absolutely not!" Archie said.

"Go away!" Dani yelled for good measure.

"Hold on," Maddox interrupted. "Maybe we can use him."

"*What?*" Jake said.

"That Nuckalavee beast Nixie described—brute strength. Well? We could use some brute strength on *our* side, too." Maddox glanced at Archie, lowering his voice. "You think your gizmo can keep him under control?"

Archie shrugged. "It's worked twice now like a charm. Still, he's rude, violent, and nasty."

"He just wants to be included," Isabelle said. "Don't you understand? This is what I was trying to tell you before, brother. The poor brute's lonely. That's why he's so obnoxious. He doesn't have a single friend his own age here."

"There's a shocker," Archie drawled. "Maybe if he wasn't always trying to rip people's arms off."

"He *could* have ripped your arms off, literally, if he had wanted to. He's not that bad. He just acts up to get attention."

"You're daft, Isabelle," Jake said.

"Can't we at least give him a chance? Like Maddox said, maybe Ogden could be useful."

"No way!" Dani protested. "He tried to kill Archie and Jake! If Maddox and Derek Stone hadn't come along, who knows what would've happened?"

"Let me try," Isabelle replied. She went to the edge of the rock-pile. "Ogden?" she called down.

"Urrrrgh."

"Listen to me. My name is Miss Bradford. I'm going to ask you a question, and I want you to answer it honestly. Do you want to be part of our group?"

"Blech," Jake muttered.

"No!" Og thundered.

Isabelle propped her hands on her waist. "Ogden, I'm an empath," she said sternly. "I know when somebody's lying. Do you? Now, tell the truth this time. Is that what all this is about?"

By the lantern light, Jake could just make out the sight of Ogden lowering his head. "Yes, ma'am," he finally admitted. "But I know you don't want the likes of me around! You think I'm a monster."

"You're not a monster. Well, you don't *have* to be one. You can choose to be nice. Then we could all get along. But if you want to be our friend, there have to be a few rules."

"What rules?" he rumbled in a sullen tone.

"Friends don't attack one other. That's the first rule."

"Or bite other people," Archie pointed out.

"And certainly not eat them," Jake added after remembering Dr. Plantagenet saying that pureblooded rock trolls tended toward cannibalism now and then. He'd had enough of that today on Caliban's island, thank you very much.

"If you can agree to be nice and do as we say, you can come back up and join our quest," Isabelle declared.

"I can?" Ogden ventured.

"Yes. We'd be very pleased to have you. Wouldn't we, everyone?"

Their mumbles were less than enthusiastic.

"We're smaller than you, so you have to be gentle around us and not step on anyone. Can you do that?"

"Yes, ma'am," Ogden answered, surprising them all with his docile tone.

But Isabelle has that effect on loads of people, Jake thought.

"Good. Then you may come up now."

Dani shook her head. "I hope you know what you're doing."

"Don't worry. He'll be all right," Isabelle assured them.

But as Og started climbing up the rock-pile to join their company, Jake leaned toward Archie. "Make sure you keep that gadget charged up, coz."

"Better believe it," Archie said.

CHAPTER TWENTY-EIGHT
And So It Begins

*D*ivide and conquer...
From the Gryphon's aerie, they split up to see to their separate tasks in preparation for their coming clash with the Bugganes.

Nixie couldn't believe that all these near-strangers wanted to help her. For the first time in ages, she had hope. She had friends. She was terrified of how they might be punished for it, but she decided to let them try, considering they wouldn't be dissuaded, anyway.

Archie even went so far as to procure a wand for her to use. She didn't dare go back to her room to retrieve her spare, so he borrowed one (without permission) from his mother.

"Don't worry, she won't even miss it," he assured her upon returning from the Bradford family suite. "Both my parents are at the ball tonight. They don't really use magic much, but Mother always packs a wand on their journeys, just in case."

When he handed it to her, Nixie clutched it to her chest with more gratitude than she could express. She did a few quick spells to try out the borrowed wand and get used to it, making a nearby flower sprout twice as tall and open. Then she doused the lantern and relit the flame a few times with a flick of her wrist, and concluded her trials with the old illusionist's classic of making a rabbit magically appear.

For some reason, Dani O'Dell winced at that and looked away with an expression of dread. Nixie didn't ask why. As the rabbit bounded off into the woods, she let out a sigh of relief, finally feeling whole again, and used the wand to fix her sprained ankle.

Then Archie took her to one of the wizard-scientist's basement-level laboratories beneath Merlin Hall. He had been given permission to use the lab any time he liked. It had everything they'd need: cabinets full of magical ingredients and chemical compounds, as well as burners and beakers, microscopes, and centrifuges arrayed on a couple of long worktables.

Best of all, it had no windows or mirrors for Jenny Greenteeth to come through. Nixie felt relatively safe.

With no time to lose, they both got busy in their respective fields of expertise, working in companionable silence. To Nixie's amusement, the protective young scientist made her wear thick, oversized work gloves and safety goggles in the lab. She supposed he had a point, since she was mixing up a potion of the most poisonous ingredients she could find to throw on Jenny Greenteeth.

Malwort assisted her, running back and forth along the shelves to fetch the jars and vials she asked for.

Nearby, Archie assembled everything he'd need to build his contraption for catching the Boneless.

As it turned out, the wand for Nixie wasn't the only thing he had "borrowed" from his mother's belongings. He had also taken her rabbit-fur muff. If Nixie found this odd, the two additional pieces of equipment that he requested from the gnomes were even stranger: a mesh dog kennel and a gardener's four-wheeled handcart.

The rest of the stuff he needed he found right there in the lab: four large Leyden jars, a roll of tin leaf, a lot of copper wire and sharp clippers to cut it with, and a large ball of solid amber with a hole drilled through the middle.

"What's that for?" Nixie knew that amber had many magical uses and was especially revered for its healing properties, but she was surprised when Archie revealed it had scientific applications, too.

"Haven't you ever heard of amber being called 'the electric fossil'?"

She laughed. "No."

"Well, it has electric properties. Even the ancient Greeks knew about that! That's why they originally named it 'elektron,' after the sun. They fancied it was made out of sunlight—oh, never mind, you'll see."

Nixie smiled. He really was a strange boy, but then again, she had no use for normal.

Once he had all his necessities collected, the young Dr. Bradford rolled up his sleeves, loosened his bowtie, and got to work.

First, he propped a stool under the handcart to hold it up while he pried off a back wheel. Then he threaded the amber ball onto the rear axle, murmuring to himself in satisfaction when it fit just right. He pulled the rabbit-fur muff up *over* the amber ball and heaved the cartwheel back on, tightening it securely with a wrench from his tool-bag.

Dusting off his hands, Archie turned his attention next to the dog kennel. He unrolled the tin leaf, slicing off as much as he needed with a blade. He proceeded to hammer the shiny silver foil along the edges of the kennel, creating a device he called a Faraday cage.

When the cage was lined with the metallic foil, he affixed the dog kennel to the flat bed of the cart, with the kennel door facing the ceiling. He tied a long rope to the door's edge so he could yank it shut from a safe distance.

Cheerfully whistling fragments of a tune, he took out the four Leyden jars. These he likewise secured to the bed of the cart, two on either side of the kennel.

Lastly, he wired the whole mysterious contraption together, running strands of copper wire from the rabbit fur to the Faraday cage, attaching them to it in several different places. He ran an additional wire to each Leyden jar and, finally, from the Leyden jars to the Faraday cage. When he had twisted the last wire into a knot to hold it in place, he let out a *whew* and turned to Nixie with a smile. "*Voila!* The Boneless Catcher."

By this point, even Malwort looked confused.

Nixie lifted up her safety goggles and bluntly said: "Explain."

"You know how the Boneless can float through walls?"

She snorted. "Nobody knows that better than I do."

"Well, it's not going to be able to get through these walls." He tapped the dog kennel. "I've turned this metal kennel into an electrified cage. If it stays inside, it'll be fine, but if it tries to slip out, it's going to get a small but painful electric shock."

He now had her full attention. "Go on."

Archie pointed to the amber ball. "What I've built here is a very simple, ancient generator based on technology going all the way back to the Greeks, as I said. We'll roll this handcart to wherever we decide to set up an ambush for the Boneless. But along the way, you see, while the cart is in motion, the axle rotates the amber ball, which rubs against the rabbit fur, generating static electricity."

"Ohhhhh..."

"The rabbit fur also serves as a collection material, storing up the energy created. Then these wires carry the stored charge up from the rabbit fur to the Faraday cage—and to the Leyden jars, which are basically just big batteries, for a little extra oomph. So, basically, I've put a charge on the Faraday cage to make sure the creature stays inside."

Nixie shook her head in amazement.

"Of course, the charge on the Leyden jars will run out eventually, but by then, the Boneless will have received a few shocks and hopefully will have learned that touching the cage walls equals pain. So, if it's got any basic intelligence at all, he won't keep trying that. Negative reinforcement, we call it. Just like I'm doing with Og"

"You really are a genius."

Archie looked abashed at her praise. "I still have to test it, of course, to make sure everything is wired up properly, but it should work. The design is solid. Child's play, really."

She looked at him in surprise at this last remark, marveling to think that one of the foremost inventors of the day—quite the darling of the Royal Society—should have built this contraption for her sake. "That's the nicest thing anyone's ever done for me," she blurted out, staring at him.

Archie's eyes widened behind his spectacles. "Oh!" He turned beet-red and looked away. "Well, er, um, you're welcome. We just need to tell everybody not to touch the cage. W-whoever does will end up getting the shock intended for the...the Boneless."

"So, how do you propose to get him in there in the first place?"

"So glad you asked!" Looking a bit relieved at the change of subject, he marched over to the other worktable, where his second project was underway.

He had a mortar and pestle out, along with a small scale and a variety of powdered substances in jars.

Nixie read the label of the largest jar aloud. "Sea salt?"

"I'm putting together a desiccant to force the Boneless to change form from a vapor to a solid." He shrugged. "Same general concept as throwing salt on garden slugs. Of course, unlike them, I don't intend to kill it. Just dry it out long enough to let it turn nice and crispy. As soon as it has some tangible substance and isn't, well, a cloud, then I'll wrestle the little bugger into the cage if I have to. Or maybe Jake could help with his telekinesis on that, come to think of it..."

"Where is your cousin, anyway?"

"Oh, he went to borrow a piece of veterinary equipment from the

Green Man who runs the zoo, Dr. Plantagenet. It's a large medicinal sprayer that I saw the doctor carrying when they went off through the Grid with the Texan. It'll be perfect for dispersing a cloud of my desiccant powder all over the Boneless. Jake said he'd get it for me."

"I see, and considering we're talking about an ex-thief..."

Archie laughed. "I don't intend to ask *how* he means to acquire it."

Nixie smiled but hoped Jake didn't get in trouble for her sake. Then again, trouble did seem to be a normal part of that boy's life.

"So, ah..." Archie gave her a hesitant glance. "How'd you fare all day with my cousin in the paintings? He can be, shall we say...brash, at times. Cocky."

"You can say that again. But he was fine. Of course..." Nixie cast him a mischievous sideways look. "He *did* try to kiss me."

Archie nearly dropped the whole jar of salt. *"What?"*

Nixie started laughing. "It wasn't really his fault. There was this Cupid in the Boucher who attacked us. Jake got hit in the leg with a golden arrow..."

She told Archie the whole story, and it was the first time she had ever seen the amiable young gent scowl.

"I can't believe he did that! So—what did you do in response?"

"What do you mean?"

Glowering, Archie lowered his voice to a scandalized whisper: "Did you kiss him back?"

"Ew, of course not," Nixie said. "I punched him."

Relief spread across Archie's freckled face, and his smile returned, albeit wryly. "Atta girl. Well, then."

A devious gleam sprang into Archie's sparkly dark eyes. She could fairly see the wheels in his genius mind turning. Feeling she had said quite enough, Nixie went back to her potion while Archie busied himself making the desiccant, weighing, measuring, mixing, and pounding everything from gypsum to activated charcoal into an ever finer dust, all meant to dry the Boneless out.

"Say, Malwort," he spoke up a few minutes later, when the arachno-sapiens returned with the vial of blowfish poison Nixie had asked for from an upper shelf.

The spider set it down gingerly before her, and she patted him on his fuzzy, spotted head with a doting smile.

"Malwort?" Archie repeated.

"What?" The spider tore himself away from Nixie and gave him a wary sort of spider-frown.

"Would you mind getting me the calcium sulfate?" Archie asked.

"Cal-cee whuz?" He had clearly been enjoying the game of fetching ingredients for the witch, but he didn't look too keen to do the same for Archie.

"A white powder. Up there."

Nixie gave the little fellow an encouraging nod toward the shelves. Seeing this would please her, Malwort scampered off.

"It's amazing he can read," she remarked, watching the spider leaping nimbly from shelf to shelf until he found the jar Archie had asked for.

Archie nodded. "I wonder if Uncle Waldrick taught him how."

"You should ask him."

"He's in prison."

"I meant ask the spider," Nixie answered with a grin.

"Oh." Archie chuckled ruefully. "Have to say, I'm a bit surprised Malwort isn't scared of you. He's deathly afraid of brooms, and after all, you are a witch."

Malwort, who was just returning with the calcium sulfate, nearly dropped the jar and froze in the middle of the worktable. "Broom? Eek! Where?"

"Oh, it's all right, Malwort!" Nixie soothed him. "Don't worry, I only use my broom for flying."

"You like flying?" Archie nearly shouted, turning to her in sudden amazement.

"Love it," Nixie said. "Why?"

"Because I invented a flying machine! Flying is like—my favorite thing in the whole world! I mean, we should go out flying together sometime! Unless—er, unless you'd rather not."

"No, it sounds fun," Nixie said, blushing.

Suddenly, they both become extremely embarrassed and hurried back to work.

"Ahem. So how's the potion coming along?" Archie asked a few minutes later.

"Oh, I don't know." Nixie brushed her floppy black bangs out of her eyes with a weary sigh. "To be honest with you, I don't know what else to try." She shook her head. "I've already used the most extreme magic I can think of on Jenny Greenteeth, but nothing's worked. Why should this time be any different? Hemlock, wolfsbane, belladonna... I mean, what else can I add?"

"How about hydrochloric acid? Pretty nasty stuff."

She shrugged. "I suppose it can't hurt."

"Oh, yes, it can. Spilled a drop on my hand once. Here, I'll get it for you. Spider: stay. It's too dangerous for you." Archie started moving toward the shelves, then turned around, his brow furrowed. "Actually... Hmm." He stared into space for a moment, off in genius-land.

"Hullo?" Nixie prompted in amusement when his voice trailed off.

He blinked back to awareness. "You say this hag apparition started out as a nursery bogey, and it was centuries of children believing in her that made her come to life."

"That's right."

"Well, then...wouldn't it be logical that *disbelieving* in her somehow might make her disappear?"

Nixie gave him a skeptical frown. "How do you disbelieve in something that's throwing you across the room?"

"Not really sure..." He shook his head, pondering again, then he shrugged. "Magic's not my forte, so take it with a grain of salt. But to me, it just stands to reason that if belief is what originally brought Jenny Greenteeth into existence, then maybe disbelief is the key to, well, unmaking her. Perhaps fear is the very thing that gives her strength."

Nixie stared at him for a long moment, then looked at her ingredients again and echoed his "hmm."

* * *

Meanwhile, Isabelle, Maddox, and Dani ventured out across the moonlit grounds of Merlin Hall to scout out their enemies. They had to confirm—from a safe distance—if the Headless Highlander was still haunting the path in the woods where Jake had seen him before, and if Nuckalavee was still lolling about in the naiads' stream.

After all, they couldn't defeat these Bugganes if they couldn't find them.

Dani had Jake's telescope. While she scanned the landscape through the night vision lens, Isabelle couldn't help sending worried glances in Maddox's direction.

All this talk of war had chilled her to the bone.

He caught her eyeing him nervously and smiled. "Don't be scared," he teased in a low tone. "I won't let the monsters get you."

She blushed. "It's not that."

"Good. I was about to be insulted if you thought I couldn't keep you safe."

She suppressed a dreamy sigh at his mild brag, but hesitated to share what was on her mind, since the Bugganes were probably enough to worry about.

He marched on, and she had to walk faster to keep up with his long strides, Dani trailing a few paces behind.

"Maddox?"

"Yes, Miss Bradford?" he answered in amusement.

A sound of distress escaped her. "Are you going to go to the war, if there is one?"

"If they tell me to, of course. Why?"

With the guarded look he gave her, Isabelle wished more than ever that she could read him, but he was a brick wall. It was so vexing! She just had to muddle through like any other girl, bewildered by the stoic silence of boys.

"It's just—if you had to go and fight, I'd worry so. The Dark Druids, Maddox. They can do worse than kill you. You do know that, right?"

"A Guardian goes where he's needed, Miss Bradford. Oh, don't look like that," he chided softly when he saw her wide-eyed stare.

"I should hate for anything to happen to you," she blurted out.

"No worries. If it does, I'm sure the healers will fix me right up." He flashed a smile and chucked her under the chin.

"Maddox! Can't you just—"

"Isabelle! You can't ask me not to be who I am," he said impatiently. "Now, you ladies stay here," he ordered, making it clear by his tone that this topic was not open to discussion. "I'll be right back."

"Shouldn't we come with you?"

"Nixie said the Scot vanishes if he sees more than one person alone."

She also said if he sees one person alone, he kills them, Isabelle thought.

He gave her a maddening look of total confidence. "I'll be back before you know it."

"Be careful," she insisted.

He ignored her, pivoting toward the woods. She stood fretting on the castle's long driveway while he strode off across the meadow, heading for the opening in the woods.

Toward the danger.

Dani arrived by her side and took her hand, giving it a squeeze. "He'll be all right, don't worry." She hesitated. "It's just a stupid ghost."

Like the sort Jake faces all the time.

Dani did not need to say that part aloud. They were both thinking it.

Isabelle glanced at her, grateful for the redhead's sturdy presence at her side. But when Dani met her gaze, she could see the same fear in her eyes, and no wonder. Jake, for all his roguery, had the exact same tendency toward heroics as Maddox. Dani gripped her hand a little harder.

Growing up's horrid, Isabelle thought. And falling in love with a boy for the first time was even worse.

* * *

Dani shared Isabelle's tension as they waited for Maddox to come back from the woods. Every second dragged. Isabelle borrowed Jake's telescope from her but then couldn't bear to look—and couldn't bear *not* to look, either. She was in a bad way, Dani mused, looking askance at the older girl.

For her part, she was finding her gift of common sense to be a bit of a burden right now.

We're just kids. Why aren't we telling the grownups? Why do we have to do this by ourselves?

She chewed her lip uneasily and conceded that, of course, the grownups had bigger things to worry about, since they had just found out that they might be headed for a war.

A war! Dani couldn't even imagine it. It didn't seem real. Maybe the vampire was just making it up to scare everybody. That sounded like the sort of thing a vampire would do.

As for the Bugganes, Jake had declared that, together, they could take these creatures on, and far be it from the baby of the group to be the tattletale.

Just then, Isabelle gasped, looking through the lens.

"What?" Dani barely got out, when suddenly Maddox came charging out of the woods with a yelp.

"I see it—the apparition!" Isabelle breathed, and Dani did, too, while Maddox sprinted toward them.

But just like Nixie had described, the moment the Headless Highlander realized the girls were there, it stopped chasing Maddox and faded back into the shadows like a wisp of fog, leaving only a long, dire bagpipe note hanging on the night like a warning.

"Holy Mother!" Upon rejoining them, Maddox leaned forward and braced his hands on his thighs for a moment, catching his breath. "*Whew.* I'm gonna need a bigger sword."

"Brave warrior," Dani teased, laughing at how he had bolted in dread just like Jake had. She couldn't resist.

Maddox sent her a playful scowl and tweaked her nose. "You go talk to him and see how *you* fare, pipsqueak."

"Yes, but you see, I'm too smart to do that," she replied.

Maddox straightened up and shook off his brief fright. "A Headless Highlander! Well, you don't see that every day." He seemed quite chagrined at having fled the ghost in front of Isabelle, but of course, she was gracious, as always.

She patted him on the shoulder. "Good work. At least we know now he's in there."

"Let's go find the other one."

"Nuckalavee." Isabelle nodded. "It's supposed to be some sort of animal, so I should be able to read it."

"You'll be careful," Maddox told her sternly. "I don't want you getting too close."

They started flirting again. Dani found it a little annoying, even though she knew how happy Isabelle was to have met Maddox.

Ever the loyal lady's companion, Dani hung back to give the pair some room. She was happy to let them chat together, as long as *she* was there to act as chaperone.

Heading down the driveway toward the stone bridge, Dani could hear the water nymphs singing along with the frogs and the light babble of the stream. It was very beautiful and made her feel like nothing bad could ever really happen.

"I wonder if the others are making any progress," Isabelle remarked.

Dani wondered, too.

* * *

Jake did not know how *he* got stuck with Troll Boy.

Well, actually, he did. Og was about to become his accomplice in a burglary. Which probably meant that an ex-pickpocket wasn't the best influence on the lumbering, child-like monster...

Nevertheless, as they crept through the zoo, with all its supposed nighttime dangers, Jake was surprised—and a trifle worried—at how quietly the big lug could sneak.

When it came to stealth, Ogden Trumbull was a natural. Disturbingly so, given his rock troll instincts.

Having already dealt with one cannibal today on Caliban's island, Jake kept a close eye on him as they crept toward the thatch-roofed cottage that housed the veterinarian's office. He had the Bully Buzzer in his pocket and was not afraid to use it if Og so much as looked at him wrong. And yet...

Poor thing. Og still had no idea why he kept having these painful "fits," as he called them. For the past few minutes, he had been confiding in Jake about his sudden, inexplicable health problems.

"Maybe I should have Dr. Plantagenet check me," he rumbled anxiously. "A person shouldn't be falling down like that for no reason!"

"Aw, I wouldn't worry him," Jake assured him in a whisper. "You probably just have a virus. It'll pass. Don't worry, you'll be fine. Are you feeling all right now?"

Og shrugged. "I think so. Just a little sore from falling off the rocks."

"See? Maybe you're getting better already. Right! So, er, there's the office." He pointed to the cottage nestled in the landscaping ahead. The windows were all dark. "You said Dr. P. keeps the front door locked, right? So what's the best way to get in?"

"Shh!" Og froze and suddenly pointed to a particular tree nearby.

Jake squinted at it in the darkness, then glanced at his large companion. "What?"

Og folded his hands together and tilted his head to mimic someone sleeping. Jake's jaw dropped. He looked at the tree again, more closely this time, and realized, sure enough, it was the Green Man fast asleep for the night.

Dr. Plantagenet had doffed his white lab coat; all his roots and vines were showing. His trunk was covered in bark, and his feet were sunk deep into the ground. Jake's stare traveled over the Green Man in wonder. His eyes were closed serenely, and his face looked leafier than before.

When he twitched a little at the flutter of a bird amid the branches of his head, Jake ducked down, his heart pounding.

After a moment, he was satisfied that the zookeeper wasn't going to wake and nodded toward the cottage. He and Og continued on, tiptoeing past the sleeping Green Man.

Their task this night was relatively simple. Archie needed to borrow one of those big sprayer gizmos that Dr. Plantagenet had used to treat the dracosaur, and Jake was going to steal it.

The irony, of course, was not lost on him. Dani and Gladwin had just finished clearing his name of false thieving charges, only to have him go and steal something in earnest.

But, of course, he would return the sprayer as soon as they were done. In truth, the kindly Green Man probably would have lent it to him willingly if he only asked, but they didn't want adults asking questions. Besides, Dr. P. was sleeping, anyway, Jake rationalized. *Why wake him?*

More importantly, Nixie had been very firm in insisting that they not include adults in this. Magic meant everything to her, and she was afraid of getting kicked out of Merlin Hall if the Elders heard about her banishing the Bugganes from Castle MacGool—considering that the evil laird had then fallen prey to a lynch mob without his ghouls to protect him.

Not that that was *her* fault.

To Jake, it sounded like the tyrannical Clan MacGool had brought their fate upon themselves, terrorizing their people. Personally, he was more concerned about Nixie's safety if the Dark Druids discovered her role in the affair.

If they'd been willing to wipe out half the village with a plague to punish the locals, who knew what they might do to the young witch who had started the whole thing by banishing the Bugganes?

Jake didn't want to risk it. It was bad enough that the Dark Druids had found out about his killing Garnock. If Nixie could be spared the same fate, they had to try. Otherwise, the Dark Druids would probably come after her, too—whether to kill or recruit her.

Jake shuddered at the thought of those devils winning Nixie over to their side. If they could gain a magical prodigy of her ability as a future member of the Dark Druids, she would be a serious enemy to contend with for many years to come. Jake was not about to let that happen. *They* were her friends now, and they were going to help her. Show her she wasn't alone. It was very much the same thing that Dani, Archie, and Isabelle had done for *him* just a year ago, when he had been a half-feral street kid.

Time I passed on the favor.

At last, he and Og reached the cover of the shadows beside the veterinary cottage. Og pointed to an open window on the upper floor, and then gave Jake a boost up on his massive shoulders. Jake stepped onto Og's thick head and climbed in the window.

Inside the cottage, he hunted around until he found the doctor's spare sprayer on the bottom shelf of a rack full of veterinary supplies. Moving silently, he picked it up, slung the leather strap over his shoulder, and glided down the stairs to the front door.

He slipped out, pulling it closed behind him. "Let's go!" he whispered to Ogden.

"That was fast!"

"Come on! We've got to get this to Archie."

They raced away from the cottage before they were seen. Once they cleared the grounds of the zoo, Jake made Ogden carry the sprayer in case anyone asked about it.

Troll Boy was known for helping Dr. P. with different chores, so nobody ought to think twice about it. However, if they did, *Jake* did not intend to be the one who got caught with the thing!

Anyway, he doubted anyone would bother them as they hurried toward a side entrance to deliver the sprayer to Archie in the basement.

While they were crossing the broad stretch of lawn between the palace and the zoo, a burst of light suddenly appeared at the waypoint, heralding the now-familiar sight of a portal opening up.

Jake stopped in his tracks as the blue circle of light appeared in the darkness. He still found the whole thing utterly irresistible.

"Look, Og, one of the Lightriders must be coming in off the Grid!"

"So? Hurry up!" Og urged.

"Hold on, I want to see..."

"But somebody's coming! Look over there, by the bridge!" Og pointed up the driveway.

Jake squinted into the darkness and could just make out three figures, two in dresses. "That's our friends, you dolt. It's Maddox and the girls. Don't worry—"

His words were cut off by a scream from the pair of adults who suddenly staggered through the portal.

A bloodied man hung slumped over, his arm slung across the shoulders of a fierce female Guardian. The woman held him up with one arm around his waist while brandishing a sword in her free hand.

"Help us!" she bellowed, dropping the wounded Lightrider none-too-gently on the grass, and turning to ward off anything that might have tried to follow her through the Grid.

Jake was already in motion, racing automatically to her aid, never mind that he was just a kid. If nothing else, his telekinesis might be of some use, as it had been when Tex had arrived wounded.

"Og, take the sprayer to Archie—now!" he yelled back over his shoulder, pointing toward the palace.

"What are you gonna do?"

"I'm going to help them. Go!"

Og looked startled but ran off to do as he was told.

In the distance, Maddox must have also seen what had happened and heard the shout for help, because he left the girls behind and sprinted toward the portal, approaching from the opposite direction.

The Guardian woman thrust her sword blade down into the turf, where the weapon stood upright, in easy access for her to grab if she needed it again.

As the boys pounded toward her, Jake shouting for the gnomes, she bent and yanked up the sleeve of the Lightrider's coat. They could see her urging him to punch in the coordinates.

While the wounded Lightrider struggled to lift his hand to shut the portal using the Flower of Life device embedded in his arm, the woman bellowed toward the palace, "Gnomes! Help! We need a doctor here!"

The Lightrider pressed the crystal chip buttons with crimson fingers, and the Guardian moved her long duster coat back to glance down at her side.

She wore men's garb—vest, shirt, trousers, boots—and a weapons holster slung around her waist. But it was not her unladylike clothes that caught Jake's attention. It was the blood seeping through them.

He saw her hands shaking and realized she was badly hurt, as well. The moment the portal vanished, she fell to one knee with an angry sound of anguish.

Glancing furiously toward the palace, she spotted Jake coming. "You, boy! Fetch the gnomes! My Lightrider's injured. I don't think he's going to make it."

"I already did. They should be here in a trice. What happened?"

"We were ambushed, obviously!" she snarled, her face a mask of fury. And then she faltered, cursed with pain, and passed out from blood loss on the grass.

Jake's eyes widened. Panic filled him. *"Gnomes!"* He turned around, but there was still no sign of the palace helpers.

Perhaps they hadn't heard the shouts for help, what with the noisy ball going on inside.

When he spun back around, he was hugely relieved to find Maddox arriving on the scene. "What do we do? They're both hurt bad. We've got to get them inside!"

"Lightrider first," Maddox clipped out, skidding to a halt by the waypoint.

Jake had never been so glad for the battle training that had obviously taught the future Guardian how to be cool-nerved in a crisis. Immediately, Maddox crouched down by the now-silent Lightrider and felt his neck for a pulse.

Jake held his breath. "Is he dead?"

"Pretty close."

"What about her?" He pointed at the black-haired warrior woman. "Be careful, she's mean. Could probably cut your throat in her sleep." Unconscious—and no longer enraged—she actually had a pretty face. Jake hoped she didn't die. "She said they were ambushed."

The boys exchanged a grim glance as they realized the Dark Druids were probably behind this, making good on their promise to punish the Lightriders for him having killed Garnock. Jake flinched with guilt at the thought that the blood of these two agents was on his hands to some extent.

Maddox stepped over the Lightrider's inert body and grabbed the unconscious woman's shoulder, turning her over to check her for a pulse.

But the second he saw her face, Maddox drew back with a gasp of alarm.

"What is it?" Jake exclaimed. He had never seen the Guardian kid rattled before.

Suddenly Maddox looked terrified.

"What's wrong? Has she died?" Jake cried.

Feeling herself being moved had revived the Guardian woman ever so slightly. Her eyes opened to slits; she seemed to be fighting to stay conscious. But the moment she saw Maddox, a soft smile skimmed her lips.

"Oh...hullo, son," she mumbled, and then she passed out again.

Jake's jaw dropped. He looked at Maddox in astonishment. "That's your mother?"

"Birth mother," Maddox said through gritted teeth, managing to regain his composure enough then to check the gaping wound on her side.

"I thought you were the son of a blacksmith—"

"Adopted!" Maddox barked at him. "Not that it's any of your business!"

Jake blinked. "Well, don't just stand there! Take her in to the doctors!"

"It's not protocol," Maddox answered in a strangled voice. He moved back toward the man. "I must see to the Lightrider—"

"Are you daft? Hang protocol! She's your mother, man! Go!" Jake ordered him with all the lordly authority he possessed. "I'll see to the Lightrider," he added, even though he feared the poor sod was already dead.

At the very least, on death's door.

Maddox glanced from one bloodied victim to the other as though he didn't know what to do. Instinct visibly warred with duty on his square face.

"Take her in," Jake ordered fiercely. "What's wrong with you? You can't let your own mother die! Go!"

"A-all right." Still looking shaken, Maddox bent down and gently picked her up, lifting her into his arms. She moaned, her head hanging back. "You have to get *him*, though."

"On it!" While Maddox strode off carrying his mother, Jake marched over to the Lightrider and started trying to wake him up with a few light taps on his cheek. "Sir, sir, can you hear me? We have to move you, all right? This might hurt, but we need to get you inside."

No response.

"Blast it!" Jake whispered. Unfortunately, he wasn't as strong as Maddox and could not lift a grown man in a dead-weight state. All he could do was hook his arms under the Lightrider's armpits and start dragging him backward toward the palace.

When the man groaned in pain at the movement, Jake suddenly remembered he had telekinesis.

336   E.G. FOLEY

He cursed at himself for forgetting his ability and smacked himself in the forehead. Why did that always happen whenever he got flustered? Would he never get used to having magical powers?

He let the Lightrider lie flat on the grass again, took a deep breath, and used his telekinesis to levitate the wounded man gently off the ground.

Just then, a troop of gnomes came rushing out to help. Maddox had been yelling for them as he sped toward the palace carrying his mother, and they had finally heard him once he neared the front doors of Merlin Hall.

Two gnomes held the doors open for him; Maddox disappeared inside. The rest trundled out in formation to retrieve the second victim.

"Oh, thank you." Jake stepped back in relief and let them take over from there. It was what Sir Peter had done, after all, when Tex had arrived.

Jake watched them anxiously, but it was hard to read their wizened little faces. They barely reacted to anything and didn't say a word, simply did what needed to be done.

He couldn't help wondering if they showed no surprise because maybe this sort of thing happened to Lightriders all the time.

In short order, they hefted the unconscious Lightrider up onto their shoulders and glided him away toward the palace, all their little legs going like a caterpillar.

"Red," he said to himself with a sudden inspiration. While the gnomes hurried their patient inside, Jake turned around and raced back toward the zoo.

Even though Red's molting process was not yet complete, surely *one* scarlet feather on his wings must be grown in enough by now to have been infused with its usual healing powers.

Barely three minutes had passed since the portal had opened, and as Jake pounded toward the entrance of the zoo, Isabelle and Dani were only now catching up.

"Jake! What's happening?" he heard the carrot yell in the distance, but he did not linger to explain.

There was no time, not with these people's lives at stake.

Desperate to reach the Gryphon's aerie, Jake raced on, ignoring all the strange and dangerous animals roaring at him as he passed.

CHAPTER TWENTY-NINE
Calm before the Storm

A n hour later, the one perfect feather Red had offered up had worked to close the Guardian woman's gaping wound.

Her name was Ravyn Vambrace according to her son, who paced continually outside her room. A pair of Elders and an old, grizzled, Guardian were in there with her now, asking questions about what exactly had occurred.

As for the Lightrider in the adjacent bedchamber, the Gryphon magic had brought him back from the brink of death, but he remained in a coma-like state, stable but unresponsive—the result, they feared, of some new Dark Druid magic.

Jake sat fidgeting on a bench in the hallway, waiting with Maddox as a gesture of moral support. After all, his own mother had died violently at the hands of an evil man: Uncle Waldrick.

Somehow, this made it all the more important to him to make sure the other boy's mother lived. The doctors had informed Maddox she'd survive, but he waited, wanting to see her for himself, however briefly.

Jake watched him pacing. "Would you sit still? You're making me dizzy."

"Can't."

Jake pondered for a moment. "I see the resemblance but I still can't believe she's your mum."

"No," Maddox corrected him in a prickly tone. "She's my *mother*. Not my mum. My Mum is at home right now, getting ready for bed after cleaning up the supper she would've cooked as usual for my Pop, got it? Ravyn might've given birth to me, and for that, I'm grateful. But that is the extent of our connection."

Jake winced. "Kind of cold if you ask me," he muttered. He

couldn't even imagine how it would be to have two mothers in one's life when he had never known one.

Maddox sent him a warning look that said he did not wish to discuss it further, and then he changed the subject. "We found the Headless Highlander and Nuckalavee, both where you said they'd be. So, we should be all set when the time comes."

It wouldn't be long now. Jake nodded. "Good."

They fell silent for a minute. He tried not to pry. He really did. He wasn't Dani, after all. But he could not shut up about it.

"Did you always know you were adopted?" he ventured. "When did you find out? Was it a shock?"

Maddox glared at him.

"Hey, if anyone knows how you feel, it would be me. I spent most of my childhood in an orphanage, you know. Always wondered what it was like for those lucky kids who got picked."

This rather pitiful admission made Maddox frown but relent. "I was never in an orphanage," he mumbled. "She gave me up at birth. I was taken to my new family straightaway."

"Why didn't she keep you?"

"So I could have a better life! You think she'd want to drag around a baby on her missions, idiot?"

"Easy!" Jake chided. "I know you're upset, but she's going to live because of my Gryphon, so you don't have to bite my head off."

"Sorry," he grumbled. "I do appreciate it. I just... Seeing her is never easy."

Jake paused until, once more, curiosity got the better of him. "So, who's your real father, then, if not the blacksmith?"

"You really don't know when to quit, do you?" Maddox exclaimed.

"Not really, no. Aw, come on, you can tell me. I mean..." He almost couldn't bring himself to ask. "It isn't Derek, is it?"

"What?"

"Well, he obviously thinks you hung the moon, so—"

"As if Guardian Stone would ever father a son and then refuse to marry the mother! He could never do something that dishonorable— obviously!" Maddox snarled, very much like how Guardian Vambrace had snarled at him outside.

"Then who?" Jake persisted, well aware he was being a pain.

"Not that it is any of your business," Maddox finally said, "but let's just say...that my father outranks yours."

"But my father was an earl. Hold on!" Jake suddenly gasped and shot up from his chair. "Is it the vampire prince?"

"Oh, please. He and Ravyn were only friends. They served on Derek's team on small group missions for a few years. And by the way, Janos isn't a real prince."

"He's not?"

"No!" Maddox scoffed. "He was just a normal Guardian who got fed up with his lot. Ask me, he's nothing but a deserter and deserves to go before the firing squad. Again," he added firmly.

"Again?" Jake echoed.

Maddox seemed glad to talk about Janos rather than discussing his own story. "Years ago, the three of them were out on a mission when they strayed into vampire territory. Little did they know, the vampires needed males. Their men kept getting killed by mobs of angry villagers. So, the vampire queen offered Derek the chance to join them. When he said no, she went after Janos, his right-hand man. Janos took the devil's bargain, even though he knew that deserting his post would mean the firing squad."

"Why would he do such a thing?"

Maddox shrugged. "He couldn't resist the temptation. Stay young and strong and live off vampire riches forever? Never die, after years of risking his neck to protect VIPs who half the time don't even bother to learn a Guardian's name?

"He also must have realized that the vampires' immortality would help him to survive any punishment the Order tried to give him. So, would you believe he had the nerve to come back to Merlin Hall and turn himself in once he had undergone the change?"

"Really?"

"That's why everybody hates him. He's the most arrogant bloody creature on the earth. Once the vampire queen had turned him into one of the undead, he came back here to resign and offer his insincere apologies. The Elders had him clapped in irons, but all he did was smirk. Then they tied the blindfold and marched him up against the wall."

"For the firing squad?"

"Aye. He knew exactly what he was doing, too, that smart aleck. He stood there and *let* them shoot him. But, of course, he didn't die. Imagine the Elders' dismay when the bullet holes immediately healed and Janos walked away unscathed. In his mind, he had paid his debt, as per the rules. The Elders were flummoxed, but what else could they do? He had gone before the firing squad. He offered to let them hang him, too, if it would make them feel better."

Jake grinned at the audacity of this bloke, even though Derek didn't like him.

"The Old Yew interviewed Janos privately and became convinced that it was in the Order's best interest to let him go. I guess the Father Tree and enough of the Elders believed Janos when he said he wasn't going to cause any trouble, and that he could actually be useful there among the vampires. As a long-term spy or something, deep undercover."

"Seems he kept his word about that much," Jake said. "So if he started out as just an ordinary fellow, how come he calls himself a prince?"

"The vampire queen made him one, gave him a big chunk of territory to reign over for her." Maddox looked away and hesitated. "My birth father..." he added in a low tone, "now, he's the real thing."

"What did you say?" He stared at him in shock. "*You* have royal blood?"

"Don't tell Isabelle!" he said fiercely.

"Why not?"

"Because I'm illegitimate, Jake!" Maddox exclaimed, his cheeks flushing. "'Bastard' son of a foreign prince. Do you know what that's like?"

"No," Jake said wonderingly.

Maddox looked away. "Seventeen years ago, Ravyn was assigned to protect the royal egomaniac. They had a whirlwind romance, then went their separate ways. Nine months later, I was born. You see, that's why Guardians are not supposed to dally in romantic affairs! I wish your cousin could understand that. And if you tell her any of this, I will thrash you. I mean it."

"I'm not going to! But, er, she is an empath. She'll know I'm hiding something. Why can't she read you, anyway?"

He shrugged. "No idea, but I have to say, I'm glad. I wouldn't want any girl poking around in my head."

"So...did you ever get to meet him? Your birth father?"

Maddox sighed. "Every few years he sends this whole elaborate escort with a pompous line of horses and carriages out to Pop's forge to come and pick me up. Real discreet." He rolled his eyes. "His lackeys take me to His Royal Highness so he can inspect me, see how I'm coming along. It's a long trip. Across the Channel. It's just a tiny kingdom in the Alps."

"Is he nice?"

Maddox shrugged. "I don't know. He's not too bad. Kind of a fool. But I guess he means well."

"Does he spoil you? Does he give you lots of stuff? I mean, if he's royalty—come on!"

Maddox just looked at him.

"Well, you know how adults are when they feel guilty, and he must feel at least a little guilty about you! Giving you away and all."

"Hey, I'm happy with the parents I got. I could not have asked for better. But...actually, he offered to make me a duke. I refused."

"What? You refused?"

"I'm a Guardian, Jake! What would I do with a dukedom? It would just weigh me down. Besides, I don't want his money or his power. I don't want anything from him. I have everything I need already. My Mum and Pop, be they ever so humble, gave me more than a prince ever could. They loved me from the first day Derek brought me to their door. All they ever wanted was a son."

Jake pondered this for a moment.

"Anyway," Maddox said with a shrug, "His Highness would have had me raised in the castle. Lord knows they have enough rooms. But Ravyn wouldn't let him."

"Why not?"

"She was afraid that, when the Kinderveil lifted, I'd become a target and a pawn in court intrigues. I mean, once my Guardian abilities started coming out, I might outshine my birth father's legitimate sons, and that would have got me into trouble. It's not healthy to outshine a royal prince. More importantly, Ravyn just wanted me to have a simple, normal life for as long as I could. And I have. I'm grateful for her choice! Still, it's kind of awkward when I see her. I'm just glad she survived." Maddox paused and turned away, his expression darkening. "But I'll tell you what, I'm going to find out who did this to her."

Voices on the other side of the chamber door alerted them that Ravyn's interview with the Elders was ending. A moment later, the adults came out, Maddox went in, and Jake was left sitting all alone.

He watched the Elders and the old Guardian stride down the

hallway, off to plan the Order's response to this shocking provocation.

Unable to shake off the conviction that all of this was his fault, Jake got up, filled with restlessness, and went in search of the others.

He found his friends having snacks in the inglenook of a huge, drafty parlor at the far end of the hallway. Og sat on the floor, too big to fit on the benches built around the great baroque fireplace. As he joined them, he reported the latest developments and told them Maddox would be along shortly. Then they could get down to business dealing with the Bugganes.

He had just helped himself to a slice of cheese off the snack tray when Gladwin fluttered in to see them.

"Gladwin!" Dani seemed particularly glad when she swept across the room and hovered nearby.

"Sorry. I only came to say goodbye," she said hastily. "All the royal garden fairies are being sent out to deliver messages to Lightriders everywhere to warn them to be extra-careful. More Guardians are being dispatched, too. That's why I came to find you." Gladwin turned to Jake with a sad look on her tiny face. "Derek is leaving. I thought you'd want to know so you could see him off."

Jake paled. "They're sending Derek out?"

Gladwin nodded. "You'd better hurry," she added, so they did.

Maddox caught up just in time to go rushing outside with them. Out on the still-bloodied lawn near the waypoint, Derek stood with Tex, who was waiting to escort him through the Grid to heaven-knew where.

A third person joined them—a scantily-clad djinni. She had kohl-lined eyes full of a devious sparkle and a belt of silver coins around her bare waist that tinkled when she walked. She carried the colorful glass bottle that was her home on a strap over her shoulder, and both men looked quite glad that she was there.

Jake wondered what sort of powers she might have.

Miss Helena came running out, apparently having also just heard the news that Derek had to go. Henry was a few steps behind her, no doubt knowing how upset his twin would be to learn that her beau would be the first heading off into danger.

No doubt Derek had volunteered.

Jake and the other children stood out of the way, rather distraught, but they could hear Derek and Helena's exchange.

"Where are they sending you?" she asked anxiously.

"We're going to scout out the ground around the Black Fortress—

at least, where it was last seen. They've probably moved it by now, but we've got to track it down."

Jake did not know what that was, but Helena paled at his reply. "Let me come with you. You know I can help—"

"Yes, you probably could, but I don't want you anywhere near there. Besides," he murmured, "you have to stay here. Keep your claws sharp in case anybody comes near them." Derek nodded toward the kids—and spotted Jake watching them.

Their beloved governess looked heartbroken, but Miss Helena lowered her head, accepting his answer with a nod of resolve. "Very well. But you had better come back to me unscathed!"

Derek kissed her on the forehead. Helena hugged him, then looked at Tex and the djinni, who waited nearby. "Take care of him for me."

Tex grinned and tipped his hat. "Will do, ma'am."

The djinni merely tapped her bare toes on the ground, obviously impatient to get underway.

Then came the hard part. Derek turned to the kids to say goodbye. As soon as he looked at them, they all rushed forward and swamped the big man, hugging him from all sides.

Laughing softly, he put his arms around them all. "Now, now, I'll be back before you know it."

"Please be careful, Derek!" Dani begged him. "We need you!"

It was true. Jake felt a threat of tears rising in his eyes. No wonder the warrior's last name was Stone—heaven knew he had certainly become their rock over the past year, at least for Jake and Dani.

They were the last two who still clung to him, refusing to let go even after the others had gone to wish Tex and the mysterious djinni a safe trip.

Wiping away a tear, Dani reluctantly stepped away from Derek, knowing Jake would want a moment alone with his mentor.

Jake looked up at the tall, rugged man with his wild mane of dark hair, a short scruff of a day's beard on his jaw. He shook his head as the threat of tears got stronger.

"This is all my fault," Jake whispered. "You shouldn't have to do this. If I had never fought Garnock—"

"Hey. Listen to me." Derek took him by the shoulders and held him at arm's length to stare sternly into his eyes. "You are not to blame. These are evil wizards we're dealing with, Jake. Starting wars is simply what they do. If it wasn't you killing Garnock, they'd have simply found some other excuse. Now, you keep your eyes open and look after everybody for me. Your Aunt Ramona's going to be taking you lot out of England for a while. For your own safety."

"Where?"

"I don't know. Somewhere they wouldn't think to look for you. Just in case."

"You think they will come hunting for me, then?"

"I don't want to worry you," he said tactfully, "but it's possible. Even so, you'll be quite safe. You've got Red to protect you—he's almost done molting. And Helena—you saw in Wales how fierce she can be when anyone threatens one of her charges. And of course, Lady Bradford. Between you and me, your aunt is one of the most powerful witches who ever set foot in Merlin Hall. She doesn't often use her skills, but when she does, look out. Oh, and I'm also sending Maddox with you till I get back. I know he's not a full-fledged Guardian yet, but he'll fill in the gaps. I figured you'd prefer someone closer to your own age instead of having another adult breathing down your neck."

"That's for sure."

"So, you think you boys can get along?" Derek paused, looking from Jake to Maddox, who stood nearby. "It's important to me that you do. You both mean a great deal to me."

Jake and Maddox exchanged a glance. "Yes, sir," they both answered, with very different looks on their faces than when he had forced them to apologize to each other back in dragon-land.

"Now, Dani girl," Derek said, turning to the carrot, "I'll want a full report on these two blockheads when I get back. You're to let me know if you see any fighting."

Dani saluted him. "Yes, sir. But I'd only be a tattletale for your sake!"

He rumpled her hair, then squared his broad shoulders and stalked toward his colleagues for this mission.

Jake took a deep breath and somehow swallowed down his roiling emotions, nodding at the Lightrider. "Careful out there, Tex."

"You too, boy. *Vaya con Dios.*" He punched the Grid coordinates into the Flower of Life, and the portal appeared.

"Finally!" the djinni said, rolling her dark eyes. She drew a nasty curved knife from its sheath at her side. "Let's go hunting." Dainty yet sinister, she sauntered to the portal, bells jangling. Then she stepped inside, and *whoosh!*

Off she went.

"See you soon," Derek said. Then he, too, stepped into the portal and turned into a man-shaped cloud of tiny golden molecules, all of which whisked off down the ley line in the next instant, bound for who-knows-where.

Tex glanced back over his shoulder and tipped his hat with that mad twinkle in his blue eyes. "Yee-haw," he murmured.

Then he took a big stride forward with his alligator boot into the tunnel, and swept off on the adventure.

Seconds after he had dematerialized, the portal winked shut.

The lawn was dark once again and Miss Helena was fighting to hold onto her composure. "Children, it's almost bedtime."

"Oh, Miss Helena!" they started to protest, for they still had to free Nixie from the Bugganes tonight.

She held up her hand amid the chorus of their complaints, in no mood to argue with them right now after watching Derek go. "Fine! Amuse yourselves a while longer, then. But *stay out of trouble.*" She directed this warning at Jake, then pivoted and hurried back into the palace. They heard a low sob escape her as she ran.

Henry had been standing there silently. He gave the kids a rueful look, then strode off after his sister to try to comfort her. When he had gone, it was just the kids. They looked around at each other, realizing anew just how serious this was, to say nothing of the dangers they were about to face personally tonight.

"Everybody ready?" Jake asked at last.

Maddox nodded. "Just need to get my weapons."

"My stuff is ready back in the lab," Archie said.

"My potions are as ready as they're going to be. It's in the lab, as well." Nixie hesitated, looking around at them. "You really don't have to do this for my sake. It's not too late to back out."

"Nonsense," Jake told her gruffly. "We all need our friends more than ever now."

Everyone nodded, moving closer into a tightknit group.

They looked around at each other for a long moment, then Jake swallowed hard.

"C'mon, you lot. We've got monsters to fight."

CHAPTER THIRTY
The Battle of the Bugganes

The wheels on Archie's handcart made an ominous clatter and squeak that echoed down the long, dim hallway where they had decided to stage their ambush.

Maddox had advised that they start with the least threatening foe, and that meant the Boneless.

This preliminary skirmish would give them a taste of what they were up against, and more importantly, would eliminate a nuisance enemy. Then Boneless couldn't get in the way and complicate matters when it came time to deal with the scarier Bugganes.

They chose their battleground with care, picking a spot that the creature was known to haunt—the same lonely corridor where Jake had chased the Boneless on the night they had first met Nixie.

Tonight, however, they weren't leaving anything to chance.

Jake and Maddox went ahead, systematically removing any mirrors off the walls so Jenny Greenteeth could not come through and interfere with their capture of the Boneless.

In tense silence, the two-boy advance team locked away all the mirrors and shiny objects they found in an empty parlor. Whatever reflective surfaces they came across that could not be moved, such as windows without drapes, they covered them with black oilskin raincoats.

This left the watery hag no point of entry. Not only did the black oilskins let in no light at all, but they were also waterproof, which they reasoned might help, since Jenny Greenteeth was associated with water.

A few yards behind Jake and Maddox, Archie pulled the handcart with an unusually grim expression on his face. The moment of truth would soon be at hand. He had not been this nervous since he'd had to give his presentation at the Invention Convention in front of Mr. Edison and Mr. Tesla; he was, however, confident in his contraption.

It should do the trick. The rotating motion of the amber ball rubbing against the rabbit fur had already charged up the whole mesh surface of the Faraday cage. With an occasional spark from the Leyden jars, the cage seemed eager to receive its prisoner.

The girls walked cautiously beside it. He had warned them all not to touch the metal, lest they get a shock.

As for the desiccant, Isabelle was carrying the sprayer over her shoulder. Frankly, she was the only one Archie trusted not to break the big glass jar beneath the nozzle if anything went wrong. Moreover, she knew how he worked. For years, his sister had acted as lab assistant for him now and then.

Lastly, Ogden Trumbull padded along softly, bringing up the rear. The big half-troll kept watching behind them for any sign of the Bugganes. So far, nothing.

Which was good.

For this gave them time to get into position once they found the perfect spot. Nixie was to be the bait, but Archie assured her he wouldn't be far away, nor would the others. Nixie nodded bravely and looked into his eyes, determined to trust him—to trust all of them.

"Archie, you've really thought of everything," Dani remarked, gazing at his Boneless Catcher in awe.

"I hope I have. Nixie's safety depends on it."

"Come on, everybody," Jake ordered. "The Boneless isn't going to show itself if it sees all of us hanging about. Let's get out of sight." He glanced at Nixie. "Good luck. Don't worry, this is nothing compared to that Hieronymus Bosch painting."

"You can say that again," she said with a wry smile. "Boneless isn't as bad as those awful Torso Men."

Jake smiled back, then they all sought out hiding places, crouching down behind the heavy baroque furniture here and there in the hallway. Maddox nipped around a nearby corner, keeping Dani behind him. Jake and Isabelle followed Archie into the darkened room right across the hallway; he pulled the handcart just out of sight, but the cage door was open and the electrical charge hummed along the metal wires. They made Ogden hide by the window, through which a little starlight gleamed.

Out in the corridor, Nixie began to wander back and forth, making a show of looking at the paintings, just like she had been doing the other night the Bugganes had attacked her.

Everyone waited in their hiding places with bated breath, Maddox knowing that his sword was of no use against the Boneless, Jake equally well aware that he, too, could do nothing, not even with his telekinesis.

The ball was entirely in Archie's court, and he had never been more ready. Heart pounding, he took the sprayer from his sister and slipped the leather strap over his shoulder.

As an afterthought, he took off his bowtie and tucked it into his pocket. Jake looked at him in amazement in the moon-silvered darkness.

Archie just shrugged. There was a time and a place to be a gentleman, and it was definitely *not* when some slimy blob of a creature set about harassing a chap's young lady. No, indeed. Boneless was in proper trouble now, Archie vowed. Then he set his jaw and gripped the nozzle on the sprayer.

He did not have to wait long.

Eventually, the Boneless glided through the solid stone wall of the corridor and floated toward Nixie. Formless as it was, its face came and went, but even Archie thought it looked happy to see her.

"Oh, not you again," she greeted the creature in contempt, taking a step backward toward the room where Archie waited. "Shove off! I'm in no mood for your tricks."

Boneless played its usual game, zigzagging across her path to prevent her from walking away. Little did it realize she was moving it into position for capture.

"Oh, you missed me, did you? You and your friends had to go a whole day without harassing me, eh? Poor Bugganes!" she taunted— and right then, Archie made his move.

He kicked open the parlor door with a barbaric yell and lunged out into the hallway, taking aim. He pulled back the handle on the sprayer and doused the unsuspecting Boneless with the desiccant.

Nixie dove out of the way of the arc of powder, which, in seconds, proved to have the desired effect.

Boneless didn't know what hit it.

As the sea salt and gypsum and silica began evaporating the water out of it, Boneless could no longer maintain its cloud-vapor form, but started materializing. For the first time perhaps *ever*, it had weight, and though it could still float, this strange experience startled it. It had to strain to fly.

But Archie was already on to the next step. He whirled around and grabbed the handle of the cart, hauling it out into the corridor. "Jake!"

"Got it!"

Now that the Boneless had substance, a tiny shove from his cousin's telekinesis helped to tap the creature down through the square top opening of the electrified cage. Boneless actually whimpered in confusion, but Archie showed no mercy, yanking the rope he had attached to the cage door.

"Ha!" It slammed shut, and the sturdy metal latch clicked at once into place. Through the mesh of the dog kennel, Boneless stared at Archie in shock.

By now, the creature, thought Archie, resembled a giant, floating potato chip.

With a face.

A face that wore a look of confusion as the crisped Boneless hovered in the middle of the cage.

"That's that! You're good and caught now, aren't you?"

Boneless glared and tried to zoom through the mesh walls. When the spark flashed in its face, it squeaked with pain and zoomed backward, but only succeeded in sparking itself in the rear, and squeaked again.

"Don't touch the cage walls," Archie instructed the creature succinctly. "You cannot pass through them, understand? Now, we're not going to hurt you, but you're not getting out of there. Your days of bothering Miss Valentine are through."

Boneless whimpered pitifully with fright, and Archie almost felt bad. But he shook his head sternly. "It's no good. You're going to stay in there until I've figured out what the deuce you are." Archie turned to his friends to give the all-clear, and only then realized everyone was cheering for him.

Nixie was clapping the loudest and gazing at him in starstruck delight.

"Here, here!" Jake shouted amidst the hubbub, clapping him on the back, but Archie barely heard a word.

As calmly debonair as he acted on the outside, nodding his thanks in answer to their praise, on the inside, all he could do was keep shrieking to himself: *She likes me, she likes me!*

* * *

"Next up, Nuckalavee," Jake announced a few minutes later, glancing around at his accomplices. "Let's go."

Off they went, out into the landscape, trying to look casual as they walked past a group of adults.

No doubt the kids made a strange sight with their Boneless in a cage on the handcart, Leyden jars sparking; Isabelle the debutante nonchalantly carrying the sprayer on her shoulder, in case their prisoner needed another puff of the desiccant; Og the Troll Boy lurching along after them, trying to look as innocent as his homely snout could manage.

Jake, for this leg of their mission, was carrying a great loop of heavy rope on his shoulder, while Maddox had a crossbow slung across his back, a spear in his hand, and a look on his face like he knew just how to use both and would not be deterred.

"Oh, hullo, good evening," Dani said sweetly to the staring strangers as they all walked by.

The adults gawked after them. Jake hoped they weren't friends with Uncle Richard and Aunt Claire.

Or worse, Great-Great Aunt Ramona.

"This way," Maddox clipped out as they proceeded up the drive. "Nuckalavee's upstream of the bridge, hiding in the reeds. That's where we last saw him, anyway. Nixie, have you got your potion ready?" The warrior boy glanced at the young witch.

"Ready," she replied.

Obviously, this close to the water, they had to anticipate the possibility of Jenny Greenteeth joining the party while they were engaged in killing Nuckalavee.

For that reason, Jake ordered Archie and all three of the girls to keep their distance on the drive, staying well back from the river. Best not to tempt the watery hag if it could be avoided.

Divide and conquer, he reminded himself. *One Buggane at a time.*

As they neared the water-horse's hideout, they heard a single note from the Headless Highlander's bagpipes echoing ominously from the woods.

Jake and Maddox exchanged a dark glance.

Neither of them knew what to expect from the fabled, skinless water-bull, but they definitely weren't looking forward to facing down the murderous Scot with his massive claymore.

"Shall we?" Maddox said.

"Wait, Jake, don't forget this!" Dani handed him his birthday telescope with the night vision lens. "Good luck."

Jake took it and gave her a cheery wink.

"Be careful, Maddox," Izzy said fretfully.

Maddox turned and kept walking backward toward the fight, spear in hand, as he gave them a final warning. "If Nuckalavee should get past us and heads in your direction, hit him with the desiccant," he said. "Nixie said the beast has got no skin, right? That'll hurt like salt in the wound—should drive him away if he comes anywhere near you."

"Good thinking!" Archie said. "Sis?"

"I've got it," Izzy said with a pleased nod at her hero's advice.

Malwort, meanwhile, sat on Nixie's shoulder while she reached into her big black bag and carefully lifted out a few of the small, glass, globe-shaped vials in which she had stored her deadly potion. These were meant to break on impact. If Jenny Greenteeth came anywhere near her, she would throw them at the hag like grenades.

Dani O'Dell watched her intently.

Nixie looked askance at her. "How's your aim?"

"Ask me five older brothers," the redhead replied with a fierce smile, which Nixie returned before offering her one of the stoppered vials.

"Here. But mind you don't drop it. It's extremely poisonous. In other words, could kill you."

Dani nodded and took the glass globe gingerly.

Jake and Maddox headed for the river—but they were missing someone.

"Come on, Og!" the Guardian called. "Here's your big chance to show us what you've got. Time to put those muscles to use!"

"Go, Og!" Archie cheered him.

The lonely Troll Boy looked delighted at the chance to be a part of the monster hunt (instead of being the monster himself for once). Og dashed after the two young, would-be heroes. Jake tossed him a loop of rope. Maddox glanced at him in amusement, then loosened his throwing arm like an athlete before the javelin competition.

As they approached the river, they glanced at each other, signaling for silence. Then they crept stealthily down the grassy banks below the bridge to the water's edge.

Jake had a loop of rope ready in his hand, just like Tex had used to catch the dracosaur.

Their plan was simple, really.

Jake was to lasso Nuckalavee and hold him in place just long enough for Maddox to plunge the spear into his side.

Of course, things rarely went according to plan—unless you were Archie and tested it a hundred times in advance, working out the flaws. Jake's style ran more along the lines of flying by the seat of his trousers, but it usually worked for him.

He hoped it worked tonight. After finding out he may have just singlehandedly started a war between the Dark Druids and the Order, he did not think he could take another disaster.

"I don't see him," Jake whispered, scanning the flowing current through the night vision lens of his telescope.

He squinted, trying to find the outline of those long, horse-like ears he had spotted before amid the reeds.

Og sniffed the air, trying to scent the beast. "Oh, Nuckalavee, where are you?" he rumbled in a low-toned singsong.

His acute Guardian senses on high alert, Maddox cocked his head, hearing a ripple of water that did not quite fit with the river's blend of soft, steady rhythms.

Jake shook his head. "Maybe we're too—"

"Shh! I hear something." Maddox paused. Jake listened, straining his ears. "It could be just one of the naiads splashing but I'm not—"

A trumpeting roar cut off his words as Nuckalavee suddenly charged.

His glistening bulk rose out of the current and barreled toward them, churning the river into whitewater as he came.

"Steady!" Maddox bellowed, dropping to one knee and bringing up his crossbow with a smooth motion.

Jake's pulse slammed in his ears. The cry of fright died on his lips. Nixie had said the water-horse was horrible, but her warnings fell short of the sheer horror of the monster charging at them.

Skinless Nuckalavee was a nightmare, twelve feet long and as tall as Jake at the withers.

Its open mouth was huge, maybe two feet wide, its jaws unhinged in a most unnatural manner; its legs as thick as tree trunks as it came crashing up the muddy bank straight at Jake; its small, piggish eyes gleaming scarlet in the darkness. The moonlight flashed on its vicious-looking tusks as it stampeded toward him.

Still, what left Jake standing there frozen in shock for a split-second was the impossible horror of a creature living without skin. Despite the darkness, the scarlet hue of Nuckalavee's exposed, pulsating flesh and striated sinews was obvious.

Jake felt queasy, staring at it.

"Rope, Jake, rope!" Maddox shouted, letting fly an arrow and hitting Nuckalavee squarely in the side.

The beast hardly seemed to feel it. It did not slow down but turned slightly toward Maddox with an angry snort.

Jake hurled the lasso, already sure the effort would fail. Even if he got the rope around Nuckalavee's neck, he could no more stop the charge of that demonic water-bull-horse-hippo-thing than he could have stopped a train.

He tried, anyway, throwing the loop of rope at the beast.

Unfortunately, Jake was no cowboy and had not made the loop wide enough. Instead of falling neatly around Nuckalavee's neck, the rope only just slipped over the beast's wide-open mouth.

Jake pulled the lasso, snapping Nuckalavee's jaws shut. The jolt nearly ripped his arms from their sockets when the monster shook his head in fury.

"Little help!" Jake yelped.

"Og, get the rope!" Maddox bellowed.

The half-troll was suddenly there, leaping to Jake's side and taking up the rope in both of his huge gray hands. While Jake's muscles were no match for the wrath of Nuckalavee, Og's brute strength was another matter.

He pulled backward with all his might, skidding down onto his haunches in a mighty tug-of-war with the beast.

Monster versus monster.

Given that Nuckalavee now seemed intent on rushing at Maddox, eager to gore him, Jake was suddenly grateful to have the half-troll on their side.

Og stopped Nuckalavee several feet away from Maddox, who had just set his crossbow aside in favor of the javelin.

Nuckalavee shook his head in rage, as if a bee had got into his ear.

Maddox blinked off the fleeting shock of surely seeing his life pass before his eyes, then threw his spear at the beast.

Of course, his aim was true. He was a Guardian, after all.

With a wicked zing, the spear sliced through the air and plunged into the flank of Nuckalavee, who let out another roar, only slightly muffled by the lasso around his snout.

The beast's bellow loosened the lasso a bit. Nuckalavee still could not unhinge his jaws like before, but he was working to be able to open his mouth wider.

"Hold him, Og," Maddox ordered. "Steady!"

The boys backed away as they watched the creature swing his horrid, skinless head about and take the handle of the spear into his mouth, pulling the blade out of his own side.

"That's not good," Maddox murmured.

With one stomp of his front foot, Nuckalavee cracked the spear like a twig.

"Hey, you!" Og yanked on the rope to get control of the beast—but to the horror of all three, the rope snapped.

Jake gasped.

Maddox uttered a curse as Nuckalavee looked at him again, his red eyes glowing with wrath. The frayed end of the rope now dangled from his head like horse reins dropped by a clumsy rider.

Steam fairly came from his nostrils as Nuckalavee homed in on Maddox.

To his credit, he did not look anywhere near as terrified as Jake felt in that moment.

Maddox glanced down to check his footing as he took another cautious step backward, reaching down slowly for his crossbow.

Nuckalavee lowered his head and pawed the ground like a bull getting ready to charge.

Jake feared his ally was doomed if he didn't do something quick. He spotted a large boulder at the river's edge and was suddenly inspired, levitating it from several feet away.

Moving slowly, wary of the black-haired boy with all the sharp objects, Nuckalavee cornered Maddox by the base of the bridge.

Though still unarmed, Maddox stood his ground, his hand inching toward his crossbow. Obviously, he was afraid of making any sudden movements with the creature so near.

But the second Nuckalavee roared at Maddox, Jake sent the boulder flying.

It hit Nuckalavee in the back.

Trumpeting another furious bellow at the interruption, the bogey-beast whirled around, forgetting about Maddox for a moment. Instead, those glowing, piggish, malevolent eyes focused on Jake.

Nuckalavee charged.

The earth shook as the water-horse stampeded toward Jake like he wanted to pound him into dust beneath his thick, webbed hoofs.

Jake flung a bolt of telekinesis at him, but Nuckalavee was four thousand pounds of furious Scottish legend.

The monster broke right through the wall of telekinetic energy Jake flung up with both hands. If it had been built of brick, he doubted it would have held.

I'm going to die, he thought as Nuckalavee's massive bulk bore down on him.

But suddenly, Og leaped onto the beast's back and grabbed the trailing end of the rope, yanking Nuckalavee's head to the side, like a horse under bridle.

"Hold on, Og!" Maddox shouted.

Og did. Astride the water-horse, the half-troll clung to Nuckalavee with his knees and one over-long arm. With his other hand, Og clutched the single rein and refused to budge as Nuckalavee began bucking with redoubled fury.

Jake and Maddox watched in open-mouthed shock as Og attempted to break Nuckalavee like one of Tex's mad cowboy friends in a hideous monster rodeo.

"Yee-haw," Jake breathed.

But Nuckalavee had no plans of giving up anytime soon. Before they could think what to do to help, the skinless wild bronco bolted off across the fields with Ogden holding on for dear life.

That quickly, they were gone, swallowed up by the darkness far across the fields.

The girls came running down to the waterside with Archie, having seen them bolt past.

"Is anybody hurt?" Isabelle shouted.

"We're fine! Did you see that?" Jake exclaimed.

Archie's head bobbed. "Og rode off on Nuckalavee!"

"Come on, we need to go after him." Maddox shouldered his crossbow and started marching up the slope.

"Are you daft?" Jake retorted. Maddox stopped and turned in

surprise. "We're never going to catch them! We don't even know which direction they went. And even if we could, what then, exactly? Your weapons had no effect. My telekinesis was practically useless. If Og hadn't been there, we would both be dead. Our only hope is for Og to stay on the beast's back long enough to tire him out. Breaking Nuckalavee might be the only way."

"*Breaking* Nuckalavee?" Nixie cried.

"Well, he's a water-horse, isn't he?" Jake shot back.

"He'd better not fall off," Maddox said uncertainly. "Because if he does, that beast will flatten him."

"Are you two sure you're all right?" Isabelle insisted, glancing from Maddox to Jake and back again.

The boys nodded.

"I still think we should try to help him. We can't leave him out there to face Nuckalavee alone," Maddox said.

"He did better against the beast than we did," Jake answered with a shrug.

While they all stood peering into the darkness, their backs to the water, trying to spot Og and Nuckalavee, nobody noticed the three-foot whirlpool that began turning in the river.

Maddox was the first to glance over his shoulder, feeling a prickle of danger on his nape. "Everybody," he said calmly, "get away from the water."

They did as he said, rushing back from the bank, even as Dani asked him why.

He didn't have to answer. For at that moment, Jenny Greenteeth rose straight up out of the river, standing atop a waterspout.

This was the first time most of them had beheld the drenched, gray-haired hag with her muddy gown, gleaming eyes, and long, tiger-like fangs dripping with algae.

"Oh, dear little witch, how we've missed you!" she hissed at Nixie. "Enjoy your journey through the paintings? I hope so. It'll be the last trip you ever take!"

Nixie started to lift her arm to throw the potion, but Jake reached over and stopped her discreetly. "Not yet. You can't throw that in the river. It'll poison the naiads," he whispered. "Wait till she comes up onto the land."

"*Well,* look at you with all your pretty friends. Why wasn't I invited to the party?"

"They're not my friends," Nixie started to say automatically.

"Oh, yes we are," Jake declared, moving in front of Nixie, bristling. Maddox did the same.

"I warned you about this." The hag floated forward atop her spinning column of water. "Their deaths will be on your head."

Just then, a whimper from inside Archie's contraption made Jenny Greenteeth look over toward the drive. When she saw the Boneless in the cage, she let out a shriek of furious disbelief.

Leaping off her waterspout onto the bank, Jenny Greenteeth zoomed past them, moving with the same weird, supernatural speed Jake remembered from the art gallery.

In the blink of an eye, she was up on the graveled drive beside the cage.

"Oh, my poor Boneless, what have these horrible children done to you? You're all dried out! Hold on, I'll have you out of there in a trice!"

They ran after the hag as she reached for the door of the cage to free the Boneless.

"Get away from there!" Archie warned. "Don't touch my invent—"

"Aaaiiee!"

Jenny Greenteeth screeched, flung backward by a large electrical shock upon touching the Faraday cage.

Unfortunately, it did not kill her, but only made her furious as it threw her to the ground. Though she looked like a crone, she jumped up like a gymnast, and in her wrath over the capture of her pet, she curled her claw-like fingers, and a bright green ball of energy appeared in her hand.

She hurled it at the cage.

The whole contraption toppled over, handcart and all. But when the cage struck the ground, the dried-out Boneless shattered into a hundred pieces, destroyed.

Jenny Greenteeth recoiled at what she had done.

Archie clapped his hands to his head. "You've killed it! Oh, what did you do that for? We weren't going to hurt it. We were just going to study it!"

Jenny Greenteeth was aghast. "L-look what you made me do, you horrible monsters! This is all *your* fault!" Her frightening stare homed in on Nixie. "Wasn't it enough that you killed the MacGools? Now you're responsible for killing Boneless, too!"

"I didn't kill those people and you know it!" Nixie cried.

"Indirectly you did, you little murderess. You banished us from the castle and stopped us from protecting them, and they died! It's your fault, horrid girl!" Jenny Greenteeth flew at Nixie from across the grass.

"Oh, no, you don't!" Dani bellowed, hurling the first poison globe at her.

Jolted out of her frozen state of terror, Nixie threw hers, too.

Both vials hit the hag and broke open, splashing the deadly potion all over her.

The hag let out a howl.

"It's working!" Archie cried.

Nixie faltered, amazed to see this was so.

"Hit her again!" Dani shouted. "Come on, everybody!"

They reacted swiftly, everyone grabbing vials of potion out of Nixie's black bag. Jake and Maddox, Archie and Isabelle all pelted Jenny Greenteeth without mercy.

She tried to block them from hitting her, but as the potion started to work, smoke began rising off her everywhere.

The hag threw back her head, convulsing, and roared at the night sky.

But when Jake reached to get another globe, Nixie's black bag was empty. The fanged, old bogart witch had been hit with their full arsenal, and not a one had missed.

Jenny Greenteeth seemed to be getting smaller, melting down into herself.

"I'll get you for this, Nixie!" she hissed. "You're never getting rid of me!"

"That's quite enough of your threats!" Archie stepped forward, taking up his lady's cause. "Now look here, madam. The fact of the matter is, you don't even exist. So go away and don't come back!"

"How dare you!"

"You will leave Miss Valentine alone, do you understand? Try coming back again, and you're going to get even worse!"

Jake and Maddox glanced at each other in surprise as the boy genius gave Jenny Greenteeth what-for.

"You're nothing but a glorified nursery bogey, and for your information, we all left the nursery long ago. We are not afraid of you. Not one bit!"

"Ah, but *she* is, my fine young gent." Hunching down in pain, Jenny Greenteeth sent Nixie a knowing evil eye.

"No, I'm not!" Nixie shouted, but she wasn't very convincing.

Jenny Greenteeth cackled even as she melted smaller. "I'll be back."

"Oh, shove off, you nasty old thing!" Archie snapped, taking a step toward her, quite fed up.

"Only if you come with me, dearie!" With that, Jenny Greenteeth grabbed the boy genius and whooshed up the road a few yards, dragging Archie with her.

She plunged over the side of the bridge and disappeared underwater.

"Archie!" Jake shouted as they all raced back down to the river's edge.

"Get back, it's a trap!" Maddox roared at the girls, tearing off his coat. "Back away, Jake. I'll get him."

"I'm not going anywhere. He's my best friend!" Ignoring the warning, Jake rushed into the dark river, searching frantically for his cousin, Maddox just a few steps behind him.

"Archie! Archie!"

Both boys waded out until they were waist-deep in the river, feeling around below the opaque current for any sign of their friend. At the edge of the water, the girls were half-hysterical, calling his name.

Nixie's patience snapped, though only a minute or so had passed. She headed for the water. "I'm going in. This is my fault—"

"No, Nixie!" Despite her own panic, Isabelle somehow managed to hold her back. "It's you she wants!"

Dani suddenly had an idea. "I'll go get the naiads!"

She bolted off toward the water nymphs upstream for help. A few minutes later, hearing the girl's panicked screams, a few of them came swimming at top speed to find out what on earth was wrong.

When Dani told them, they sped off under the bridge and joined the hunt for Archie and the hag.

The swift, fierce naiads found them, too, and attacked Jenny Greenteeth. Baring their claws and taking swipes at the hag underwater, they were able to distract her long enough for Archie to lunge up once out of the water, glasses gone.

Jake rushed toward him, splashing wildly with every stride, but his cousin only had time to gasp for air before Jenny Greenteeth pulled him under again.

She, too, surfaced, but only long enough to hurl her green energy spheres at the naiads zooming around her.

They were hit one by one. Struck by the same explosive blasts of magic that had thrown Jake and Nixie into the foxhunt painting, the naiads were knocked unconscious.

Two floated away, carried off by the current, while one was actually tossed up onto the banks and hit her head against a rock.

Jenny Greenteeth submerged again with a cruel cackle.

Then the water went calm.

CHAPTER THIRTY-ONE
Nixie's Nightmare

Nixie felt her whole world crashing in. Her worst fears were coming true before her eyes, and in that terrible silence, terror overtook her, freezing her where she stood. This was eons worse than the hag drowning her cat. She couldn't believe she had caused this, had brought about the death of the first boy who had ever noticed her.

Possibly the kindest human being she had ever met.

She felt like she couldn't breathe.

"I can't find him," Jake said, turning to them in despair. He suddenly punched the water and screamed at the river, *"Give him back!"*

Isabelle was sobbing.

"Help me," a soft voice rasped nearby. "Can't...breathe." The injured naiad had woken up and was unable to reach the water by herself. Her head was bleeding, and the gills along her ribcage strained to breathe. Dani ran over and helped to roll her back into the river, while Maddox, hating inaction, refused to give up. He took a deep breath and dove in to search underwater.

Alas, even the sharp eyesight of a Guardian was of little use in a murky river, with nothing but moonlight to illuminate the watery world below.

Nobody else knew what to do.

"We have to help Maddox," Isabelle said in a shaky voice. "We've got to find my brother." She stepped into the water, but Nixie grasped her arm.

"Wait." Staring at the current, she remembered something Archie had said in the lab.

"If belief is what originally brought Jenny Greenteeth into existence,

then maybe disbelief is the key to unmaking her."

"I don't believe in you," Nixie uttered, her voice barely audible. "I don't believe in you," she said again, a little more loudly.

Isabelle turned almost angrily to her. "What are you talking about?" she demanded.

"Do you hear me, Jenny Greenteeth? You're not real!" Nixie shouted at the water all of a sudden, fists clenched by her sides. "Say it with me—please!" she implored the others.

"That we don't believe in her? How absurd! We all just saw her. How much more real can she be?" Jake flung out, tears in his eyes. "She just killed Archie!"

"No." Nixie barely had the strength to tell them her idea. "Archie said that since she's a nursery bogey—created by belief—then maybe disbelief could *unmake* her. He said it would work."

Isabelle flinched. "If my brother said it would work, it'll work. I don't believe in you!" she shouted wildly at the river.

Dani joined in, running back from helping the naiad. "I don't believe in you, Jenny Greenteeth!"

The grim look on Jake's face said that he thought it a pointless exercise, but he was desperate enough to try anything, so he joined in, too.

When Maddox came up from another fruitless underwater search, his clothes sopping wet, his hair plastered to his forehead, he heard their chant, and though a bit confused, he echoed their refrain.

"We don't believe in you!" all the children shouted.

The river began to churn.

It seemed their chant had certainly got Jenny Greenteeth's attention, and this time, when she rose from the river, her wrinkled face was filled with utter malevolence.

"I don't believe in you!" Nixie yelled at her.

"What have you done with my cousin?" Jake shouted.

"Jake, the chant!" Dani told him.

"Fine. I don't believe in you!" he continued, saying it with the others, but everybody knew this was between Nixie and the hag.

"You are done tormenting me. You are not real," Nixie vowed.

"Then why are you so terrified?"

"I'm not. You're nothing," said Nixie. "You don't even exist. I don't believe in you!"

"Stop saying that!" the hag screeched.

"I don't believe in you. Children made you, and we can unmake you, too. You're not real. *Go back into the nothing that you came from!*" Nixie shouted with all the witching power she possessed.

Jenny Greenteeth howled, her head thrown back, the moonlight gleaming on her algae-covered fangs. She had already been sorely assaulted by the potion, but this—five strong-willed youngsters denying her existence—was more than she could take.

The murderous hag began convulsing. Smoke rose in plumes from her body. Her bony hands curled with rage, her face contorted with pain.

"Nooooo!" she screamed. Then she suddenly exploded, a circular wave of green-tinged magic barreling out in all directions from the point of her destruction. The power of it blowing past them shook the kids off-balance. They had to catch themselves, and then Jenny Greenteeth was no more.

They stared at the river.

"We did it," Dani breathed.

But any joy Nixie might have felt at this victory was destroyed, for as soon as the hag had vanished, Archie's body floated up, facedown in the river.

He wasn't moving.

Panicked beyond words, Jake and Isabelle both sprinted into the water to retrieve him as the current started gently carrying him away.

"No, no, no," Dani was uttering, while Nixie just stood frozen, too horrified to move.

Maddox helped them carry Archie up onto the grass, where they turned him on his back. His eyes were closed; his face looked tinged faintly blue in the starlight.

"Archie!" Isabelle screamed, trying to wake him. "Please, he's not breathing."

Jake started screaming for his Gryphon.

"Move back, there's no time!" Maddox pushed everybody out of the way and leaned with both hands on Archie's chest.

He started trying to pump the water out of his lungs, but Nixie saw Jake staring at the far bank of the river, his face ashen. He was so still, standing riveted, that she had the awful feeling he was seeing Archie's ghost.

"It's not working!" Isabelle sobbed, watching Maddox try to revive him.

"Is he really...*dead?*" Dani whispered in a strangled tone, clinging to Isabelle.

"*No.*" Nixie had been standing a few feet away, feeling utterly powerless. But something about that word, with the weight of its terrible finality, galvanized her into motion.

With jerky steps, heart pounding, she gripped her wand and marched over to Archie's side, dropping to her knees.

Holding the wand in both hands, she closed her eyes, searching deep within herself for her power, the deepest source of her magic. At last, amid her panic, she laid hold of it and calmed down enough to start to work.

She thrust the wand straight up at the dark sky, opened her eyes, rose to her feet, and began murmuring to the elements.

A strong wind suddenly blew; clouds gathered; thunder rumbled.

"What are you doing?" Isabelle asked amid her tears.

Nixie did not break her concentration to answer. Her will, so fierce and focused, dropped down into that place where the rest of the world ceased to exist. There was only her and the inscrutable magic that had somehow poured out of the very core of her from the moment she was born and made her who she was.

The wind blew stronger, the air shifting at her command; a great thundercloud gathered overhead. Magic thrummed through her veins.

At the edge of her awareness, Nixie saw the others back away when the first thin, bright, beautiful lightning bolt barreled down to kiss the tip of her wand like a greeting from a friend. It was ready to oblige her.

The electricity in the air made everybody's hair stand on end. The gale swayed the trees and made the river froth, and there she was, in the center of the storm.

"Archie," she whispered. Lowering herself slowly to her knees again, she lay her left hand on his chest, where his gallant heart had stopped. Her right still clutching her wand, she ignored the fact that she had never attempted anything of this magnitude before. "Listen to me. You are my friend. Please don't leave. We need you here, so much. You're not done yet. Think of all the inventions you still have to make." Her words broke off, but tears streaming down her face, she had so much more to tell him silently.

I know this world hurts. Especially for people like you and me, who really don't fit in. It's dark and it's full of mean people who don't understand us, and it must be so tempting to leave and go into the light, but I'm begging you to stay. Jake needs you. I need you. And if anyone can make this awful world a little better, it's you.

"Come back, Archie. *Now!*" She pointed her wand at him and uttered the command, and the dainty lightning bolt she'd captured flew into his chest.

It jolted him from head to toe. Jake spun around, as though seeing the ghost fly back into the body, and then he cursed in amazement as Archie suddenly coughed.

Isabelle let out a strangled sound and Dani made the sign of the cross, while Maddox quickly helped him to sit up. Water poured out of his mouth. Coughs racked his shoulders, and his eyes flew open as he took a huge gulp of air.

"You're alive," Jake whispered. Without warning, he lunged at his best mate and caught him up in a bear hug, his eyes squeezed shut. Isabelle put her arms around them both, weeping with astonished joy. Dani, also crying, flung herself into the group hug, while Maddox stared hard at Nixie.

You just brought that kid back from the dead.

He didn't have to say it aloud. Though Nixie was totally drained, the shock of what she had just accomplished with her magic at the tender age of twelve had also shaken her to the core.

She dropped the wand as though she had been clutching a viper.

CHAPTER THIRTY-TWO
Bagpipes at Dawn

"**N**ow, now, no need to make a fuss," Archie scolded them all with affection, finally getting a little annoyed with everybody hanging on him so.

The way they were all staring at him made him feel just a wee bit freakish, and nobody wanted to explain what the deuce had just happened.

Red was almost as confused as he, apparently having just come running in answer to Jake's call. The Gryphon had arrived on foot since he could not quite fly yet.

Having their large, feathered friend on hand was always a comfort in dangerous situations, to be sure. But Archie wondered just how bad the hag's attack on him had been, because neither Jake nor Dani nor Isabelle would let him walk out of arm's reach.

Nixie kept her distance, meanwhile, but watched his every move with wide, haunted eyes, and Maddox was even more taciturn than usual for a Guardian.

Archie hardly knew what to make of it all. *Must've passed out or something,* he thought. *Maybe inhaled a bit of the river.* Beyond that, he did not care to think about it. All he remembered was a big, black void around him, and a light in the distance.

"How did you know to do that with the lightning? How did you know that would work?" Jake asked Nixie.

"I-I don't know. I read *Frankenstein,* you know? With the electric eels? And the mad scientist used lightning to bring the monster to life."

"I'll pretend I didn't hear that," Archie jested in exhaustion.

But he was quite sure they were mistaken. There was no way he could have been literally dead. He refused to believe such a thing. His legs still felt a trifle wobbly as he stood up and, rather desperate for a return to normality, went over to check on his ruined experiment.

Perhaps it could be salvaged, he thought while everyone continued hovering about him.

"Can you see all right without your glasses?" Dani asked anxiously.

"Well enough. I've got another pair in my room."

"Do you want me to go and get them for you?" Isabelle offered.

"No, sis, I'm fine! Now, everybody, please, let me see to my invention!"

Just then, they heard galloping hoofbeats coming from across the fields. Everybody tensed.

"It's Nuckalavee!" Dani cried. "What do we do?"

Red growled, the still somewhat scraggly feathers on the back of his neck bristling as he moved to the fore to protect his children.

"Halloo!" a deep voice rumbled from the darkness.

"Holy..." Jake uttered.

Ogden Trumbull waved to them from astride the Nuckalavee's back, then reined in with a violent tug on the rope from Jake's broken lasso. "Whoa, boy!"

"You have got to be joking," Maddox breathed, staring in disbelief as Nuckalavee obediently slowed.

Red relaxed a bit, realizing the threat was not quite what he had assumed.

"Look at me!" Og shouted in triumph. "I got a pony!"

Archie hooted with laughter as Og made the hideous, skinless beast walk tamely over to them.

"He did it, he tamed Nuckalavee!" Dani cried in amazement.

"Do you think Dr. Plantagenet will let me keep him?" Og asked eagerly. "You think he'll be impressed?"

"Uh..." Even Jake's sarcasm failed him.

"*Everybody's* going to be impressed, Og," Maddox assured him.

"Well done," Isabelle murmured, shaking her head in shock.

"Ain't he a beauty? First horse that's ever been strong enough to carry me." Og gave his skinless mount a proud pat on the neck.

Everybody winced, but their heads bobbed up and down dazedly. No doubt, as a half-troll, Og had different standards of beauty.

"And we get along 'andsomely, too," Og added. "He tried to throw me for a bit, the old rascal. We had a grand tug of war. But I taught him who was boss, then he settled down, nice and gentle. Well!" Og declared, with a beaming smile that made him considerably less ugly. "Think Nuckie and I'll go for another gallop. That's fun, ain't it, boy? Tallyho!" Og kicked the ghastly water-horse in the sides and rode off on him.

Everybody looked around at each other and started laughing incredulously.

"Doesn't look like Nuckalavee's going to bother you anymore," Archie told Nixie.

"And maybe Og won't be so mean to everybody, either, now that he's got a 'horse' to keep him busy," Dani said.

"All due to my brilliant cousin's Bully Buzzer," Jake declared, throwing his arm proudly around Archie's shoulders. "You tamed Og, and Og tamed Nuckalavee. Which was convenient, considering the beast was trying to kill us."

"Well done," Maddox agreed, nodding at Archie.

Archie gave a modest shrug but couldn't help frowning as he looked down at his ruined experiment, hands on hips. "Dash, it really is too bad about the Boneless, though. Can't deny I'm disappointed."

But then a very peculiar thing happened as his friends gathered around to consider the situation.

Some of the river water still dripping off Archie's clothes, and Jake's and Maddox's and Isabelle's, trickled across the ground and into the broken pieces of Boneless scattered at their feet. The dried-out bits started swelling like little sponges sucking up water. Puffing up one by one, the pieces started to levitate.

"Blimey! Just add water," Jake said.

Red tilted his head in confusion. "Becaw?"

Dani gasped. "It's coming back to life!"

"Not it," Archie said, staring. *"They!"*

Each new, miniature Boneless had a face.

And all the little faces were smiling.

Tittering laughter came from the horde of itty-bitty pranksters as they found themselves not just alive, but in good company, each one surrounded by several dozen copies of itself.

"Ohhh," Archie said in belated understanding. "Of *course*! I should've realized!"

"What?" Jake asked.

Archie gestured at them. "That's how amoebas replicate! Cell division. Why didn't I think of that? Well, you're pretty clever, aren't you?"

The teeny Boneless pranksters flew around, pestering them all just a bit, even Red, before zooming off in a hundred different directions to cause trouble.

"Come back! Oh, botheration," Archie huffed.

"At least at that size, they can't do too much damage," Jake offered with a shrug.

But to Archie's surprise, one of the diminutive Bonelesses flew back and smiled eagerly at him, bobbing back and forth in the air.

"What do you want?" he asked it. "Can I help you?"

It chirped at him in a high-pitched flurry of, well, not quite words, but the tiny Boneless seemed to know exactly what it was saying.

Archie furrowed his brow. "Why aren't you flying away?"

It stayed.

"Hold on—unless you want to be studied?"

"Bee-bi-bee-bop," it replied cheerfully.

Isabelle cast her brother a wry glance and translated as best she could: "'You said you wouldn't hurt us. We believe you.'"

"I won't, I promise!" Archie told the tiny thing.

"Beep-boo!"

"It agrees," Isabelle said.

"Really? Well, all right, then!" Archie exclaimed, brightening. "Maybe my experiment is not a total loss, after all! Come along, little fellow. We're heading back to Merlin Hall to regroup now, what?"

"That sounds like a good idea," Dani said and yawned. "It's getting really late."

"I daresay it's almost morning," Isabelle agreed.

"Help me get this cart up," Maddox said to Jake, but as the two boys went to push the handcart back up onto its wheels, the mood of joviality faded.

For a long, lone, ominous note of bagpipe music floated out across the grass from the direction of the black woods.

It filled them with dread.

No wonder the bagpipes had been used in warfare for centuries to strike fear in the hearts of enemies, Archie thought. The dire tune sounded like a warning.

Or a threat.

Jake stared toward the woods, reminded anew that this wasn't over yet. "Maddox, take everyone inside."

They glanced at him, fear on all their faces save the Guardian's.

"What are you going to do?" Dani asked anxiously.

Jake kept his gaze fixed on the forest. "I'm going to finish this. Alone," he added when Red growled. "The Highlander disappears if more than one person sees him at a time, remember? We've got no choice. It has to be one-on-one."

"Then let me go. I've trained for this," Maddox said.

Jake shook his head. "Sorry, not this time, my friend. You may be the Guardian, but I've already conquered bigger enemies than this." *And bigger enemies than you have,* he did not add aloud.

Maddox frowned.

"He did kill Garnock," Archie pointed out cautiously.

"It's too dangerous, Jake," Isabelle insisted. "After what just happened..."

"What choice do we have? We have to finish this, or he'll just keep coming back and haunting Nixie. Look, the Highlander's an apparition," he explained, "and I'm the only one out of all of us who can see ghosts. If he tries to play hide-and-seek and attacks while he's invisible, then none of you stand a chance against him. Not even you, Maddox. He can't get away with that with me, though, because I can see him. Besides, I can't risk losing any of you again." He glanced meaningfully at Archie, but Nixie stepped forward.

"This is my fault. I should be the one to face him, Jake. He's only here because of me—"

"Nixie, his sword alone is taller than you are. No," Jake replied. "I promised you my friends and I would free you from the Bugganes, and I keep my word. Especially after what you just did...for Archie."

"Yes, but you needn't do it alone!" she insisted. "Jake, you just proved to me that everyone needs allies. I think there's something I can do."

"I'm listening," he said.

Nixie told him her plan.

* * *

A few minutes later, satisfied with their strategy, Jake set off across the field alone. Unfortunately, Red was not having it.

The Gryphon galloped ahead of him and stood in his path to block him, all four paws planted.

"Stand aside, boy. As much as I'd love to have you with me, it won't work. I have to do this alone."

"Caw!" Red shook his head angrily.

"Aw, don't worry, you old mother hen. I know he's got no head, and that is rather disturbing, but look on the bright side. He hasn't got any magic powers, which means at least he's not as bad as Garnock, anyway. All he's got is a really big sword. On the other hand, I've got the advantage of a having my head. That's got to count for something."

"Caw becaw?"

"Oh, and I've got Risker, too," he added, holding up his very sharp magical dagger, a gift from Odin after his heroics (if he dared say so himself) in the land of the Norse giants.

The worried Gryphon let out a low yowl of disapproval.

"Now, now, you and I will have plenty of adventures in future. Trust me, this won't take long."

Red sat down on his haunches in protest, abruptly unfurling his wings when Jake tried to walk around him.

"Phooey!" Jake spat out the taste of feathers and scowled at his pet. "Would you grow up?"

It was nice to say it to somebody else for a change instead of having it said to him. Red snorted in reply, considering that he was about nine hundred years old, at best estimate.

Jake patted him on the head. "Don't worry, I'll be fine! I can do this. Don't you believe in me?"

"Cawwww," Red complained.

"I'll be right back! Now, no more. I'm ordering you as your master to stand aside. Go and wait for me with the others. Watch Dani for me," he added, knowing that would get the stubborn beast. The Gryphon adored the carrot-head quite as much as he did.

Red scowled at him, but what more could he do? Jake would not be dissuaded. With a huffy little snort, Red rose and padded back to stand guard over Dani and the others.

When Jake glanced back to make sure the Gryphon wasn't following anymore, he saw that Nixie had her wand out, which made him feel a good deal better.

Truly, he still could not believe what he had witnessed back there, her bringing Archie back to life. It was bloody unnatural. But the thought of seeing his cousin's dazed ghost wandering along the far side of the riverbank back there made him want to puke.

He shuddered and thrust the image out of his mind. He could not afford to be distracted right now, and besides, there his cousin stood, alive and well, with the others.

Jake gazed at all of them for a moment. He might be an orphan, but right there, he thought, was his family.

And he knew he could fight any number of Headless Highlanders for their sakes. Determination filled him while the first glimmer of dawn danced along the horizon and the sun began to fill the great, invisible ley lines with power.

Taking one last, good look at his friends waiting there for him shored up his courage. Jake turned and headed for the woods, ready to do what had to be done.

Just like a real Lightrider.

Fortunately, he was one aspiring Lightrider with a past as a thief. His vast experience as a London pickpocket was about to come in handy, as he had long since mastered the art of slipping away from larger people who were trying to catch him.

Nevertheless, his heart pounded as he stepped into the woods and glanced around, his senses on high alert, the blood thudding in his veins—where he hoped it all remained by the time that this was over.

Looking around in all directions, he took a few, slow, cautious steps down the path into the Scot's territory. The leaves crinkled under him, and the trees soughed in the night breeze.

"Hullo? Oh, Headless?" he called. "Anybody home? Thought you might want to talk after losing your friends. So sad about Jenny Greenteeth. She's dead, you know. Oh, wait, you can't talk. You'd need a mouth for that."

The Headless Highlander appeared, a mighty, looming figure cloaked in fog, the bagpipe silent under his arm.

Jake stopped at a wary distance. "Oh ho, there you are. The big, braw warrior who thinks he's brave for terrorizing a little girl! And here I thought you Highland types liked to pride yourselves on your honor. But I guess there's a bad one in every bunch, eh? Nice skirt," he goaded. "Maybe you can borrow one of Nixie's sometime. So, is that the plaid of the MacGools you've got on? Your clan, eh? Yes...about them."

Jake narrowed his eyes. "Ask me, they got what they deserved."

The bagpipe let out an angry burp as the Headless Highlander exchanged it for his long, deadly claymore.

Jake's eyes widened as his gaze traveled down the length of the blade. The sword really was taller than Nixie. In fact, it was taller than him and might even have been taller than Maddox. It was hard to say in the darkness.

He couldn't even imagine how the Scots of old could have lifted such a weapon in a battle of any duration. It dawned on him that those blokes must have been as strong as oxen.

Blimey. A bead of sweat ran down his face, but he held his ground, glancing about to check his footing all around the path and the surrounding, leaf-strewn woods. He noted the location of some rocks here and there, a slim fallen log. He could not afford to trip. The Highlander was much bigger, much stronger than he; to make up for it, he'd have to be quick and nimble.

And clever. Not to mention as obnoxious as possible.

"Provoking the spirit" was a well-known technique in psychic circles, and Jake should have known he'd have a knack for it, considering how skilled he was at provoking the living when he chose. And sometimes when he didn't.

Just ask Dani O'Dell, he thought rather more merrily than the occasion warranted. But that was just gallows humor. In truth, he was nervous.

Very well, he was shaking in his boots.

But he refused to admit it to himself, let alone to the apparition. The angrier he could make the ghost, the better their plan would work.

"You know, instead of blaming Nixie for what happened, maybe you big, bad Bugganes should've blamed yourselves. I mean, really. You weren't even strong enough to withstand the magic of a witch who's only twelve years old! That must be so embarrassing! How many hundreds of years did you haunt that castle, only to be thrown out by a wee lass? I guess that must have stung, finding out you're not as tough as you thought. Hmm," he said. "You don't look very tough to me, come to think of it. Perhaps if you had a face..."

Headless wasn't big on conversation for obvious reasons, but Jake could have sworn he almost heard the warrior's battle cry as he came charging at him, the giant sword poised to skewer him.

Jake darted out of the way with a pickpocket's irksome agility, and turned, laughing. "Ha! Missed."

Whoosh. The blade sailed above his head: Jake ducked just like he used to do from the constables. "Missed again, laddie!"

He dove to the side, then twisted to avoid another thrust.

"You're really bad at this, aren't you?" he chided the kilted killer. "How'd you lose your head, anyway? Take it off one night before bed and forget where you put it in the morning? Must've had too much of that famous Scottish whiskey—"

The Headless Highlander charged him again, his footsteps thundering across the ground, and this time, he sank his blade into the narrow trunk of a young tree behind Jake. Splinters flew.

"Oops, missed *again!* Poor you."

Jake ran past the apparition and kept taunting him, dodging the big, violent chops of the terrible claymore as he led the ghost steadily toward the edge of the woods.

Nixie, you'd better be ready, he thought. *Almost there...*

"Why don't you cross over, anyway? Sweet person like you. Don't you want to go to heaven? Oh, you've murdered too many people, is that it? Well, I suppose that *is* a problem. Don't you like hot weather?"

Whack!

"Easy! You almost nicked me there. You're mean!"

Jake tricked and teased and goaded the Headless Highlander, enraging him with his insults, until, at last, the apparition had followed him out past the edge of the woods. He had ordered his friends to make sure they stayed out of sight because he did *not* want to have to go through this again, what with the Highlander's habit of vanishing as soon as he was seen by more than one person.

Ah, but Nixie's plan did not require anybody else to confront the ghost directly. All it needed was just a little magic.

Any minute now...

Jake was breathing hard. "Isn't that thing getting heavy?" he asked with cheerful insolence while the warrior menaced him, the point of the claymore weaving before his eyes.

The Scot heaved back and swung the blade, the metal flashed, and Jake leaped backward—but then, disaster!

He tripped over a stone in the field and went sprawling on his backside in the grass.

The Highlander lifted the blade high.

"Nixie, now!" Jake shouted as the towering apparition loomed over

him in all his unearthly wrath, the claymore poised to slice him in half length-wise.

Jake rolled out of the way of the vicious blow that slammed down into the turf, just as a familiar voice in the distance yelled something that sounded like, *"Aperio!"*

At Nixie's command, the false darkness the little witch had conjured to hide the dawn dissolved, suddenly washing the Headless Highlander in the bright rays of the sunrise.

The warrior's fierce, missing head appeared briefly as he stood immobile with surprise; he had shaggy red hair and a big red beard, and his battle-scarred face wore a look of shock. He stood trapped in the glow of the morning sun flaring up behind him from over the horizon.

His whole brawny body started to smoke, much like Jenny Greenteeth's had. The evil he had wreaked in all his centuries could not withstand the sun's rays. He threw back his head and bellowed in stunned agony—realizing only then, too late, that Jake had tricked him into coming out of the shadows.

Then he turned to ash, crumbled, and blew away.

Jake stared, wide-eyed, barely daring to exhale, let alone to let himself hope that their plan had succeeded.

But it had.

Jake sat up and slowly looked around in the bright morning light. No trace remained of the last, most fierce of the Bugganes. The Headless Highlander was gone, sword and all, with naught but a final, ferocious note from his bagpipe.

"Whew!" he said, blowing his forelock out of his eyes with a big sigh of relief. Then he flopped back onto the grass in nerve-racked exhaustion, his arms wide, his heart still pounding.

In the distance, he heard his friends anxiously calling his name. They had not dared peek at the fight until that moment, for fear of scaring the Highlander away and causing their plan to fail.

Jake sat up again to show them he wasn't lying there dead. "It's all right, he's gone!" He grinned and threw his fist into the air in victory.

Seeing this, a cheer went up from his companions. They all came running, everyone laughing and talking at once as they clustered around him.

"You did it!" Isabelle said.

"I'd say we all did," he answered. "Certainly couldn't have done it without Nixie."

Archie and Dani pulled him to his feet, one by each hand. Red bumped him in the hip with his head like an oversized housecat, and Nixie smiled from ear to ear.

"Quite a team, eh?" the little witch ventured.

He squeezed her bony shoulder. "I'm just glad you're on our side, missy."

"Hear, hear!" Archie beamed at her.

"Jake, that was brave—well, either brave or mad," Maddox said, offering his hand. "Either way, Derek would be proud."

"Actually, Derek would be furious," Jake said wryly. "But thanks." He shook his hand, then gave the older boy an affectionate clap on the shoulder.

All this time, Dani was jumping up and down beside him in uncontained excitement, as she often did, talking nonstop at a hundred miles a minute. Not that much of it made any sense, Jake thought with a smile.

Meanwhile Malwort, perched on Nixie's shoulder, kept trying to catch the itty-bitty Boneless zooming around Archie's head.

While the kids exchanged a last round of hugs and claps on the back, Red lifted his head and crowed at the dawn like a common rooster rather than a magnificent royal Gryphon.

Everyone looked at him in surprise, then started laughing.

"What on earth is that supposed to mean?" Dani exclaimed with a quizzical glance at Isabelle.

She shrugged. "I think he wants breakfast."

"Excellent idea! I'm starved," Jake declared, throwing his arms around the two nearest him and steering them toward Merlin Hall. "C'mon, you lot. Let's eat! I'd say we earned it."

And so they went, all together.

CHAPTER THIRTY-THREE
The Crystal Ball

After staying up all night to defeat the Bugganes, everybody went straight to bed after breakfast and, consequently, missed the last full day of the Gathering. But there was no chance of them missing the farewell festivities that night—namely, the much-anticipated Crystal Ball. The gala that marked the end of the Gathering took place each year in the center of the maze, so that the Old Yew and his ancient offspring could feel included.

Jake and Archie donned the dreaded tuxedoes for the occasion. Presently, they loitered in front of Merlin Hall, waiting for the girls to finish getting ready—though that could take all night.

Looking dashing in their formal clothes, the boys leaned against one of the big stone lions that flanked the wide front steps. Hands in pockets, they watched the endless stream of guests leaving the palace and filing into the maze. It reminded Jake of how nervous he had been going in there for his Assessment. Only three days had passed, but it felt like a lifetime ago.

Meanwhile, he and his cousin chatted about the fact that the fairy market had already disappeared. All the itinerant magical vendors had packed up their wares and moved on.

"Guess we'll see them next year," Jake remarked.

"Say, coz, do me a favor," Archie said abruptly. "Don't tell my parents I died today. I think they'd be...a little upset."

"I won't, believe me! How are you feeling?"

"Tired. I could've kept sleeping. That reminds me, I had the strangest dream."

"Oh?"

"I dreamed I was in my lab at home when Leonardo da Vinci, of all people, walked in, picked up a piece of chalk, and helped me figure out some problems with my submarine."

"The bloke who invented the Enchanted Gallery?"

Archie gave him a long-suffering glance. "He did a lot more than just that, Jake."

"Er, I knew that."

"Anyway, strange…it seemed so real! Somehow I managed to wake myself up and wrote down everything he told me to fix. I'm going to try it as soon as I get home."

"What if it works?" Jake asked. "What would that mean, do you suppose?"

Archie blanched. "I'm not sure I want to know."

"Maybe he really came to you in a dream."

"Jake, he's been dead since the early 1500s."

"So? Ghosts are obviously real."

"But not to me. I'm a scientist."

Jake looked at him. "Maybe the Kinderveil is lifting."

"Please don't say that! I don't want any powers. It's enough trouble having a big brain."

"You might not have a choice," Jake said kindly.

He didn't want to upset his cousin after what he'd already been through today, but he instantly suspected that, if it wasn't the Kinderveil lifting, Archie might have returned from his brush with death with the power of prophetic dreams.

Jake knew it was possible, because he had talked with other psychic-medium kids during the Gathering who had reported having gained their abilities after surviving terrible accidents or illnesses, like scarlet fever or typhus.

But he did not press the issue. He knew his cousin well enough to grasp that any sort of magical or clairvoyant ability would be completely at odds with how Archie saw himself. He was just grateful that Archie was alive.

"Hey-ho, here's one of ours!" Archie said, sounding eager to change the subject as he gave a cheerful wave to Maddox. The young Guardian had just stepped out of the wide double doors of the entrance hall onto the top of the stairs.

"Nah, that can't be Maddox St. Trinian," Jake teased. "He would never put on a tuxedo."

"Guess that means you're coming to the ball?" Archie asked.

Maddox joined them with a shrug, resting his foot on the step above. "Not to go would be bad form."

"I didn't think you owned a tuxedo," Archie said.

"It just appeared," he said. "Whether it came from the gnomes or from Ravyn, I don't know. At least it fits."

"Guess we better be ready to catch Isabelle in case she swoons when she sees you," Jake said with a grin.

Hand to brow, Archie imitated a lady fainting. "Quickly, the smelling salts!"

The boys laughed at the general silliness of females. But they all stood up the moment the young ladies appeared.

Miss Helena stood behind Isabelle, Dani, and Nixie, looking proud of her work in spite of her lingering worry over Derek's absence. The girls looked quite fetching.

Isabelle wore a lavender dress trimmed with white lace, and Dani wore a green that matched her eyes. But as pretty as they both looked, somehow it was even more startling to see Nixie arrive wearing a splash of color rather than her usual all-black. Granted, there was still black in her dress, along with the crimson, but at least it was a start. Much to their amusement, she had tied a tiny bowtie around Malwort's neck, so even the spider would look smart for the occasion.

"Everyone ready?" Miss Helena inquired.

"Shouldn't we wait for Uncle Richard and Aunt Claire?" Jake asked.

"They're already there," she answered. "Shall we?"

They all started down the rest of the stairs in a group.

"One moment, please, children!" a crisp voice called from behind them.

"Aunt Ramona!" Jake greeted her.

The Dowager Baroness stood tall and stately in her dark indigo gown. With her gray hair gathered in a severe bun, her lips pursed, her knife-hilt cheekbones etched with disapproval, they instantly realized the Elder witch did not look happy.

"Good! You're all here," she said. "I should like to speak to you, please. Yes, all of you. This way. Follow me."

Glances were exchanged. *Uh-oh.*

"Miss Helena, you may wait in the entrance hall."

"Yes, Your Ladyship." The governess stepped aside but sent Jake a startled look that demanded, *What did you do now?* He lowered his gaze and followed his aunt.

All the kids exchanged worried looks as Aunt Ramona led them down the hallway and into an empty parlor.

"Shut the door, thank you." When Maddox had pulled the door closed behind the last of them, everybody waited tensely. "Sit, please." She gestured to the center couch.

The three girls sat down in a tidy row; the three boys went and stood behind the couch, leaning against it.

Aunt Ramona swept them all with a piercing gaze. She rested her hip against the writing desk before them. "I heard the most interesting tale today from Dr. Plantagenet."

Gulp. Jake's heart pounded.

"You know that unfortunate half-troll boy, his assistant? Well, it seems Ogden Trumbull showed up at the zoo this morning with a ghastly creature called a Nuckalavee, asking if he could keep it as a pet. Fancy that! He would not say how he came by the beast, but the doctor noticed that one of his large medicine sprayers was missing, as well."

Archie sent Jake a subtle, panicked glance. They had slept all day and hadn't had a chance to return it yet.

"I don't suppose any of you would know...anything about that, would you?" Aunt Ramona inquired.

Maddox drew breath to speak, but Jake stepped hard on his foot to keep him quiet. Knowing Aunt Ramona, she probably already knew the answer, anyway. Admitting to everything would only have lost them a smidgen of her respect.

"Hmm," Dani said noncommittally.

Jake took it further. "What's a Nuckalavee, ma'am?"

Aunt Ramona pursed her lips—perhaps in disapproval, or just maybe, holding back an exasperated smile. "Look it up," she said tersely. "In any case, we leave in the morning, so be ready, and that goes for all of you. Miss Valentine will be coming with us. And the spider, I suppose."

"I will?" Nixie echoed in surprise.

"I spoke to the Elders on your behalf, Miss Valentine. They said you could either remain here at Merlin Hall to continue your education or be entrusted to my custody for more personalized attention. I surmised you would rather come with us so you could be with your new friends. I hope I was not mistaken?"

"No, Your Ladyship. Thank you, I am grateful," Nixie murmured, though she looked a little torn about having lost the freedom she had enjoyed, roaming the countryside with the gypsies.

"Good. Because the Elders agreed that a young mage of your abilities can by no means be left unsupervised. I am afraid, Miss Valentine, that you will always have a target on your back for recruitment by the Dark Druids—just like Jake. We can't let that happen to either of you, especially now." Aunt Ramona did not explain that comment, but obviously, it had to do with the threat of war that they, as mere kids, weren't supposed to know about. "Don't worry, you will be quite happy, in any case."

"Yes, ma'am." Nixie lowered her gaze, while Archie grinned from ear to ear.

"As for you, Mr. St. Trinian."

"Yes, my lady?" Maddox stood at attention.

"You'll be coming with us, too. All the equipment and clothing you will need for your new assignment will be provided for you, as per protocol."

He sliced a nod, concealing any twinge of hurt pride he might have felt at the reminder of his relative poverty. "Guardian Stone informed me of my assignment before he departed, ma'am."

"Any questions?"

He looked askance at Jake. "Permission to throttle my charge as needed on occasion?"

"Oh, I'd be grateful for it, believe me," she answered in amusement. "Within reason, of course."

Jake scowled while Isabelle tried to hide her joy at the news that Maddox would be coming with them, too.

"Very well, then. Off we go to the ball. You are dismissed. Except for you, Jacob. Remain behind with me for a moment, please. You may rejoin your friends shortly."

That sounded like trouble, but he did not dream of disobeying the Elder witch. "Yes, ma'am."

While the others left the room, sending him discreet, worried glances, Jake started mentally rehearsing possible excuses for his most recent round of mischief.

His aunt studied him intently. "I'm afraid I have some rather troubling news for you, Jacob. You've probably heard by now about the vampire prince who arrived the other night. Well, I'm sorry to have to tell you that the reason for his visit concerns you. He came to bring us warning that the Dark Druids may have discovered your defeat of Garnock the Sorcerer. I don't wish to scare you, but we're going to have to be very careful with your safety for a bit. They may...want revenge."

Jake nodded but did not bother explaining that he already knew.

She arched a brow. "Well, you don't look too rattled by the news. You're a very brave lad. Which is good. You'll have to be, if you want to become a Lightrider."

He kept his gaze down as he recalled Janos saying that the Dark Druids were targeting Lightriders now.

"We'll return to Gryphondale and sort out our affairs, but very soon, I shall be taking you and the others abroad. Someplace where our enemies wouldn't know to look for you. Think of it as a nice, long holiday—at least, until the unpleasantness dies down a bit."

"Where?"

"Oh, somewhere pleasant, to be sure. The seaside is nice this time of year, and I daresay you children would enjoy the ocean. The Mediterranean, perhaps. I was thinking the south of France or one of those lovely Greek islands. Unless you'd prefer the Italian coast?"

Jake looked at her, wide-eyed. As if he'd know! "Whatever you think best," he answered eagerly.

She nodded. "There is quite good Society in Naples these days, what with all the consumptive Englishmen living abroad. Yes, Italy, I think. I have many friends there... 'Twould be good for your education, as well. And the food! You in particular will appreciate that," she added with a knowing smile. "Any questions?"

"Not really."

"Very well, then, come along."

Jake hesitated, wondering if she had got in trouble with the other Elders for trying to hide his secret. He also wondered if Derek had volunteered to go for the same reason—because of his involvement in keeping Jake's feat quiet.

Crossing to the door, Jake's thoughts strayed back to how his battle against Garnock had unfolded this past autumn in Wales.

His aunt paused and turned to him. "Something on your mind?"

"What about the people who helped me?" He could not hide his worry. "I didn't defeat Garnock alone. Isabelle was there. Emrys and the mining dwarves helped me. Red, Derek, Helena. Those ghosts in the town. They all had a hand in it."

"We're taking measures," she assured him.

"And what about Celestus and the other three angels who came down at the end? If they hadn't arrived, that huge demon could have busted out of the underworld to terrorize the Earth."

"La, child! You needn't worry about the angels, for heaven's sakes! The Dark Druids' evil is powerful, but they don't have anywhere near the capability to harm one of the Light Beings." She paused. "I mean, there were stories in the ancient past, long, long ago, of that happening every now and then... But that knowledge has been lost for at least a thousand years. So, don't worry your head about all that. Just concentrate on being a boy a while longer, why don't you? Lord knows being thirteen is hard enough."

Jake smiled ruefully and hugged the old woman, then they left the parlor and rejoined the others.

His friends were waiting in the entrance hall, looking impatient to get to the party.

"Did you get in trouble?" Dani whispered as he approached.

"Nah, but guess what! They're taking us to Italy!" he confided in her ear.

"Italy?" she echoed in excitement.

"Aye, the beach! But you can't tell anybody yet."

Halfway across the entrance hall, Jake suddenly felt a small jolt of lightning run through his entire body, making his arms and legs go rigid. His eyes bugged. He stopped in his tracks. "Ack!"

"Jake! What's wrong?" Dani cried, right beside him. She grabbed his arm to keep him upright.

Just as quickly as the sensation had burst through him, it stopped, leaving him slightly dazed. "What the...ugh."

As the spasm wore off, he became aware of the sound of hilarious laughter from behind him. He turned around and found Archie belly-laughing with a downright devilish twinkle in his dark eyes.

"Got you, coz!" He held up the little controller in his hand.

Jake's jaw dropped as understanding filled him. "You Bully Buzzered me?"

"That's for kissing Nixie! Aw, come on, you know you had it coming! And Og didn't need it anymore."

"Wait." Dani turned to Jake. "You kissed Nixie?"

"No! I mean—not exactly!" he stammered.

"Actually, he missed," Nixie said in amusement.

Maddox turned to him, lifting an eyebrow. "You *missed?*"

"Ugh." Blushing scarlet with embarrassment, Jake hid his face in his hands.

Archie, still snickering over his diabolical revenge, sauntered over and peeled the two brass nodes off Jake's back where he had surreptitiously planted them earlier.

"Now we're even, coz," he said with a jovial slap on his shoulder. "Aw, don't worry, you'll be fine. I cut the voltage in half."

"Guess I deserved that," he mumbled to him.

Nixie shook her head at them both, rolled her eyes, and walked away. Archie strutted after her.

"Seriously. You missed?" Maddox drawled while Isabelle went ahead. Then he, too, walked away, chuckling and shaking his head.

Only Dani was left glowering at him, her fists planted on her waist.

Jake threw up his hands. "It wasn't my fault! It was a Cupid arrow! What do you care, anyway?" he challenged her. "Jealous or something?"

"You're *gross*," she replied. Then she pivoted on her heel and flounced off with a huff.

Jake heaved a sigh, slid his hands into his trouser pockets, and strode after his party with a grumble under his breath.

Outside in the balmy spring evening, the rose-pink sunset was fading, slowly revealing a dark blue sky full of twinkling stars. It was too beautiful a night to stay annoyed for long.

Soon they arrived in the center of the yew maze and found it lit up like a fairyland—which, of course, it was. Huge purple amethyst geodes sparkled, with candles set inside them. Dramatic quartz crystal formations in many different colors were set up here and there and lit from behind so they glowed.

There was music to enjoy. An elven orchestra played on mysterious magical instruments, while Constanzio, King of the Tenors, dazzled the psychic-mediums present as he sang along, crooning dramatically into the spring night.

Jake listened with pleasure, and wondered if everyone in Italy would prove to be as jolly as the opera ghost.

He supposed he'd soon find out.

At that moment, the mighty Crafanc-y-Gwrool, otherwise known as Claw the Courageous, but more commonly called Red, made his entrance. The Gryphon came flying over the outdoor ballroom, soaring in a circle as his eagle-eyes searched the crowd for Jake.

People pointed at the magnificent beast above, but Jake waved, delighted to see his friend could fly again. "I'm down here, boy!"

"Caw!" With a few beats of his wings, Red descended. The people around Jake moved back to clear a spot for the regal beast to land. In the next moment, his lion paws hit the ground with a graceful pounce.

"Look at you!" Jake said admiringly as the Gryphon marched proudly toward him, resplendent in his new array of bright scarlet feathers. The smattering of gold ones winked like tiny flames in the torchlight. "Why, you're handsomer than ever!"

"Becaw," Red replied with his beak in the air, as if to say, *Oh, yes, I know.* He tapped his tufted tail in time with the music. Jake scratched his pet fondly on the back.

"*Hors d'oeuvre,* sir?" Maddox drily offered the Gryphon as he returned from the refreshments table.

"He likes anything with salmon," Jake said.

"Here." Maddox tossed the beast a tiny salmon ball crusted with almonds.

Red caught it in the air, but this small taste of his favorite food only whetted his appetite. "Caw!" With a flick of his tail, he padded off in the direction of the refreshments.

"He'll eat the whole tray of them, likely," Maddox said with a smile.

Jake nodded. "And possibly the table."

"He looks good."

"What a relief to have him back to normal. I do wish I knew why some of his feathers grew back in gold, though. I wonder what it means."

"Oh, he didn't have those before?"

"No! And if the red ones have those amazing healing powers, I can barely imagine what the gold ones do."

"Go ask Dr. Plantagenet. Bet he'd know. He's right there," Maddox said, gesturing with a celery stick smothered with soft cheese.

"Where? Oh, crikey." He spotted the Green Man escorting a female of his kind across the ballroom, flowers sprouting from the twigs that crowned her head.

At once, Jake turned away and hid his face behind his hand to avoid being seen.

"What's the matter? Go ask him. He's a magical veterinarian. If anyone would know about the feathers—"

"Can't! I'm too embarrassed," Jake said. "He must've seen me stealing the sprayer last night. That's how Aunt Ramona must have known. I could've sworn he was asleep!"

"Well, you can quit hiding. He's looking right at you."

Awkwardly, Jake glanced over and met the Green Man's gaze. He raised his glass of punch to him in a token apology as Dr. Plantagenet sauntered by with the Green Lady. The mild-mannered veterinarian sent him a pointed look in answer, but nodded politely.

"Where did you and Archie leave the sprayer, anyway?" Maddox asked after they had gone past.

"We hid it in our room. Why?"

"I could go return it for you in a little while."

"You're that desperate to escape?"

"Frankly, I'd rather be welding," he muttered. "Or at least fighting goblins."

"Oh, come on, it's not that bad for a ball."

Maddox let out a wordless grumble of frustration and did not seem to know where to look. "Yes, but your cousin keeps staring at me!"

Obviously, he did not mean Archie.

Maddox rubbed the back of his neck with an air of tension. "I think she wants me to ask her to dance."

"So, why don't you? Don't tell me the mighty Guardian is scared of a girl."

Maddox scowled at him. "It's not going to happen. I'm on duty."

"You are not on duty!" Jake scoffed. "Lord, you're such a stick."

"I am not a stick."

"Yes, you are. Believe me. You need to loosen up!"

"How am I supposed to do that? Look at me! I look like a penguin for starters! You and your cousins might be aristocrats, but me, I'm not used to all this. All these people in their finery and jewels..."

"So? You're a prince's son."

"Illegitimate!" he reminded him defensively, as though it were a badge of honor.

Jake shrugged. "Well, you might want to try to acclimate because you're right. I am an earl and this is the kind of life I'm going to have, and if they've assigned you to be my Guardian, then I think you better get used to it."

Maddox growled under his breath.

"As for Izzy, don't worry, she'll forget about you soon. Chaps are always falling in love with her. She'll find somebody else."

Maddox turned and glared at him.

Despite his claims to the contrary, this was apparently not what the lad had wanted to hear. He grumbled and stared forward, like a sentry alone on the night watch.

"Maddox," Jake prompted in amusement.

"Of course I like her!" he finally admitted in an angry whisper. "How could anybody not? She's...beautiful. She's one of a kind. But it's out of the question."

"Why?"

"Let's just say that seeing Ravyn again refreshed my memory about the consequences that can result from a Guardian getting involved with someone in a way they shouldn't. I don't intend to make the same mistake. It wouldn't be fair to Isabelle. I just wish she'd take the hint. I don't want to hurt her feelings, and I know I will. I'm too blunt. I always say the wrong thing. Maybe...you could talk to her for me."

"Me? Crikey, no. I'm not getting in the middle of that, thank you very much. Tell her yourself."

"Ah, Maddox! There you are. How smart you look, son."

"Ravyn." At once his posture stiffened, but he bowed to his birth mother, who joined them without warning.

Jake took a wary step backward. Even dressed in a chocolate-brown, satin ball gown, the tall, athletically muscled Guardian woman was an intimidating person. He was quite sure she had any number of weapons hidden around her person, concealed perhaps in the puff of her long bustle skirt. He would not want to get on her bad side ever.

He could scarcely imagine, if she had kept Maddox, what her brand of motherly discipline would have been like. She'd have probably had him running drills at the age of five.

Guardian Ravyn Vambrace looked from one boy to the other, no doubt sensing that neither was overjoyed to see her.

Jake found her slightly terrifying, and Maddox had all sorts of conflicted emotions concerning his birth mother. But although she sensed the lack of welcome, no self-respecting Guardian was easily chased off.

"I want to thank you boys for your assistance when I arrived. That was bloody awful," she muttered, then tossed back a shot of some strong drink as easily as the male warriors did.

Blimey, Jake thought. "Er, how's your Lightrider, ma'am?"

"Better, thanks to your Gryphon."

"Happy to hear it," Jake said. "Well, if you'll excuse me." He nodded with respect to the fierce-eyed lady, who obviously wanted a moment alone with her son.

And I thought my family history was complicated, he mused, returning to his friends.

By now, only Dani was around, standing next to one of the large, beautiful quartz formations for which the Crystal Ball was named. She greeted him with a sour glance as he rejoined her.

"So. There you are, Mr. Kissy Face."

He just looked at her, then changed the subject. As if he weren't already embarrassed about it enough. "Where's Archie?"

"Where do you think? He's out there dancing his little feet off, as per usual. You should try it sometime," she added with a pointed look of reproach.

"Oh, I see. You want to dance, too."

"We are at a ball, aren't we?"

"It appears so."

"Well?" she exclaimed, muttering, "Blockhead."

"Fine! Come on, then." He grabbed her forearm, more like a constable arresting her than any sort of proper young gent. "Let's get this over with."

"You are so rude. See, this is why I knew you'd succeed at provoking the apparition," she scolded, even though she went along with him. "It's too bad they don't have a special Assessment just for beastliness because you'd win."

"*You'd* win," he retorted.

It was easier to bicker than to think too much about the fact that they were holding hands. But then Jake remembered he had something to say to her, and he couldn't concentrate on where to put his feet until he got it off his chest. "Dani."

"What?"

He pulled her back from the thick of the crowd of dancers and stared at her. He suddenly discovered that trying to speak from the heart was way more embarrassing than unwittingly trying to kiss someone under the influence of a blasted Cupid arrow.

"Um..."

"Hello?"

He looked away. "I...er, I wanted to thank you for clearing my name. The whole Queen's flag debacle. I really mean it. That could've *ruined* my chances of ever becoming a Lightrider, but because of you," he forced out, "I've still got a shot."

She looked stunned at his earnest tone, then smiled prettily. "'Oy, us rookery brats gotta stick together amongst the toffs 'ere, savvy?"

He smiled ruefully at her use of their old city cant.

She lifted her hand and fixed a wrinkle in his cravat. "I told you, I'm not going to stand by and let anybody rob you of your dream. Even if I think it's daft and that you're gonna get yourself killed. You've already lost enough. Besides, it was kind of fun getting back at those skunkies."

"Even if it meant you getting turned into a bunny rabbit?"

Her eyes flew open wide with a sudden look of dread. "You found out about that?"

He grinned. "Sticking Powder, eh? How I wish I would've seen that."

"Who told you?" she cried, aghast.

"Dani, everybody knows. It's the biggest bit o' gossip at the Gathering."

She looked briefly horrified, then realized he was teasing her and walloped him. "No, it's not! You're horrible."

Jake was laughing. "I try," he said with affection. "I can just picture you with whiskers and the cute, floppy ears..."

"I hate you. Are we gonna dance or what?"

"Sure, carrot. That name's got a whole new meaning now, doesn't it? Carrot...rabbit, get it? Heh."

"You think it's funny I got turned into a monster for your sake?" she exclaimed, but he could see that she was trying not to laugh. "Lucky for you Gladwin put me back!"

"She should've waited till I could take a picture with Archie's camera."

"Oh, shut up," Dani grumbled.

Then they attempted to sort out the dancing, and Jake felt about as graceful as Ogden Trumbull, though he tried to act normal. Dani put her hand on his shoulder, and he rested his hand gingerly on her waist. It was all too bizarre to him, but she seemed happy. *Girls.* He shook his head to himself.

"Jake?" she asked at length.

"Yes, Daniela?"

"Things are going to change soon, aren't they?"

"They always do." He looked into her green eyes, feeling protective of his trusty little sidekick and strangely philosophical after their battles of the previous night. "But one thing will never change," he said abruptly. "You and I will always stick together." The second the words left his mouth, he realized the cringing, awful mushiness of what he had just said and turned three shades redder than his Gryphon. "I mean, all of us, that is. Archie and Isabelle and Derek...uh, everybody."

"Of course. I-I knew what you meant." She nodded vigorously, staring at the crystal nearby.

"Hey, there's Archie and Nixie!" Jake said rather desperately. "I have an idea. Let's go ram 'em!"

Dani seized upon the game, too, and they put the moment's awkwardness behind them. Laughing like two rascals, they interlocked their fingers and thrust their front hands out like a battering ram, then sashayed toward Archie and Nixie, bumping them so they stumbled, only to be bumped in return.

Their raucous laughter and jolting about in the middle of the dance floor illustrated why youngsters under sixteen were not usually invited to a ball. But it seemed to Jake that, when it came to being kids, they all had best enjoy it while it lasted.

EPILOGUE
The Captive

M eanwhile, still standing at the edge of the Crystal Ball, Isabelle decided to do it. She had fought with herself about it since they had arrived, but when she saw Archie and Nixie and Jake and Dani all having fun out on the dance floor, she couldn't hold back anymore. In that tuxedo, Maddox just looked *too* handsome.

If he was too shy to ask her, she'd ask him—though this would have horrified even *her* lenient governess. She swallowed hard, steeled her courage, and then slipped away from Miss Helena, who was distracted anyway, in some fierce, private conversation—more like an argument—with her twin brother, Henry.

Mother and Father were also busy, chatting away with the haughty contingent from King Oberon's court.

Maybe if I just give him a tiny bit of encouragement, he'll ask me first.

One dance was all she wanted, really. That would be more than enough, especially now that he was coming home with them to Gryphondale.

She understood he was to stay at Jake's, but Griffon Castle lay just across the fields from her own home of Bradford Park. Why, they could see each other every day now if they liked...

Her heart pounded as she made her way toward him through the crowd.

Earlier today, at her wit's end about why she could not read him, she had sought out the expert from the Healers and Empaths session while everybody else had been catching up on their sleep.

"I just don't understand why I get nothing off him," she had confessed to the Elder empath.

"My dear, haven't you ever heard?" The kindly woman had taken Isabelle's hand between her own. "It means your fate is somehow tied to his."

"My fate?" She had stared breathlessly at her. "Does that mean I'm going to marry him?"

"No, not necessarily. Fate can show up in many different ways, dear. The only thing that can be said for certain is that this person is going to be extremely important in your life. You're not permitted to read him because, if Fate's plan were revealed to you too early, then what's supposed to happen might not happen at all. And besides, it's good for us *not* to have our usual advantage over others sometimes. Don't you think?"

"I suppose." She had heaved a sigh. "I just wish I understood him."

"Talk to him."

"He's a Guardian. He doesn't talk."

"Not everybody uses *words* to speak."

Isabelle understood what the woman had meant, so as she approached Maddox, she vowed to be patient until she could figure out his preferred "language." When it came to Guardians, she supposed that actions spoke louder than words.

She smiled shyly at him as she approached. "Good evening, Mr. St. Trinian." She smoothed her dress and clasped her hands behind her back as she sauntered toward him.

"Miss Bradford." He gave her a gentlemanly bow.

"Are you enjoying the ball?"

"Uh..."

She chuckled at his inability to lie. Well, she supposed she wasn't surprised. He wasn't the ballroom type. But at least he was here. Might that have something to do with her?

Heart pounding, Isabelle braced herself to speak the boldest words of her life. "Perhaps you'd like it better if we, er, joined the others?" She gestured hopefully toward the dance floor.

He gave her a long, hard stare. And one didn't have to be an empath to understand that this meant no.

"I just don't think that would be a good idea."

"No, you're probably right. I'm sorry," she blurted out, turning away in humiliation so sharp it nearly stole her breath. "Never mind. I-I don't know what I was thinking," she stammered, backing away.

Then she turned around and fled.

Maddox shut his eyes. This was going to be torture. For both of them. Because all the while, in his pocket, he'd been gripping the small silver unicorn brooch he had made for Isabelle at the forge the very first night he'd seen her.

He had fashioned the delicate piece with such care, but he had not been able to bring himself to give it to her yet, and probably never would. For he knew full well that, once he did, there'd be no turning back.

* * *

Isabelle ran to the edge of the Yew Court and asked a gnome to show her the way out. It was all she could do to hold back tears at his rejection.

She was so angry at herself for being a fool.

At the moment, she was glad she could not read him. She did not want to know what an idiot he must think her!

In any case, the gnome led her safely to the exit of the maze, where Isabelle mumbled her thanks, picked up the hem of her long skirts, and strode toward the palace.

If this was how it was to be between her and Maddox for the future, she needed some time alone to adjust to his rejection before they all left together for Gryphondale tomorrow. Oh, how would she endure having to see him every day after that?

Walking toward the front steps of the palace, she stopped when she saw a flash of light out on the lawn at the waypoint.

Another portal was opening up. She turned, shading her eyes and squinting toward it.

Is that Derek coming back?

Her own evening had been ruined, but at least Miss Helena would be comforted if her Guardian beau had come back safely. Rather than going into Merlin Hall, Isabelle was drawn toward the portal to see who it was.

As she looked on, the Guardian who leapt out of the pulsating tunnel of light was not Derek, but a towering mountain of a man packed with muscles, his skin as dark as coffee. She had seen him around the Gathering before. She did not know his name, but it would have been difficult to miss anyone that huge, nor fail to hear his loud, jolly laugh on occasion.

Catching his balance, the big, imposing Guardian stepped out of the way to await whichever Lightrider he was protecting.

A moment later, the princely wood elf, Finnderool, stepped through. Isabelle recalled Jake saying that the graceful fellow had taught the first half of the young Lightriders' session.

Finnderool had not arrived alone, however.

Presently, Isabelle saw that he was escorting someone through the Grid—a brown-haired man with a big, full beard, whose massive frame stood as tall and nearly as broad as the nearby Guardian, only this man was dressed in the uniform of a prisoner.

"Urso!"

Without warning, Prince Janos stepped out of the shadows, his arms wide.

Isabelle went instantly on her guard at the sight of him.

"Janos!" The big, brawny prisoner managed to give the elegant vampire a hearty bear hug despite his chains. "Knew you wouldn't leave me to rot, *mein Freund!*"

"Never." Janos laughed and gave the shackled man a comical kiss on his bald front pate, then clapped him on both mighty shoulders. "Ha, ha! So good to see you, you old grizzly! But, Lord, you stink!"

Urso laughed like a pirate. "I hope the smell offends you! Took you long enough! A whole year, you useless bat?"

"Sorry, it couldn't be helped. But, look! I finally got the medicine that landed you in that dungeon in the first place." Prince Janos held up a decanter of shining purple liquid.

"*Ja,* is good. I heard from the wood elf that they let you have it. Now your babes will grow up strong like their uncle, the Bear!"

"Right you are. Take these shackles off him. He's been released," Janos scolded Urso's captors.

"Not yet. Watch them," Finnderool advised the Guardian, pulling up his sleeve to enter new coordinates into the Flower of Life device embedded in his arm. "Well, gentlemen, let's not dawdle. I've got things to do. Unless you two would rather *walk* back to the Carpathians?"

"Get me home!" Urso boomed.

Janos clapped him on the back. "My brides will cook you the biggest feast you've ever seen."

"Eh, I'd rather catch it myself. It's been too long since I hunted!"

"My forests are yours," Janos said warmly.

"Land of the misfits," Finnderool muttered. "DuVal, are you quite ready?" the wood elf called into the darkness behind her.

To Isabelle's astonishment, Henry strode past her toward the portal.

"Henry!" she cried abruptly. "What are you doing?"

This must have been the cause of the sibling spat she had witnessed between him and Helena.

"Oh...Isabelle," the boys' tutor said awkwardly, turning to her. "Why aren't you at the ball?"

She did not care to explain. "You're leaving?"

"Er, I'm afraid I must go...for a while. Tell Archie that he's to be the tutor until I return. Tell him Jake needs to keep working on his long division. Let them all know I'll be back soon, would you?"

"But where...? You can't be going with them?" She gestured at the vampire. "He can't be trusted!"

Until that moment, Prince Janos had been pointedly ignoring her, but now he sauntered toward her and Henry. "Are you coming or not, DuVal?"

"Excuse me, Izzy, I must go," Henry murmured regretfully, and then he went to consult with Finnderool about the journey through the Grid.

Isabelle looked at Janos, at a loss. "Why is Henry going with you?"

"Well, if it isn't my future bride," he greeted her with an ironic smile. "Oh, I'm sorry, were you talking to me? And here I thought you despised me."

"I do. But I still want to know why our tutor's going with you to the Carpathians."

Janos sighed, as though considering how much he could safely tell her, then he shrugged. "Very well. The fact is, Henry means to do a little spying for the Elders."

"Spying?"

"The wolves in my forests can talk to him more freely than to me. They may have useful information."

"I see." Isabelle absorbed this with a chill.

Henry wasn't a spy! He was a scholar and a teacher. Never mind that he had fangs that could rip a person's throat out in his wolf form. She knew he never would.

She looked at the vampire in distress. "Please, Prince Janos, don't let anything happen to him. He's like family."

He smiled wickedly at her. "For your sake, anything, mademoiselle."

He bowed and walked away.

She shook her head, barely knowing what to make of him. *What a slimy scoundrel.*

"I heard that," he said smoothly and smiled over his shoulder. "You can come with us if you like. My homeland is very beautiful. And wild. None of the usual rules there, Isabelle. You might like being bad if you tried it for a change."

"No, thank you," she replied.

"Ah, well, your decision. Give Guardian Stone my best. If he makes it back alive."

She ignored the cruel, casual remark. "Henry, please be careful."

"No worries, Izzy. I'm pretty indestructible in wolf form. Look after Helena for me, would you? She's rather a mess right now."

She nodded sympathetically. "I will."

Then they set out on their journey through the Grid. The Guardian led the way, leaping into the portal. The Bear went next.

Henry squared his shoulders and followed bravely.

When it was Price Janos' turn, he paused to send her a piercing look. *Farewell, beauty.* He placed the thought into her mind, disturbingly, as he had done before. *Tell your cousin Jake that I'll be calling on him soon. The boy is more important than he knows.*

"Don't you dare," she answered softly.

"Go," the haughty wood elf commanded, unaware of their telepathic exchange.

With a taunting glint in his eyes, Janos blew her a kiss goodbye, then stepped into the portal to take the medicine to his hideous vampire hatchlings and his many wives.

As if he needed another—namely her!

Yuck, she thought with a shiver. *Bloodsucking charmer.*

But she knew he was only toying with her. For some reason, it seemed to amuse him.

As she turned away, she hoped she did not seem as forward and annoying to Maddox as Janos did to her, with all of his too-suave flirting. Even more than that, she hoped Henry would be safe, and still more fervently, she hoped their efforts could avert a war.

The portal vanished, and as the dark of night returned, she

wondered where Derek had gone. She was not privy to that answer, but one thing was certain. He was a Guardian, so it was bound to be a place full of danger.

But not even Isabelle knew how right she was.

* * *

Through binoculars, Guardian Derek Stone scanned the Black Fortress carefully. They had been lucky enough to find it, considering the Dark Druids' stronghold had a nasty habit of magically disappearing and showing up again in some far-flung location. For now, at least, the Order had pinned it down, and here they were.

Though his battle senses were on high alert, his weapons within easy reach, Derek was thinking of the kids, hoping they were safe.

He crouched out of sight behind some boulders alongside the inimitable Tex.

They were waiting for Aleeyah to return. The djinni could move with an incredibly light step. She had gone ahead to scout out the faint sliver of light coming from the bottom of a door near the base of the building.

"Any sign of 'er yet?" Tex whispered.

"No," Derek breathed.

"So," he said at length. "What about you and that little shapeshifter gal o' your'n? You gonna marry that Miss Helena or what?"

"Not now, Munroe! Honestly." Derek shook his head in disapproval.

"Easy, pardner, just flappin' ma gums to pass the time."

"Oh, you're bored?" he retorted in a whisper.

Tex gave him a droll look, whittling a piece of wood while he waited, and obviously appreciating the knife in his hands, given the nearness of pure doom.

Derek homed in on a flicker of motion in the darkness, tensing. "Here she comes."

Aleeyah glided out of the night, bounding lightly up the rocks despite being barefooted. She vaulted over the boulders without a sound, her curved knife in hand, and crouched down between the two men.

Only then did the little magic bells that adorned her ankle and her waist begin to tinkle again—as if they'd been holding their breath.

"What did you see?" Derek asked urgently.

She shook her head. Given her skill at hiding her emotions, she was difficult to read, but even Derek could see that the djinni looked shaken. "I don't know how to tell you this."

"What?" the men asked in unison.

Aleeyah glanced back toward the fortress with a look of anguish. "They have a prisoner in there. He's guarded by demons."

"Demons?" Tex echoed in grim shock.

"Two of them."

"Then that's a high-value prisoner," Derek murmured.

"You might say that," she agreed in sarcasm.

"Well, lil gal? Don't keep us in suspense. Who they got in there? A Lightrider? It is, ain't it? Well, come on. Let's go mount a rescue!"

He started to stand up, but Aleeyah pulled him back down.

"No, Munroe! That would be incredibly foolish, even for you," she said sharply.

"Why?" Derek asked.

"Because the prisoner is an angel." She stared at them. "That's the light coming from under the door. They had him in chains. I...I think they're torturing him."

Derek stared at her, a chill running down his spine. "But that's impossible. They don't have the power—"

"I know what I saw."

Tex was glowering at the fortress, sizing it up with a dangerous look coming over his sun-leathered face.

"We need to get back and tell the Elders about this," Aleeyah whispered.

"Naw, we ain't goin' nowhere till we get that feller outta there. Now, come on, ya'll, or I'll do it my dang self. But you ain't gettin' home without me, remember? Let's go." Six-shooters at the ready, the mad Lightrider crouch-walked behind the rocky ridge that wound down to the Black Fortress.

Derek and Aleeyah exchanged a slightly exasperated look. But neither of them protested.

They both knew he was right.

"Ladies first," Derek whispered wryly.

Aleeyah snorted under her breath, silencing her bells again with a mystic wave of her hand. Taking out a second dagger, she followed the

Texan, a nasty curved blade in each hand.

Derek braced himself, bringing up the rear. He glanced around to make sure they had not been discovered and then shadowed his fellow spies.

This is bad.

If the Dark Druids had somehow recovered the ancient knowledge of how to take down one of the ethereal Light Beings—the strongest race of all known creatures—then the Order, indeed, the entire world was in more trouble than anyone had yet suspected...

The End

Want More Gryphon Chronicles?

Join Jake, Dani, Archie, Isabelle, Maddox, and Nixie on a seaside holiday where the kids definitely plunge into adventure WAY over their heads! It's sink or swim as they discover the underwater...

SECRETS OF THE DEEP

The Gryphon Chronicles: Book 5

Some lost treasures were never meant to be found...

With the Dark Druids after him and a magical war brewing, thirteen-year-old Jake Everton must lie low for a while, so his Elder witch aunt takes him and the gang on a long beach holiday, out of harm's way. But sure enough, Jake plunges into trouble once again when he meets a feisty royal mermaid on the run.

Princess Sapphira, daughter of King Nereus, recently ventured into the deep and stumbled upon a powerful artifact from ancient Atlantis. But the mysterious orb holds deadlier secrets than she ever suspected, and now every power-mad tyrant in the Seven Seas wants it—especially the dread, undead pirate king, Captain Davy Jones. When the legendary Lord of the Locker invades her father's kingdom and takes her little sister hostage, demanding the orb in exchange, Sapphira blames herself for the catastrophe and means to hand it over. But Jake finds out that if Jones gets the orb, he'll use its power to drown the world in a second Noah's Flood!

Now it's up to the aspiring young Lightrider and his friends to help the mermaid rescue her little sister *and* save the world from the same watery doom that drowned Atlantis—if Jake and the headstrong princess don't strangle each other first!

Turn the page for a Sneak Peek...

CHAPTER ONE
The Exiles

In the damp, suffocating blackness before dawn, Jake Everton, the thirteen-year-old Lord Griffon, stood before his parents' white marble mausoleum. He'd come to say goodbye.

Around him, unseen throughout the wooded grounds of Griffon Castle, flocks of birds screeched and clamored almost angrily for sunrise. Dew dripped off the spider webs. An eerie morning fog hung over the broad lawn. The wafting curls of mist, indeed, the whole atmosphere churned with unseen threat, and Jake was eager to be gone.

For a long moment, he stared earnestly at the locked iron grate between the pillars of Lord and Lady Griffon's stately tomb.

He wished he could somehow surmount this implacable barrier between them, the living and the dead, but it was impossible. So, hat in hand, he just lowered his head.

"Well, Mum, Dad," he forced out at length with a resolute but rather painful smile, "I just wanted to pay my respects before we leave on this supposed Grand Tour. I don't know where we're going, exactly, or when we might be back, but you needn't worry. Aunt Ramona's taking us someplace the Dark Druids will never think to look for us. Well—mainly me," he added in a taut whisper. "I'm the one who started all the trouble. And, er, well, now it seems they sorta want to kill me."

But as the ever-burning memorial flame in front of the mausoleum sent shadows twisting like phantoms over its mossy marble doors, there was still no sign that his parents could even hear him.

"Hullo?" he muttered a trifle impatiently, waiting.

As always, no answer. Jake clenched his jaw. Blast it, what good was it being able to communicate with spirits when the dead you most wanted to talk to never showed themselves? *Where are you? Why do you always ignore me? Am I such a disappointment?*

He squared his shoulders, though, and reminded himself he had survived without them just fine for most of his life. He managed to nod. "Very well," he said in answer to their continued silence. "I can understand why you'd disapprove of me. Yes, I might've been a thief for a while to survive. But at least I'm not a coward," he added in a fierce whisper, staring hard at the shadows as if to challenge them.

"I'm not afraid," he vowed. "You think I *want* to go to ground somewhere? Of course not. I'd rather fight than hide, same as you. Same as Derek, o-or Tex. But the Elders won't let me. They say I'm just a kid."

He glared at the tree-shaped insignia of the Order his parents had served so bravely. It was carved above the mausoleum doors, below the gryphon rampant of the Everton family crest.

"But so be it," Jake conceded in resentment. "After all, I've got to think about the others."

With a restless glance toward the drive, he saw his sleepy fellow travelers up and dressed and carrying the last of their things out to the two heavy-laden carriages parked in front of Griffon Castle.

Under a mound of traveling trunks strapped to the roof of each, the coaches waited to take them to the coast, where they would then board a ship across the Channel to start their Grand Tour, pretending all the while that they were not going into hiding and running for their lives, but merely off on holiday.

Ah well. Despite their pretense, all six kids going on the journey understood the threat just as well as their two adult chaperones. That didn't stop any of them from being excited about the famous sights they'd see along the way.

Even better, Great-Great Aunt Ramona had promised to end their wanderings at some fancy seaside villa, where they would lie low in luxury until it was safe to return to England.

Even though Jake knew it would be fun, he hated knowing that *his* actions, his stubborn decision to destroy Garnock the Sorcerer in Wales, had turned everyone he cared about into targets for a cult of evil warlocks.

Blimey. He shook his head and heaved a grim sigh. Well, it was a little late now to be finally thinking about the consequences, wasn't it?

As his best mate and cousin, Archie Bradford, the boy genius, had summed it up recently in a philosophical mood: *"It's Newton's Third Law, coz. For every action, there is an equal and opposite reaction."*

Indeed.

But if Jake had known at the time that his blowing up Garnock might become the opening salvo in a great magical war between the Order of the Yew Tree and its age-old enemies, the Dark Druids, he probably never would've done it.

Only, he had.

And frankly, his getting murdered for the deed might be the best-case scenario.

Yet there was hope even now that war might still be avoided.

Jake's rugged idol, Guardian Derek Stone and that wild cowboy, the American Lightrider, Agent Josephus Munroe, better known as Tex, were out there somewhere on a spy mission with Aleeyah the Djinni, trying to figure out exactly what the Dark Druids were up to.

Even the kids' shapeshifting tutor, Henry du Val, had been sent off to take part in the effort. Henry had gone to faraway forests ruled by the dashing vampire double agent Prince Janos, to listen in his wolf form for any whispers amongst the bad-leaning species of wild animals—wolves, bats, ravens, snakes. Some of them might have information, and Henry was tasked with sniffing out any clues.

Poor Miss Helena, Jake thought with a frown. He really didn't know how the girls' elegant governess could stand to look at him these days, considering that Henry was her twin brother and Derek was her beau.

If anything happened to either man all because of *his* actions, Jake knew he couldn't live with himself.

As it was, he had to remind himself continually of what Derek had said to him before he'd left: that it wasn't *really* his fault. That the Dark Druids had been looking for any excuse to renew hostilities for a very long time. They'd never be happy until they controlled the whole Earth, Derek had said. The Order of the Yew Tree had always stopped them, and always would. Nevertheless, every hundred years or so, the blackguards took it into their twisted minds to try yet again.

Any semblance of a reason would have sufficed, Derek had assured him with a fatherly squeeze on the shoulder before he'd gone.

Jake just wished *he* hadn't been the one to give it to them.

"Jacob!" Great-Great Aunt Ramona called sternly just then from across the sweeping lawn.

He turned, and with the predawn darkness beginning to fade to gray, could just make out her tall, prim, very proper figure.

The Dowager Baroness Bradford was no ordinary aristocratic old dragon lady. She also happened to be a powerful white witch, and an honorary Elder of the Order. "Come and make sure you have all your things," she commanded. "We'll be leaving in a trice!"

"Yes, ma'am! Be right there," he shouted back, then turned hesitantly one last time to his parents' ornate tomb.

Considering he might not make it back alive, this seemed like the closest chance he'd ever get to give them a proper goodbye. Then again, he might be joining them pretty soon in there if he didn't watch his back.

"Right. Well, we're off, then," he murmured. "Like I said, no need to worry about me. Aunt Ramona's got everything in hand. The ol' girl's sworn to keep us safe, even if she has to use magic again, and you know how she feels about that."

Silence.

"So, if you have any parting advice for your son," he added hopefully, "now's the time. I'm listening... Dani says I never listen, but if there's anything at all you'd like to say to me..."

Jake closed his eyes, waiting with his supernatural senses finely attuned for any subtle answer.

When still none came, he flicked his blue eyes open angrily and lifted his gaze to the dark dome of the sky, feeling unspeakably abandoned—and rather enraged at his parents. Honestly, was Heaven so comfy that the earl and countess, dead for over a decade, couldn't be bothered to spare him one moment of their shining blasted eternity?

True, he admitted, Dr. Celestus had said they might not be *allowed* to visit him like other ghosts did once they had fully crossed over. And that one would know, since the mild-mannered, *seemingly* human physician had turned out to be a bona fide angel, wings and all.

Oh, forget it, Jake thought, turning away. He could barely remember his parents, anyway.

With that, he stalked away, but he must've been more on edge about the looming threat than he'd realized, for when the greenery nearby suddenly rustled, he nearly jumped out of his skin.

He reached at once for the magical dagger at his side, Risker—but it wasn't some assassin of the dark arts come to murder him.

"Becaw!"

"Blimey, Red! You nearly made my heart stop," Jake muttered, clutching his chest with a belated chuckle.

"Caw?" The family Gryphon tilted his head as he prowled out of the leafy shadows, a magnificent, graceful, lion-sized version of the carved one above the mausoleum doors.

His heart still pounding, Jake welcomed the noble beast with a smile and threw an arm across his neck where the feathery part of Red's head met the tawny fur of his lion body. "Come on, boy, you can walk me to the carriage."

"Caw," Red said sadly, nudging Jake's side with his large golden beak.

"Aye, I'm going to miss you, too. But don't worry; you'll be joining us soon. It's not like we can take you with us traipsing through museums and cathedrals. Once we've seen the sights and get to wherever it is we'll be staying, one of the Lightriders will bring you to me through a portal, all right?"

"Jake!" a high-pitched voice piped up from the drive before the castle entrance. "Hurry *up*! You'll make us miss the ship!" Dani O'Dell held up what appeared to be some sort of tin. "I've got snacks!"

His lips flattened into a sardonic line. "She always knows how to bribe me," he remarked to Red, then called back, "I'll be right there!"

After Dani had bounded up into the first carriage, Jake looked wryly at Red. "Well, you heard the carrot-head. Guess I'd better step to it."

"Ca-caw," Red said sternly as they walked across the lawn.

"What, look after Dani? She looks after me. Don't you know that by now?" Jake paused mid-stride, however, when a thick twist of fog ahead began to churn and suddenly whirled into the shape of a friendly spirit of his acquaintance.

"Ahh, there you are, *ragazzo*!" the fat, jolly opera ghost greeted him, materializing on the lawn a few feet ahead of him.

"Constanzio! Well, this is a pleasant surprise." The King of the Tenors had helped Jake get through his Assessment just a week ago or so. "Shouldn't you be haunting Merlin Hall?"

"I had to come to see you *bambinos* off, of course! I could not let you leave to visit my beloved homeland without wishing you a proper *buon viaggio*."

"Huh?"

"Bon voyage, my charming lad! Ahh, you are going to love Italy,

Jacob! It's so beautiful!" Constanzio kissed his fingertips in the Italian style as he strolled floatingly beside Jake and Red as they continued toward the castle. "Such food! Such culture! Such art! And the ladies, heh-heh? You are old enough by now to spot *le donna bellissime*, I think?"

Jake snickered, but admittedly blushed. Having just turned thirteen a few days ago, he was feeling terribly grown up.

Laughing, Constanzio attempted to tousle Jake's hair with a ghostly hand. "Aha, I already know the girls chase you, you young scoundrel."

"Nah, it's just the castle and the earldom, that's all," Jake denied, puffing up his chest nonetheless, ridiculously pleased.

"Well, don't flirt with them in Italy, or you'll anger their papas," Constanzio warned. "Trust me. They're very strict down there."

"I don't even know how to flirt," Jake said with a snort.

"Wise lad. Don't learn. It only causes trouble. Now, heed me. I have some thoughts on your itinerary. In Florence, do not forget to see the doors of the great Baptistery. In Rome, you must toss a coin in the Trevi Fountain and make a wish; this is essential. And in Venice, you must ride on a gondola beneath the Bridge of Sighs—"

"I don't know if we're actually going to Venice," Jake interrupted. "Aunt Ramona says the Dark Druids are strong there."

"Oh, that's right." The famous dead tenor snapped his ghostly fingers. "Pity. I forgot—a few of their dreadful founding families did get their start there centuries ago among the old Black Nobility. Never mind Venice, then. There's Naples! The great, gilded opera house! Ah, I sang there many times. Standing ovations! The shouts of '*Encore!*'" He sighed. "How I miss them! I sang in most of the magnificent theaters of Europe, from Sicily to St. Petersburg."

"Oh, I don't think we're going as far as Russia. Aunt Ramona promised us we'd wind up somewhere on a warm, sunny beach. She says we're doing France first. Maybe Belgium? I hear they have outrageous chocolate there. Anyway, I'm not sure which port she has us sailing into. She's been keeping everything fairly secret to confuse *our friends.*"

"Understood. Well, I'm sure you'll be, as you British say, safe as houses, once you are away from here. Her Ladyship knows many cloaking spells, and now you've got Miss Valentine, as well. I hear young Nixie is as brilliant a student of magic as your cousin Archie is with his inventions."

Jake nodded. "Maddox St. Trinian is coming, too. Do you know him? He's a Guardian apprentice, but he's sixteen, so he's only got another year or two of his training. He's kind of a dull stick, but he can fight. Derek sent him along to watch my back while he's away."

"That is good. But let's not forget your own prodigious skills."

Jake sighed, for the compliment merely reminded him of the parents from whom he'd inherited his two supernatural gifts—and who apparently had nothing to say to him. The telekinesis had come from his sire, the ability to communicate with ghosts from his dam.

Constanzio misunderstood the reason for his gloomy exhalation. "You'll be fine out there. Just try to have fun and enjoy yourselves. That, my boy, is what Italy's all about." The late, great opera star gave him a roguish wink.

Jake managed a smile. "Thanks for coming to see me off, signore. Say, would you keep an eye on Red for me while I'm gone?"

"Why, it would be my honor." Constanzio bowed to the Gryphon, who bowed back.

"Aunt Ramona has arranged for one of the Lightriders to bring him to me through a portal once we figure out where we'll be hunkering down for the long term. But he gets lonely." Jake turned to his pet. "Now, Red: you'll be staying at the menagerie at Merlin Hall again for a while. You made yourself a very comfortable nest while we were there, as I recall, and the nice Green Man will make sure you have all you need. But you've got to promise me you won't eat any of the Dreaming Sheep."

Red snuffled at his teasing remark.

Jake gazed at him. "I'll miss you, boy. It'll be hard being separated. But don't worry; we'll be together again in a few weeks, and then we'll have loads of fun. I promise." Jake hugged his large pet, feeling a bit of a lump in his throat.

"Becaw, caw, caw," said the Gryphon.

"Of course I'll be good! Aren't I always?" Jake exclaimed.

Red huffed and shook his feathery mane.

Jake laughed. "You know me too well." He turned to the ghost. "Constanzio, you must promise to bring us any news of Derek and Tex the moment you hear something. And Henry, too, of course. If they come back from their missions while we're away—"

"I'll be sure to tell the gents where to find you. Well! Since the other children cannot see me, do give them my warmest regards... And I shall *GO!!!*" he sang, lifting his arms out theatrically to his sides.

He then went into one of his trademark flourishes, and held the final note for an impressive length of time: "Constanziooo must go... Go, go, go, go, *GO...!!!*"

Laughing, Jake applauded until his showy ghost friend disappeared. "What a ham."

"I heard that." Only Constanzio's round head reappeared, grinning. "Ciao, *ragazzo!*" he said, and disappeared.

"Arrivederci, signore!" Jake said to the empty air, which was the sum total of all the Italian he could speak, aside from *ragazzo*, which apparently meant *boy*.

The little preview of Italy's sights and sounds from Constanzio suddenly made Jake eager to get their adventure underway. Jogging the rest of the way to the castle through the dewy grass, he took a final brief walk-through of his home to make sure he hadn't left anything important behind.

He took one last, hard look at his family portrait over the fireplace in the great hall. The painting showed Lord and Lady Griffon—blond, handsome Jacob, and dark-haired, blue-eyed Elizabeth—both beaming with happiness and life, while Jake, as a baby, sat on his mother's lap, looking plump, contented, and thoroughly indulged.

Jake narrowed his eyes at the portrait. Looking at it always made him feel like someone had stuck a knife in his heart.

But with no desire to prolong the danger to his companions here in England a moment longer, he pulled the castle door shut and left, commending his home to the care of his former frog servants.

Though sad to see him go, the neatly uniformed butler, footmen, and maids were mostly grateful to have been turned back into humans some time ago.

"Do hurry, Jacob. That is quite enough dawdling," Aunt Ramona clipped out, checking in her little beaded handbag to make sure she had everybody's passports.

"Yes, ma'am." Jake strode toward the first carriage, the driveway gravel crunching underfoot.

Archie waved from inside the second coach, where he sat with Miss Helena, Nixie Valentine, and Maddox.

Jake sent them a casual salute in reply, then bounded up into the first coach, while Aunt Ramona gave the driver some final instructions.

He slumped into his seat on the maroon leather bench across from Dani. Cousin Isabelle sat beside her.

The girls were both smartly dressed in long, fancy traveling gowns, and between them sat Teddy, Dani's little brown Norwich terrier, wagging his wee stump of a tail and wearing a wide doggy grin.

He was becoming quite the little world traveler, that pup, but Dani would not have dreamed of leaving him behind. Not when he was small enough to fit in her satchel.

Jake looked at the redhead. "Did I hear something about snacks?"

Dani pulled out a tin of what proved to be Scottish shortbread, but she let him take only two of the sweet, buttery biscuits before putting the lid on it firmly again. "You're not goin' to eat them all in the first five minutes! Who were you talking to?"

"Constanzio came to wish us a bon voyage."

"How nice!" Dani said sweetly.

Jake tilted his head, finding her more curious every day. He had known Dani O'Dell for years—and she knew *him* better than anyone— but things felt a little different of late between them in ways he couldn't quite describe. All he knew was that Miss Helena's educational efforts and Isabelle's ladylike influence had started turning the rough-and-tumble rookery lass into quite the respectable young miss.

Just then, the Elder witch joined them.

"Finally!" Aunt Ramona huffed. The footman closed the carriage door politely behind her, and, at last, they were off.

Jake waved out the window. "Bye, Red! Tell Gladwin we'll send her a postcard!"

Red reared up and posed, wings out, in a parting salute, then he flew up to his favorite aerie on the castle roof.

As the shiny black coach rolled down the long drive, creaking under its mountain of baggage, Jake looked across at Dani. Her green eyes shone with excitement for the journey ahead.

"I cannot wait to see Paris! I *never* thought I'd ever get to see the world." Dani swung her feet just a bit, her tan boots laced up to where they met the hem of her shin-length gown, and she bounced happily on her seat, much to Jake's amusement. "This is going to be amazing! We're going to see so many marvelous old things! Old churches, old paintings, old palaces, old ruins..."

Jake quirked a half-smile. "I had no idea you liked old things so much, carrot."

"Old things have *presence*. I mean, just look at Her Ladysh—" Dani suddenly stopped herself, aghast. Wide-eyed with her blunder, she gulped and lowered her head, her cheeks strawberry. "Never mind."

Jake stifled a chortle and kicked her lightly.

Dani sent him a mortified look.

"I'm sure she meant it as a compliment," Isabelle said with the utmost delicacy, her lips twitching.

Aunt Ramona's eyebrow arched high. "Indeed."

Well, people *did* speculate that the Elder witch might be as much as three hundred years old, Jake thought with a grin.

"Humph," said Her Ladyship, then she gazed out the window, her stern lips pursed like she was holding back a chuckle.

And at last, their Grand Tour got underway.

The Complete Gryphon Chronicles Series:

Book 1 – THE LOST HEIR
Book 2 – JAKE & THE GIANT
Book 3 – THE DARK PORTAL
Book 4 – RISE OF ALLIES
Book 5 – SECRETS OF THE DEEP
Book 6 – THE BLACK FORTRESS

And don't miss out on the holiday fun...

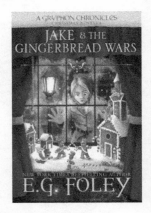

It's Jake's first Christmas with a family, but nothing's ever quite what you'd expect. Celebrate a Victorian Christmas with a Gryphon Chronicles holiday novella.

JAKE &
THE GINGERBREAD WARS

Peace on Earth, Goodwill to Men...And Gingerbread Men?!

ABOUT THE AUTHORS

E.G. FOLEY is the pen name for a husband-and-wife writing team who live in Pennsylvania. They've been finishing each other's sentences since they were teens, so it was only a matter of time till they were writing together, too.

Like his kid readers, "E" (Eric) can't sit still for too long! A bit of a renaissance man, he's picked up hobbies from kenpo to carpentry to classical guitar over the years, and holds multiple degrees in math, science, and education. He treated patients as a chiropractor for nearly a decade, then switched careers to venture into the wild-and-woolly world of teaching middle school, where he was often voted favorite teacher. His students helped inspire him to start dreaming up great stories for kids, until he recently switched gears again and left teaching to become a full-time writer and author entrepreneur.

By contrast, "G" (Gael, aka Gaelen Foley) has had *one* dream all her life and has pursued it with maniacal intensity since the age of seventeen: writing fiction! After earning her Lit degree at SUNY Fredonia, she waited tables at night for nearly six years as a "starving artist" to keep her days free for honing her craft, until she finally got The Call in 1997. Today, with millions of her twenty-plus romances from Ballantine and HarperCollins sold in many languages worldwide, she's been hitting bestseller lists regularly since 2001. Although she loves all her readers, young and old, she admits there's just something magical about writing for children.

You can find the Foleys on Facebook/EGFoleyAuthor or visit their website at www.EGFoley.com. They are hard at work on their next book.

Thanks for Reading!

CPSIA information can be obtained
at www.ICGtesting.com
Printed in the USA
LVHW091957170419
614605LV00002B/236/P